POINT VENUS

Michael Moran has led a varied and adventurous life. Born and educated in Australia, he spent his twenties wandering the islands of Polynesia. He later studied the piano and harpsichord in London. He has written on a diversity of subjects, ranging from British art and architecture to the music of the French composer François Couperin. Posted to Eastern Europe shortly after the fall of communism, he now lives and works in London.

Michael Moran

Point Venus

BRANDL & SCHLESINGER

B O O K   P U B L I S H E R S

First published by Brandl & Schlesinger Pty Ltd
24 Wilberforce Avenue Rose Bay NSW 2029 Australia

The characters in this novel, with the exception of the historical figures, are all figments of the Author's imagination.

This project has been assisted by the Commonwealth Government
through the Australia Council, its arts funding and advisory body.

National Library of Australia
Cataloguing-in-Publication entry:

Moran, Michael, 1947-.
Point Venus.
ISBN 1 876040 08 4
I. Title
A823.3

Cover painting: *Poedooa, the Daughter of Oree* by John Webber (1752-1793)
© National Maritime Museum, Greenwich, London

Map of Norfolk Island © British Library, London

Cover and book design by András Berkes

Printed and bound by Alken Press, Smithfield

*For Norfolk Island and its unique people
both past and present but especially
in memory of Jeanie who has
reached 'that beautiful shore'
with love*

AUTHOR'S NOTE

The origins of the language spoken on remote Norfolk Island in Oceania must be among the most dramatic in history, unfolding as it did from a notorious love affair. The language is descended from Pitcairnese which evolved in the settlement on Pitcairn Island founded by the Bounty mutineers and their Tahitian lovers and 'servants' in 1790. Today, the Norfolk Islanders are a bilingual people who take justified pride in their language. It is a colourful amalgam of various forms of regional English and Tahitian. The conventional English spoken to visitors is softly accented in the manner of an educated Scot or North of England speaker. It is quite unlike the common varieties of Australian or New Zealand English.

As *'Norfolk'* is an oral language, a prescriptive spelling and pronunciation has not yet been established and variations abound. The author has adopted the phonetic spelling system pioneered by Alice Buffett (a 7th generation direct descendant of mutineer Matthew Quintal and his Tahitian wife Tevarua) and Don Laycock (Senior Fellow in the Linguistics Department of the Australian National University) in their book *'Speak Norfolk Today'* (Himii Publishing Company, Norfolk Island 1988). Readers are also referred to a more academic analysis and description of Pitcairnese and Norfolk in *'The Pitcairnese Language'* by A.S.C. Ross, Andre Deutsch, London 1964. In light of the above, the author has attempted to capture the idiom of Norfolk rather than a transliteration.

ACKNOWLEDGEMENTS

The author wishes to acknowledge the assistance given by the Scott Polar Institute in Cambridge concerning the early life of Lady Jane Franklin and to Professor Edgar Wind for his neo-Platonic interpretation of paintings by Sandro Botticelli. Mr Nicholas Wragge-Morley rendered me invaluable advice on matters of military detail.

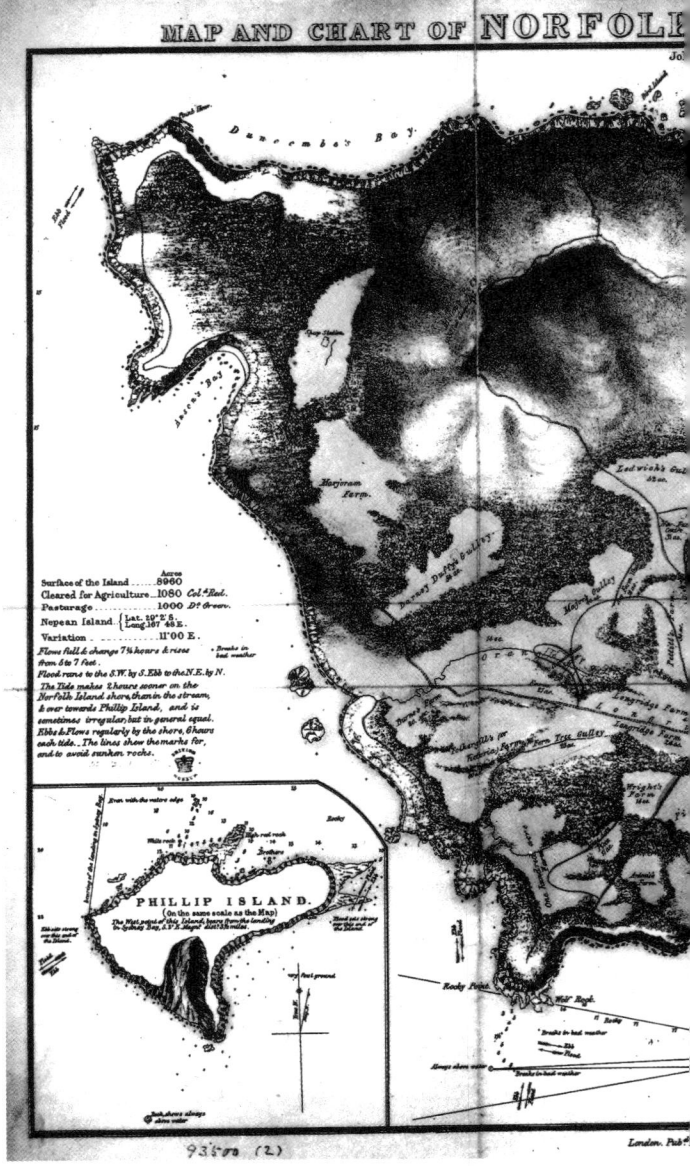

Surface of the Island 8960
Cleared for Agriculture ... 1080 Col.ᵈ Red.
Pasturage .... 1000 D.ᵒ Green.
Nepean Island {Lat. 19° 2' S.
              {Long.167° 48' E.
Variation .... 11°00' E.

Flows full & change 7½ hours & rises
from 5 to 7 Feet.
Flood runs to the S.W. by S. Ebb to the N.E. by N.
The Tide makes 2 hours sooner on the
Norfolk Island shore, than in the stream,
& over towards Phillip Island, and is
sometimes irregular, but in general equal.
Ebbs & Flows regularly by the shore, 6 hours
each tide. The lines shew the marks for,
and to avoid sunken rocks.

PHILLIP ISLAND.
(on the same scale as the Map)
The N.ᵉˡ point of this Island, bears from the landing
in Sydney Bay, S.W.b.S. dist. 4½ miles.

London. Pub.ᵈ

SLAND FROM ACTUAL SURVEY, 1840.

wsmith, 1842.

Scale of Chains or 1 English Mile.

42 by J. Arrowsmith, 10 Soho Square.

'...*not a Clowd was to be seen the whole day and the Air was perfectly clear,*
so that we had every advantage we could desire in Observing the whole of
the passage of the Planet Venus over the Suns disk: we very distinctly saw
an Atmosphere or dusky shade around the body of the Planet which very much
disturbed the times of the Contacts particularly the two internal ones. Dr. Solander
observed as well as Mr. Green and my self, and we differ'd from one another
in observeing the times of the Contacts much more than could be expected.'
From the Journals of Captain James Cook concerning
the observation of the Transit of the Planet Venus for the Royal Society
from Point Venus in Tahiti on 3rd. June 1769

'...*the unity of Venus is unfolded in the trinity of the Graces...*'
Pico della Mirandola
Conclusiones de modo intelligendi hymnos Orphei No.8, 1486

'*I... wish we could meet to talk over the many prisons of life – prisons of stone,*
prisons of passion, prisons of intellect, prisons of morality and the rest.
All limitations, external or internal, are prisons – walls, and life is a limitation.'
Oscar Wilde in a letter to Cunninghame Graham
in 1898 concerning *The Ballad of Reading Gaol*

CHAPTER I

'If my friends enquire of me, tell them I am somewhere
in the South Seas' (spoken 'in a jeering manner')
James Morrison
Boatswain's Mate and mutineer
His Majesty's Armed Vessel *Bounty*

*D*awn. The flying-boat *Pacific Trader* slipped her moorings, taxied away from the buoy and faced into wind. A choppy sea threw spray at the inner propellers as the outboard engines opened to full power. As she gathered speed, arcs of water obscured the windows and waves pounded the hull. The nose lifted, and she finally pulled off the surface of the harbour to climb laboriously into the rising light beyond the mainland. The slow states of change in the banks of cloud passing beneath gave me time enough to meditate on the full mystery of my escape to the island.

I gazed out under the broad wing and felt a sudden elation at having finally broken the sterile bondage of the city. I was hoping this almost irresponsible flight would help me avoid the frenzy of an ambitious career, the concealed hollowness of realised hopes, the cultivation of the approved measure of guilt, the approved measure of despair.

I tapped the pocket of my jacket, took out the buff-coloured box of 'Chaliapine' and lit one of the thick Russian cigarettes. I abandoned it in the corner of my mouth, letting the smoke wander about my face while I glanced listlessly through the window at some vapour rushing from a vent. The gentle movement and aromatic tobacco induced a profusion of fragmented memories.

I recalled hours spent in the prison of the family, watching the heat shimmering from the surface of the suburban street through a grille set in the pink wall. Boredom, stillness, anxiety, unfulfilled promise. Friends often spoke to me through this ironwork. Conflict over the serious study of music as opposed to a practical, remunerative career had reached the incendiary stage. Eight to ten hours piano practice, counterpoint and harmony each day at Sydney Conservatorium had trapped me in a cycle of sterile intellectual endeavour. It always seemed faintly absurd to be playing Mozart and Bach through the searing Australian summer, rocks trembling and cracking in the heat haze, kookaburras alighting in the eucalypts in the park, laughing at me working in the cool gloom of a music-room. Healthy surfers rode the waves in sunlight while I explored the dark cavern of the European soul.

Reviews of my early concerts as I worked towards my Performer's Diploma were ambiguous.

"The Paul Seagrave recital of Schumann last night at the St. George Chapel revealed a rare and promising talent. However, his approach to the Symphonic Studies Op.13 betrayed a tantalising inability to control a headstrong and excessively passionate virtuosity..."

Faith in myself began to seep away, escaping like slow blood from a punctured vein. Shattered nerves caused harrowing lapses of memory before the audience. My spirit seemed to be in conflict between the intellectual culture of Europe and the irresistible physical attractions of the Antipodes. The combat compressed me painfully between these magnetic polarities, and the pressure had become insupportable. I could not face the looming destiny of a failed concert career and I desperately wanted to escape the assaults on my inner life that social performance dictated. There had to be an alternative to the barren imperatives of duty and permitted behaviour. Flight was a compelling alternative to my present misery, and I dropped out in my final year.

I had applied for the post of Broadcasting Officer on remote Norfolk Island, a thousand miles east of Australia across the Tasman Sea. This had been advertised in an obscure journal with the rider 'Fair knowledge of music required'. This would be my chance to break free, to evade my responsibilities, if you like, to run away. I spat off some shreds of tobacco and glanced down at the sea.

My memories seemed accidental and random in their shape and relationship, the process of thought being like an artist in mosaic

I once observed in Ravenna, contemplating mounds of coloured glass, his tweezers indecisively poised whilst assembling the picture. I traced a fumbled education, my family attached to the diplomatic corps in Russia and France – reckless drives along the Pacific coast at dawn – reveries in parks beside still ponds with young girls met by chance – affected moods of sentiment and morbid idealism – the coloured stockings of my Polish lover – wine, swimming, sunbathing, harsh heat, wild salt on the lips after slaking the thirst for love – barbecued steaks on the vine-covered patio attached to the dining room of our Wilkinson house below the sacred aboriginal terraces, cool water trickling from the fountain sculpture, its sound mingling with the cry of parrots and the perfume of gardenias – fierce arguments with parents over the rental of a tower overlooking the ocean, a place to think and write – infatuations and betrayals – desultory piano practice. My identity was utterly fragmented, yet I had somehow found the will to pull the pieces together, act positively, leave the city and set up on the island permanently.

The acrid smoke of the 'Chaliapine' jolted me away from the window and the discs spun by the propellers. I focused again on my immediate surroundings. A disturbance had erupted toward the rear of the aircraft, the passengers turning as one to stare at an elderly man clutching his chest. He appeared to be gasping for breath. The passengers seated in the vicinity looked on like watchers at a fire. He recovered, but it seemed as if this sudden pain was an ominous sign of the secret heart of our destination, known in the Nineteenth Century as the *Isle of Death*.

A change in the pitch of the engines and the groan of hydraulic pumps indicated that the flying-boat was beginning its descent. There was a good deal of increased activity within the cabin as the destination drew near. I was moved by a pleasant anticipation of this new phase in my life. Such flights from one reality to another, from one self to another are seldom deeply considered. The streets outside my room had lead only to libraries, destinations of the intellect, the competition of words in the erection of worlds. The aircraft banked to the left and the island appeared, low and green on the horizon.

The main island strangely resembled a heart. Mostly it was was a patchwork of lush green, but in the valleys, where the land had begun to erode along the edges of the cliffs, scars of brown and white blighted the surface. Bays and inlets lined the precipitous coast, fingers of rock pushed out into the sea like supplicant palms. Stately pines covered much of the island, growing in dense stands on slopes and ridges, lining the tortuous roads, planted in groups around the colonial buildings fringing the beach. Some stood solitary and alone like men of dispossessed temperament or disinherited mind, some clung fearlessly to the edge of the cliffs. The rust-pink roofs of island dwellings and farms were scattered randomly about. An intriguing pentagonal shape lay submerged beneath the turf within some ruined walls near the lagoon. It was as if layers of green velvet had been stretched over a recumbent body. I could see two hills rising through the haze, swathed in impenetrable foliage, and on the right one of the denuded off-shore islets. It was coloured in many shades of red, mauve and brown – arid, barren, a few struggling plants in the hollows. The water surrounding the main island looked preternaturally transparent as though illuminated from below, the shallows milky blue alternating with the darker shapes of coral banks, falling off to the cobalt of the deeper ocean.

Now the *Pacific Trader* was on her final approach over the lagoon. The pitch of the propellers altered as we floated towards the turmoil of the reef, and we were buffeted by updraughts as we passed over the cliffs. The tops of pines and the roof of a chapel flashed beneath the wings. She skimmed the surface of the lagoon, settled in a shower of spray and taxied up to the moorings.

A customs official in shorts, long socks and polished brogues came aboard from a launch to fill the interior with insecticide before dealing with the passengers. Warnings against forbidden imports of raw meat and live rabbits were read. We took seats in a lighter, and were towed across the foaming waves breaking over the reef. A breeze carrying the perfume of pine resin ruffled my hair as I disembarked at the pier. A rusty crane squeaked softly as it swung in the wind.

A taxi driver took me to the guesthouse named *Almira's*. We drove up a steep hill and along a deserted road, turned into an entrance across a cattle-grid of rollers that set up a tremendous rattle and drove across a paddock past some grazing cows. A white picket fence stretched in incongruous starkness across the front of the house. Semi-tropical plants and shrubs, hibiscus and bougainvillaea concealed the entrance. The uprights of the broad verandah that supported the gable blended with the palm trees round about to create the ambient repose of a Polynesian sanctuary.

As I stumbled slightly over the tufts of grass, I vaguely hoped that in this place I would be initiated into another learning, an alternative to the intellectual analysis which so corrodes the instinctive faculties. It was a self-conscious search for a measure of intuition to balance the weight of reason. The justifiable claims of the heart over the desert of good sense. Perhaps here in Oceania there might be a respite from the pressure of building a conventional middle-class career. I lifted the latch and swung the white gate open. Laughter poured out from the dark interior, floated across the verandah and pandanus palms, breaking over me with an energetic and astonishing irreverence.

I wandered up the stairs, walked through the dining room and came to a doorway which led directly into the kitchen. It was filled with exotic odours, laughter and conversation. Some island women were cooking on a huge Aga stove and joyfully bustling about with pots of vegetables and meat. A vast pan of sweet-smelling red fruits – guavas – simmered at one side. Cats negotiated their way across the floor. Some guests were sitting at a long table at the far end of the room. Dressed in garish Polynesian shirts and muu-muus, they laughed and poured out generous whiskeys, knocking the bowls of hibiscus as they reached across the table. The room overlooked a tropical garden with avocado, guava and palm trees.

'Es ai hau glehd f' si yuu! Kam in a' haus darl!'[1]

An elderly island woman seated with the guests was smiling and beckoning. I was struck at once by the nobility that lay in every line of the woman's face. Her plaited, black hair was curled into a bun which accentuated her straight forehead. The olive skin of her cheeks shone with a gentle luminosity, almost reflected in the darkness of her eyes.

'Ai es Almira.'[2]

She introduced me to the guests and the island women, Teio and Mau. 'This is Paul Seagrave from Sydney. He's the musician who is taking up the post of Broadcasting Officer on Norfolk.'

'Darl, yu laik wan whiskey, nort? Join aa family!'[3] Almira said.

Her voice broke into infectious chuckles as the spirit tumbled into the glass. I was to discover some of my happiest island moments in her company at that table. The restful afternoon settled over the island and red parrots flashed through the trees seeking their nests. The mood seemed to be one of intense pleasure and compassion for the foibles of men, bubbling laughter with the briefest moments of semi-serious repose. She lent back, opened the refrigerator and brought out a plastic box.

'Tek wan piis dieh fish darl,'[4] she said authoritatively, pushing the container in front of me. It looked like a raw fish marinade, and it tasted delicious. 'What is it?'

'Tahitian fish darl. Go orn, tek sum mor! Es guud anieh?'[5]

And so began my addiction to this exotic dish. Almira's emotional largesse expressed itself with striking generosity through the food.

'What brings you to the island?' asked a guest.

'I've come to set up a broadcasting facility.'

'Will we hear you on the air then?'

'I suppose so.'

'We've got a celebrity here, Almira!'

They turned back to their drinks. There was a deal of tedious conversation concerning air fares, duty free goods, exchange rates and time differences, so I soon left the table to unpack. I was tired after the flight, and I lay on the bed, listlessly watching the patterns of light on the curtains. Erotic fancy played in my mind. Lethargic clouds and the vibrating fingers of a palm frond disturbed by the wind were shadowed on the wall by the hard shafts of sunlight. In taking this journey I had abandoned the love of a dancer, Alexandra. An air-letter lay on the table, and my mind turned over the melancholy contents once more.

Madras
March 17th 1974

Dearest Paul,

You asked me to write to you. That was strange. I could not let you know how I felt although that meeting between us was so strong. I used to be an absolutist at eighteen and I gave myself entirely to you. Now that you have decided to flee the city to Norfolk Island,

I will become a relativist in relationships – no longer a matter of surrender, merely an expression of affection…

This fragile record remained a tantalising shadow in the glass of possibility. Her judgement was definitively accurate in one respect – the island was the beginning of a process of purification.

However, on this first afternoon I contrived slothful fantasies around memories of her erotic dance improvisations. The cheerless pleasures of masturbation filled the moment as the drained letter fluttered to the floor. There was certainly no indication that I was being carefully, secretly observed through the glass louvres of my bedroom.

I awoke from an anxious sleep near dinner time. I decided to change my clothes, have a shower and a drink before facing the other guests. Nearly everyone had gone out for an evening walk and a warm silence pressed about the house. The early spring sun was still high, and I walked down to the hire-car office to rent a jeep. I hoped to do a little exploration of the island before reporting to the administration offices next morning.

'Watawieh yuu darl?'[6] Almira affectionately called as I entered the kitchen. I noticed with delight the lilting Norfolk – a mixture of English and Tahitian, the unique language of love that emerged from a mutiny of the senses aboard the *Bounty* long ago in Otaheite. I was soon to learn the manner in which this beautiful tongue had been forged from the fierce passion of the English sailors for their Tahitian lovers.

'We speak Nor*folk* and not Nor*fik*!' Almira would insist impatiently. The tiny difference in pronunciation mattered a lot to her.

To visitors, standard English was proudly spoken with an educated Scots or North of England accent, quite unlike Australian or New Zealand usage. Norfolk was used exclusively when the islanders were talking among themselves. The languages were often mixed. Almira paid me the compliment of often speaking to me in Norfolk. The intonation carried such warmth and affection.

'Tek wan whiskey f' yuu, go on,'[7] she said with that blithesome laugh again. The language seemed to transcend all worldly griefs, floating effortlessly above failure.

'Yu gwen aut a' Bucks Point f' breakfast morla?'[8]

'What do you do, exactly?'

'Wi gwen aut lorng em cliffs, f' kech aa sunrise over daa ocean en haew breakfast rern a' fia, anieh Teio?'[9]

'It's beautiful, it's the best time,' Teio said, with a finality of intonation.

'You'd better be up by five, darl, or you'll miss the magic moment! Last time it was so windy the coffee blew out of the cups and the bananas out of their skins!'

Almira chuckled and nudged my arm, indicating the Tahitian fish with a nod.

'Yu orta staat a' lern f' tork Norfuk suunes yu s'anpaek yus behg!'[10]

My enthusiastic consumption of food was considered the greatest of compliments. The women sang away amongst themselves the stories and gossip current in the air.

'Peli s' get wan sheep en hi nor wornt et.'[11]

'Huu es et?'[12]

'Tracy Young. Shi gwen a' fallow haim a' dem ends f' earth en mor!'[13]

I slipped out on to the verandah and sank into a cane armchair. I watched the dusk through the Norfolk Palms and Rau Ti, wisteria and bougainvillaea, sunlight firing the vibrant pink bracts. A breath of air set the palm fronds in motion, the coarse leaves rubbing together, parting the silence.

Two dogs erupted on to the lawn, chasing each other between the red-throated hibiscus, followed more lethargically by a woman. My first glimpse was of a beautiful oval face with lustrous dark eyes, golden skin, sensitive yet sensual lips. Her dark hair was luxuriant, slightly crinkled, falling back at an angle to her forehead down to her waist, caught up by the breeze. A blue flowered sarong was tied loosely around her waist and a loose yellow top outlined her breasts. She walked barefoot. The limbs of Polynesian women are somewhat short, slightly heavy but perfectly proportioned. She quickly disappeared behind a Butterfly Tree.

A few minutes later, I noticed her observing me between the slim pillars that supported the verandah. She was gazing at me with great intensity, curious yet wary. I leaned back with my Scotch and Russian cigarettes and prepared a masculine smile. She fled at once like a startled bird, threatened by the intuition that is carried on the electrical connection between eyes, between souls. I was discomforted by this wordless, how shall I name the feeling – 'summons' fits well enough. I failed to dwell on the incident as I had heard the ruder summons of the ship's bell outside the dining room signalling the commencement of dinner.

The table was heavy with island dishes. A few guests were already seated, questioning Almira about the method and ingredients.

'Daa es mada darl! Green banana dumplings cooked in milk. Tek et f' yuu.'[14]

As I helped myself from the platters, I heard the wind agitate the leaves in the garden, a slow rustle stealing in through the window. Heavy clusters of palm fruit arched down from the crowns of the tall trunks. The fading light was marked by the distant bark of a dog or bird call. I turned my attention from a haze of half-formed questions to the cool interior lit by a single lamp. The dark oak table was covered with a lace cloth. Subdued silver placings, tropical flowers in cut crystal bowls, candles waiting for nightfall and pine-panelled walls gave the room a tender ambience, a nostalgic hastening of the soul to the Victorian past of this 'smallest of Her Majesty's Colonies'. I had already begun to dream, to succumb to the enchanted seclusion and joyful listlessness induced by the island.

'*...the moment of his Horrid act of ingratitude*'
Captain William Bligh

Almira's had been built in the late Nineteenth Century for *Almira's* father, a direct descendant of Mr. Fletcher Christian, that young member of an ancient and respected Manx family who joined the crew of His Majesty's Armed Vessel *Bounty* as Master's Mate in 1787. He became captain of the mutineers for a time, a prince of the '*allurements of dissipation*'.

At the beginning of my residency on Norfolk Island I was aware of the popular accounts of this notorious tale. Later researches revealed a more complex set of psychological relationships. The long, solitary period the mutineers spent on Pitcairn's Island following the firing of the *Bounty* resulted in a scarcely known parable of sexual betrayal, murder and redemption. This was the historical landscape against which the contemporary descendants chronicled in my story played their parts.

The aim of the expedition to the great Southern Ocean was to collect breadfruit plants from Otaheite for introduction into the British Caribbean colonies as a source of cheap food for the slaves on the sugar plantations. Ironically, when the fruit finally arrived in the West Indies, after the curtain had fallen on the '*Grand Opera*' of the mutiny, the natives refused to eat it. The Cornishman, Lieutenant William Bligh R.N. – ultimately known as '*Breadfruit Bligh*' – was given the command. He had gained invaluable navigational experience under Captain James Cook on his Third Voyage as Master of H.M.S. *Resolution* in 1776.

The *Bounty* was an extremely small vessel, 215 tons, taken from merchant use for a naval transport and converted to carry the plants. Sir Joseph Banks had advised modifications to the 'Great Cabin' which involved a leaded floor and system of water runways beneath containers for more than a thousand breadfruit saplings. This reduced the living space, so the sailors had to live packed close together. The ship was simultaneously undermanned and overcrowded – fatally.

Bligh was the only commissioned officer. He had an all-volunteer crew, but no detachment of Royal Marines to enforce discipline on this long voyage. He knew the odds were stacked against success, and he smouldered that he was *'but very indifferently used'* by the Admiralty on what they considered a minor enterprise. In the event of a disaster, rescue from these remote islands was unlikely. He had to look for a high degree of mutual support and trust from his officers. It would not be forthcoming.

Circumstances combined to create fertile conditions for a mutiny to flourish alongside the botanical specimens. Bligh had courageously beaten the ship into the teeth of winter tempests for weeks around Cape Horn, before finally coming to anchor at Tahiti, some eleven months after breaking out into the Channel from Spithead. The welcome was overwhelmingly friendly when the *Bounty* entered Matavai Bay on Sunday, 26th October, 1788. As she lay off *Point Venus*, her figurehead, a female in a green riding habit, witnessed a display of erotic nakedness in the sparkling water that might have put her to the blush had she not been carved of wood.

'In less than ten minutes the deck was so full that I could scarce find my own people,' Bligh wrote. They were to be there almost six months, nursing the rooting plants in their pots and waiting for the easterly winds that would take them through the Endeavour Straits. During these weeks the crew were also nursed like tender plants by the perfumed bodies of Tahitiennes.

The memories of Georgian England, the *'blue-eyed violets of Devon'* and recollections of the *'odiferous young ladies of Billingsgate'* dissolved in the pure water of the lagoons. Protestant moral idealism insisted on control over the sinful inclinations of the body. The damnable delights of the gin-palace doxies, the miseries of *'Signor Gonorrhoea'* contracted in the *'stews'* of Limehouse could scarce stand comparison with unashamed passion in a palm-thatched hut with these healthy devotees of sexual delight, *'the fair ones ever willing to fill your arms with love'.* As the sailors languished through the tropical nights with these South Sea creatures, scars pressing against silken skin, their sense of duty started to fail. Desertion, sleeping on watch, thefts by natives, neglect of the sails so that mildew rotted the cloth, all were symptoms of the narcotic effect of Polynesia. Many seamen formed deep attachments, but the austere Bligh remained true to his Betsy and only studied Tahitian customs.

Bligh became increasingly desperate as trust in his officers disintegrated. He had the qualities of a despot. His choleric outbursts were accompanied by inconsistent gestures of thoughtfulness. Many of the crew were reduced to wretchedness. His standards were fastidious and he was passionately devoted to the details of naval procedure, an imperious man unbridled in pride.

'By God Sir,' he swore, *'if it is not great to you it is great to me'.*

He introduced many innovations to the crew's diet, signed on a half-blind fiddler for their dancing, and installed a permanently fired stove for drying the men's clothes. Most important of all, he set up a system of three watches, which greatly reduced the strain of the long voyage. Yet under stress his language was frequently intemperate – describing one man as *'a damn long pelt of a bitch'* – and he indulged in such *'violent Tornadoes of temper'* as could break the spirit of his junior officers.

On 4th April 1789, the floating greenhouse that was the *Bounty*, loaded with a plentiful supply of fruit, hogs and goats, glided away past the reef after an unforgettable twenty-three weeks in Otaheite. High on the masts, on the deck and swimming in the wake of the armed vessel, many hearts parted in painful sympathy with the sea.

Three weeks elapsed, and Bligh's contempt for his officers and crew inflamed like a boil from the scurvy. His bursts of hysteria did nothing to ease the difficult return to naval discipline. Fletcher Christian was crushed by abuse and unreflecting harshness which acted destructively on his febrile and unstable temperament. He sported Tahitian tattoos on his buttocks now, and suffered from *'violent perspirations, especially on his hands so that he soils anything he touches',* according to Bligh.

His worldly aspirations had been thwarted early in life. When he was four his father had died. At sixteen, while at school with the poet William Wordsworth, his dreams of following the family tradition and going up to Cambridge as a young gentleman to prepare for a distinguished law career had been shattered by his mother's bankruptcy and his brothers' financial deceit. William Bligh was only ten years older than Christian, and he had become his mentor and financial support, blind to his faults, a surrogate father against whom Christian would finally rebel. Christian was the son Bligh had never possessed, who would ultimately cause him fierce anguish.

The Royal Navy was not a vocation for Fletcher Christian. He took to it as a way to improve his social expectations. His cousin had already snatched away the beautiful heiress Isabella Curwen, of whom Romney has left us such an elegant portrait. Sentimentally, he named his Tahitian lover Isabella and was generally considered *'one of the most foolish young men I ever knew in regard to women'*. His Naval career showed great promise, and he had been singled out for special responsibility aboard *Eurydice* and *Britannia*. Perhaps because of their close emotional ties and Christian's sensitive financial dependence on Bligh, this insufficiently robust temperament was overwhelmed by his mentor's wounding abuse, bruised to the point where *'tears were running fast from his eyes in big drops'*, tears of humiliation and rage. *'Flesh and blood cannot bear this treatment,'* he cried. In a final characteristic outburst of anger, Bligh had cut Christian with savage invective and publicly degraded his protégé and second in command as a petty thief.

'Damn your blood you have stolen my coconuts.'

Later that day Bligh inexplicably invited Christian to dinner, but Christian refused. His mind in turmoil, he was unable to face the long passage through the Endeavour Straits. The atmosphere of tension, heightened by the dangers of navigation, would make life aboard intolerable. Christian impulsively decided to desert alone on a raft to the island of Tofua. That night, in a bout of deep irrationality, he did away with his personal belongings and tied a heavy weight around his neck. His mental anguish was extreme. As he came on deck after a fitful sleep to take his watch, a distant volcanic island in eruption was lighting the dark sky. A whisper came to his ear from a tempter, Able Seaman George Stewart, that *'The people are ready for any thing'*, and he determined instead to take the ship in a burst of suicidal freedom.

Mutiny on the high seas in the Royal Navy was punishable by death under the Articles of War. This tortured Byronic figure merely wished to abandon worldly ambition and pursue his dreams of escape, perhaps of revolution. The erotic dances, sexual games and worship of beauty that almost two centuries later crushed my own heart in a vice, lay deep at the heart of the mutiny. It was a leap from the crags of reason into the cleft of chance.

Bligh was dragged raging from his cabin just before sunrise on April 28th, 1789, clad only in his night shirt. Christian *'looked like a Madman, 'is long hair was luse, 'is shirt Collair open'*.

'Mammoo,[15] *Sir, mammoo or you are dead this Instant!'* he screamed at Bligh, now tied to the mizzen mast. Christian pressed a bayonet against his chest.

'Blow his Brains out,' drifted on the breeze.

'You have dannled my children on your knees!' Bligh pleaded as he was forced into the launch. Was this the way to repay past kindnesses? Remorse seemed to flicker across Christian's distracted features.

'That, – captain Bligh, – that is the thing; – I am in Hell, – I am in Hell!'

Christian was now in command, and he set Bligh adrift in the launch with eighteen local crew and a handful of navigational aids to ensure his survival on the perilous 3,900 mile voyage from Tofua to Coupang in Timor. *'Huzza for Otaheite!'* drifted from the *Bounty* over the water. Breadfruit plants sailed through the air and bobbed on the Pacific swell.

The mutiny gave William Bligh a terrible opportunity to display his gifts, will, foresight, attention to detail and superb skill at navigation, on the greatest open boat voyage of all time. The mutiny had given Fletcher Christian the terrible opportunity to explore the dark cells of passion, betrayal and murder in the dark nights of Paradise.

Through her father, Almira was a seventh generation direct descendant of Fletcher Christian. The coat of arms of the Christian family above the fireplace gave *Almira's* a fanciful amalgam of sensational history and warm Polynesian hospitality. I felt an obscure kinship with Fletcher Christian. My own relocation to the island was the result of a similar failure of nerve and ambition.

I turned my attention to the faces of my fellow guests. Three English naturalists in safari drill were discussing the distribution and description of lepidoptera on the island.

'Of course the host plant for *Papilio ilioneus ilioneus* really ought to be *Capparis nobilis,* known as "Devil's Guts" locally.'

'Why do you say that, old man?'

'Because when irritated the larva will protrude a pair of prongs from behind the head!' He chuckled at this droll observation.

Next to me sat two mature, rather handsome ladies from the mainland. One was a college bursar, the other an archaeologist who was studying the remains of the penal settlements. Her historical knowledge was impressive, and she had the hooded eyes of a hawk. Opposite sat a stockman, visiting the island to advise on the management of cattle, because the thin animals disappeared over the cliffs at an alarming rate. He sat tall, quiet and self-conscious in a naive way, bright pink blotches showing through the scorched skin, ears set at an odd angle. A few other guests were seated around the table, all possessed of colourful fragments of island lore. At the far end sat the stockman's antithesis, a tubby, effeminate and talkative individual, touching everyone within reach. John was disconcertingly knowledgeable about Siamese cats. I helped myself to some Tahitian fish after Grace was said.

'Do you know,' John said to us all, 'that these cats have five more muscles in each ear than normal cats? They can leap vertically too, directly on to your shoulder from the floor! I have two Blue Points, one Lilac Point and two Brown Points. They are so gorgeous and passionately affectionate!'

The bursar seemed to see him as an enthusiastic child. She smiled patronisingly.

'I have a Burmese Blue in Point Piper,' she said.

'I do hope you have a scratching pole for the little dear and a substantial litter tray. The absolute minimum depth of litter…'

'Well, the only cat I'm familiar with,' the archaeologist observed, 'was made of nine tails of knotted and weighted cowhide that fell dull and heavy upon the flesh.'

This sabotage of the gay mood caused a gloomy silence to descend. I turned away to see Almira bringing in a platter of roast pork and red guava jelly. Beside it on the hand-loomed island cloth she placed a steaming bowl of kumera. Attention fixed on the food and the silence of inadequacy was transformed into the silence of anticipation as the plates were piled high.

One of the hungrier guests took hot potatoes and yams directly from the serving dishes before the girls had a chance to place them on the table, much to the consternation of a guest who persisted in wearing white sunblock on his nose after dark. Silence. The stomach often manages to still the ramifications of the mind. Almira watched her friends eat with evident vicarious satisfaction, her face generously glowing from the kitchen doorway.

'Yu laik sam yorlyi swiit tieti?'[16] she asked, holding out a large platter of sweet potatoes. Murmurs of assent.

The bursar started the conversation on a point of history.

'The French captain of *L'Astrolabe,* Jean-Françoise de la Pérouse, described the island as *'only a place fit for angels and eagles to reside in'.*

'Daa mait bii true darl, bat es plenti dem devils orn Norfolk!'[17] Almira laughing again. A veritable litany of quotations erupted, vying with each other to express disgust.

'Governor Darling referred to it as *'a place of the extremest punishment short of Death.'*

' *"The ne plus ultra of convict degradation"* according to Sir Thomas Brisbane'. Clearly the college bursar was a scholar.

' *The picture presented was a Cage full of Unclean Birds,'* quoted the curator of insects.

'They feared the depravity of this place more than death itself.'

'Men utterly irreclaimable and steeped in crime to the very lips.'

'Ocean Hell.'

The litany of horror cascaded around the table rolling off the tongues with delight.

'Sodom Isle.'

'Women were paraded naked before the male convicts in anticipation of a flogging on the triangles. Commandant Foveaux *revelled* in physical abuse.' The archaeologist at this moment seemed possessed of a mission.

'The Villain's Home.'

'The island where Satan never slept!'

'Moral gangrene ate their souls!'

'Oh dear me! So much evil in such a beautiful spot,' wistfully commented one of the ladies, unmindful that she had touched on a central mystery.

The stockman became uncomfortable with the academic tenor of the conversation and attempted to lighten the atmosphere with a contemporary assessment.

'Well, you know what they say – the island for the newly wed and the nearly dead.' Smiles and a slight pause by the masticators, eyes meeting, heads nodding.

'Slaughter Bay', I said, 'Headstone Point, Bloody Bridge, Gallows Gate, Murderers' Mound...' This contribution exhausted my knowledge of the signposts of suffering. The guests ruminated over the flaccid emotions that the idea of violence creates in the inexperienced mind over dinner. Silence resumed, broken only by the clink of silver on porcelain.

At this early stage, the island's history had only a superficial interest for me. The conversation remained part of the general touristic chatter as we approached the dessert and coffee. I had no deep knowledge of the ghastly traces of torture impressed on the night air up on the mountain, the plastered grain pits where convicts were abandoned to scream and starve. I was still a victim of studied dualities and enforced polarities, the contradictions and omissions of my education. Evil and beauty still appeared to be opposites early on.

Night began to press close about the house. Almira lit the candles and threw wide the French doors to the verandah. Dessert promised to be a complicated affair. Each diner was given a tray with a small bowl of brandy, one of brown sugar, one of whipped cream and an egg-cup of flaming alcohol. Pieces of pineapple in boat-shaped skins were brought in. Almira explained the steps in this ritual of gastronomic completion.

'Tek wan piis pineapple. Dip et in aa brendy, den the brown sugar and hold it in the flame. When the sugar's melted, pop it in the cream and then straight away eat it. Tell em if you don't think it's the best thing you've ever had! Es swiitan![18] Don't burn your tongue on the hot fork or you won't be talking any more nonsense!'

We experimented with the procedure under her careful gaze. A recording of Pitcairn Hymns filled the house with haunting melancholy. The male voices expressed a yearning, troubled by an inexorable sense of loss. Dusk lay close, the flames were reflected by the dark panelling, palms whispered in the night. We heard this plaint for the lost Garden of Eden, drifting on the air.

There, everlasting spring abides
And never withering flowers;
Death, like a narrow sea divides
The heavenly land from ours.

This music, artless and unaffected, was the first I encountered on the island. A fragile enchantment settled over us.

'In the Congo I used to grind the coffee with the butt of my pistol.' The moment was ruptured by the naturalist in boxer shorts as he lit his Calabash pipe.

'Yu mas haed plenty taim on yus hends or nort much koffee,'[19] Almira said. She had an instinctive ability to deflate any pompous remark.

∞

'...*it appeared like a great rock rising out of the sea: it was not more than five miles in circumference and seemed to be uninhabited; it was, however, covered with trees, and we saw a small stream of fresh water running down one side of it. I would have landed upon it, but the surf at this season broke upon it with great violence... it having been discovered by a young gentleman, son to Major Pitcairn of the marines, who was unfortunately lost in the Aurora, we called it Pitcairn's Island.*'

Captain Philip Carteret,
Account of a Voyage Round the World
in H.M.S. *Swallow*, 1767

The colonial house radiated an atmosphere of piety and innocence greatly at variance with the accounts of the mutiny. After the overloaded launch carrying Bligh and the loyalists had faded from view '...*Mr. Christian Himself took possession of Mr. Bligh's Cabbin...*' and the *Bounty* got under away for Tubuai in the Austral group. Uniforms were made from old sails edged with the blue material from Christian's jacket – an attempt to restore the symbols of authority and intimidate *'the Indians'*. As they arrived at Tubuai, the whole bay resounded to the unearthly music of blown conch shells. The ship was surrounded by canoes carrying aggressive native men with weapons and their women *'young and handsom having fine long hair which reached their waists in waving ringlets... Sent to Snare'*. Thefts resulted in bloodshed, with natives dying in canoes holed by grapeshot from the *Bounty's* cannon.

The crew considered the island suitable to settle. They returned to Tahiti to obtain livestock and female company, the prices of both negotiated with highly prized red parrot feathers. At the newly named Bloody Bay in Tubuai they began to build the ambitiously grand *Fort George*, the site again purchased with the plumage of parrots. But their presence led to civil war among the three island chiefs, and passions for women and grog so diminished Christian's authority that Tubuai was eventually abandoned. As the mutineers contemplated their alternatives, the *Bounty* dropped anchor for the third time in Tahiti at *Point Venus* in September 1789. *Point Venus*, where Captain James Cook had built *Fort Venus*, a fortified observatory, to observe the transit of the planet Venus across the heavens for Admiralty navigation charts in June 1769 – Venus, goddess of Love. The Fates were now managing their destiny.

Some twenty-eight mutineers and Polynesians finally began an epic voyage in the South Seas searching for an uninhabited, isolated island on which to hide. During this protracted wandering, Christian discovered Rarotonga. The natives stole an orange, whose descendants still flourish there. His skill at navigation preserved his leadership on the undermanned ship. He was searching for remote Pitcairn's Island, which he realised had been incorrectly mapped. On January 12th, 1790 they finally sighted the fertile and picturesque outcrop of Pitcairn, and, *'with a joyful expression such as we had not seen on him for a long time past'* Fletcher Christian decided to end his remarkable 8,000 mile, nine-month exploration. The *Bounty* had found her final resting place.

The great Pitcairn tale was not yet completed when Matthew Quintal, floundering in an alcoholic haze, set fire to the carpenter's storeroom.[20] The *Bounty* burned to the waterline, and useful timbers and fittings were lost. With this purgatorial fire began the eighteen years confinement of the outcasts. The island would become a forcing-house of passion for the nine Europeans, six native men, twelve women and a baby.

Bitter resentments began early. The mutineers divided Pitcairn among themselves with dictatorial arrogance, effectively making the natives slaves. The mutineers had each stolen native *'wives'* from Tahiti and now called them by English names – Isabella, Susannah, or Prudence. The death of Faahotu from scrofula left one of the mutineers, John Williams, without a *'wife'*. Toofaiti was *'taken'* from Tararo, a Raiatean native from the Society Islands, and *'given'* to Williams. She lightly agreed and changed her name to Nancy. Tararo fled to the wilds and plotted revenge on the whites, but the native women always told their white lovers of any plans hatched by the native men. Murder and birth pursued a perverse rhythm. Massacre increased the choice of women for those men who survived, yet bloody incidents proliferated.

Two of the native women lured the last two native men to their deaths. Teatuahitea tempted Tetahiti to her treacherous body, and then, when the satiated man finally fell asleep in a sexual stupor, Susannah crept into the hut and struck him across the throat with an axe. The blow failed to kill and as he flailed ineffectually, she split his skull with another ferocious stroke. The scalp of one native victim and the arm of another were sent as murder proof when belief among the men faltered. Fletcher Christian was shot in the back with a musket at close range *'whilst digging in his own field'*. In this way, eleven men were murdered in the four years to October 1793.

The women were treated brutally. Matthew Quintal bit off his wife's ear during a fierce argument, and threatened the rest of the community with death. The women responded with impotent conspiracies from remote places of concealment. William McCoy threw himself off a cliff, crazed with ardent spirit distilled from ti-trees and sugar-cane in one of the *Bounty's* copper kettles. Matthew Quintal was finally murdered by the ladies' favourite, Edward ('Neddie') Young. The quantities of blood splashed on the walls of the house by the frenzied wielding of the pole-axe in this *'justifiable homicide'* terrified the remaining women and children. Neddie died from an asthmatic complaint in 1800.

The lone surviving mutineer, John Adams (alias Able Seaman Alexander Smith) subsequently had two violent dreams where he saw visions of the flames and punishments of the Hell that awaited him. These were experienced while drunk on liquor from the *Bounty* still. The Archangel Michael loomed above to attack him with a dart for his transgressions. He embraced the Word of God forthwith, and he followed the angelic commands to instil the faith into the hearts of the remaining community.

In the minds of pious Victorians, the ancestors of the characters within my present story had enacted a parable of the fall and the redemption. The *'evil'* outlaws and their *'depraved'* Polynesian concubines had eaten of the apple of sexual licence and become beasts whose activities would blanch with horror the blood of a believer. All appeared lost when the Word was made manifest through the *Bounty's* Prayer Book and Bible, given tongue by the solitary survivor of the massacre. The community was transformed into an idyllic Christian brotherhood. Such a revolution was living proof of the power of the Gospels. This *'miracle'* became the matter for innumerable Victorian sermons on damp mornings in cold, stone churches in the English counties. Within England's seething cities, it was a ray of hope.

The Pitcairn Islanders came to possess the innocence of childhood. Remote from the influence of European and Polynesian civilisation, the community reflected the essence of neither. They expressed the joy of infancy entirely without guile, wickedness or the sophistication of adult life.

'Money no use to us. If you give me money, I throw it in the sea.'

The richness of the island allowed the friendship and trust of barter to prevail. But the community had soon outgrown Pitcairn, the tiny *'Rock in the West'.* Drought, famine and influenza set upon them.

In 1856, Sir William Denison, Governor General of the Australian Colonies, with the blessing of Queen Victoria, resettled the Pitcairners in the remains of the disused island penal station, Norfolk Island, 4,200 miles west across the Pacific. He considered the new establishment a form of *'experiment'* to preserve the Pitcairners from outside influences and corruption. They fatally misinterpreted this move as a form of land gift, and failed to press him for an exact rendering of their precise status. Generosity of intent rather than precision in law was more their natural culture, and they imagined him to be of similar heart. This notion of *'gift'* remained their interpretation. So was inflicted an invisible wound which was later to fester so painfully and so destructively.

This Third Settlement was the last Victorian experiment in a perverse laboratory of suffering. A fateful irony had placed this group of pious folk in what was once known as *'Old Hell'*, a place formerly devoted to moral reform through torture of the body, a place of toil, of *'punishment short of Death'*. Their virtuous souls had been maintained on Pitcairn in striking opposition to their heritage of intoxication with violence. They now dwelt in a setting once occupied by *'the vilest outcasts of society'*.

The purity of the original redemptive ideal had been diluted through the passing years, but echoes of the bells of piety still sounded in the souls of the older descendants. The old Pitcairn Hymns were often sung during warm, peaceful evenings of devotion in pine-panelled island homes.

CHAPTER III

'Ah, questo amor funesto obblia – ella e d'altri...'
('Ah, forget this ill-fated love – she is another's...')
Raimondo
'Lucia di Lammermoor' by Gaetano Donizetti, 1835
Act II Scene 2

I slipped into the kitchen for temporary relief from the intrepid insect experts, and I was surprised to find yet another group of people eating and drinking. They were more convivial than our educated friends and they joked loudly and bawdily with the island women working there. A ginger cat dozed on the long window-sill in front of the glass louvres. The tin rat-protectors, suspended like short skirts around the palm trunks in the garden outside, could hardly be seen in the failing light. The first moths were already beating against our bright reflections in the glass.

My eye was drawn to an islander seated apart, detached from the active life of the room, concentrated within himself. He had the bearded face of an adventurer, and his discerning eyes brushed one's face, absorbing detail, judging and assessing. His gentle, cultured voice seemed to carry within it concealed worlds, capable of arousing unaccountable emotion. Meeting him resembled a simultaneous encounter with two people, one propelling the mechanism and making the requisite social gestures, the other a vulnerable, soulful being, heavily guarded within. He ambled into the sitting-room and in the shadow of the Christian escutcheon he replaced the hymns with another music.

Suddenly, like the strike of a serpent, doom-laden chords worked in horns and tympani insinuated the breath of tragedy into the carefree atmosphere at *Almira's*. For this joyful house to be invaded by music of such sepulchral gloom was completely unexpected. The prelude to *Lucia di Lammermoor* in these healthy surroundings astounded and fascinated me. Part of my attention was taken up with domestic activity in the kitchen, but one ear strained for the opera. The glittering harp of the moonlit fountain rose above the orchestra and general kitchen chatter. I shivered at Lucia's premonitory apparition of blood-reddened water, ecstatic yearning for Edgardo, the low moan in the wind.

Curiosity drove me to look through the gauze curtains into the darkened room. From my concealed position on the verandah, I could see his hunched figure staring at a television screen. He was watching a transmission that was being specially relayed from the Sydney Opera House. The scene was the Great Hall at Lammermoor Castle. Edgardo, that instrument of immoderate passion, had thrown back Lucia's ring and was furiously crushing his own into the ground with his boot. Music of convulsive emotionality swept the tenor towards self-slaughter.

This tragic illusion of falsehood appeared to overcome the islander. With a sudden movement he lunged for the machine and switched it off. For some moments after lighting a cigarette he sat slumped, defeated, as if some vital organ had been severed. The darkness was marked by night insects, laughter from the kitchen and the arcing point of light from his cigarette. I returned to the company in the kitchen and in time he drifted listlessly back there with no sign of emotion. No attention had been paid to the music of the opera or his involvement with it.

Almira suddenly appeared preoccupied when she caught sight of him. 'Yu gwen ap in a' styk desdieh?' she asked.[21]

'Noe,' he replied, glancing furtively away.

'Mind yu tek daa stuff ap Sarnum's orn Jieh Ie Roed.'[22]

He nodded, silently left the table and wandered toward the rear garden. No-one bothered to notice him leave.

Wondering about this, I walked out alone on to the chilly verandah. The moon was rising behind a stand of pines. Moths whirled around the coachlamps in frenzied spirals towards the flames. A sable shell had descended over the island, condensing the peace in excruciating density. The pastness of the place came flooding to a singularity and the brain waited in this cell for a respite from the pressure, as if for a birth. This coincidence of the consummated and the anticipated gave island nights an intensity and pregnancy that teemed with intuited life, haunted by the suffering of felon souls. That night was the first manifestation of such metaphysics and I became profoundly uneasy in the face of these concealed forces.

Without warning, a powerful motorcycle flayed the darkness, cleaving up the drive beside the house, across the paddock, gun-fire of the cattle grid, to accelerate down the main road. It was a blast of violence into the peace of the evening. The islander of *Lucia* sat astride the machine, bare-chested in shorts, with a large hunting knife strapped to his thigh. Through the gloom I was astonished to make out a Collie dog seated on the petrol tank between his arms, bracing itself against the wind.

Almira was clearing up around me. 'Whoever is that?' I asked.

'Da es mais boy Nathan,'[23] Almira replied in a voice deprived of warmth, the voice of long suffering and neglect.

'He was married to Mareva,' she said, 'but they're separated now.'

I desisted from further questions.

Night had closed over the island like a vast, soft moth nestling into the hills and valleys. The blackness was of an intensity and depth I had never encountered in the city. Stars never before seen were scattered on indigo wings above us like hectic crystals. Presentiments of passions beyond the reach of the intellect flitted about with the insects.

'Kam in a' haus en light up a' fire darl!'[24] Almira called brightly.

It had already been set, so I simply applied a match. My mind gradually emptied of thought as I stared into the heart of the flame. The other guests drifted to bed and I was alone.

Slowly the wind began to rise to achieve a final terrific force, a tremendous clamour from the foliage of the palms in the garden. The fire had consumed itself and burned fitfully. I hurried across a pool of illumination cast by an outside lamp. Sounding like no other tree, the pines creaked and sang through the black gale. The atmosphere of the old island home was strong in my room, the deeply stained board and batten construction, the amber lamps. I placed a pale blue wafer of poison in the mosquito machine, and a deathly fragrance filled the chamber.

During the night, what seemed to be a thousand fingers scratched on the galvanised iron while rats squealed along the rafters. A torrential downpour woke me, falling on the roof and broad leaves with a deafening patter. It was as though I was lying in a cave beneath a forest waterfall. I remained in a blissful half-dream, snug and warm, protected and safe.

Before dawn crept about the horizon, a bird began to sing through this tropical turmoil. I lay in the dark, listening to the pure arabesques of melody rising above the tempest. The storm began to abate with the lightening sky and the bird flourished a final cadenza of isolate rapture. I rose, dressed quickly, and walked to the coast to watch the sun rise over the ocean.

CHAPTER IV

'When the Tree of Knowledge fell, an era ended.'
'Cracky' Christian

$\mathcal{T}$here were practical reasons for my presence on the island and these soon took a more positive shape. I had been contracted by the Norfolk Island Administration as the Broadcasting Officer. My duties required me to supply programmes and shipping information for some six hours per day – local and national news schedules, musical material, various programmes from the BBC Transcription Service. The cramped transmission room was in the former wine cellars of the Officers' Quarters of the New Military Barracks, a Second Settlement complex of buildings completed in 1836. The call-sign, *VL-2-NI*, was unremarkable and sterile, belying the occasionally surrealistic nature of the broadcast material. The equipment was rudimentary at the outset, and on a good day the signal from a transmitter the size of a shoebox could be just be received on the other side of the island.

Once, notices for the residents had been shown on a huge pine called *The Tree of Knowledge*, situated in a magnificent avenue of three hundred and seventy-five pines, planted during the convict period. The construction of an airfield by the Americans during the Second World War had necessitated its tragic felling. Now the radio station was meant to replace it. A typical Local Notice from the early period of the station might have read:

PUBLIC NOTICE CONCERNING TRESPASSING STOCK

'A red cow over the past weeks has continually trespassed on portion 24ma9 which is reached by a right-of-way over Mrs. Quintal's land between Mrs. Buffett's and Mrs. Young's houses at Stockyard Road. It is not known where the cow enters but when seen it usually leaves by jumping the cattle grid at Stockyard Road or else the grid into Mr. Matthew McCoy's house property and from there, jumping a fence on the hillside. Considerable damage may result from this continued trespass. Owner is untraceable. Appropriate steps will be taken after Saturday August 27th.'

I wondered about the 'appropriate steps'. An element of weird humour crept into the Local Notices, which developed greatly in scope after the station was relocated and upgraded following a serious fire. But following the move *'up country'*, I always remembered with nostalgia the original cellars of the Officers' Quarters for the amount of claret drunk in Regency style during *'official transmissions'* and the atmosphere of wartime espionage that prevailed late at night beneath the flagstones.

Early each morning I would park my jeep near the foaming rocks and spend some moments musing over the panorama laid out before me. Through the aromatic sea mist I could see the ruins of the Pentagonal Prison, elegant Government House on its symbolic eminence, the hump beneath the undulating pasture that revealed the site of the Lumber Yard. The blatant statement of power expressed by the ziggurat staircase to Major Anderson's Commissariat Stores left no doubt as to the martinet mentality of the majority of Commandants. Then, still further, beyond the sea wall, the surf breaking over the bar at low water and the recumbent red lion of Philip Island, formerly used for shooting expeditions by the officers of the garrison. As I walked south along the compound, past the corner turrets and loopholes in the wall of the Old Military Barracks, the treacherous waters around Nepean Island showed ingenuously mineral-blue in the morning light.

Two black guns on scarlet carriages were placed before the entrance to the New Military Barracks, now the Administration buildings. They had been salvaged from H.M.S. *Sirius*, the flagship of the First Fleet which was wrecked on the morning of March 19th, 1790. The romantic idealist Lieutenant Philip King R.N., Commandant of the First Settlement, had previously warned in his geographical report that *'when the flood runs to the westward, it sets very strong around Nepean Island and Sydney Bay'*. Despite these observations, he was forced to watch grimly on the shore as the coral reef tore out the heart of the warship. Captain Hunter had misjudged the flood-tide, the wind had capriciously shifted to the south-east and *'having fresh stern way, she tailed on the reef and struck'.*

The surviving colonial buildings showed strong contrasts in the nature of the accommodation provided for the Detachment. The New Military Barracks was an impressive if brutal example of Colonial Georgian architecture. The walls were a soft honey-yellow with dark brown dressed stone to the windows and doors. Minor details faintly echoed the Palladian harmony of the terraces of Georgian London and Bath, but the robust function of a Newgate was more in evidence. Along the main street known as Quality Row, a number of Regency colonial villas nestled in tropical gardens.

The Officers' Quarters, my destination, was a building not without refinement, having graceful verandahs to the ground and upper floors, supported by slim white pillars. The upper gallery had a delicate white balustrade encircling the structure. The officers, after dining in the mess and taking a glass of Fine Old Military Port, would stroll or sit in pleasant coolness discussing a recent shoot, reading Lord Byron, recovering their wits after a strenuous ball or admiring the fine views over Slaughter Bay. The suffering within the prison was invisible to them during those terribly beautiful sunsets behind the ridges of pines. Only the sea sound of the reef was punctuated by the music of the convict bell. The mass grave called Murderers' Mound remained a sentinel of death on the periphery of the settlement.

The discrimination and artful sensibility of Miss Jane Austen's secluded characters, her deflations of snobbery and measured severity towards her creatures had little place on Norfolk Island, yet the island 'Establishment' was often drawn from their class. As for the convicts, the thieves of the great Wen, the Irish political rebels out of Cobh Harbour and the gentlemen forgers from Spitalfields, they were considered examples of an unforgivable failure of self-discipline and character which transportation to the colonies and the lash were bound to cure. One convict received 30,000 lashes in sixteen years, *'yet the man is hearty and well and in no ways concerned'* remarked a Governor. Any subordination of the lower orders was supported by that unexpressed complicity which exists between the jailer and the jailed to perpetuate the system for their mutual benefit. The habit of coercion and its attendant vices infected the very stones of these grim convict piles.

Lieutenant King remained true to the moral imperatives of the time, and took as his mistress a female convict, a *'mantua maker'* from Worcester, convicted of stealing a dimity petticoat and other items of a delicate nature. He had two natural sons by her, on whom he lavished great affection. A flaring up of the gout prompted an application for leave, and he returned to England and married his cousin at St. Martin-in-the-Fields in London. He returned to the island as Lieutenant-Governor, and he found his mistress had meanwhile begun to live with a convict, but his wife warmly accepted the two children into the family while she herself was pregnant. Life in the colonies presented many such examples of the bewildering compassion of the female heart.

My later investigations into the deeper shadows of the First Settlement revealed blemishes in the Regency idealist. An *'excess of manly sentiment'* expressed itself in the flogging of a female convict on her naked back, stripped, wrists tied to the tail of a moving handcart. A later Commandant, Major Foveaux, ranged the male convicts in a circle where they could watch the *'backscratcher'* work the naked woman on the Triangle, delighting in her agony and shame. Women were forced to danced naked on the mess tables of the Garrison, the *Dance of the Mermaids*, with numbers painted on their backs so the officers could more easily recognise their favourites and urge them on to assume more lascivious and depraved sexual positions during the port. The bellman would sell a fine specimen as a slave for ten pounds and one *'more used'* for a bottle of rum.

The evangelical satisfaction of whipping the transgressor, together with the fear and bitter resentment arising from the isolation from England, merged in an obsession to punish rather than reform. The traditions of the public school hero-floggers and the Navy's common use of the lash combined in the colonies to sail perilously close to the aphrodisiacal pleasures of unfettered power. The inescapable sexual cycle of dominance and submission rapidly turned these isolated, occasionally desperate Commandants into *flagellant voyeurs*, addicts of pain, addicts of the weighted cat softening in its tub of beef-brine and bluestone.

While I worked as Broadcasting Officer, I met more and more people at nearly all levels of island society. It was a place of extremes. The pious homes of elderly Pitcairn descendants gave way to the shockingly crude Carmel (known by the *cognoscenti* as *'Cream Caramel'*) a bar prostitute from Kings Cross, who assured me, in a frantic burst of sensitivity, that she played 'classical piano', more specifically *'Sonatas by Haydn... from the original, mate'*, as she massaged my groin with her calf.

I engaged in interminable bouts of drinking with the lighterage workers and listened to their stories of unloading the visiting ships, dropped loads and heroically salvaged loads. I was invited to receptions at Government House for the visiting Australian Cabinet, and I entertained the inebriated politicians with spirited Chopin on an ancient Broadwood upright. Here I was introduced as the Broadcasting Officer 'who's got three women up the duff simultaneously Ha! Ha! Ha!'

Almira, being a Polynesian patrician and sensitive to social class, maintained a close relationship with each Administrator and his wife during their posting to Norfolk.

'Darl... Tek wan pineapple en sam carrot daun a' Government House – go orn.'[25]

Most Administrators were Navy or Air Force officers, who were great sources of diverting anecdotes over coffee and cognac on the cool and spacious verandahs of Government House.

The station became my vehicle for self-exploration and improvement, and this made me suspect to the minute public within range of the transmitter. I was tolerated, even enjoyed, but I was still a 'blow-in'.[26] Sunday evening broadcasts were devoted to classical music. This was particularly popular with the English settlers and increasingly so with the Pitcairn descendants, who were innately sensitive to music. It was an emotional release for me to be able to communicate my excitement with particular performances. One Scotsman mounted a regular 'Opera Season' complete with engraved invitations. The 'performances' were on gramophone records in the tropical gardens of his mansion. I indulged in gargantuan series devoted to single composers, a four month series on Hector Berlioz with readings from the *'Memoirs'*, six months on Beethoven.

The Officers' Quarters were gutted by a mysterious fire. The studio was moved to bigger premises in the centre of the island on New

Cascade Road, the road leading to the old whaling station. Transmissions from this location were in constant jeopardy from the cows munching cable in the aerial enclosure or calling their calves through the stable door of the studio, or sheltering during rainy nights under the entrance awning and making diarrhoea over the locks.

As I was digging my way in early one morning through the mess, an English settler in boxer shorts arrived in a Land Rover to deliver an early Local Notice. He glanced about him at the 'khaki decorations'.

'You know, if this sort of thing happened at the BBC in Portland Place', he said, 'the doorman wouldn't be at all pleased.'

Cockroaches took up residence in my trousers during the night, and then started crawling while I was reading the news. A concerned listener brought me an enormous can of insecticide tied with pink ribbon. During more extreme sessions the telephone would ring on air. The Official Secretary from Kingston regularly accused me of obscenity, obscure forms of blasphemy (there were many denominations on the island to offend) and outright political subversion. A catalogue of floggable offences were cited. All quite justified as I approached my work in high spirits.

∽

The theme music from the Marlon Brando version of *'Mutiny on the Bounty'* opened broadcasting each day.

'This is VL-2-NI broadcasting on a frequency of 1570 kilohertz. It's just coming up to eight o'clock. Here is the Local News and Notices for Wednesday October 12th.'

'The Great Seal of Norfolk Island is to be returned and displayed in the Historical Museum. It is to held on perpetual loan by the Administrator of the day. This symbol of loyalty to the Crown and emblem of freedom, this vital link with the United Kingdom is again in its rightful place.'

'The newly appointed Commonwealth policeman affectionately known as Wyatt Earp was successfully rescued from the surf yesterday afternoon after being thrown in from the Kingston Pier by a group of islanders who wished to establish their superior affection and authority through this initiation ceremony. This time-honoured custom is performed thoughtfully at high tide and is intended to warn rather than mutilate. No charges have been laid.'

'A worm count of dung will be made by the Department of Health over the next six weeks.'

'A set of convict trumpet irons in good condition have been found during excavations at the New Gaol near the Hampton Isolation Punishment Cells. These are to be restored by the resident archaeologist, Mr. Voussoir.'

'A rabbit has been sighted running free on the island. It has not yet been ascertained if the creature is a buck or pregnant female. The possible repercussions of a litter of rabbits born in the wild is potentially disastrous to the flora. Accordingly a $50 reward had been offered by the Administration for the carcase.'

'The bookmark working bee at the Wives and Mother's Club has been cancelled for this week.'

'The Wives and Mother's Club Fashion Parade will begin this evening at 8.00 p.m. An attractive range of lounge and night wear, mix-and-match undies, bikinis, panty girdles, full and half slips, stretch love undies in ravishing colours such as Blueberry, Wild poppy, Persian Plum and Crushed Ruby. Hope to see you there.'

'A container of valuable bull sperm has disappeared from a Post Office Box in Burnt Pine. The police are investigating this unusual crime.'

'A replica of Captain Bligh's open boat will soon set out to duplicate the 3,900 mile voyage he made after the mutiny aboard His Majesty's Armed Vessel *Bounty*. He was set adrift 25 miles southwest of Tofua and passed Fiji, the Great Barrier Reef and Timor. The anniversary is on May 2nd. and the boat will depart from the same position. Period dress will be worn.'

'Nicky and Willy and Uncle Bertie present Music from the South Seas at the Paradise Hotel tonight. This will include the Tahitian Fertility Dance by Teehuteatuaonoa. Pie and prawns will be served.'

'SHIPPING NOTICE: The *M.V. Jacques del Mar*, which due to bad weather had to sail before cargo unloading was complete last weekend, is due next Friday.'

'Finally I have two lost notices:
First of all a chrome hub cap was lost in the Burnt Pine shopping area some time on Tuesday afternoon. Please return to "Hoof" Quintal at the crusher.
Secondly a notice from the Island Hospital – Lost: Walter Christian. If he is found could you please return him to the hospital as soon as possible.'

'This is VL-2-NI at three minutes past eight. A song for a special lady by the great Jim Reeves *"Stand By Your Window Tonight".*'

The radio station benefited from the local community spirit. Scrumptious warm Apfelstrudel and cream was sent round to the studio in the late evening by The Garrison Club, a local restaurant. Baskets of wild limes, lemons and oranges were delivered as a gesture of appreciation by listeners. The post of Broadcasting Officer was an ideal appointment for an emotionally burnt out young man.

CHAPTER V

Tropic Bird – Phaethon rubricauda

On such an historic island, it was impossible to escape the intimations of past experience that surrounded me or prevent the mapping of my personal destiny on to the dismal background of the convict ruins. Natural beauty possessed no force for moral regeneration among the prisoners or their keepers. I became fascinated by the mysterious conjunction of the exquisite scenery and the morbid, unrelenting cruelty practiced by men at the Ultra Penal Station. I encountered their fragmented spectres as they flitted by, unsummoned yet inescapable by virtue of the contained nature of the place. You must understand it was an island, a place of concentrated power in the wilderness of the ocean.

Little in this Paradise was as it first appeared. As I peeled back the layers of time, a world of kaleidoscopic complexity began to enfold me. To Captain James Cook, the Master of H.M.S. *Resolution,* who discovered '*Norfolk Isle*' on October 10th. 1774 together with Reinhold and George Forster, his Polish 'philosophers', the outwardly sound plantations of pines that covered the island seemed to offer the finest wood for the Masts and Yards of the Fleet. '*...the chief produce of the isle is Spruce Pines which grow here in vast abundance and to a vast size...*' he wrote in his Journal of the voyage. The branching did not begin until high up the massive trunks but later the timber fellers found that behind the bark the wood had decayed, too risky for use in large ships.

The melancholy years of the First and Second Settlements had strangely insinuated themselves into the wind and seemed even to infect the innocent pairs of fairy terns riding the updraughts along the valleys. The setting sun caught the branches of the white oak and whitewood which glowed palely like the drained blood vessels of a convict hand thrust out from the grave. As the history crystallised in my mind, I became uneasy when confronted with the merely picturesque.

One was irresistibly seduced away from conventional morality in such a pagan Arcadia. The ambiguous quality of the air caused the upright, the self-righteous and the depraved alike to be inspired by a desire for natural pleasures and passionate sexuality, for freedom from spiritual and physical fetters. Throughout its history, the sensual, yet in the same breath, celestial air of Norfolk Island has profoundly challenged the received ideas of those who chose to settle there.

'There's a beautiful girl out here wants to meet you,' Almira called. I came out of my room but was rather tongue-tied when I saw the exotic island woman I had glimpsed in the garden, standing on the verandah, confident and without a trace of shyness. I could almost feel the sexual heat radiating from her.

'Watawieh yuu? Ai es Paul,'[27] I managed to stumble out.

'Wael, thaenks. Yu el tork Norfuk guud, anieh?'[28] Her laughter sparkled like the sea. 'He'll be popular, this one!'

'I knew I shouldn't have introduced you two,' Almira seemed as ambiguously pleased as Mareva.

'Will you be long on Norfolk?' Mareva asked.

'Quite some time I should think. I'm running the radio station and I might start a business.'

'Yes, I know why you're here,' she said rather mysteriously.

'Where do you work on the island?'

'Here and there. Mainly up at the hospital, in reception.'

We looked at each other for fractionally longer than was comfortable, always a sign of mutual attraction.

'Ai staaten.'[29] Mareva suddenly said. 'Ai gwen naawi.[30] It's so hot here! See you later orn, Paul. Bye, Almira!'

She turned away with such an erotic glance and movement, I felt as if a powerful magnet was pulling me along. It was the fascination opposite temperaments instinctively feel for each other. We were both alert for an adventure to fill the vacuum that follows any significant change in life.

I often reflected later on the social risks she took in becoming my lover. Island men deeply resented mainlanders mixing with their women. The confined atmosphere concentrated these feelings as it had done since the First Settlement, when soldiers from the detachment of the New South Wales Corps enticed wives and lovers from the huts of time-expired convict men. There were violent incidents in the rain forests. Watching eyes were everywhere.

Mareva was descended from one of the most violent *Bounty* mutineers, a murderer who brutalised the native women on Pitcairn. She had inherited from her knife-scarred ancestor a will to fly in the face of established authority, and she combined this with the natural pleasures of her Tahitian soul. This curious alloy was fired in the crucible of our passion. She stilled my mind to analysis and intellectual rumination with burning caresses, ancient kisses. Intelligent in ways I had not anticipated, separated from her husband Nathan, she insinuated herself with gestures and dance calculated to arouse my deepest erotic feelings.

We explored the ruins and island topography until layers of time rose in my mind like stacks of plaited mats. I began to explore the moral wilderness that lay beneath what appeared to the uninitiated as *'only a place fit for angels and eagles to reside in'*. I looked forward to the future – carelessness, love of pleasure without guilt, beauty and sexual games. Simultaneously I looked backward into the old years, into the island's past, the pain of thwarted idealism, the cold austerity of control and punishment. The dawn shadows of the barracks pressed down more heavily each morning as I went in to broadcast, although the freedom of the night and Mareva's silken skin had swept away the living death of history. Excesses of moral reform had been carved into the hearts of the convicts and the abominable grunt of ravishment and despair were still imprisoned in the air. Deprived of the hearts of men they had been given those of beasts.

Mareva and I went on egg collecting expeditions to the barren offshore islands, laughing with the breakers, guiding a small fishing boat through the opening in the dangerous reef that guarded the entrance to the lagoon. In October we gathered the eggs of the Whale bird, the Wide-Awake. The yolk was vibrant orange in colour with a fishy taste not unlike caviar, and it was a delicacy among the islanders. At low tide she would lead me along a creek bed to Bumboras, a magnificent reserve that opened to the sea above a crescent of sand, fringed by pines in a curve like a giant order of columns. We climbed over the mounds of smooth, rounded rocks collecting hi-his, small shellfish. Time expanded to stillness. As we clambered out beyond the headland, a classical view of the gold-ochre buildings emerged across the slow-breathing ocean like a face from beneath a scarf disturbed by the wind, a living picture of the old Second Settlement. The tidal pools among the rocks, some shaped like skulls looking out to sea, had trapped Rainbow Fish, wonderfully banded in luminous blue and yellow. Dappled by sunlight they swam in panic across and back across their prison, finally leaping over an isthmus of shallow water to an adjacent pool. There they remained despite desperate efforts to escape and ultimately hid themselves in the eroded spaces and shelves beneath the water.

I watched Mareva in awe, her dusky, luxurious body clad only in a fragment of flowered cloth bending over the hot mineral-blue pools, ivory-black hair tumbling over her breasts as her short fingers deftly removed the tiny spiral shells. In silence she pointed to spiny sea urchins, what appeared to be bunches of submerged grapes that glittering like glass through the ruffled surface, brain coral and yellow starfish. We swam and watched the white terns glide.

A trek around the base of a cliff infested with the burrows of the Ghost Bird took us to the secret beach known as Second Sands. A wild cavalry charge of waves crashes over the crags here – sea spray, sea sound, sea spume, perfume of salt clear air. Her dark eyes captured mine and the sun revealed her strong legs through the thin fabric. She stood on her toes in the sand, trembling a little as we embraced. The sarong dropped from her waist as we fell towards a patch of dappled shade under the pines. We came together for the first time, and she moved languidly as I touched her. Her perfume rose and mingled with the stronger odours from the ocean and the floating kelp. We spread ourselves cooling and exhausted in the breeze, like lizards resting on warm boulders.

Towards dusk, lethargy overcome, we cooked the shellfish in a pot on the beach, teasing out the tiny morsels of flesh with a pin, enjoying the intimacy of the moment. The purity of the air allowed us to see with great definition the changing patterns of light that swept over Philip Island in the distance. We listened to the inner life of the sighing surf and watched a pair of rose-white Tropic birds (*Phaethon rubricauda*), with their long tail feathers like two streamers of vermilion light, trailing in the wake of their arc over the waves.

CHAPTER VI

Paulina

*O*ne evening, Mareva suggested we visit a remote house she had discovered in the Reserve near Bird Rock, abandoned some time before by an itinerant Scotsman. It was on the far side of the island, down a boggy track, where we had to leave the jeep. Darkness was almost upon us when we ventured into the forest, and I became apprehensive as the dense foliage closed in and the sepulchral cry of the Boobook Owl, the Mopoke, made me to clutch Mareva's hand. She giggled blithely, and as we passed an old convict saw-pit she pointed ahead.

Scattered about the floor of the jungle there were countless glowing points of light. Small, luminous fungi were sprouting everywhere between the damp, dead leaves. I left the path and bent down to examine this strange phenomenon of fallen stars, and she knelt beside me and stroked my head with strange compassion. All I could hear was the hum of insects and the murmur of the distant ocean. Her hair and perfume descended over me like a languorous cape, but as I turned my lips towards hers, I was discomforted by the sight of a trickle of dark, red sap meandering down the trunk of the Blood-wood Tree against which we were leaning. I rose nervously and she fluttered away like a leaf from my shoulders. We continued along the rutted track, now led only by her instinct and the luminous mushrooms. A darker area lay ahead, and she went before me, whispering, 'Weit'.

She disappeared inside. The vast night slowly enshrouded me in a teeming blanket of intuition. A window was gradually illuminated as she trimmed the wick of a hurricane lamp. The amber light bobbed insecurely, alternately glowing and fading as she came to the front door. She held the lamp forward.

The walls appeared to be made from old packing cases and tea chests. We could even make out some faded lettering. The roof had collapsed into some of the rooms and we had to step over rotting timbers, while in the dark unknown objects crunched and broke underfoot. We came to a back room that seemed inhabited, with primitive landscapes of the island cliffs in rough oils on the walls, pink hibiscus in a tumbler of water on a makeshift table and a mattress in one corner covered with a Balinese cloth. Rush matting covered the floor.

I realised this was her nest, the secret love haunt of a feral creature, a place where she could play the games of sensual oblivion she knew so instinctively. She did not care for me in any conventional romantic sense, she was simply curious about my sexual experience, murmuring I was beautiful, like the ocean wind. She beckoned me with a graceful gesture, her hand moving downward and drawn gently towards her. As Mareva lay back on the crimson dragons printed into the Batik, impudent hair crept above the margin of cloth that had loosened around her thighs during our walk under the forest canopy.

The touch of her skin left me breathless with excitement. I felt I was being drawn into oblivion by her voluptuous body. The lethargic caress of her tongue brought me punishing explosions of pleasure. She moved powerfully yet gently like the sea in summer. The lamp flickered and began to go out as she gave little shudders, the aftershocks of bliss. As we rested, my buttocks nestling into her belly, I felt the heat of Venus radiating against me like a warm shell at the edge of the cool ocean. We drifted into sleep as the distant surf hushed over the rocks.

Strong sunlight and birds woke me the next morning. While she slept, I slipped from under our light covering and wandered about, waking up. No coffee in this abandoned place. Now I could recognise broken packets of children's sweets on the floor. Around the battered entrance a climbing yellow rose grew in wild profusion. A chicken-run leant at a fantastic angle, twisted wire, weeds and rusted coops. Blasted trees, dense stands of lantana and a variety of climber known locally as 'Devil's Guts' (nasty spines erupt along the sterile branches) were threatening to consume what remained of the old house. I turned over planks and pieces of old packing case in that same desultory fashion as when one picks over what remains after a death. The trickle of what had once been a stream drew me over to a crude water wheel slumped on a broken axle. Ferns and mauve Clematis were growing between the twisted vanes and out of the cracks in the rock.

A rough concrete generator box stood nearby, and I saw the gears and cogs of a mechanism, a driving shaft and gearbox welded solid by rust. Wires that had carried the current led off into the bush, their broken ends hanging from the tree branches. Jammed in a corner among the confusion of iron, there was an old leather kit-bag covered in dust and mouse droppings, the brass hasps rotting away from the frame, the lock corroded.

I carried it back into the house and sat down on the end of Mareva's mattress. Sunlight poured in through the empty window. The gentle movement of her crinkled, brown hair on the pillow showed she was awake.

'Wathing yu bin duu?'[31] she asked sleepily.

'I've just been wandering around. Strange fellow, that Scot, living way out here. So difficult to get to. I found an old bag of his in the generator house.'

'Es samthing en et?'[32]

'It's locked.'

'Erpen up daa thing! Mait bii treasure ensied!'[33] Her almond-shaped eyes were alight.

'That's not very likely,' I said. I prised a long, rusty nail free from the wall and used it to try to force the hasp open. Mareva draped herself over my shoulder and nibbled my ear.

'What did this McLachlan do on the island?' I asked.

'Hi bin werk durn aa Admin. at Government House mostly in dem gardens. Hi bin paas master f' miekmiek. Hi bin s'baeli ap orn a' bied – got wan hili or bin m'hoen.'[34]

The leather parted from the frame and the bag was open.

'Oe Noe! Es em maad oel buuk,'[35] she moaned, more interested in running her hands between my thighs.

'Stop it Mareva. This could be interesting.'

She scratched me playfully and went to the mirror on the wall, holding strands of hair across her face and mouth, pulling absurd faces. There were four books in the bag, one slightly smaller than the others, each protected by its own marbled case. I took out one volume bound in yellow morocco, fitted with a patent Bramah lock. A faded coat of arms had been embossed in gold on the cover. My excitement rose as I picked the lock, and the South Pacific sunlight fell on a ruled and paginated notebook, each page covered in minute handwriting, impeccably neat with scarcely any correction, written in sepia ink. I leafed through, glancing at entries.

∞

"Journal of my Visit to Italy, Education at Geneva,
Dark Meditations on the Death of Major J. Wellesley
Journey to Van Diemen's Land aboard the 'Fairlie' 1836"

Florence, April 26th 1828
In the Boboli Gardens

The month of May, *ce mois sacré!* How soft are these days of spring in Italy, no chill damp that descends, no dangerous sea-mist to cling. My indisposition is now passé & the sun has quite elevated my mood. I have befriended a waif, a street cat which lies at my feet. The water splashing from the cylix fountains, the silent gestures of the statuary provide a most cheerful and happy music.

Last evening we listened to Madame de Staël but her countenance is not nearly so ugly or her skin as tawny as our journalists relate (her profile is *'as frightful as a precipice'* says Lord Byron; *'she has the effect of a torpedo upon me'* says Adolophe). Her hair is black, if it be her own. Her mouth is unpleasant but her complexion is fair & her dark eyes brim with vivacity *'c'est un oeil qui éclaire toute sa personne'*. While talking she strokes & pinches her nostrils & twirls in her fingers a piece of paper twisted into the form of a flower. I believe the absence of this trifle renders her dull & mute. Perhaps she should rid herself of it perpetually for her voice is loud and disagreeably hoarse. She paid assiduous attention to me with the liveliest suggestions as to my costume in her *trainant* style, removing the broad ribbon from my blue willow hat & tying it around my waist to appear highly un-English and *farouche*.

Next morning M. de Rocca was also present who sat mysteriously apart, silent, in great *déshabillé*, wrapped in a great coat. He enjoys the reputation of being a violent, passionate & sensual cavalry captain.

'*Vous ne parlez pas, mon cher,*' said Mme de Staël.

'*O, ce n'est pas çela, Je ne parle pas parce que je n'ai rien a dire,*' insolently replied this tall, somewhat handsome young man.

'Speech is not his language,' observed a caustic Mme de Staël.

She transformed herself into some silent and magnificent tempest of gloom & vexation on hearing this, furiously twirling her twig & went on to some commonplace observations about rough weather on the Grand Canal in Venice. The Gondolas were something between love & death she said. I felt cold & trembled at this premonitory dark thought.

Later I discovered *en passant* that Mme de Staël had secretly married John de Rocca, a man twenty-three years her junior!

Geneva, May 14th 1828

My instructor, Mr. Cornelissen, took me riding early this morning as the mist was rising from the placid surface of the lake. We traversed some magnificent alpine pastures scattered with Spring flowers in a multiplicity of colours. I cantered quite fast. The violent motion threw my petticoats into disorder, &, shocking to relate, they rose above my knees. Chill winds from the mountains lifted my habit like a light kerchief & it served just to shade my garter from observation. Mr. Cornelissen was maliciously amused at my misfortune, tittered away behind me & made various caustic remarks on the fine figure I might cut in Hyde Park. I should have been dull indeed to cry yet could scarcely restrain from changing colour.

Pressed flowers and desiccated leaves fluttered to the floor as I turned the pages. I carefully replaced these pathetic traces of an experience so remote from my own.

Florence

Fiesole – Villa Mirandola
Following a visit to the Uffizi Gallery

May 20th. 1828

(Copy of a letter)

Dearest Selina

Here I am lately cast again into the world of Art Studies in Florence. I await a letter from you with impatience & have heard nothing from England for weeks. Thank you for the French patterns – *ravissant!*

I suffer from a surfeit of pictures & sculpture! Such colour & passionate genius for composition! I cannot appreciate more than a few pictures on any occasion before my mind aches from excessive stimulation. My companion & tutor was Signora Berardi, a beautiful yet diminutive Florentine lady, a scholar of the Renaissance who possesses more than superficial powers of observation & was trained as a painter in Ravenna. She dresses in the Handsome Italian Manner & revealed some of the mysteries. I felt engaged in an initiation, as these pictures resemble Nature not one whit – so unlike our dear English watercolours. Such a superabundance of flesh in the Italian pictures with such a marked absence of drapery! At length we arrived at the *'Primavera'* by Sandro Botticelli painted for Lorenzo di Pierfrancesco de' Medici in 1477. It hung in the villa at Castello.

We contemplated it sitting as I was excessively *fatigué*. It being the Spring season in Italy, I hoped to understand more of this country's botanical specimens through contemplation of the scene, but found it dominated by a host of dancing ladies engaged on a pic-nic, one of whom was fleeing the grave dangers posed by a licentious gentleman springing from the trees. The only other gentleman (also partially clad) was indifferent to the assembled company & pursued his luncheon with a staff in the surrounding orchard of golden fruits. Their delicate features were beautiful but gave little indication of the character of the possessor. Signora Berardi was amused by these interpretative efforts and hastened to inform the *Signora Inglesa* that the picture had an *allegorical* purpose. At the risk of straining your optics, look at the small engraving I enclose.

The gentleman on the right in the elucidation remains dubious, despite the Signora's great cleverness of exposition. He represents Zephyr or the Spring wind, a *'breath of passion'* pursuing the next figure, the timid unadorned earth-nymph Chloris. When caught she is transformed or metamorphosed into Flora – her whole personage covered in the most exquisitely painted Spring flowers. In a sonnet by Lorenzo de' Medici one finds the line *'la primavera quando Flora di fiori adorna il mondo'* (*Spring, when Flora adorns the world with flowers*). Signora Berardi informed me that this was the beginning of the drama entitled *'The Metamorphosis of Love in the Garden of Venus'*. The central figure is the moderate Venus of Nature assisted by a blindfolded & wanton Amor flying above, the little peach about to release his flaming shaft. The next group are three interlaced dancers called the Three Graces – Virtue, Beauty & Sensuality – who perform in a mysterious dance knot, the significance of which I have not the brain to encompass, despite Signora Berardi's best efforts! What a maze!

Dearest, I approach the conclusion of my *'Discourse'*. I am left to explain Mercury, the gentleman on the far left. He leads the Three Graces, a mystagogue, a *'probing intellect'* who plays with the clouds in order to *'reveal the mysteries'*, an *interpres secretorum* whose desire is to reveal the truth through poetic dissimulation. The complementary forces of love are here displayed. *The Argument* of the painting is to turn from the world & contemplate celestial love through the intellect in Mercury's winged shoes but then to re-enter it again in clear knowledge upon the breath of passion.

Well! My tympanums and brain cracked at this presentation of the *'persona sofistica'* Botticelli & I would fain disbelieve painters had such intellects! Signora Berardi was amused in her venomous way with the irritation & disbelief written on my countenance. I have lately returned from the gallery & written you this *'Chapter'*.

Selina my dear, how I long for our simple English pictures *sans allégorie!* Nature presented in her truthful sense, *sans philosophie &* wordiness. I yearn for my beloved Suffolk landscape, my parish churches & our picturesque John Constable – now what clouds are *those!*

Geneva, December 1828

Letter from the Honourable Lieutenant L – H – L

The receipt of this was as water to the parched wanderer in Ismailia! I took this precious communication with its full seal & entwined initials to my pretty bedroom that overlooks the Lake to Mont Blanc, gazing at the slow clouds moving across the azure sky.

'Will he be gentle with me?'

'Will he request me to be of his party at the Grand Ball at Lady Bedingfield's?'

The paper he uses is made by hand at Bologna & always resists my efforts to cut it. I seem to see his languishing dark eyes smiling at my struggles to obtain his words. It is not without reason he is known as 'The Magnetiser' by the more envious of our admirers.

Later

Both my questions wonderfully & affirmatively answered!

I was astonished and excited by these journals, discovered in such enchanted circumstances. Mareva was growing restive with my indifference to her, and she had begun caressing me, nuzzling, fingers gently exploring, her head butting the base of the binding and making it hard to concentrate.

'Please, Mareva!' I said. 'Just let me *be* for a while!'

But she was making the moment into a contest between herself and the book, and this time she was victorious.

Paulina Wellesley, the author of these journals, could only have been young when she wrote these brittle first effusions on love. My age? And how curious that her name was so similar to mine. I wondered if she might be a distant relation to the great Duke of Wellington. She seemed to be an uncommon young woman, intelligent and passionate, vivacious, a gifted diarist. My imagination was fired instantly.

Mareva's motion was insistent now and I felt myself dividing, my mind preoccupied with my discovery whilst my body involuntarily climbed the knotted rope of passion. I leant over her magnificent body and selected the smallest case from the wretched bag. Again a volume in a yellow morocco binding, with the crest and entries on rose-coloured paper. The first page was untidily inscribed.

'Commonplace Book – fragments from my Reading and Poetical Works by Lord Byron, devised by P.W. Begun on the Banks of Lago Maggiore one perfect Sunday Evening in 1828'

*'Earth cannot show so brave a sight
As when a single soul does fence
The batteries of alluring sense,
And heaven views it with delight.*

*Then persevere: for still new changes sound
And if thou overcom'st, thou shalt be crowned'*

Andrew Marvell – from
'A Dialogue between the Resolved Soul
and Created Pleasure'

'"On revient toujours, toujours à ses premiers amours."...
"Love's young dream" is sadder but more true.'

Jane G. 1816

Then I had to shut my eyes, distracted by Mareva's physical insistence, her head beneath my hands. A wild scent drifted on the air and the rhythm intensified. I let fall the book. I shuddered with the pleasure – the cycle was spent – that moment of conscious oblivion had passed. She tilted up her head and through her superb hair of the night, her unfocused eyes wore a look of soft triumph, her lips glistening with affection, her face as if seen through shallow water.

Two unopened journals were left, but I was in a tumult of inner contradictions. I needed to lighten the atmosphere between us. I suggested we walk along the cliffs near Elephant Rock, and then on to *Almira's* for supper. We would separate as we approached the more inhabited parts of the island. I put the broken Gladstone bag under my arm and we set off down a fantastically tangled bridle path toward the sea.

'I hope you're going to let me read those things,' Mareva said. 'I'm not stupid, you know.'

'I've never thought that. I just thought you'd be bored.'

'I think a lot,' she said. 'Things you'd never dream of.'

We climbed over giant roots like tendons stretched across the path. At the cliff edge, the whole foaming coastline, open sea and sky, pines and gliding terns, breeze and sea sound drew me up and out of the internal gloom that had overtaken me in McLachlan's house. We walked along the crumbling, dusty cliff margins, passing heart-shaped flowers dusted over the grass. The night-scented jasmine, heated by the sun, mingled with the perfume of Mareva's warm body as she moved before me trailing a pink-throated hibiscus in her hand. She turned and kissed me suddenly, enfolding me in soft passion.

'Mmm… Daa was nais,' she said. 'Have you had many lovers?'

'Well, a few, I suppose. But none like you.'

She expected no literal answer, and she seemed gratified.

The colours of the rocky coast there had an inner luminescence, radiant green new growth draped over the rusted earth, the cobalt ocean streaked with silver-white foam. I glimpsed the sea intermittently through the pines as we passed along the high track. Pale areas of clear water suggested a submerged city with crumbling towers thrusting above the surface. The tops of these monoliths were covered with waxy foliage, and Masked Gannets rose and alighted from the edges of stagnant ponds on them, while below, the surf broke over fractured boulders. Vast peninsulas of rock jutted out into the sea like ancient lizards suddenly struck down and fallen on their sides, heads dangling beneath the waves. Mareva indicated a stone elephant emerging from its house to drink from the ocean. Crimson and blue parrots speared with precision and sharp cries through the sunlight. Emerald doves started up from the swathes of shrubbery climbing the slopes. Cicadas racketed in the pulsing heat.

We walked in silence along the track and lay finally in a hollow fringed by lilac Goats-foot Creeper and made love again, surrounded by huge weathered pines festooned with pale, silver lichen. The pines and White Oaks had been bent by the wind into fantastic arabesques, clinging frantically with their exposed roots to the side of hills, some fallen, some partially bare, some deformed with twin crowns, many tapering to a spear point like giant toothpicks. Water poured unceasingly in and out of the arches of the sunken cathedral and surged against the basalt shafts of Organ-pipe Rock.

'I hope Nathan wasn't spying on us from the bushes,' Mareva said. 'He would've seen plenty to talk about.'

'So you still think about him, then?' I asked.

'I'm a bit frightened of him, I suppose,' she said cautiously. 'But you'll protect me, won't you?' She kissed me light-heartedly.

I had already begun to feel the islanders knew something about us and were looking at me differently. Islands are dangerous places, like pressure cookers without valves. But Mareva revelled in the risk, and her real fear of detection was lightened by a curiously joyful nervousness. A Brown Noddy had swooped down for an insect and was hovering just above us, riding and adjusting to the wind. The natural magic of physical love in this high place, the purity of desire, were so foreign to my city existence.

We walked on through the aromatic wetness of the forest, and the glades filled with the bell-sound of insects, and then back to that shattered margin of cliff. We passed small green depressions in the turf, and saw patches of white feathers, a skeleton of a wing, a drop of blood. Mareva told me that at dusk or just before dawn, feral cats waited in the hollows for the delicate fairy terns. The birds floated on an updraught, trimming tail and wing, adjusting their weight with finesse to the columns of air, and the cats lunged up from below the bird's line of sight and dragged them down into these amphitheatres of death. Occasionally a stronger gust would disperse a few snowy feathers, which settled again tentatively, like ashes.

We came to the crest of a hill. Two thin horses, one grey, one chestnut, stood sleeping in the sun on the opposite side of the small valley, their hindquarters on the very edge of the cliff facing away from the sea. In the breeze, their manes and tails streamed like war banners towards the interior of the island. Among the gaunt thorn trees where they were standing, a cow skeleton was trapped in a green bog. The stillness of this scene, its ancient immobility, silenced the expressive faculty.

Mareva left me shortly before nightfall. 'See yu morla,'[36] she whispered, before she took the dusty road to her shack on the hill.

I arrived at *Almira's* shortly before dinner with my prize. After dinner, I went out to the verandah during the long twilight to read the first of the journals, to explore that perilous time zone which lay between Paulina Wellesley and myself in the contained secrecy of the island night. The guests had now either retired to bed or set out for the Paradise Hotel. I made myself comfortable in a bamboo armchair, took out the buff, leatherette-covered box containing my cigarettes, and began to read.

CHAPTER VII

*A Voyage to Van Diemen's Land aboard the
Indian built Barque 'Fairlie', 1836 by Paulina Wellesley*

*Evening, Friday August 26th. 1836
Aboard the Barque 'Fairlie'*

I am indeed fortunate to be travelling with my Uncle, Sir John Franklin, the next Lieutenant-Governor of Van Diemen's Land, & the vice-regal party. Such adventure! Once my piano was safely packed & despatched from Devonshire Street I was anxious to be off. We have left London behind us at the height of the season & all the giddiness of the drawing-room & the bal-masque. The ship is vastly overcrowded, as our party was mentioned in the Ship Advertisement. There are some fifty-two children sailing steerage & three pregnant women! It is two years since my dear father Major Wellesley, a distant cousin and ADC to the great Duke, was placed to rest from St. James's Chapel, Spanish Place. A soldier's daughter born in Bengal is accustomed to travel, although this journey bears little resemblance to passages in the East India Company's service. What generous hearts Sir John & Lady Jane have to take me in as a ward & assist me with my slender financial prospects & solitary situation. Sir John was the first man to unfurl the British Flag on the coast of New Holland at the age of 14! Oh! I am in such high spirits this evening & long for the future, however unknown, in this infant society.

September 20th. 1836

Could add little to my Journal – crippling seasickness off the Scilly Isles. It was impossible to stand or sit. There is no ship's hospital & already a corpse on board! Intense & awful excitement off the coast of South

America at night when a whaler bore down on us with momentous inevitability, lights ablaze. That we should crash together, enter the next world with our fate sealed beneath the waves was clear! Mercifully, our paths divided.

I am taking sketching lessons from a Scottish artist who is emigrating to the colony. This will be of value when painting foreign landscapes. Many pleasant hours stretched on the deck with Captain Maconochie's children. They are permitted to read anything *except* the Bible. Lady Jane has arranged some evening lectures on the deck & Captn. M. features prominently. He delivered his first from the poop, the subject of which was 'The Natural History of Man'. The other ladies & myself found his constructions preposterously vain. He possesses many peculiarities of disposition & habits of thought. He argued that we whites owe our skin colour to civilisation. The secretion that blackens the skin of the savage is atomised in proportion to intellectual development, flies upward (once it is released by civilised thought) & is thence converted into grey matter or the organ of mind. His words savoured of materialism & excess faculty of imagination. Other lectures included Metaphysics & Phrenology which scarcely avoided putting the ladies to the blush with such mention of physicality.

Michaelmas Day 1836

This halcyon weather has meant many hours on the deck with eyes closed or if open, perusing the beautiful things in Mrs. Edgeworth's works. The shark-fishing today caused me much apprehension as I leaned out of the stern windows of the cabin. The victim's mighty thrashing with his tail almost broke the windows! We all watched the disembowelling with much squeamishness on my part, although Lady Jane took her usual scientific notes with furious curiosity of the awful organs emergent, the savage smells & yellow fluids, the still twitching spine after filleting. We partook of a little of the flesh at breakfast but I fear I looked rather reticent & sulky à l'anglaise. Lady Jane even learned the use of the harpoon.

I was horror-struck by a disgustingly massy fish called a squid which had been pecked at by two lice-infested Cape Hens. The teeth of the tentacula of the monstrous specimen were cut out & the fleshy envelope removed – the company received a number of teeth each – disagreeably amusing – all the young ladies developed *'Neptune's Fingers'* & smelled in consequence dreadfully fishy for some days. Portions were prepared with curry for the dinner table. It was ventured to be *'pretty good'* but I desisted, being considerably prejudiced by its marked lack of vitality when discovered.

At sea on board the Barque 'Fairlie'
October 10th. 1836

We have engaged in all manner of absurd theatricals to fill this long period of leisure & peacefulness. Latterly *'The Maid of Genoa'* has kept us vivacious & gay with shivers & shrieks of horror, horror, horror! I must say I found unexpected relish in playing my role as *Hag of the Tomb* & have become passionately fond of coquetry, appearing disarmingly pretty with white ostrich feathers in my hair. I began, for my own amusement, a flirtation with Monsieur Timidité, the Archdeacon. How will it proceed?

Cape of Good Hope
Table Bay
November 10th. 1836

A tremendous salvo of guns heard this morning as a mark of respect to Sir John by Sir Benjamin D'Urban. We chose lodgings in Long Market Street & are to be here for some three weeks. The weather is gloomy but Lady Jane is determined to explore Table Mountain at the earliest opportunity. We have made the acquaintance of the traveller Dr. Smith, who in his modest fashion, has offered to guide us to the summit. Sir John & Captain Maconochie are violently opposed to the expedition.

November 15th. 1836

The ascent to the summit took five hours, but the view of Cape Town was so splendid it repaid the effort to overcome the fear of my excessive intrepidity. Many flowers were picked for subsequent botanical classification.

M. Timidité deserves to be renamed M. Rapidité for the speed at which he descended, clutching his Blackthorn stick & yellow chrysanthemums, in scarcely three hours. Of necessity I tied my print dress up around my waist.

Quel Horreur! It came *quite* above my knees and I felt rather bold climbing before M.T.... I trust the breathtaking geological vista as we climbed distracted him from the splendour of any revelations I might be making.

Cape Town
November 24th. 1836

In the final week of our stay, Lady Jane, as adventurous as ever, suggested an excursion into the interior. Our party set out in wagons for *Hottentot's Kloof*, the pass at *Frenchhoek* & the Moravian settlement at *Genadendal.* We encountered some women convicts at an African prison & their screeching forth persuaded me that wild creatures in the jungle would be easier to tame. I trust my position in Van Diemen's Land will provide me with every opportunity of avoiding the agitation of the soul that worked on me in their presence.

Christmas Day 1836

It is a slow & stormy passage from the Cape – some three weeks & two days have elapsed! Certainly today is a day of limited festivities. The never ending motion & the noise! We are unable to sit or even stand still without practising a variety of gymnastics just to retain the perpendicular or horizontal. A horse & box were carried overboard. Between the decks an absolute *danse macabre* took place during the storm. Dead dogs & goats flew about, another horse was flung down the quarter hatchway among the men & broke its legs. Timbers rolled like matchsticks smashing arms racks & lockers. The constant dampness penetrates everything – you eat, feel, drink, see and sleep in it! When the decks are noisily scraped, water oozes into your cabin through the cracks, the fowls peck & scratch without let up, ducks do the *unmentionables* & smell, the teak timbers groan & creak continually, gravity slams the doors – the Master informed us that this Barque left the Calcutta shipyards some 25 years ago but quickly assured his dismayed listeners of its staunch construction! The calmest temper & stoutest nerves shatter under this constant duress. Just five minutes silence is the *summum bonum* of our aspirations!

Hobart Town
On board the 'Fairlie'
Early morning, January 6th. 1837

A great pulse of excitement thrills through me now that we are arrived. My new life (even yet with the same ears & eyes) is about to open like a Morning Glory!

Lady Jane has confided the agenda of today's official engagements to me. At eleven the members of the Executive Council with the Commandant of the Troops board the vessel & then Sir John makes his public landing. I have no idea which costume I shall choose now that I am projected into this association with fame & undreamed of social position through a gesture of chance. The ladies are to walk quietly in the gardens of Government House whilst the various speeches of welcome are addressed to the fearless explorer. Everything is quite beautiful here, strangely possessed of a homely English aspect. I am not very fond of Captn. M's offspring. They appear excited to do exactly as the whim takes them, with little coercion or discipline. Come, I shall permit nothing to mar this glorious Summer day and embrace the future as happy as a princess!

Government House
Hobart Town
February 24th. 1837

We are confidently settled into our newly adopted way of life & it is more agreeable than I could have imagined. Sir John was escorted upon arrival by three hundred horsemen & above seventy carriages! His reputation as a great explorer had preceded him. The climate is temperate rather than excessively hot. Government House commands beautiful views of the Derwent River & the surrounding scenery is always reminiscent of England. It appears a prosperous colony with little intrusion of the fearsome convicts (as we were informed of them in England). Some have been trustworthy house-servants to settler families for periods of twenty years & more! It is quite possible for fashionable ladies to walk about with no fear of harm or insult. Nevertheless, I have encountered vastly more snobbery than I would have conceived possible in so small a community. Invitations to Government House are interpreted as analogous to presentations at Court! The Military Officers occupy the first set in society.

The island seems to be flourishing & prosperity is much in evidence. Many of the buildings are constructed of brick & some detached houses possess verandahs covered in plants in the manner of a domestic forest. Some have fine views of the harbour. The great basaltic columns of Mt. Wellington dominate the horizon. In the gardens mulberries, cherries, currants, raspberries, strawberries, gooseberries, apples, pears, quinces & medlars abound in a profusion that reminds me of Botticelli's *Primavera* in Florence.

There is a great deal of dancing here, of which the young ladies are passionately fond. Many of the Gentlemen and Officers ride very handsomely & display their skills at the races in various *'Cups', 'Ladies Purses', & 'Town Plates'.*

There is even a flourishing theatre! I satisfied my hunger for the fantastic when the vice-regal party thrilled to the terrors of *The Black Caverns of St. Bruno* and *The Nun of Messina.* We were accompanied by some officers & their ladies. My escort was an English gentleman farmer settled here from an ancient Manor in Cornwall, a Mr. James Worth. We returned to Government House for a *petit souper* in high spirits and repeated snatches of remembered dialogue, the gentlemen over their port & the ladies over tea. We were quite done up by our terrifying escapade. Next month, a sentimental theatrical piece *The Dumb Boy of the Pyrenees* and *The Broken Dagger* will be staged. Mr. Worth is an excellent mimic and shares my love of the drama & its transports, so has again requested the pleasure of my company. He is become good friends with Sir John & Lady Jane & has excellent connections in the colony. We are to visit his cottage at *Risdon,* where a portion of his farmland is situated, next Sunday. With characteristic mischevious wit he has invited us to *'Breakfast'* though we will scarcely arrive before the middle afternoon. Lady Jane is convalescing there after a recent illness.

The Quaker missionaries Messrs. Backhouse & Walker have written with much perception of their recent visit to the colony: 'The state of discord and selfishness which very generally prevails among the colonists is a subject that soon forces itself painfully upon the notice of visitors among them, notwithstanding the pleasing impression that may be produced, especially at first, by the general intelligence and hospitality of the community.'

A disturbance in the dark palms in the garden took my attention from the Hobart Town theatre. Nathan, brooding dark and silent, passed up the drive on foot. I put down the journal as Almira brought me some coffee.

'Tuu mach readin' brings orn wan early death,'[37] she said, smiling though as she spoke.

The innocence and gaiety of Paulina had begun to affect me. This butterfly newly broken from its chrysalis was gliding unprotected about the perimeter of a penitentiary. How would she react to the realities of her situation? Would I find a family portrait? What would she look like? How had her journals come to be on Norfolk Island, late *Gomorrah Isle?*

My knowledge of Van Diemen's Land warned me she would find enough horrors there to satisfy her Gothic imagination – the slaughter of the natives, the convict settlement and the rabid divisions within the settler's community. I skimmed over much froth and bubble concerning preparations for the Prince Paul of Meckelburg-Schwerin's ball *'in costumes of 1788'* – petticoats of white *gaze satinée de Lyon,* crimson velvet and black satin corsets *à la paysanne* – all this in such contrast to Mareva's complete physical availability *sans lingerie.* This was all too remote from the grim reality of a *'separate-treatment man'*[38] lashed bloody on the triangles, about to develop holes in his *'maggoty back'*[39] from carrying lime. I slipped a yellow volume from its marbled case.

Mr. Worth of 'The Manor of Trevalor'
Crackington Haven, Cornwall at Risdon in V.D.L.

Copy of a letter

Sunday evening
'Trevalor', Risdon (Restdown)
March 1st. 1837

Dearest Selina

A day of travel never fails to place my mind in a fluid & impressionable condition. Our party (Sir John, Eleanor, two young officers & our maids) crossed the Derwent by means of ferry-boats – ourselves in one & the horses in the other. Mr. Worth courteously rode down to the landing place on a fine hunter & we were transported to Risdon by one of his better class of convict coachmen in a rather broad, somewhat stout, colonial-built conveyance, a variety of gig with a seat behind for the convict servant. The keen edge of the still morning had given way to a pleasant warmth as we rumbled through the scented air, quite alive with birdsong. We were welcomed with gentlemanly hospitality by Mr. Worth. In truth it bordered on the excessive but then one hears great reports of his talented farming methods & other achievements, so I anticipated an uncommon temperament.

The windows of his dining-room (containing furniture in a variety of native woods & a sumptuous Turkey carpet) command a most beautiful view, perhaps the most inspiring since I left England. Mt. Wellington is the chief object that draws the eye in the landscape. The title 'Organ Pipes' is given to the dolerite rampart near its peak. It could be regarded as the brow of the mountain, a counterpart to the human face. The sun sparkled like gems on the broad Derwent, the surface speckled with a variety of vessels, steam and sail. The river reminds me exquisitely of the Cumberland Lakes. It is skirted by gentle slopes & flat meadows of powder green grass, shading to darker hues approaching the water. The cottage is most commodious & in wondrous close connection with animals & nature. Mr. Worth's background is an absolute mystery but his bearing is so youthful & distinguished, I incline to a high country set. I noted that although his manner is not overbearing, the assigned convicts in his service react promptly & instantly in his presence. The servants included a gentle female domestic or 'lady-wire' Eliza – most unusual in the colony, where one of the Government House laundry-women is a child murderer!

Lady Jane was in the small drawing-room near some open French windows to the verandah & lawn. She was reclining on a chaise-lounge &, indomitable as ever, struggled to her feet when we entered. She was pale of countenance but appeared much improved & clasped me warmly. Simplicity & informality are much to her taste & mine but she commits the grievous colonial sin of being 'very clever' & is much harassed by the malicious & the jealous. She partially supports Captain Maconochie's views on the reformation of Penal Discipline & this attracts scorpions of all varieties, particularly the 'Arthurite species' who understandably support the principle of assignment (Mr. Worth's admirable convicts are surely proof of the system's felicity). Captn. Maconochie deems it *white slavery* & burns with a disconcerting fervour.

If those who are scurrilously using Lady Jane to batter Sir John's convictions could have seen his open and generous solicitations to her this evening, they would surely cease slandering her & endangering her health. I trust I shall never engage in the ferment that lies beneath the surface of this outwardly placid colony, basking in the summer sun & so miraculously endowed with Nature's gifts.

'Make yourselves comfortable ladies after *such* a demanding journey. Tea & cakes will be served on the lawn presently.'

Mr. Worth indicated that we recline informally on rugs placed under a stand of grey-green Eucalypts close by the verandah, which was weighed down by swathes of scarlet geraniums. He began to discuss the improvements he had made & the principles of land management that have given Risdon the reputation of a stylish & highly ordered establishment along traditional English lines.

'My father Sir Hawthorne Worth was a "liver" before he ran aground,' laughed Mr. Worth.

'How so?' queried Sir John.

'We had the Manor at Crackington Haven, our seat near Tintagel. It once belonged to the half-brother of William the Conqueror, the Earl of Mortain. There were no roads for our carriages, so he had 'em built. Improved the land, plantations of fir, a fine duck decoy for shooting. I remember postilions in livery when we attended St. Gennys Church on the cliff as children. Wilberforce did for us on the sugar plantations in Jamaica.' A touch of bitterness betrayed itself.

'In consequence you set out for VDL?' observed a young officer (Roger Conway of the 50th Regiment I believe).

'Forced into it. We tried harder than most to introduce our slaves back into the community in Jamaica. Didn't abandon 'em. They loved us, those slaves, with uncommon affection. Sir Hawthorne was impartial, compassionate but severe. The way we should treat these.' He indicated his assigned convicts waiting dutifully nearby.

'Captain Maconochie would perhaps disagree,' commented Lady Jane in a wry fashion.

'Domination is a product of will, not of learning. Character develops through disciplined obedience. My father was adored by his Cornish tenants & enormously improved the surrounding area.'

Mr. Worth briskly rubbed some mud sparks off his Wellington boots &
suggested we walk a little around his property. (His grey eyes are quite
thrilling when they rest on one). The gentlemen walked ahead, no doubt
continuing their warm discussion of penal matters which is inevitably
roused in all gatherings in the colony. We halted near the kitchen garden, a
walled structure adjacent to the servant's quarters.

'I raise early-ripening vegetables in here. The beds are constructed at a
forty-five degree angle to the horizontal to catch the sun. We had 'em in
Cornwall – very successful they were too'.

He also showed us some ghastly man-traps and manacles arranged in
decorative patterns for apprehending bushrangers & escaped prisoners. Lady
Jane took a scientific interest, but I thought them terrible machines.

Along the meandering river a narrow path had recently been cleared &
I strolled arm-in-arm with my Aunt who sought my opinion on her attempts
to introduce evening parties in the *conversazione* style for the pretty
Vandemonian girls. I dreaded exciting her displeasure by the truthful
preference I had heard for *'carpets out & military bands & dancing in'*.
Many of my friends disliked *'being stuck up in rooms full of pictures &
books & shells & stones & other rubbish with stupid preaching about
philosophy & science'*. She was relieved of the necessity of considering this
opinion by the scattered groups of our party moving towards our cottage
for dinner. Doubtless I would have succumbed to dissimulation to avoid
taxing her emotions still further.

Dinner at 'Trevalor' was a delightful *al fresco* affair, as the bay windows of
the dining-room were thrown open introducing the vista into the house.
Mr. Worth exercises his command system toward his convict servants with
silent intensity. They are predominantly agricultural labourers from the rural
districts in England.

'Thieves of circumstance, not thieves of the heart,' he remarked with surprising discrimination.

This gentleman has pretentions to taste & is a rare virtuoso. I have not
felt more at home since my arrival in the colony. The light faded toward
eight o'clock & in keeping with his spirit of scientific improvement, our
host lit some of his new *Argand* colza-oil lamps, which showed the
delicious cherries & mulberries to great advantage, seeming to enhance
their taste as well as their appearance. Whilst the gentlemen played
billiards & smoked, we ladies retired to the drawing-room where Lady

Jane took up her favourite topic of female education. I lapsed into a reverie near the French windows, sleepily watching the saucers with glass domes containing trapped butterflies that had been placed at random about the verandah.

Government House
Hobart Town
May 12th. 1837

Nervous indisposition has prevented me from continuing this journal for some weeks. My last entry was completed in such a peaceful dream, few would have credited the drama that the morrow would bring.

Sometime during billiards, Mr. Worth broached the idea of an opossum shooting expedition to the gentlemen. It would last the whole of Sunday evening. They scattered enthusiastically like so many coloured balls to their rooms to dress. Mr. Worth appeared promptly, attired in a short olive-green jacket & long leggings, both rather tight for my taste & a slightly feminine straw hat. A powder flask protruded from one pocket & over his shoulder a wide belt, for the shot I imagine. He twirled a dog whistle although no animals were to be seen & adjusted his monocle with needless flamboyance. He is quite the *'pattern card'* in some respects! The other gentlemen were decked out in undress military fashion except Sir John who has gallantly decided to forgo the pleasure & remain with his sweet convalescent. Their guide was to be an old opossum hunter. Mr. Worth ventured a brief biography with hunting associations.

'Scrope Kemp is our man. The old hound was a sheep-stealer, transported to VDL & set himself up as a bushranger. Fine turtle.'

'Did you bring him in, James?' queried a young officer.

'Soon as we got a scent we had a good run, but we never killed. An awkward customer. Took weeks to capture.'

'Does he still break cover?' asked another young blood, grinning.

'There is not a more faithful or honest servant under my command,' he observed severely.

My love of theatre prompts the detailing of such language as gentlemen never use in the company of ladies. The household was asleep when they returned with their inedible treasure. Hot coffee & breakfast buns were miraculously produced for the adventurers.

Later that sunny morning it was suggested that we have a pic-nic at Grass Tree Hill. The household used up the entire mobile force of carts & carriages at *'Trevalor'* to retire to this spot, which gives a beautiful elevated view of the town & harbour. There are great numbers of these *Grass Trees*, so named because of their crown festoons of long grass-like leaves. They were in many shapes & sizes: tall, short, bent, straight & lent a curious character to the scenery. The glossy, brown leaf-bases form interesting whorls on dead trees. We sat beneath some sombre & melancholic Eucalyptus Gums. The bark had formed into long streamers & rustled desiccate, without joy. However, from the litter of champagne corks round about it seemed that *someone* had been strenuously combating the lifeless atmosphere. Many trees had died, some were blown down & lay in all directions. Distant shots from our intrepid hunters disturbed the Diamond Bird – a tiny, dainty jewel of life, gold & amber in shade with silver spots. Wattle & honeysuckle flowered about us in profusion but were bound to conceal native rats & snakes.

I turned my back to the prospect & with the assistance of my Claude glass managed to do some sketching of this picturesque domain whilst the food was being prepared. The light in VDL is soft but clear, the untroubled air giving a great serenity to the temperate marine landscape. In the distance, convict road gangs proceeded like clanking ants & smoke issued from the sod hut of a settler on the shore.

The adventure of the food! *'Stuck-up kangaroo and bacon'* makes very good eating! The kangaroo cutlets are two or three inches broad & a third of an inch thick. They are speared on a sharpened wooden stick, one above the other, and a piece of bacon is placed on top. This construction is then driven into the ground close to the fire. The heat melts the bacon fat which then drips on to the cutlet, and thus cooks them as they are occasionally turned. Kangaroo hunting is considered good sport by the gentlemen. There was talk of setting up something similar to the *Bathurst Hunt* which sports buttons embossed with a dingo's head! I reflected in some amazement at the gulf that now separates these exotic experiences from our civilised roast lamb served on the Spode 'Blue Italian' in Devonshire Street not one year ago.

Mr. Worth was very solicitous of my comfort & we discussed the similar shock he had received when newly arrived in the colony. I am much drawn to him as he radiates such self-assurance, power & capacity for life. Yet beneath

this stern, handsome yet negligent figure I suspect a man of culture &
refinement. He was tireless playing childish games with little Eleanor & is
ceaseless in pointing out this or that feature on the Derwent. His friendship
is important to me despite the customary malicious rumours in this tight
little community of the social élite that cast doubt on his reasonableness.

We returned to the cottage unprepared for the unspeakable drama of the
evening. The usual diversions were proceeding after dinner (the gentlemen
wielding the dice-box) when (with I reflected later, a slightly excessive
dramatic flair) Mr. Worth came into the drawing room & announced that
some bushrangers were only some three miles off & would attack *'Trevalor'*
within hours! This intelligence prompted an immediate response from Lady
Jane: 'You have a boat, James! Might we not flee *instantly* across the water
to Hobart Town?'

'*Will* you trust me, ladies, with your lives?' James replied with killing
melodrama. He clearly feared we would not wish to navigate miles of sea in
a diminutive vessel at night.

'Nothing to worry about!' shot in Sir John. 'We are all *fearfully courageous explorer chaps!'* amid much laughter from the officers of the 50th.
Regiment known as the *'Blind Half Hundred'* – hardly encouraging in this
instance!

Lady Jane hurried along the placid Mrs. Williamson & Eleanor (who
was near asleep) & her timid maid who had been nursing her through the
illness & myself. The horrors were upon us as it was rumoured that these
fiendish men turned to murder & cannibalism at the slightest provocation.

'Scrope! Get me my pistols & top boots!' ordered Mr. Worth with
immense authority. My Aunt's maid was fussing about the necessity of
conveying pillows & lime-water for her health.

'Fiddle-*de-dee* of the lime-water!' called Lady Jane.

In five minutes we were in the boat laden with these 'necessities' as well as
a barometer in a velvet-lined case. Two officers were left in the house under
orders to bar up all doors & windows. James (immensely strong physically)
pushed off from the creek between two hills that looked down on the
cottage. He put his shooting coat over my shoulders to warm me against the
chill evening breeze. The occupants of the vessel lapsed into silence &
personal reflections on our plight. The lapping of the water against the hull,
the creaking of the timbers & faint lights on the shore accompanied us for
some twenty minutes until we arrived at the wharf in Hobarton.

The sail unfurling in the wind, the gloom, the silhouette of the posted lookout at the bow, the thrill of the dangerous & wretched creatures that might yet pursue us & the calm confidence of James caused me to feel as though I had become a player in one of Lord Byron's tales. Lines from 'The Corsair' tumbled through my brain:

'Few are his words, but keen his eye and hand.
"Steer to that shore!" – they sail. "Do this!" – 'tis done:
"Now form and follow me!" – the spoil is won.
Thus prompt his accents and his actions till,
And all obey and few enquire his will;
To such, brief answer and contemptuous eye
Convey reproof, nor further deign reply.'

He accompanied us to Government House where we were all taken into the warm, domestic security of candles & carpets. Our maids saw us to our rooms directly with much compassionate cooing & miscellaneous hot beverages.

At the entrance to the House, as James removed his coat from my shoulders, he *violently & unmistakably pressed my hand!* Those ever so slightly grey glittering eyes with their black lashes set the blood coursing once again through my veins with an abandoned force until I was fit to die! He importuned me for a lock of hair... Have I encouraged this attachment or contrived it in any way? Any fool could see I was uncommonly moved in his presence. When I felt my colour go & I became agitated it would have scarcely been concealed by the lamps.

I rushed into my Aunt's sanctuary, the dark, cold menagerie to collect myself alone before returning to the unsettled company. There, among the shells, snails, toads, stuffed birds & reptiles, weapons of savages, specimens of wood & stone fossils, my nerves ceased their jangling, yet the while my flickering candle threw grotesque shadows from these objects against the walls.

After sitting quietly for some time I became aware of something near me insinuating itself, a presence in that bizarre museum! Icy fingers of fear squeezed my already exhausted heart. I slowly turned & there stood a figure, *an ancient black figure,* a naked young woman draped in a scarlet cloth, *a lubra.* I cried out, grew faint with horror. Consciousness departed.

I awoke slightly delirious in my bed some hours later. My Aunt was smoothing my cheek & murmuring comfortingly. What had I seen? Whence had the vision come? In the sudden access & superfluity of feeling attendant on that day, my memory had failed. I had mistaken the stuffed, juvenile lubra, a prize exhibit in Lady Jane's collection, for a corporeal being. Reason began its slow triumph over Imagination but my sensibility was cruelly weakened. Such a paroxysm of experience prevented the continuance of the generally dull catalogue of events that comprise my journal.

CHAPTER VIII

Fletcher Christian Esq., at the 'Paradise Hotel'
Norfolk Island

*P*ages had been torn and some lines heavily scored out. The passages seemed to relate to Mr. Worth. I gazed through *Almira's* dark garden into the clear Pacific night and reflected on the document. Had McLachlan read the journals in his isolated cottage, or was my eye the first to rove over these secrets of illusioned youth? A love story had begun to unfold in tandem with my own. Paulina had to rein in her emotions with such violence, where I permitted mine complete abandon. We were both trapped in the cruel springtime of a relationship, its extremes mirrored in the sun and wild rain of that season. I was anxious to read the other volumes to see if she had actually visited *this* island, this place peculiarly suited to eagles and angels. Almira began to switch off the lights, preparing to retire to her tiny shed behind the main house.

I sped down to the coast in my newly-acquired old MGA. It had been shipped to the island years before by one of the many company lawyers who worked on Norfolk. The island was tax-free haven, and thousands of Australian companies were registered here. There were mostly Japanese cars on the island, so I was particularly excited to find my favourite English sports car for sale. It was Hawthorn Green.

Clouds of coral dust poured into the cockpit through the rotting passenger floor as I headed for 'open night' at The Paradise, a hotel near the convict cemetery overlooking Nepean Island. Most assignations took place there on Friday evenings, and much of the population became thoroughly drunk. There was dancing to a scratch band. It was a good opportunity to eye off the latest batch of tourist girls, if you had missed the regular inspection at the airport. Sunday afternoons would be spent sitting on the roofs of our cars watching the 'talent' arrive off the plane, before collecting the mail from the Post Office. The result might be two weeks of licentiousness without guilt on either side, chains of holiday romances. We boys often compiled *'hit lists'*.

I occasionally played an upright piano in Jerry Lee Lewis style, bruising my fingers and sending broken hammers spinning into the *mêlée* on the dance floor, taking a perverse pleasure in rejecting my classical training. The liquor was duty free, which rapidly led islanders toward self-destruction. Naturally, the older, more respectable establishment figures and the reclusives could not be seen at The Paradise on any night.

As a man, it was best to prepare an authoritative entrance, as these descendants of the mutineers from *Her Majesty's Armed Vessel* threw off the veneer of domestication at the slightest excuse. Timidity was instantly sniffed out. My nickname was 'Haet'[40] because I often wore a Corsican fisherman's cap in the sports car and at the beach.

Mareva was an illicit passion that took some courage to maintain, but dicing with erotic risk was thrilling. The eyes of the island herd, struck down with boredom, waited ravenously for the betrayed secret, the suspect sexual orientation, the glimpse of thigh. I half hoped she would not be there, as suspicion already hung thick and humid in the air. I dangled a cigarette from the corner of my mouth, hunched my shoulders and walked directly to the bar, elbowing past, ordering a bourbon and ice with an air of self-confidence. The heavy musculature of the descendants gathered about me in knots.

'Heh Haet! Hello brud! Gettin' any?'

I managed a half smile. 'What?' I was smirking and manly complicity at the suggested ravishment of ladies in every direction.

'Hair pie brud. Gettin' any hair pie?' Sniggers all round.

'Seen Nathan lately?' Malicious leers.

I fled to the piano with my drink, threading my way through the crowd. The band welcomed me, even though the keyboard was inaudible above the amplified guitars and drums. During a break, I saw Mareva with some girlfriends, and she caught my eye, the whole repertoire of suggestiveness on public view. I feared it, yet it gave me status. Our 'secret' had by now become common knowledge but we continued keep up a pretence. She looked delectably exotic compared with the droves of pink holiday secretaries in cool Polynesian prints and I went over to talk to her.

'Watawieh yorlyi?'[41] I greeted them.

'Much betta if we didn't have to listen to you!' Everyone giggled like schoolgirls. 'Why don't you put an islander on aa station, someone who speaks Norfuk?'

'I'll see what I can do,' I replied.

'Da classical stuff is terrible,' a pretty islander said. 'More of that Country en Western like Johnny Cash is what we want!'

Mareva kept sucking a finger and looking at me suggestively. Everyone was aware of her flirting. Her friends exchanged meaningful glances, more inane remarks about the broadcasting station, more drinks, invitations to parties, even some compliments on my programmes and jokes. Mareva glowed with the spice of the forbidden.

By taking up with a lover from the mainland, she had in one sense betrayed her island husband, Nathan. Despite her separation from him, she was innocently following that pattern of deceit created by her ancestors almost two hundred years before. The brutal events on Pitcairn's Island were the lurid inheritance of the woman who was my island lover. The knowledge of those fates and the 'blood-fest' that followed, disturbingly crossed my mind whenever we embraced. She was named after the original Mareva, the widow of the Tahitians Teimua and Minarii. Minarii was murdered by the mutineers who were the ancestors of my own Mareva, the mutineers whose violent lives ended in death on Pitcairn's cliffs.

As I rode the flood tide of her eyes and sipped my bourbon at the bar of the weatherbeaten Paradise Hotel (itself covering the site of a Second Settlement Overseer's Hut) I became entangled in the nets of love and time, blood-passion and transience that breathed through her living being and through the ruins of the convict settlement beneath my feet. I felt we should not persist in our public intimacies. The glances of the island men were like knife thrusts. We agreed to meet at Slaughter Bay at two in the morning the following day.

But not all the islanders were so restricted in their imagination as to be preoccupied with my affairs. I parted from Mareva and found myself talking to an intelligent and humorous member of the Christian family. He was short and fair with an arresting, charismatic friendliness. We dealt with the Administrator, the Administration officials and the policy of the Island Council with summary and outrageous generalisations. As the last strains of *'When the Saints Come Marching In'* died away and the crowd began to disperse, he suggested we go to his home to have something to eat and more to drink.

The doors of his ancient Ford Falcon had been welded shut, so we were forced to climb through the windows. The headlamps cut wavering arcs through the clouds of coral dust as we made the tortuous ascent into the interior of the island. The car careered down a long drive lined with palm trees to a Pitcairner Colonial Georgian house opposite a saw-mill, with huge machines and earth-moving equipment littering the ragged lawn. It was said he would start the 1940's grader by pouring pure ether into the carburetter and lighting it.

I climbed out of the car and he killed the lights. We were instantly submerged in powder-black night, and we lurched past massive silhouettes to the open front door. He was humming what vaguely sounded like a hymn. A naked bulb blazed suddenly on the verandah.

'Kam in a' haus brud! Kam in a' kitchen f' eat something!'

He laughed like a contained explosion, wheezing through his teeth. I negotiated a chaos of furniture and dismantled diesel engines. The table was strewn with opened tins of beans, ravioli, milk cartons and bachelor snacks. Rumour had it that he was married to a beautiful fashion model from the mainland, but tonight she was not to be seen. He was said to exert a powerful fascination on young girls. Many thought he was a genius who had become the pathetic victim of his own brilliance.

A surprising number of battered history books lay on the floors and chairs, and he was already launching unaccountably into a disjointed and passionate defence of the character of Edward VIII. Two stained cups materialised from the mound of unwashed dishes. He poured some whiskey from an old Johnny Walker bottle.

'He followed his heart… always follow your heart brud. Don't give a damn for them in power! Take independence by daa throat!'

'Yes, I've been reading a selection of his letters to Wallis Windsor. He wrote secret messages on the jewels he gave her.' My voice sounded curiously pretentious to my own ears.

'To give up your Kingdom for a woman is either true love or great foolishness.' He stared into the cracked cup as if searching for parallels in his own life.

'Some say he evaded his duty in a cowardly fashion. He had a weak face and she was plain. The jewels made up for that.'

Fletcher blasted me. 'Duty! Daa es wan joke brud. More like a force of coercion for them that fears change, them that fears freedom. Saves one from having to make a choice. Follow your heart brud – passion – it never lies but can be dangerous! I should know being a Christian!' That explosive yet affectionate wheeze again. Any argument I wanted to advance suddenly became a hopelessly vain intellectual construction before his twinkling eyes.

'Don't you feel reason should prevail over the sentiments?' I asked. My reading of Paulina had already begun to affect my language. He blinked at me, hovering in the mists of alcohol.

'Yu es brekin' daa kings crown![42] Let's have some "Spam" to feed aa brain.'

I sliced some of the frightful stuff on to a piece of stale bread and began to eat without enthusiasm. He suddenly became arrogant, the gentleman slipping away.

'Never hide your feelings brud. Morals comes from them down there.' He indicated the direction of Kingston. 'The rats!' Whiskey from the cup, fumes forced through the teeth.

'Fletcher did more than his duty in those fuckin' storms dar bastard Bligh took them into round Cape Horn!'

'How long were they in Tahiti?'

'Months brud. Months at Point Venus. Months of love. Wish I'd ha bin there!'

'Was this the reason for the mutiny?'

'Nu salen! Are you stupid or something? If they hadn't listened to their hearts I wouldn't be sitting before you at this moment! You're draggin' aa chain[43] – a drink to free love on a free island!' A great cataract of mutinous laughter erupted like a Tahitian waterfall.

'Ai es want to shew you one thing rare and beautiful brud.' His voice had lowered to a tone of criminal confidentiality. He lurched out to a distant room, and I could hear a great deal of rummaging about and obscenities whose origins lay deep in the England of the

Eighteenth Century. To my great amazement he returned carrying a broken sword.

'Dieh brud es daa Abdication Sword of Edward VIII!' he announced triumphantly, fingering the broken tip. I laughed at this outrageous suggestion, but I tried to look serious as a scowl began to distort his features.

'Really? How extraordinary!'

I examined this unlikely dress-sword of an obscure regiment with its formerly bright gold, now tattered tassels.

'Dem se brek et over his shoulder when he abdicated. Se brek his heart too.'

I examined this outward sign of neglected duty. Mr. Christian slumped into a chair and instantly fell asleep. I finished my whiskey and walked out on to the verandah. There was a large bulldozer in the front yard, and I decided to climb up into the driver's seat for some amusement. With the drink and the altitude, I fell asleep just as rapidly as my host had.

I was awoken next morning by the dazzle of the rising sun. I stood up in a completely disorientated state, and took a step. The fall was about eight feet, I suppose, and it certainly brought me round with a rush. I remembered the night of drinking and Fletcher's entertaining play. Now I would need to walk home across the island. I looked in at the house, and Mr. Christian was still peacefully asleep on the verandah with the Sword of Abdication lying across his knees.

At *Almira's,* the long table had been set outside for breakfast under the palms. It was laden with great containers of pineapple and guava juice, bowls of sliced paw-paw, mango and bananas. The guests had not yet risen, so I poured myself a tumbler of juice and sat in the cane armchair to watch the fierce drama of the spring sky. Dark, grey clouds were moving fast over the island at low altitude. The pines appeared naive in shape, innocent and childish brushstrokes in a landscape painting, the branches arching upwards like widely spaced giant feathers.

I heard a sudden urgent stride of boots in the drive.

'Morning, Paul!' punched out with an exuberance that was alarming at such an early hour.

'Morning Cameron!'

The wiry, muscular Englishman accompanied by his dog, Dart, the fastest on the island, moved with a sense of purpose that belied his seventy years. He seemed incessantly at work on the fabric of *Almira's,* repairing, rebuilding, wrenching and splitting in a frenzy of expert carpentry. His belief in the rejuvenating power of work was absolute.

'Keeping well, Paul?'

You could feel that his body strained against the leash of his mind in pausing to talk.

'Fine. Beautiful time of day before anyone is up.'

'Why don't you come down to the Kentia plantation? I'll show you what I've done with the irrigation system.'

'I'd love to.'

As a youth he had sailed steerage from India to New Zealand with five pounds in his pocket. Another ninety-five, he had lent to his brother to get married. The other men in this hellish accommodation were either vomiting or playing cards, and he himself was ill with a virus. He remembered nothing with pleasure apart from the smile of a great Samoan who would lean over the edge of his bunk, talking to him as he recovered. A chance encounter had brought him to Norfolk Island to manage a plantation of ornamental palms. An English 'man of action', he was pragmatic, energetic, and had a loud voice of colonial determination and honourable authority. Unromantic on the surface, he had been deeply in love with Almira for years. She wandered in her garden in a blue satin gown among the lobster plants, citrus, avocados and flame trees, aloof, confident in the power of this knowledge. He was concerned for her health but she continued to rebuff his advances with gentle irony.

I stood in the back of the utility truck with Dart, who precariously perched his rear over the edge of the tailgate in the rising clouds of coral dust. The neglected plantation had been turned into a model farm for palm seedlings which would not mature for nine years. As we drove along the rutted, water-logged track he told me of his brushes with death – high-tension cables snaking over the ground (Dart had dashed for help), an uncontrollable blaze while burning off (Dart obeyed orders and survived) and the collapse of a bulldozer arm which narrowly missed him. Many of those who came to the island were marginals from the mainland who seemed to thrive on danger and challenge. Dart had by now abandoned his perch and was streaking along beside the truck as we headed towards the hill that commanded a vista over Philip Island.

CHAPTER IX

'Blaydes'

Rented accommodation was invariably poor, so I was pleased to find the half-completed, stained-pine cottage called Blaydes on the road to Anson Bay. It was in an isolated position, and the scene of many wild evenings with the descendants of the mutiny. Once I was ejected in the dead of night by the owner for non-payment of rent. He took possession at gunpoint and the last image I have of him is sitting up in my bed swigging from a bottle of whiskey, a rifle across his knees, as I accelerated away to his house to tell his wife about it. He only behaved like this 'under the influence' and he just needed to be rescued. Unfortunately I destroyed his prize rose beds and lawn as I turned into his drive, and I finally had to find somewhere else.

At Blaydes, cows would keep me awake at night, butting the walls as they scratched themselves or worried a horn. A few shots between those horns would send them crashing amusingly through the guava scrub gully. I often shot common starlings and rats that infested the ceilings. Starling chicks would fall between the walls to die a lingering and squeaky death. Yet this was my happiest residence.

The glow of the varnished interior, the proximity to the cliffs near Puppy's Point and the peacefulness of historic Orange Vale and the Melanesian Mission Chapel nearby made Blaydes a good place for the appreciation of poetry and music as well as a perfect lovers' retreat.

On moonlit evenings I would climb high into the branches of a pine and listen to *Tristan und Isolde* or *Don Giovanni* in the open air while drinking champagne. The passional night was my own. The notion of Tristan's ship crossing from Ireland to Cornwall, carrying the lovers in their delirium on the waves of my imagination, was augmented by the sound of the distant surf raging over the reefs below.

'where Isolde steers here before the wind,
inflamed with love's passion, to find me.
The ship! The ship! It glides by the reef!'

On sunny days I could lethargically watch the crimson rosellas bulleting through the pine groves with harsh alarm calls bursting from their throats. As they were a pest, I felt no compunction in shooting a few for sport. Alternative targets were the empty Lanson Black Label champagne bottles from the previous night's festivities. Then there was the waiting through the heated afternoons for Mareva to arrive.

Each morning I powered the MG along the winding valley roads, parting the mists floating over the fields sparkling with dew, wire wheels creaking in the slides and eating the red dust until I reached the beach at Emily Bay. I dived into the warm waters and struck out for the pontoon as the light rose over the ocean. In high spirits then, I headed for the radio station to read the early news and notices.

My life on the island began to be spiced with risks and dangers. My finances had fallen into a parlous state, but I could not summon the energy to address the problem. I suppose I was seriously 'going troppo'. The station closed in the early afternoon, and that left the remainder of the day open, a great stretch of erotic promise.

Mareva occasionally went riding with me along the deserted roads to Crystal Pool, past the stone arches of the barracks built by convicts. We trotted at an easy pace on the track between the pines, past picturesque C.C.R. Nobbs, the oldest Pitcairner store on the island. Sometimes Mareva spoke to me in English, sometimes in Norfolk, sometimes a mixture of the two.

'Do you often see Nathan?' I asked directly.

'No, but he often sees me. He's always lurking somewhere.'

'Why did you separate?'

'Because he's so strange! After we got married he would just sit on the floor, stare at me and say nothing. For days sometimes!'

She sounded disillusioned and confused. The horses shook their manes and swished away flies.

'Were you both born on Norfolk?'

'I was, but he was born in Australia. Almira was living in Adelaide. He went to the best public schools. What a waste! He changed as soon as we got married. Hi es moos ell mard f' jalis f' me en imagines things.[44] He was quite violent. I hope you're not the jealous type!'

I reflected that a man would need great self-confidence not to be jealous about Mareva.

'Did you love him?'

'Yes, until hi es a' start orn dem moods! Dar s' finish et. Hi es always readin aa mystical poetry of Saint John of the Cross. But we're not divorced yet.'

'Do you think he'll find out about us?'

'Sure! Norfolk's a small place. Everyone already knows! When I said I heard you orn daa radio hi moosa fit f' aengry![45] Watch out for that bastard "Haet" they all said.'

I was thoughtful but not apprehensive at this piece of news. Nathan seemed to be an individual possessed of complex demons. We wandered on towards the coast.

'Have you been to Sydney?' I asked.

'A few times, but I'm always glad to get back to Norfolk. I really wanted to go to art college,' she said. 'Nathan stopped me. Said I would sleep with an artist. I wish...' her voice tailed off.

'Were those your paintings in McLachlan's house?' I asked with enthusiasm.

'Yes. Did you like them? I suppose you thought they were stupid, like me!' she tossed her head.

'Mareva, I think they're beautiful. You seem to love nature and know so much about Norfolk. I've never thought you were stupid. Don't be silly! I just don't want you to change, that's all.'

'I love magic too, and dreaming. Sometimes I dream about the past history of Norfolk, even the Polynesians.' She looked out to the horizon and pulled at the mouth of her horse.

'Why don't you do a course in painting?' I pressed her.

'Why, do you really care?' She seemed edgy and trotted on ahead.

There was no time for reflection now, as I needed to steady my horse as we descended the steep slope to the rocky beach. We tied our mounts to the paddock fence near the stile, and after some 'keesen'[46] in the grass we headed at low tide towards the shelf of rocks that formed the foaming bar to the Crystal Pool. Swimming naked here was both exhilarating and dangerous because of razor-sharp corals and barnacles, but smaller pools were safe from the currents. We swam in amongst the fish and kissed in languorous abandon, and we let our tanned bodies drift and bump against the sides of the vents as they filled and emptied. The sea cascaded across the high shelf into the pool as Mareva lay open before the sun like a Polynesian odalisque, skin gleaming and hair glittering with spray.

There was never any thought then that this idyll would ever end, that Nathan might become more jealous, that Mareva herself might drift away from me to another lover among the pines. These were the perfect hours of the affair. The simplicity of this love in paradise, its singular lack of urgency, incident or drama, its slowly evolving richness were all novel to me.

Late in the afternoon we stabled the horses. Mareva kissed me a lingering farewell in the sun.

'Ai staaten,' Mareva said. 'Ai gwen ketch et ef ai es leit.[47] I hope no-one realises we are seeing each other!'

I returned to Blaydes at dusk. It was the best time to visit the nearby St. Barnabas Chapel, in a grove of English oaks near a stream and pond known in the past as Orange Vale. This was the garden of exotic citrus and berry fruits cultivated in a beautiful hollow by Major Joseph Anderson, a past Commandant of the penal settlement renowned for his cruelty. Now it was a true bower for lovers.

The chapel was completed in 1880 as a memorial to John Coleridge Patteson, the first missionary Bishop of Melanesia, murdered by natives in the Solomon Islands in 1871. A college for the training of missionaries, the Melanesian Mission, was set up on Norfolk Island in 1866. Ten years earlier, Bishop Selwyn from New Zealand had brought a group of dark Solomon Islanders with rings in their ear lobes and noses to visit the island. Melanesians are from an older, differently evolved society to the Polynesians, and they were distrusted. Some twenty per cent of the arable land was summarily annexed from the Pitcairners by the then Governor of New South Wales, Sir John Young, and sold to the mission at the bargain price of two pounds an acre. Many Pitcairn descendants believe this was the beginning of the end of their independence and identity, the beginning of the theft of what they understood to have been given them by the Crown. Their cultural isolation was effectively finished, the *'experiment'* abandoned.

Although built of convict gaol stones and wood, the chapel showed the refinement and authority of the High Anglican Church, a challenge to the simpler Pitcairn faith practised in the austere All Saints Church in the converted Commissariat Store in Kingston, pew ends modestly decorated with cornstalks. The detached bell-tower of St. Barnabas contained a bell originally destined for the mission at Santa Cruz. Both structures were designed by a London architect, although there were Oceanic echoes in the detail. The pews of precious kauri wood faced the central aisle like those in an Oxford College, but they were inlaid with mother of pearl and delicate Maori turtle-shell designs. Dark violet and orange cowrie decorated the bench ends. The floor was black and white marble from quarries in Devonshire and the stained-glass rose-window was set *"to remember those shot by the heathen whilst ministering the gospel in the islands"*. The five sanctuary windows showing the life of Christ and the Saints were by Burne-Jones, and ornate brass lamps hung from an open-beamed roof. The refined spirituality of all this seduced me without difficulty, even after a long pagan encounter with Mareva.

At close of day, with brilliant colour dappling the marble and sunlight falling across the walnut panelling, I would mount the high seat of the five hundred pipe Willis organ and throw the switch to start the bellows. The floor beneath the pedal board was hollow, and a creaking tremor and pulse would slowly take possession of the instrument as its lungs filled with air. It would start to hiss then, as the pressure reached the gentle optimum required to work the antique tracker action. The tone colour was restricted to a few rich and varied stops. Only a single keyboard was available to perform my favourite Bach Preludes and Fugues, Toccatas by Girolamo Frescobaldi or a Mass by François Couperin le Grand.

After an afternoon of love with Mareva, grains of sand under my fingertips on the stained keys, salt clinging to my skin still glowing from sun and sea, I would play the close of day away in the cool evening of an English parish church. There were no psychological contradictions here, just a calm spiritual repose. The painful contradictions of the human heart were magically reconciled through music. In the darkening pines outside, delicate pairs of fluttering white terns alighted in the branches. The island settled under dusk like an egg engulfed by the plumage of a nesting bird.

We met again that same night, down at Kingston. Mareva had brought champagne and a thin blanket. Roaming horses were making their wild sunset charge down Quality Row, tails and manes streaming. She suggested going to Cemetery Bay yet again, but I was superstitious about the place at night.

'Ai nor gwen durn aa cemetery! Ai es fried f'dem guas in taun.'[48] I said in my best Norfolk.

'Ai gwen,' she insisted. I was worried because there was no street illumination and I had already felt the eeriness of the sea-mist flowing over the ruins of the gaol. I had blundered about and injured myself on previous nights.

'Min da guas f' Billy Tin don't grab you. Hi es a set under daa tree!'[49] she giggled as we passed the Royal Engineer's Office near the pier.

After a long walk we leaned against the retaining wall near Bloody Bridge. There was a story about that name. The convicts had murdered an overseer while the bridge was being built, and they had incorporated the body into the stones of the structure. The blood seeping out through the mortar and dribbling over the stones had revealed the crime. Less sensationally, there was a Bloody Bridge in Dublin which was more likely to have lent the name. I watched the surf breaking over the reef, the area known as the Wet Quarry in convict days. The prisoners cut dripstones there to filter water, working in heavy irons and up to their waists in the tide. It was one of the most feared punishments.

The champagne cork flew into the darkness leaving a trail like an insect, and we drank and kissed, luxuriating in our freedom. The smell of spray from the reef mingled in true ghastliness with the muffled wail of the Ghost Birds that drained from their burrows. The gravestones were clustered like grieving spectators behind us. The atmosphere here was genuinely ominous and I needed more alcohol to summon up a festive mood.

'Yu gwen narwi?'[50] Mareva asked from the darkness.

'Dunna mard!'[51] I said.

It would have been madness to go swimming on a moonless night in that place. Still, we wandered down the beach. I played the fool, stalking up and down with my socks draped over my erect penis, calling on the dead, while she giggled under the blanket.

'A skeleton of a convict was found sticking out the sand last week near here! He had no teeth!' she called in the wind.

'Mind you don't step on a skull! Plenty people are buried here!'

The evil atmosphere near the mass grave of Murderer's Mound was especially strong, and we finally lapsed into thoughtful silence.

Mareva suddenly shrieked then, and jumped up.

'Something s' run or mais lieg! Es wan boohi!'[52]

'Don't be silly, Mareva,' I said. 'It's only some crabs!'

'Look over there!' she cried out.

I peered into the gloom, and then I saw the dim shape of an enormous black rat scuttling into the darkness. Then I saw a nest of frantic cockroaches, and that finally destroyed any further inclination we might have had to remain at Cemetery Beach.

Mareva set off to her shack above Kingston, the headlights of her car cutting wavering arcs in the sky. I drove back to Blaydes wondering how I would ever have the courage to secretly visit her at night. Preserving our 'secret' would involve an approach through the pitch-black ruins. But resistance was hopeless. By now I was deep under her spell, her beauty, in thrall to her macabre history, her extraordinary powers of perception and this curious predisposition to the occult.

CHAPTER X

'Drumminor'
1969/1970 Opera Season
Mr. and Mrs. R.N. Fitzroy Douglas
would like the pleasure of your company on Wednesday evenings
Dec 10th 1969 The Magic Flute Feb 4th 1970 Traviata
Jan 7th 1970 Aida Mar 4th 1970 Rigoletto
Apr 1st 1970 La Forza del Destino
at 7.45p.m prompt for an open air musical evening of Opera at 'Drumminor'
Seating (on verandah) please bring chair
Dress warmly
R.S.V.P.

*T*he appearance of this invitation in your island mail was tantamount to a summons to court. It began one of my deepest friendships, which taught me a great deal about the way to value island isolation.

The post of Broadcasting Officer put me in a position to define the nature of local broadcasting, letting me programme the station as if the island were my private domain. Television reception was poor and depended on favourable weather. Newspapers arrived only once a week. Generally, I tried to create programmes to satisfy the Pitcairn descendants, expatriate British settlers, Australians and New Zealanders. But Sunday evening was a special time where I ranged over literature and music as much for my own benefit as the audience's. A BBC dramatisation of *The Mill on the Floss* in ten episodes might be followed by the music of Brahms with readings from his letters, over a period of three months. Rare historic recordings of great pianists would be followed by a late evening Sherlock Holmes dramatisation – *"221b Baker Street, cabby!"* – a jingle of harness through the Victorian fog – peculiarly atmospheric, far out in the clear Pacific night. This sort of programming brought me to Fitzroy's attention, and I was sent the invitation to the opera series. One became an instant pariah if even a single performance was missed during the short summer season. I accepted with deep curiosity.

Fitzroy Douglas had retired early in life to Norfolk Island from New Zealand. He was a large inventive Scot with a shock of white hair, living in a sprawling Pitcairner Colonial Georgian home called Drumminor, in an enormous sub-tropical garden near the airport. The house was completely hidden from the road by pines, whitewood and oaks. Frangipani scented the air and ferns grew in abundance, clinging to the trunks of trees and even to one another. The broad verandah leading to the cool dark interior was swathed in bougainvillaea, the bracts drooping, heavy with pink blossom nearly all year. French doors opened to a study rich in Isphahan carpets, camphor chests and gramophone equipment. A swivel chair was placed before a mahogany, leather-topped desk loaded with correspondence, a Zenith world radio to one side. Two Guy R. Fountain Autograph loudspeaker enclosures the size of small wardrobes occupied corners of the room. In summer a breeze would blow up the palm valley at the rear and through the cool, timber house, and the long net curtains to the bedroom would billow out on to the verandah.

Scattered throughout the garden, he had numerous cunning inventions. One was a trip wire attached to a rat trap that would project the unfortunate rodent into a bucket where it would drown in disinfectant. When you slid back the long gate at the entrance (carefully checking you had arrived at an acceptable time – a small sign informed callers of the visiting hours) an unseen voice addressed you from the bushes, inviting you in and giving directions as you approached the front door by a circuitous and picturesque route through the property. Alternatively, this could be set to fire blank shotgun cartridges to frighten off unwanted intruders. Fitzroy and his wife had begun living in the house when paraffin lamps were the only source of illumination, long before the generator and wartime runways disfigured the island forever. They trained a pet blackbird called Mrs. Blackie, and they gave her wheaten pellets soaked in castor oil as she hopped along the railings near the kitchen.

Thousands of other birds filled their garden, all connoisseurs of the finest music.

On opera nights it was best to arrive early with your chair and cushion, so you could get a good position midway along the verandah. Sherry or tea and biscuits were available if you arrived before the 'curtain'. Most of the audience were English, and an intense colonial feeling was generated by their country-set accents as they discussed property values in East Sussex or Hove as they idly leafed through back copies of *Country Life* during the interval. Reviews of the recording we were about to hear lay casually about, and the title of the opera, with the main cast, conductor and orchestra were chalked up on a blackboard propped against a verandah post like the daily menu in a French bistro. Finally, the audience were asked to take their seats in two rows along the verandah, facing the garden, and a row of of green mosquito coils were lit and placed on shiny metal stands along the railing. The lethal perfume settled over us, creating a curious intimacy. The lights dimmed and Fitzroy made a brief announcement.

'The plot of *The Magic Flute* is quite preposterous so I won't go into that here. The music of Amadeus Mozart is on the contrary rather beautiful. There will be one interval.'

The mainly elderly audience began to nod off as the solemnity and severity of the overture gathered its massive fugal weight, transforming the garden into a natural Masonic temple. We listened to this great struggle of the spirit of mankind, the eternal conflict of masculine and feminine principles, rising mysteriously from the depths of the plantation. Night drew in, and the coils became glowing points issuing smoke. While Papageno, the birdcatcher, was playing on his bells, real parrots flashed through this arcadian grove with hurried wingbeats. Their harsh calls faded in passing, and added further charm to the fairy-tale enchantment of the opera.

During these night performances, one also became aware of the suffering imprinted on the air. Numberless tragic destinies had been agonisingly played out in the prisons of this paradise. Clouds scudded across the moon during the malevolent aria sung by the Queen of the Night, a perfect expression of the blind passions that had become the engine of damnation for the hunters and the hunted alike on the Isle of Death.

During interval, the English community would chat while they admired the complex gramophone. Recordings were ordered from London, and they took three months to arrive. Fitzroy appreciated them the more because of the wait. Each disc was washed with a secret anti-static concoction, mixed with water 'at blood heat', and then allowed to dry on lint-free cloth. To reduce vibration, the precision turntable was placed on a concrete plinth weighing several hundredweight. The enormous speaker enclosures had complex pipes inside which gave the grandeur of a cathedral acoustic to open-air performances among the trees.

He never treated recorded music as wallpaper or furniture. Listening to a disc was a special, almost sacred event, and much preparation was required. They were fond of the pianist Maurizio Pollini, and they referred perceptively to his performance of the Chopin E-minor piano concerto as the 'product of *illusioned* youth'. My favourite nights were when it was raining heavily, beating loudly on the tin roof and on the broad leaves in the garden. Then the room glowed amber, and Persian rugs, a cosy fire and music rendered all the accepted comforts of civilised life.

Current events were hotly discussed during the interval.

'They are certainly not building a High Security Quarantine Station here if I have anything to do with it!' Fitzroy expostulated on the current plan of bureaucratic horror. He often wrote punishing letters, 'bromides' he called them, to the local weekly paper, *The Norfolk Islander*.

'Did you go to the public meeting at Rawson Hall on Thursday, Fitzroy?'

'I certainly did! There's nothing like provincial politics in a smokey hall to set the pulse racing!'

Many expatriates gasped, as Fitzroy had not been 'out' into the town in living memory. He was an authentic recluse. 'Rats, black ones *they* say but I have *my* opinion, rats that would jump like squirrels onto the roofs of the station carrying brucellosis and other diseases communicable to man... I wanted to know what preventative measures were being taken!'

'I say, steady on, Fitzroy.'

'The place was a hotbed of intrigue – low lights and cold – like an illegal cock-fight. I find the whole thing patently absurd!' And he flourished a brightly coloured kerchief and bent over the gramophone to make an adjustment.

'You hardly mean to tell me that a virus cannot be carried by random gusts of air through the finest wire mesh…'

'There are millions of tiny black flies around our bungalow already,' added the limping Mr. Hunter, drawing on his pipe with the fury of an hussar.

'One would never get that drunken Commonwealth doctor out from under the kitchen table with his native mistress in a *real* emergency,' waspishly commented the prim librarian, Miss Bate.

'Now just a moment. Things have improved since my day. Amputations used to take place by candlelight at the hospital, freezing the limb in ice before removing it. And the nurses no longer sleep with the patients!'

This caused amusement among the relays of tea slaves, passing back and forth from the kitchen.

'Paul, I did so enjoy the Mendelssohn you played last Sunday on the radio. We are all so pleased you came to Norfolk.'

'By the way, old boy, if you want to… you know…'

Colonel Berry, reputed to have invented the Sherman 'flail tank' minefield clearance device, gestured ambiguously into the dark garden beyond. Various unworthy thoughts came to my mind until I saw a number of the male members of the audience standing in the shrubbery with their tweeded backs to us, pipe smoke rising, doing the 'business'.

At length a small gong was struck and we all drifted back to our seats. This miraculous work, *The Magic Flute*, 'at once childlike and godlike', moved toward its radiant conclusion of hope. Members of the sleeping audience would lurch awake during the louder dramatic scenes, and then chins would fall to chests again and heads would loll. But for me, listening to serious music was an unforgettable experience in the heavenly air of Norfolk Island.

I returned to Blaydes, the pure melodies of Mozart singing in my head. I sat on the verandah listening to the murmur of the reef and admiring the dashing Salvator Rosa sky, a full moon suspended above Mt. Bates and the clouds racing over the pines. I could not sleep. I decided to take out Paulina's journals again.

CHAPTER XI

'The picture presented on that occasion was a Cage full of Unclean Birds... who appear to gather no heartening effect from the beauties of the Creation around them, but make a Hell of that which else might be a Heaven...'
Judge Sir William W. Burton
aboard H.M.S. *Alligator*
at Norfolk Island 1834

I had been hoping to discover if Paulina had married James Worth, but I realised the vital journals of the development of the romance were missing, as was any account of her adjustment to the Vandemonian *haut ton*. A locked volume in stained green morocco was prefaced with a scrawled title, *'The Black Books of the Settlement'*. It was the most damaged of the journals and had fallen apart at the binding. The lock showed signs of having been forced. The first entry was dated:

Restdown
October 10th. 1842

On occasion I feel, in the words of the venerable Dr. Johnson, *'as ignorant as a butterfly'*. Lady Jane has been greatly unwell & is partly paralysed in one foot after a fall on a voyage to New Zealand. This has negated her plans of establishing a school of English painting in Van Diemen's Land. Of more serious import are the venemous horrors perpetrated by that sleek snake John Montagu who has accused her of hatred & intrigue – he is a *noxious animal* exercising invisible tentacula in the most destructive fashion. Lord Stanley at the Colonial Office may well recall Sir John. This occurrence only months since Lady Jane sent the white kangaroo to Queen Victoria!

Oh, the ordeals of an Australian Colony – one must be the better or the worse for it.

Hobarton
Sunday, November 5th 1843

Suffering terrible distress at the final departure of Lady Jane and Sir John from VDL. He was dressed in the full uniform of a Captain in the Royal Navy as he acknowledged the cheers of the multitude. Veterans of the Peninsular wars presented arms as he pulled towards the H.M.S. *Flying Fish.* Sir John trusted *too* implicitly when he should not & leaves as a hero but not in disgrace. Went to Lady Jane's cabin at about 4 in the morning with James but found her asleep. I stood over Eleanor's berth & wept profusely, my emotion most violent. I am bereft of life, my last civilised contact has departed! The ladies here are well-meaning but simple & plain in their tastes – my anchor has been lost & I drift rudderless in the tide. James is warm & supportive as he can be.

(There is no explanation for the gap of two years in these entries, apart from her evident despair at the departure of her aunt.)

New Town Road
Hobarton
December 1845

I remain blessed with the Franklin spirit of adventure! My aunt took such an interest in the state of the Factory Nursery & the plight of female convicts generally I attempt to discharge the moral commission that Mrs. Fry (that woman from Newgate) gave Lady Jane before she quitted VDL. James forbears in good spirit as he considers their conduct worse than any that can possibly be conceived. Female convicts are the plague of everybody's life that has them & a pest but our great engine of punishment & reform, the system of assignment, forces us into acceptance of them as domestic servants. I far prefer good male convicts of some sensibility.

The leafy avenue to success in trade or the granting of pardons lies in courtesy to convict mistresses (the first choice upon arrival is quite properly given to the Military Officers). Captn. Stewart of the 58th. Regiment humourously regaled me with this intelligence.

'I fixed my fancy on her from the moment I struck the rivet that held the manacles to her pretty ankle.'

It is common to lend them money or proffer presents. The situation is worse than France under Louis XVI!

Many young women from the workhouse or dispossessed genteel families are hopefully despatched from England by the Emigration Committee & arrive clutching their *Certificates of Virtue*, attested to by two clergymen. The cost of the passage is seventeen pounds. The hope is to reduce the disparity between the sexes & elevate the morals of the colony. Forlorn hope! Lacking Natural Protectors, they are soon vitiated upon arrival or even during the voyage. James as Police Magistrate has a deep knowledge of such unsavoury matters & forbids me to indulge my thoughts on it but my imagination is ungovernable!

Floating in my memory is the recent *visite amusante* to the Cascade Factory near Hobart with Sir John & his ADC, Lady Jane & myself & the chaplain. The atmosphere within was as loathsome as expected. James warned me not to go as he could not answer for the behaviour of these women. Many of the ladies were known as the *Royals*, prostitutes formerly in the streets of Hobarton, so designated after the names of their ships namely the *Princess Royal*. As the chaplain began his sermon they all with one impulse turned around, raised their clothes and smacked their bare posteriors with a loud report! I could scarce control my laughter at our flustered Monsieur Timidité.

Out of a sense of duty I am reading with intense boredom the lectures on prison reform given by Baron von Holzendorff at Hamburgh and Professor Mittermaier at Heidelberg which were recommended by my aunt. More divertingly, my dancing lessons have taken a daring turn and I am learning the *Waltz*. My dear, there have been more than a few *on dits* concerning my activities with James at the ball to welcome the French explorer de Courmont given by Mme. d'Argency last evening! I have recently aquired a wombat from Mr. Verracaux which waddles about the house & suffers himself to be patted by all and sundry.

(Sections missing, seemingly torn out violently.)

Aboard the Barque "Lady Franklin" at Sea
July 25, 1846

In great haste & confusion we are, after being much delayed by calms & interminable tacks, at last sailing towards Norfolk Island! We were under weigh from VDL about 2 in the morning on July 20th, but the wind was not favourable for a passage along the Western Coast so the Captain went up D'Entrecasteaux. James is pressed by duty to take up the senior post on the island, restore order & assist in the trial of some men on capital charges there. We are *sans doute* sailing into a convict typhoon! The reputation of Norfolk Island in VDL loses nothing in the telling. I have neglected this journal for more pressing activities. There was so much to prepare & packing to be accomplished – I was *determined* to take my piano although James was equally determined that I left it behind. I prevailed & stamped my pretty foot! The Captain has made over his cabin for our exclusive use but it is now such a riot of trunks, packing cases & boxes we can scarce inhabit it!

James has taken up the appointment of Commandant & resigned his commission in Hobarton. There was general consternation & regret amongst the populace at this decision (they attempted to raise his salary to retain him) but it was finally accepted & he was presented upon leaving with a valuable service of plate bearing the Worth crest.

I am perfectly wretched & can scarcely take note of the remarkable oceanic scenes & fish we encounter daily. Darting Pilot-fish, sharks & Black-fish abound while blue & silver dolphins catapult out of the water at the bow. Jelly-fish are very numerous & at night float about the ship emitting brilliant points of light like fallen stars.

Yet I cannot take the slightest joy in these wonders. I am deathly pale and little Clara violently sea-sick! Our meals in the Wardroom & occasionally with the Captain are full of amusement but the food is of dreadful monotony. Fortunately James had brought a number of casks of wine & other delicacies. The Saturday toast in the Cuddy was to *'Wives and Sweethearts'* to which the murmured refrain *'and may they never meet'* was clearly audible! I take no particular interest in the relief officers & soldiers of the detachment of the 11th. Infantry Regiment & their families that accompany us. James is not well from the motion between decks & he certainly requires a firm constitution at this moment. The reputation of the Paradise is that of one of the circles of Dante's Hell. This does not encourage me to support his strenuous opinions. We are travelling together with the three children, Clara having just recently left the breast!

The present Commandant incumbent, a kindly man, lacks the required temperament for the post & has been recalled for being too lenient. He attracts sympathy for the unavoidable inheritance of Captn. Maconochie's relaxed regime. I well remember the ungrateful experience extended to Captain Maconochie when he was Commandant by the Arthurites & Lord John Russell – his ignominious recall was referred to by the Legislative Council as resulting from *"the Freaks of Captain Maconochie at Norfolk Island upon the Queen's Birthday"*. He threw open the gaol & allowed the desperadoes to roam freely over the island for the day & drink Her Majesty's health! When intelligence of this reached New South Wales it put the colony into a veritable ferment. Needless to say the Queen enthuses over his personality & methods. This inheritance has made me doubt the wisdom of James's acceptance of the appointment, even under desperate pressure from the authorities.

The new Lieutenant-Governor of VDL has charged James to restore order & impose the regulations on a settlement on the verge of open mutiny. James does not form quite so high an opinion of human nature as our dear friend Captn. Maconochie. He considers the N.I. convicts either incorrigible or insane. We had a fiendish row in Hobarton over his ambition for the post, one of the few we have indulged since our marriage. He seeks to prove himself as the strong man of the colony, the only one with sufficient secret knowledge & detailed remembrance to curtail the murderous intents of these *'flash-men'* [53] – although I grant he *was* loath to take up the post.

'How *can* I transport you & the children into this Lazar House of crime, my dearest? Will you now give up these city comforts & friends to accompany me into danger?'

I *insisted* on taking our domestics & Septimus Thorn, our trusted music tutor. James will not be parted from his faithful Eliza, a jewel among female convicts. As to my costume, I must needs abandon my satins, pearls & ostrich plumes so expensively assembled. What form will society take in this dangerous Paradise? Will there be balls & pic-nics & calls to be made? *Quel horreur!* We are taking up residence among the Serpents in the Garden of Eden!

Government House
Norfolk Island
August 5th. 1846

The presence of the red-tailed Tropic Bird gliding in the azure above the ship together with White Terns & Brown Noddies signalled the nearness of land. The grand peak of Philip Island & behind it the rich verdure of Norfolk Island was soon to be seen. It was a fair passage of nineteen days from VDL. My reservations disappeared at this sighting of a picturesque set of cathedral spires or stone pillars which transpired to be innumerable lofty pines rising sheer from the cliffs, precipitous to the sea. The toy settlement beyond the reef was innocent & singular in effect. Despite the sombre aspect of the gaol, the island is truly an enchanted & majestical spot which caused my spirits to rise. I have even begun an indifferent sketch.

The present Commandant & some Officers as a boat party came along side in a government launch & the entire family, Septimus & Eliza clambered aboard with much shrieking from the younger family members. We took the Mail with us but would need to wait for our other convict domestics & chattels to be unloaded.

Enormous seas were breaking over the reef which protects a small bay lying before the settlement. It was explained that at *le moment critical* we would be rowed through a gap in the reef called the *Bar*. Furious activity put us on the crest of a wave & we passed safely through – 'a good run' it was termed – what excitement! James sat bolt upright in his usual theatrical manner, quizzing the scene with his monocle, a faint smile playing over his mild features. There was a great bustle at the settlement upon our arrival. Terrific & horrible cries – a veritable pandemonium of lost souls – were issuing from a building pointed out to me as the Crank Mill – the first encounter with the horrors that might await us!

We were soon inspecting Government House which was to be our home for the forseeable future. Adolphus seemed particularly excited by the sentry box placed in the inner entrance hall & *would* gallop up and down saluting & flogging his sister Charlotte despite my admonitions & those of his father who threatened to put him in irons, much to the amusement of all present!

Government House
Norfolk Island
August 6th. 1846

There was some deep disturbance at the moment of our arrival. A great shout came up from the gaol some time after James went down there to address the outcasts for the first time. I immediately feared for his life. We do not have a great *commanderie* – only some 300 soldiers to keep the 2000 inhabitants of the Inferno in check. James was extremely out of temper with the outgoing Commandant. The atmosphere was emotionally close within the house but he departed recently on the *Lady Franklin* without incident.

The Mails were finally unloaded – a heavy sea & unfavourable winds delayed the vessel's approach to shore for several days – there was a letter from Mrs. Simpkinson detailing the activities of Lady Franklin in England & her fears for Sir John on his latest expedition through the Arctic ice fields. There was a paucity of news from Van Diemen's Land & I am quite depressed to have no news of my friends. I felt truly sorry for those officers who received nothing at all – they looked in deepest dismals with their years of silent separation from home.

Some men are to be hung quite soon for their part in the bloody rebellions but my mind is more on my own new situation than the fate of these desperadoes. James dresses his huge frame to intimidate the prisoners, as if in a role for the theatre – nautical straw hat with ribbon, pistols in his broad belt, black silk kerchief, tight jacket, small clothes, Wellington boots & quizzing the offender like a basilisk with his monocle! A veritable Giaour! God prevent that he ever turns this look upon me! Yet he cannot appear *mild* before these incorrigibles. They are of the worst possible description, these men who have ignored the pleas of wife, brother, parent or friend in order to follow their grim destinies. The Catholic chaplain Mr. Valentine Onslow is an insufferable prig & sports a neck scarf & Marquis of Anglesey hat. He offers a compassionate heart towards the monsters but in a rather too self-conscious manner to my taste. It is said he neglects his family in England which is at strict variance with his moral protestations on behalf of the convicts in the colony. As a member of the *Society of Friends* James is much against chaplains & even religious instruction and observance, it being a travesty of the true Christian faith. He seems over harsh on occasion but in this he takes after his father.

'Provided the Inward Monitor tells me I am right I can proceed no matter what a man might say,' he advances as philosophy.

Government House
Norfolk Island
September 20th. 1846

It is such a grey & gloomy day I shall spend it entering my journal. Rain is driving across the island & the sea is battering the reef – a strong sea mist has set in over Kings Town & everything in the house is damp with it – mould has grown within hours! I have been so much taken up with making calls on the various officers' wives at Longridge Farm (an agricultural station apart from the main gaol) & offering so much tea here at the Settlement that I have neglected my account scandalously.

Government House is a most commodious building of eighteen rooms, constructed of stone with wide verandahs, situated on an eminence above the settlement with a dramatic vista of the reef & less pleasantly, the convict buildings. Much of the cedar furniture & pine decoration within is of convict manufacture & not in the least inelegant. Many forgers are fine cabinet makers & carvers it seems. I write at a fine fall-front secretaire. The Khandahar & Turkey rugs from Risdon look most elegant on the polished floors of the Dining & Drawing Rooms. James has wasted little time in installing his *Argand* colza-oil lamps & mirrors with the pine frames. The privies & bathing facilities are dreadfully primitive & he has promised to obtain hip baths & have two Bramah closets built.

Both our bedrooms are large & possess dressing rooms. My precious Zobel sand pictures of grazing deer are already hung. The pink bed hangings & coverlet of Italian scenes catch the sun from my window which has beautiful views over the ocean, reefs & stands of pines. Mosquito nets are *en garde*. But the confusion that generally reigns in the room! – boxes, rugs, furniture all of a muddle.

Eliza has draped James's coverlet of platypus pelts over his four poster cedar bed, his guns are lodged in their locked cases & *le tout ensemble* possesses a marked colonial dignity. Hunting is a favourite pastime for the Officers, who sail out to Philip Island to indulge their passion for sport – much to my horror. The vast dining table would accommodate a multitude of feathered and furry corpses! My greyhound *Actaeon* is happy chasing the little island geckos that forage in the rubbish around his kennel in the yard. The dashing Polish officer Captn. Zaleski of the 11th. Regiment has promised me a horse quite soon – part Arabian!

Externally, there is a substantial coach-house & stables as well as as the principal island dairy. Charming ornamental gardens were constructed by a previous Commandant & contain majestic Norfolk Island pines, a broad English oak, advocado trees & guava shrubs. I remember small specimen pines in Kew Gardens being pointed out to me by my Aunt, scarcely imagining I would visit their place of origin. The branching is more delicate & wider spaced than the Baltic pine.

I am already *bored* by the penal nature of the place, the barred windows & sentry pacing the flags outside. Why, two cannons adorn the garden! There are even two sentries within! One resides in the kitchen on a platform high above the convict domestics preparing the food & the other, already mentioned, stands in his box in the side hall.

My square piano in the Sheraton case survived the terrifying *Bar* crossing & is safely installed in the Drawing Room. The fire burning there is a welcome foil to the gloom that generally pervades at this season. Septimus has already begun to tutor Charlotte but I fear the instrument is most dreadfully out of tune! We must fit up a small bedroom as a nursery for sweet Clara. I managed to stow a few pieces of miniature furniture for it & the panoramas before quitting Hobarton. I *do fear* this constant congress of our children with assigned convicts but the necessity of their education forces me to put my trust in God.

Norfolk Island
September 21st. 1846

The Officers have proposed giving a ball in the mess although a date is not yet fixed – I anticipate a gay evening – I am much turned in on myself as relations with the wives will take some time to flourish. There is a great want of intellect & an excess of vapid thought among the island society. Mrs. Webster, who is resident at Longridge Farm, is a charming woman of good address. Charles St. Aubyn, the Medical Officer, an exceedingly handsome young man & already married, is a person of clear refinement who appears to require a friendly ear to share the intelligence of his gruesome tasks. But I fear to be drawn into any exact knowledge of the surrounding degradation. I did have a brief letter from my friends in Hobarton, the Ferrers. They may be taking up residence on Norfolk Island!

I dress plainly in cotton print dresses & straw bonnets (how dreadfully dull, dull, dull!) as I am more thrown into closer proximity to working convict gangs than in Hobarton. They are dressed in a yellow & black or grey striped uniform, depending on their status, & are known as *'magpies'.* When a free person passes they must needs stand in the ditch & doff their striped caps. Regulations foolishly require them to salute *empty* sentry boxes – one I spied this very morning was even *brightening his chains!* – a more demoniacal group of ravaged faces I have never seen. I am constantly challenged by sentries. Already reports abound of murderers taking to the bush & the island is in a constant state of excitement & alarm.

(This diary had been severely mutilated, and to continue reading I would need to order the pages and repair the binding. She seemed such a vivacious creature that I wondered what effect the hothouse atmosphere of the isolated penal settlement would have on her psychological condition. Who had attempted to destroy her journal? It was late and the ghost of Barney Duffy would be sure to be loitering in the gully. I reluctantly left my small verandah and went to bed.)

CHAPTER XII

One hair (upon my nape)
You loved to watch it flutter, fall, and rise)
Preventing your escape
Has snared you for a prize
And held you, to be wounded from my eyes
from *'Songs between the Soul and the Bridegroom'*
by St John of the Cross (tr. by Roy Campbell)

Nathan's behaviour became increasingly bizarre as his jealousy increased its hold over him. I had learnt of his love of mystical poetry, and I had met the anorexic girlfriend he was living with 'up country'. He refused to do anything constructive, despite pleading from his mother and Mareva. He had no job, and he lived from the invested capital of an inheritance. He became emaciated and grew a prophet's beard, and he spoke of going to Bali.

One evening I was having a late drink at the Paradise Hotel bar when he materialised beside me. I use this word advisedly, as he had a habit of 'appearing' in a room when you least expected it.

'Watawieh yu Haet?' he said.

'Fine thanks, Nathan,' I said, concealing my surprise.

'Yu es drinkin hard or draggin aa chain?'[54]

'Are you shouting? An Old Grand Dad please.'

'Ai bin hear yu bin drivin yus MG fast en loose krors daa island leit en aa nait.'

'At about the same speed as your Norton!' I said. I was relieved to have found a point of contact apart from the unmentionable questions concerning Mareva that remained suspended in the air like so many bowie knives.

'Yu bin see Mareva?' he asked, diffidently. At last it was out.

'Yes, I see her at Almira's quite often. Why do you ask?'

He smiled before replying.

'I want to warn you about her,' he said. 'Stay away from her, shi es bad for you.'

'How do you mean?'

'Shi es dangerous. I just want to help you. I don't want you to be hurt or polluted.'

'That's very kind of you, but we seem to getting on quite well.' How nauseatingly reasonable and middle class I sounded.

By now various islanders were nudging each other and smirking. Daffi, Goat and Hoof edged closer, a mutinous crew mouthing scarcely veiled threats. I decided to drive along the beach near Slaughter Bay for some air. *'I don't want you to be polluted.'* What did he mean?

'Yu laik wan biya, nort?'[55]

'No thanks. See you later, Nathan.'

'Bye, Haet. See yu morla, brud.'[56] They watched me leave, shifting their feet in a felonious knot.

I emerged into the cool evening. The prison walls in the moonlight at Kingston were ominous and swarming with shades. The moon seen through Gallows Gate, the loophole towers of the Old Military Barracks silhouetted against the sky, were disturbing. I went to walk inside the Pentagonal Gaol, but the atmosphere at the entrance paralysed me. I found myself falling into a march step along the old Bay Street, and was prevented from walking along the old Military Road by an uncanny pressure on my chest and in my mind. The damp smell of sea spray filled the air and through the soles of my feet I could feel the incessant pounding of the surf. The effect of this low tremor on prisoners entombed for months in the black *'dumb-cells'*, immersed up to their waists in sea-water, scarcely bears imagining. The moon was at an acute angle, the reef a faint margin of activity.

Cameron told me he had mapped a series of underground passages beneath the ruins, with some children to help him, a torch, a white stake and some string. He discovered solitary cells which were simply black pits in the ground where the prisoners were thrust like animals. They were fed through a complex series of doors which excluded the faintest gleam of light, and on Sundays at chapel, a cloth mask was tied over each man's head to maintain this isolation. Late at night these ruins trembled with the cruelties of the past.

It was late and I had arranged to meet Mareva at her grand-mother's house. There was an old piano there and I had promised to play. She loved listening to me rushing through the passionate music of Chopin. I drifted the car through the gate in some style, then I saw Nathan's motorcycle against a tree. Not wanting an awkward con-frontation, I instantly reversed out of the drive and headed back towards Blaydes, congratulating myself on my rapid reflexes. Later, she told me Nathan had been standing at the foot of her bed waiting for me, dressed in a wet-suit, hunting knife strapped to his leg, and carrying a sawn-off rifle.

'Es daa bastard Haet gwen visit you? Hi es gwen get wan biggan shock!'

'Nathan, yu mussa mard!'[57] screamed Mareva.

Apparently, when he realized I had rumbled him he rushed into the garden and jumped on his machine to chase me. I had almost reached Middlegate crossroads by the time I noticed the Norton headlight in my mirrors. I gunned the MG straight on down Cascade Road hoping to outrun or confuse him, but he stuck to my tail. I drifted the unsurfaced corners on the twisting descent to the ruins of the Whaling Station at Cascades. The wire wheels groaned under the strain, and clouds of coral dust blew through the cockpit from the holes in the passenger floor and the loose battery cover behind the seats. The seats themselves began to twist in their rusty mountings. The moon was suspended like a spotlight over the dark pines thrusting into the sky.

I snatched third coming into a steep descending left-hander through a copse and he disappeared from view. I decided to kill the lights then, and drive solely by the moon. I hoped he might think I had turned off into a farm or drive. The instant blindness was alarming, but my eyes adjusted to the reduced light, and I eventually reached the final right-hand bend down to the cylindrical silhouette of the Oil Tanks and Digestor of the Old Whaling Station. I drove as close to the retaining wall as I dared, and I hid the car behind the boiler above the surf breaking over the pebbly beach. The dim outline of the curving cliffs and sentinel pines seemed to close in on me.

Then Nathan arrived, and I saw his headlamp wavering as he drove up and down, searching the broad concrete landing place. He had not seen me, and in the end he accelerated away in a flurry of swift gear changes. I followed the sound with my ear through the curves until it faded out under the wash of the waves beside me.

Silence and the hiss of the tide. Sitting on the rusting remains of the gantry in a reverie, I imagined another time – the smell of blubber, the plash of oars, the ominous contour of a sperm whale being towed home by moonlight, the plaintive song of the Norfolk whalers floating over to the shore.

This eruption of violence both elated and frightened me. It seemed the mercurial nature of the Christian family still flowed in his veins. Events had taken a serious turn and I cautiously returned to Blaydes via a different route, Harpers and New Cascade Road, just missing a cow that wandered across in front of me, nipping under its outstretched neck. I expected to hear the motorbike as I parked beside my entrance porch and rushed inside. I shut the blinds, locked the door and switched off the lights.

As I turned over these events in my mind I became aware of a curious dampness spreading between my legs. I thought I had wet myself in fear, – something else to be ashamed of, but when I went to the bathroom to change I found my pants were soaked in blood from a deep flesh wound in my right thigh. I pressed hard and stopped the bleeding. How had I done this? I dressed it as best I could and poured myself a stiff bourbon and smoked a cigarette before sleep finally overtook me. I would need to go to the hospital and explain the injury somehow.

A chorus of birds woke me in the morning. My leg was throbbing, but I had to open the radio station and read the early morning news. There was no telephone to contact Mareva. The hospital would have to wait. I took my coffee out on to the porch, and embraced the cool air of morning. My eyes wandered over the dewy fields and pines that lay before the house floating in the rising sun. I congratulated myself on a narrow escape.

Then I gave a start. There was an odd hole in the driver's door of the MG, a bullet hole, the punctured metal gleaming through the flaking paint. There was blood on the driver's seat and the leather had been freshly holed. So perhaps Nathan had succeeded in getting off a shot from the motorcycle during the chase, and that was what had ripped into my leg. This seemed unlikely, so maybe he had lain in wait by the road as I sped home.

There was something else, too, on one of the windscreen pegs that were meant to hold the hood catches. This bloody mess was more difficult to fathom. Was it a bird? Was it an occult island warning placed there during the night? Of course! The cow I had just missed on Mission Road, hurrying home. The soft grey pulp with fine soft hairs looked like part of its lower lip. This was potentially even more serious than being shot. On the island, killing a cow, even one of those starved specimens with arthritic limbs and reversed horns, a skin stretched taut over a starved skeleton, was considered almost a worse crime than killing a man. It was punished accordingly – fines, deportations, a possible jail sentence. I had been living on the island for some nine months, and I wanted to avoid this type of embarrassment.

I cleaned up the bloodstained car and got rid of the lip, and I drove off in a mood of some depression to open the radio station for another day. My formerly peaceful private life was becoming complicated. Besides my financial difficulties, I had to worry now about my personal safety. I was missing my piano desperately. In addition I had lost my talisman hat, the Corsican fisherman's cap. I might have left it at the Paradise Hotel. It seemed a dreadful omen.

CHAPTER XIII

Platycerus elegans

The Commonwealth policeman called around to see me the following evening. He was investigating reports of shots from the area around Blaydes. What had I been shooting at? More to the point, did I have a current firearm licence? The narrow board on the verandah, bearing the corpses of ten red parrots arranged in a row, did little to endear me to him. I pointed out that they were a pest, not a protected species. He asked me about the bullet hole in the MG's door. I made up a story about a low flying parrot that I was trailing in the sights, that flew past the car just as I fired. The car was dark green like the foliage, and I had failed to see it. The constable looked sceptical. His nickname on the island was Wyatt Earp.

'Sorry brud, but ai gwen report des thing en yu mus appear in aa couirt f' explain et.'

'What will be the charge?'

'Shootin yus own car. Dieh mait be possible on aa mainland but nor here orn Norfolk!'

So, I was to be arraigned on a charge not unlike the petty charges loaded on to the convicts a hundred and thirty years ago.

'For shooting his own car – a "feeler" of 200 lashes!'

Maybe the court appearance would enhance my reputation among the islanders, if not among the Establishment. The descendants of the mutineers respected those rebellious souls a little outside the law. At least the more serious episode of the cow appeared to have passed unnoticed.

Almira always helped me when I was in trouble. Today, she had poured herself the usual whiskey and pushed the Tahitian fish in my direction when I began to tell her about the coming court appearance.

'Yu always had aa dark en evil look, darl,' she giggled.

'Will I have to leave Norfolk, do you think?'

'Daas et. Always fishin for compliments! Yu es nor bad enough, boy – sorry f' disappoint yu darl.'

We could never speak about Mareva, however. She was fond of her, and she was deeply disappointed in the way Nathan had failed to develop as a man and honour his responsibilities. The drug treatment that had crippled a fine intelligence was a torture to her imagination, and created the fear of an unpredictable future. By chance she had found a rose in one of the guest suites that I had intended Mareva to discover as a love token. The implications were obvious, but she ignored them.

The courtroom was a dark-panelled, austere chamber in the administration buildings at Kingston. A Royal Coat of Arms and a photograph of the Queen dominated the bench where the magistrate sat in judgement. I sat in a gallery waiting my turn, listening to the cases that preceded mine.

The first case involved cattle rustling. The possibility of rustling cattle on an island five miles by three defeated my imagination. While evidence was being given, a brand from the hide of one of the animals that had been slaughtered was held up for the magistrate to see. The evidence against the accused mounted up, and there was scarcely any defence.

'Case dismissed,' the magistrate declared, nonetheless.

There was consternation in the courtroom, particularly in view of the material evidence of the brand. I began to feel more optimistic.

A more serious case was that of the motorist who had struck and killed a cow near Headstone Point. The accused was a huge blonde islander wearing a curious crown of vine leaves in his hair. He was called upon to explain the incident.

'Well your honour, I was driving along the Headstone Road when suddenly this cow came around the corner on the wrong side of the road travelling at about 50 miles per hour. There was nothing I could do to avoid it. This is not the first time. This cow is guilty of negligent behaviour, endangering life, and it should have been prosecuted or put down long ago.'

The few people in the courtroom exploded with laughter and so did the magistrate.

'This is a serious Court of Law!' he finally expostulated.

'And this was a criminal cow! Now es a' daird so wi nor can ask et f' testify!'[58] replied the islander.

'Case dismissed on the grounds of insufficient evidence and lack of witnesses, including the victim.'

The next case involved an Australian resident of long standing who was a member of the Norfolk Island Local Council. He was a pillar of the community who had married one of the proprietors of a shop in the massive Duty Free shopping complex of Burnt Pine, the tawdry commercial development in the centre of the island. Their relationship had been stormy, and now he was charged with physical abuse, attempting to shove his wife head first in a washing machine while it was running. She had almost drowned, and she had received a broken arm. He admitted the act, sobbing, blaming his Irish ancestry and his black bouts of drinking. The magistrate sentenced him to five days community service, which would involve cutting scrub on Mt. Pitt to keep the walking tracks clear.

Wyatt Earp gave evidence against me about the red parrots *(Platycerus elegans)* and the offence of 'shooting your own car'. In my defence I pointed out that I was merely controlling an introduced species, escapees from aviaries during the convict period of the First Settlement, keeping down the 'feathered tribe' that were particularly aggressive towards the rare Norfolk Island Green Parrot *(Cyanoramphus novaezelandiae verticalis)*. I insisted I was performing a service for the endangered endemic species. I reiterated the account of the mistaken car shooting. The magistrate seemed unimpressed with my explanations, and I was offered a choice – five days community service, a $500 fine or two nights in the lock-up. I saw the lock-up as a chance to ape the old convict style, and I accepted with enthusisasm.

It was unusual to spend any time in the solitary cell, as it doubled as the administration liquor bond store. Normally, it was only used to detain people while they were waiting to be deported. In fact it was a 9 to 5 jail as far as I was concerned. During the day I sat around on cases of Johnny Walker and assisted in unloading and packing. Then I was taken along to the Paradise Hotel and locked in a room, which was mysteriously unlocked later in the evening to let me socialise. On the first evening I sat lethargically at the bar, looking out to sea and dreaming.

'Hey Haet! Look out aa window!' suddenly shouted an islander.

A group of the descendants were sitting around a barbecue fire in the grounds of the hotel, between two enormous curved bones known as Whale-jaw Arch. They were drinking and singing, and I saw one of them was wearing my Corsican hat. As I looked, someone snatched it off and threw it on the embers, and it flared up and burned. They all cheered and danced Indian fashion around the fire, looking up at me, waving and jeering. I wrenched open the window and threatened to fight all of them, but I was pulled back by one of Wyatt Earp's deputies and dragged off to my room, fuming.

I remained a mainlander, a 'blow-in'. Time was bringing their resentment to boiling point. Unknown to me then, there was one islander protecting me, a large, friendly fellow named Channa. He had a carefully trimmed black beard, and he held sway over the other descendants by sheer force of character. I had spoken to him often at the bar, not realizing he was my secret bodyguard. I had deluded myself that Mareva was mine alone. She was free, she was extraordinarily beautiful, and she was lusted after by most of Nathan's friends.

CHAPTER XIV

Bounty Day

*'Cloudy weather. Close in with Norfolk Island, very much disappointed in its
appearance from the present point of view... for picturesque beauty
Norfolk Island is not to be compared with Pitcairn.'*
Register of George Hunn Nobbs, June 8th. 1856

*'They (the Pitcairners) have the dress of poor people, with the feelings
of those gentleborn and nurtured...'*
Bishop John Patteson, Melanesian Mission

*T*he preparations in *Almira's* kitchen for Anniversary Day began
almost a week before the event. For some delectable specialities the
work took even longer. The day commemorated the arrival of the
Pitcairners, soaked through and seasick, aboard the government
barque *Morayshire* on a winter's day in June 1856. Some of them
found it hard to walk after disembarking, and they needed tea and a
fire to restore them to this world. Famine and disease on the lone
'Rock of the West' had forced their relocation some four thousand
miles across the Pacific to Norfolk Island. Some Pitcairners had
never seen stone buildings and they were loath to enter them at first.
The ox-carts amused them greatly, as they had never seen wheeled
vehicles before. This was hardly surprising as the Polynesians did
not know of the existence of metal or written language until the
arrival of the Europeans. Six families were so overwhelmed they
elected to return to Pitcairn. Some descendants believe that lost
documents prove that Queen Victoria gave Norfolk Island to the
Pitcairners as a *'separate and distinct settlement'*. They enjoyed separate
colonial status for fifty-two years, until the Governor of New South
Wales decided on a policy of eviction if they were unable to pay a
fixed rent.

I had now been resident for almost a year, and in some ways it was also an anniversary for me. The broadcasting station was developing well and I was known throughout the island. I had also by now opened a small restaurant and coffee lounge in Burnt Pine.

The hectic activity and large quantities of food in *Almira's* kitchen had become a familiar sight. Pots of steaming *kumeras* (sweet potato), *mudda* (green bananas cooked in milk) and *pilhi* (baked bananas) lay everywhere, ovens disgorged freshly baked granary loaves, Tahitian fish marinaded in plastic containers. There were prawns, rock crabs and crayfish, shrimps, shark, groper, garfish, trumpeter fish, red emperor, trevally, parrot fish, butterfish, clownfish, lionfish, reef salmon, vast hams, cold tongue in gelatine, brawn, Italian sausage, home-churned butter, preserves of all types, pickles, fruit salad, green salads, potato and tomato salads, macadamia nuts, guava jelly, pineapples, mangoes, paw-paw, oranges, lemons, limes, red and yellow guavas, water melons, sugar melons, strawberries, gooseberries, bananas, passionfruit, avocados, the difficult fruit of the *Monsterio Delicioso*, custard apples, pavlovas, lemon tarts, Christmas puddings, steak and blackpudding sausages for the barbecue, and finally the vast Aga stoves yielded up whole roast sucking pig, chicken and pigeon. All sorts of wines, spirits and beers were available in the usual massive duty-free quantities from the cold box. This Byzantine feast was to be packed into picnic baskets and cartons, and sent in a fleet of cars to Kingston, where most of the day's festivities would take place.

Almira presided over the provisioning from her post at the head of the kitchen table, her leg folded under her, hair immaculately arranged in a silvering bun, sipping from a glass of whiskey. Orders were gently given to the small regiment of island women, some enormous of stature, some delicate and fragile, who helped her mount the campaign. The dignity of her posture, the laughter and joy in her eyes, her unspoken authority, all proved to me that she was truly the Queen of the Island.

'Try sam a' dii darl!' she kept telling her guests, as the mountains of food passed across the table into the baskets. It was a celebration of life and her joy in it. The island chatter enveloped me like chamber music. The ginger Tom became agitated with the excitement and rushed from window-sill to garden, scampering up the trees, falling from the tin rat protectors. Tarler birds pecked at fallen guavas. The sun strengthened in a cloudless sky.

Mareva was late. She was still working as a receptionist in the hospital to make ends meet, and she was often late for our meetings, as her hours were inflexible on split shifts. We managed some freedom to be with each other, but it was never very satisfactory.

The islanders assembled at Kingston Pier in the mid-morning, and prepared to leave for the Cenotaph to lay a wreath. Many were dressed in various types of period costume, some more fanciful than others. Young boys were dressed as *Bounty* midshipmen and cabin boys, wearing straw hats with ribbons or sailors hats and braided tunics, ladies in long gowns, bonnets and shawls carrying parasols, men as Able Seamen, Captains or Admirals. Often a whole family made a concerted effort at a group image. Many appeared driving sulkies, with spirited horses brushed till they shone, decorated with ribbons.

'Watawieh yu darlen?'

'Ai se guud thank you.'

Shouted greetings filled the air from all these folk. It sounded as if they saw each other rarely. In fact they met every other day, but this was special. Meeting had never become an indifferent routine on Norfolk. On the roads, people all lifted a finger from the steering wheels of their cars, or waved when they saw a friend.

After the Cenotaph and the laying of wreaths by a member of the Christian family, the crowd wound their way to the cemetery. Here simple hymns were were sung, and modest prayers said by descendants of the Adams and Quintal families.

'In the Sweet by-and-by
We shall meet on that beautiful shore...'

Families in period costume went to Government House, to be judged by the Administrator and his wife.

Earlier in the morning, I had announced on the radio that the Bounty Picnic would take place on the grassy area sheltered within the walls of the New Gaol, near Slaughter Bay. A great many picnics had already been laid out on the grass covering the footings of old prison cells. *Almira's* was naturally the grandest, and everyone of the least significance on the island made their way over eventually to 'make obeisance' to her, lawyers, accountants, shopkeepers, councillors, alcoholics, ministers of religion, the Official Secretary, soft drink industrialists from Cascades and road workers from *'durn aa admin'*. We were joined by her daughter, whose career was everything she had wanted for Nathan. Nathan was commanded by his dark, internal world, and he never appeared at social events.

Mareva was enjoying herself hugely, and I spent a lot of time at secret language games and surreptitious play.

'You always make me laugh!' she said 'Hat always cracks me up!'

'Yu gwen f' walk durn Music Valley?' I suggested.

'Everyone'll start gossiping... ai nor gwen. Ai mait go a' Cemetery Beach en through a' cemetery later orn.'

'I'll meet you there.'

I had noticed more than a few islanders looking in our direction, drawing conclusions. Almira made sure I was constantly eating and taking part in the antics. Many of her friends were the generation of older Pitcairners who would soon pass on, taking their almost un-recorded folk memory with them.

'Have you met Cheryl?'

'I know the face.'

'Well, shi es haed et sam taim!'[59]

Gales of wheezing laughter and more whiskeys. Food and drink were handed round with effusive generosity. I was complimented on my radio programmes from all sides. Children fell into large lemon tarts. Whole sucking pigs with fruit, ribbons and paper flowers stuffed in mouth, ears and nostrils were splendidly carved with virtuoso flourishes.

'You know the last time I was on Norfolk, five years ago, I was bitten by a mosquito at exactly the same time and in exactly the same place – amazing!' observed one of *Almira's* paying guests.

'Almira, why do you sleep in that tiny shed?' asked another.

'Norfolk should have its own... and produce... there is money in that... the taxes on companies should... why don't they just kick out... the islanders definitely need...' an expert of two days trailed off, wiping *mudda* off his Polynesian shirt front.

'Orl em tauris jus law Norfuk!'[60] Almira said.

She told the story of the islander stopped by the Commonwealth policeman for driving wildly all over the road, stopping every half mile to swig from a bottle.

'Have you been drinking? Why, that's gin on the seat!'

'Well officer, you're right but nort to worry – it's only "Gordons"!'

'Daas alright then.'

There was such a contrast between the old and new generation of Pitcairners. The old folk seemed such good people with a sort of inner light of the soul, a simple piety which lent their expressions unusual dignity. An inner smile of contentment permanently illuminated their faces and shone through their eyes. All their houses and cars were left permanently open and unlocked. Theft was unknown. Loneliness was quite unknown.

'Kam in a' haus darl. Ai gwen maik wan hot cup-a-tea.'

'Daas guud. En ai es hungry!'

But the young ones often fled to the mainland for work and entertainment, breaking the continuity and sense of family, always more profound within the confines of an island.

'Dais, do you remember that alabaster figure I gave you for Christmas? Where is it?' asked her husband, a bronzed, erect old gentleman with close-cropped hair.

'Yes, of course I remember. Well, ai es fraid ai got sumthin f' tal – I alabastered it on the tap,' she said with a certain piqued satisfaction.

A smile filled her knowing eyes, and her white hair stirred lightly in the breeze. This dry humour was typical of the old islanders. This lady was also the organist of the St. Barnabas Chapel.

I drank cups of *'switzel'*, tea served in scooped out lemon halves. More laughter and stories, acres of fish and plantations of roast sucking pig. The traditional cricket match on the Kingston Oval was about to begin – the *Bounty* side, dressed as Georgian seamen, against the All comers. This gave me a perfect reason to leave the feast. Watching such a match with no time ceiling to the day was a magical recreation. It also gave me a passable reason to rendezvous with Mareva.

The approach from Quality Row to the road above the cemetery was covered by a sinister tunnel of trees just short of Murderers'

Mound and Bloody Bridge. There was a tremendous surf running, the spume like graceful hair curving in an arc, lacing back in the wind. Huge seas were breaking over Nepean Island, and dappled shades of blue passed across the surface as the sun played with the changing light. Islanders with straw hats and long bamboo rods were fishing off the rocks with their children. Struggling fish were flicked from the sea on hooks, to be tossed into baskets on the sand by a lady in an enormous blue cotton shirt. A barbecue fire was burning further back, sheltered behind rocks.

The Kingston cemetery at Norfolk Island was a picturesque and magnificently sited place of burial near the shore, with memorials from all the layers of history of the various settlements. The detailed inscriptions on the headstones depict the heartbreaking destinies of free men and prisoners. The naive carving of inscriptions of the few First Settlement headstones was deeply affecting. In the distance I could see Mareva wandering among the graves, and I went to join her.

'Wathing yu bin do?'[61] she asked me as I came up.

'Eatin, drinkin and laughin...' I kissed her passionately.

'Es yu ever pat in orn aa sturn?'[62] she smiled wickedly.

'What are you talking about?'

'Sametimes wi es kam durn hier en make love orn aa graves!'

'Mareva, yu mussa mard! Beautiful, intelligent but mard. Read this.' I pointed to an ornately carved scroll on a headstone.

Sacred to the Memory of Charles Turner aged 20 years
Private of Her Majesty's 99th. Regiment of Foot
who was accidentally drowned when fishing at Rope Rock
on the 1st. October 1850

'He was one of the three who drowned that day. They say that the convict Barney Duffy cursed them when they discovered him living in the hollow trunk of a tree. They drowned in the sea off Headstone Point.'

Mareva was always full of macabre information. If a cock crowed in the middle of the night she would leap up in bed, and cry out, 'Someone's just died!'

Sacred to the Memory of George Wade William
only child of George and Fanny de Winton who
departed this life 13 January 1850
aged eleven months and twenty five days

The sense of isolation and grief upon losing a child on a Pacific island, a remote penal settlement, can only be guessed at. It suddenly struck me that this was the period of Paulina's residence and I wondered if she would describe births and deaths in her journal.

Here lies the body of James Saye
who died June 21 1842
Aged 35 years
Stop Christian stop and meditate
On this man's sad and awfull fate
On earth no more he breathes again
He lived in hope but died in pain.

I dwelt for a moment on the crude skull and crossbones and trumpeting angel on an adjacent gravestone.

'Mareva, do you love me?' I blurted out as we approached the southern end of the cemetery. She seemed more intensely alive at that moment than ever before.

'You always were romantic, Paul, but don't be so serious. I'm not going out of one marriage straight into another.'

'But that wasn't my question, Mareva. Do you love me?'

She remained silent at first, swamping me with her eyes and cascading hair.

'Don't spoil things,' she said then. 'Ai staaten!' She skipped off joyfully towards the Bounty Day festivities again, and she turned after some time and beckoned me to follow. I realised she was not as entwined with me as I had thought, and now I feared she would start to rove among the men. In this sometimes terrible emotion called love, whatever you imagine invariably comes to exist. I followed her without conviction, and before leaving the cemetery I noticed another headstone sentiment that matched my emotions.

For like a lily fresh and green
I am cut down and no more be seen

We risked walking together until we reached the Golf Club, at the beginning of the noble run of colonial mansions known as Quality Row. Then I allowed her to set off ahead.

'Yu gwen a' Bounty Ball des nait?'[63] I asked.

'Sure. I'm going to enjoy myself. We can talk, even dance but no kissing in public. Please don't hang around me looking as if you'd lost your dog. Come up and see me later on.' She gave me a wonderful complicit look, and we parted.

I did not spend much more time at the 'prison feast'. I soon left Almira, who had reached that stage of subtle disconnection from reality brought on by the pleasure of giving food, the presence of her grandchildren and the whiskey and water. Cameron had joined us, and his practical demeanour set everything in order. He would manage the logistics of the return. She often made cruel remarks about him, but it was clear true affection always lay beneath the barbs. She would never allow her better nature to get the upper hand.

The Rawson Hall was just a wooden barn, but most important public meetings on the island took place there. It held a place of real affection in the hearts of the residents. I had occasionally gone to the cinema, the 'Rawson Hall Talkies', on Saturday evenings with Mareva, and fumbled a few intimate explorations during the double feature.

The hall was always beautifully decorated for the Bounty Ball with local plants and flowers, Norfolk Palms and agricultural produce, ferns and streamers. After one or two Pitcairn hymns and a Benediction the dancing could begin in earnest. The whole island seemed to be there, dignified elderly islanders, ladies from Jane Austen novels with their Captain Wentworths, young blades and babes in suggestive and fashionable clothing, children in sailor suits, the resident millionaires, tourists with cameras, and expatriates of all nationalities on the island. I noticed the modern Princess Potocka, a member of an ancient Polish line, far from the Palace of Łańcut now, dancing in her 'vertical' style.

An event like this gave me a chance to meet people I would not otherwise have met socially. There were many social classes on the

'*Madeira of the Pacific*', particularly among the immigrant community and within their own national groups. Less obvious were the distinctions among the Pitcairn descendants. My broadcasts of the Local Council threw a spotlight on the social undercurrents, and they brought me into contact with all sorts of prejudices. It made for turbulent politics, which by and large I remained detached from.

The Administrator was not interested in music so I had little cause to visit Government House. Occasionally I delivered a gift of vegetables or melons from Almira. She used such visits to introduce me to the inner circle, as if she was an ambitious mother. Administrators were disposed of with swift, poisonous darts if they had no 'kum frum'[64]. Occasionally an administrator and his wife loved the island *and* the islanders, working hard for the community. Almira became a regular visitor only if she felt they had the best interests of Norfolk at heart.

It was expected that this Administrator would put in an appearance at the ball with his wife. This was a courageous move, as the islanders deeply resented any bureaucratic interference from Australia. The Norfolk Island Council was only an advisory body, and it could always be overruled by the Minister. The islanders were bitter about this, and it made them aloof at such gatherings.

Many expatriates adopted superior advisory roles on Norfolk long before they were entitled to comment. I had noticed this at *Almira's* within a few hours of arrival on the island, and I came to resent it. 'Blow-ins' were often rich former businessmen, and they meddled in the local politics as a form of escape from the inactivity of retirement.

Mareva arrived dressed in a short black skirt, black stockings, high heels and tight leopard-print top. Her tanned skin glowed with residual sun and her mane of burnished hair cascaded over her shoulders. Her eyes were wildly alight. I had never before seen her so provocative or alluring in public.

I realized this was all meant to make her the centre of attention for everyone, not just to excite me. I kept losing sight of her in the throng. Who was she dancing with, who was she exciting now? The music was a mixture of styles, and occasionally I would play the piano with the band, but my main attention continued to be fixed on Mareva and her dancing partners. A slow poison seemed to have entered my heart. This was the first time she began to drift away from our relationship and as a sort of trivial revenge I flirted with some of the tourist girls visiting the island. One in particular, who danced alone.

Mareva put on the full repertoire of suggestiveness. 'Come to me after the ball,' she whispered in my ear, her tongue deftly exploring. But she kept looking over my shoulder at other couples and flirting with her eyes. My stomach was in a knot. She pressed her body against me and I closed my eyes with pleasure like a cat. The musicians took a break.

'Why are you dressed like that?' I hissed as we made our way to the bar.

'Yu es a real bore, and no mistake,' she replied grumpily.

'You're becoming like all the rest,' I lashed out.

'Sexy, you mean,' and she flounced off.

From then on she made her mood clear to me by dancing with the most handsome and muscular of men. I noticed she seldom chose islanders, and they stood in a resentful clump at the bar, unable to summon up courage to approach the pretty tourists. To my surprise Nathan wandered through the crowd and stood at one side, detached, as though he despised them all. His thin girlfriend in a sarong fiddled with her beads and laid her head on his shoulder. They soon disappeared, but not before he gave me a penetrating glance that cut across the room like a laser. I retired from the field.

'I forgive you. Let's dance again.' Mareva had joined me on a bench under some palms. I put my hand on her golden thigh and moved towards her.

'Kiss me,' I said. She did so with abandon, and then everyone at the ball knew for sure.

The radio station had made me a local celebrity, and my coffee bar had become a popular, even *risqué*, place in the small hours. Mareva seemed thrilled by my reputation, cultivated as it was along Fletcher Christian's lines, a failed career and great foolishness in the company of Tahitian women.

I drifted around the hall moving among the social cabals.

'Hey Haet, gettin any? Ai hier yu bin talkin a' Nathan. Wataweih daa poor bastard?'

'Paul, my dear chap, Richter's performance of *Faschingsschwank aus Wein* on Sunday was superb. Looking forward to the death of Paganini! Keep it up, old boy!'

'More Country and Western on our station, mate! The old Jim Reeves – *"Bottle, Take Effect!"* It's a beaut! You can't *like* that opera crap can ya? Opera's for the minority, mate. And pooftahs, of course! Ha, ha, ha.'

'Es yu openin up daa coffee lurnge afta aa Ball, eh Haet? I want three hundred toasted ham and asparagus sandwich and a cup of chino. My advance order!'

'It is my considered opinion that more time should have been spent broadcasting an analysis of the Butland Report. Would I be correct in thinking that it is more in the public interest?'

'Brud, ai gwen florga ears orf youse face if you nor stand aside!'[65]

At this point I decided I had had enough of the Bounty Ball. Mareva was nowhere to be seen and my emotions were in turmoil. I left the Rawson Hall and climbed into the MG. I had started the engine and was about to leave when she suddenly materialised beside the door and leant over me. Her perfumed breasts fell forward, just touching my face.

'Where are you going?' she asked. She looked around nervously as she lay over me.

'I've had enough of it, Mareva. I'm tired and I need some quiet. Will you come with me?'

'No, no way. I'm staying. The night is young, and I'm having a *great* time. See you later, then.'

She kissed me as if devouring soft fruit and flounced off again back into the hall. I watched that tiny skirt twitching as she disappeared among the parked cars, and I ached with a mixture of desire and sick rejection. Perhaps I was in love with an idea, the sensual Tahitienne with the fantastic history, rather than with a real person. I was still unable to balance my life between the mind and the body. I powered the MG away from her up Grassy Road, neatly drifting the sharp left-hander into Mission Road, taking the slight right kink in third with wire wheels groaning and finally into top, racing through the old Orange Vale to Blaydes.

That night I sat reading the journals on the verandah for many hours, listening to the yearning moonlight harmonies of Debussy's *Pélleas et Mélisande* and the youthful passion of Berlioz's *Harold in Italy*. Only as the first glimmers of dawn crept about the pines and warmed the sky beyond the cliffs did I lay down the embossed slip-case and head for bed.

CHAPTER XV

'The executioner... was... a broad-chested, sturdy-limbed figure, broad-faced and bull-necked, who had won his freedom by taking two bushrangers single-handed at Port Macquarie. But in the struggle he had received a cut from a hanger across the mouth, that opened it to the ears, and left a scar over his face that was alternately red and blue. Yet he had good-natured eyes. Whilst pinioning the arms of one of the men, he suddenly recognized him and exclaimed: "Why, Jack, is that you?" "Why, Bill," was the answer "is that you?" He then shook his old friend by the hand and said: "Well, my dear fellow, it can't be helped."
From the *'Autobiography of Archbishop Ullathorne'*, 1891
concerning his visit to Norfolk Island in 1834

Government House
Norfolk Island
October 13th. 1846

My day is punctuated almost to madness by the convict bell which is suspended from a post near the corner of the house, adjacent to the new flagstaff – seven times it is sounded over the Settlement by Clane the Bellman during the day, beginning at 5 a.m.! *"Turn out, you d...d souls,"* I was shocked to hear him mutter. I remembered being awoken in happier times by the great tenor bell of St. Peter & St. Paul in Lavenham. Ah! my beloved Suffolk, departed so long ago. Will I *ever* return to the pastoral calm of life in England? My sense of *duty* continues to prevail & I must needs banish such cruel thoughts, but to be placed in this den of iniquity is indeed *a great trial.*

It was a beautiful spring morning, so I set off with *Actaeon*, my energetic greyhound, for an early walk through the Settlement & picturesque Officers' Gardens. Eliza had looked to the children & placed them in the care of Aeneas de Meuron, one of the schoolmasters at the school for free inhabitants. This gentleman convict had been transported for fraudulently obtaining the sum of ten pounds by means of a false cheque upon Messrs. Coutts and Co., Bankers.

There was an unconscionable degree of activity around the gaol & I was prevented by the guard from proceeding far along Military Road. Three bullock carts loaded with coffins trundled towards the dripping machineel trees concealing the Burial Ground. James rode past me without acknowledgment looking severe and preoccupied, accompanied by some Officers & his Superintendent. The Catholic Chaplain, Rev. Valentine Onslow, followed soon afterwards, running along in an alarming fashion, quite out of temper, his vestments flying in the wind. It appears these rough boxes contained the bodies of the men responsible for the murderous July Mutiny, those executed this morning on the New Drop. What a quite horrible beginning to a perfect day! May their souls be redeemed upon entry into the *next* paradise, their last vision being of the beautiful shores of *this* one. I consoled the widow of one of the murdered officers yesterday & comforted his three children now left defenceless in the world. The chaplains give no succour here & rarely attend to their duties.

I had decided to give some of the officers & wives of the 11th. Regiment a pic-nic at Orange Vale & we left the Settlement at midday by way of Longridge Farm. There is a pleasant carriage at Government House (built by convict labour under a previous Commandant – Major Anderson of the 50th. Regiment) which I put to good use. *Actaeon* leapt with joy & high spirits about the beautiful gardens that are situated in a Gully with a sparkling stream rippling through it. The soil is a rich red. All the delights of Paradise are here – Lemons & Citrus, Coffee, Bananas, Strawberries, Loquats, Pomegranates, Melons, Pineapples, Olives, Peaches, Guavas, Figs and Cabbage Trees. A great misfortune is that the Orange trees were unaccountably cut down by Commandant Morisset as supplying sustenance to any convict who absconded to the bush. I have never heard of anything so vexing! Green parrots and cooing pigeons will approach one tamely, singularly without fear – one can reach out and take them. *Actaeon* sat back and barked at them in a frenzy! This arcadia, together with the natural abundance of produce, make one feel one could be inhabiting the Garden of Eden. The Norfolk Pine abounds & we set up our tents & tables under a magnificent spreading English Oak.

Captn. Zaleski was most attentive to me. There is something very captivating in his countenance, something of the Polish wildness in his glittering eyes mixed however with sweetness & tenderness. He has beautiful teeth & when he smiles the effect is delightful. Captn. Vane had arranged a fiddler & after much drinking the Officers danced on the green or played cards until well after the sun set, resolutely pursuing their reputation for 'hard living'. There was even a fight between a young officer of the 11th. and one of the gentleman who received a bloodied nose – and this all before the ladies!

I returned to Government House with the Medical Officer Charles St. Aubyn & Ensign Coffin, who managed as an excellent coachman. We noted some fine prospects & parrakeets & I determined to return soon with my sketch pad and Claude glass. Charles seemed preoccupied & spoke of the appalling circumstances surrounding the present state of discipline of the convicts. James is presently constructing a hospital to improve their health & talks about setting up a proper school.

'These are men of the most vicious & uncurbed passions. We entertain the utmost faith that Mr. Worth will exert the strictest coercion. He has a fine reputation for regulation & order,' he commented rather seriously, as we passed a number of bucolic sheep gambolling on a hillside in the dusk.

'Before Mr. Worth arrived the convicts were stealing those Government sheep in every direction!'

'Do the men greatly outnumber us?' In posing this question I foolishly worried my own personal sense of dread. A reef-gang with their diving bell were ceasing the day's work in the distance near Nepean Island, leaving the Wet Quarry like ants. They had been cutting dripstones & boiling salt.

'Fraid so, maam. But the military contingent can contain them, cant you, Ensign Coffin?' he smiled up at the coachman.

An unpleasant smell from the Swamp Creek heralded our arrival at the Settlement, but before the question could be affirmatively answered a convict suddenly rushed at the carriage from behind a wall, waving his straw hat and uttering imprecations in horrible & disgusting language. Ensign Coffin laid the whip across his face and he fell back – it was then I noticed that most of his nose had been torn away & scarred, his face fearfully mangled & monstrous. I was close to fainting as we turned into the drive from Military Road & Charles was most solicitous with medicinal applications. I would retire to my bedroom as soon as I satisfied myself as to the welfare of the children – Charlotte was playing a Gavotte on the piano with Septimus & Adolphus taming his lizard with insects & nectar in the yard. Eliza was in constant attendance & a bobbing pig-tail indicated the presence of our industrious Chinese domestic Wu Li. As I was closing my door I heard James say, 'Life is going to be difficult for them in this moral wilderness – the men are like wild beasts – but there it is.'

'One of the beggars rushed the gig! Someone had taken a mouthful of dog's nose from the devil!'[66]

'That will be Richard Ryan – better known as Hellfire Dick – with me on Cockatoo Island – a real wild Irishman from County Wicklow. I know him – a murderer and pirate – a fearful ruffian. Fifty-six times before the Bench. A depraved & dissolute man.'

'The dungeon life of Naples compares favourably with this island, James,' smiled Charles, in an attempt at lightness.

'Tell Superintendent Gaudin to get Potts to take the tails. Give Ryan a feeler[67] and strap him down! Give him the gag! I want him muzzled and on the stone.'[68]

James's voice seemed to change colour under the influence of this convict argot & a fierce expression, the like of which I have *never* before seen, suffused his features. He turned violently & looked out through the barred window over the reef as if searching the horizon for miscreants. His monocle dangled on its cord.

'Your wife, sir…' Charles indicated my pale presence.

'Paulina, please take your rest. You must be more circumspect & stop this gadding about! Good evening, Charles, most grateful for your trouble.'

James fixed his monocle & retired to his study & I to a troubled sleep. He had *never* spoken in such a fashion to me before. I know he fears for us dreadfully but such imperiousness! Our joyful youth in VDL seems to be passing away, to be replaced by what? I am becoming fearfully constrained by the limits of this island. The final bell for the day was rung & echoed mournfully through the house as I drifted into Lethe with nostalgia for England.

(The binding was loose and clearly sheets had been lost or removed.)

Norfolk Island
November 23rd. 1846

So much time to dispose of on Norfolk Island! I engage myself in writing my journal & long letters to the La Trobe sisters in Switzerland to occupy my mind. There is such a want of intelligence among the ladies.

Charlotte is making great advances with Septimus as her music tutor. His story is of such a romantic nature I must set it down briefly.

Born in Devon of a French mother, this unfortunate young man developed an excessive sensibility even to a degree of *mental imbalance*. This has most certainly been exacerbated by the terrors of transportation but he remains an excellent musician despite all.

While living in London he aspired to a connection with Amelia, the daughter of a baronet – Sir Somerville Learmonth. Septimus comes from a humble background but was thrown into the company of Amelia by chance when visiting her father's house in Upper Wimpole Street. His mother was engaged as a domestic in the establishment. He is an exceptionally handsome young man & they spent many idyllic hours in the Regent's Park where he finally fell violently in love. His passion became ungovernable. She carelessly neglected to mention that her betrothed was on service abroad with his Regiment which unfairly compounded the young firebrand's hopes.

Major Villiers – Amelia's beau – inevitably returned from India & had a mysterious confrontation with Septimus in Golden Square concerning an intercepted love-letter written in French. Septimus called him out before witnesses. The Major refused the challenge on the grounds his rival was 'no gentleman' & turned on his heel. Septimus became infuriated, drew a pistol & against all etiquette fired twice at the retreating figure, unfortunately hitting him with swan-shot in the nether regions! James always maintains that convicts are only partially sane! Septimus was tried & sent to Newgate under sentence of Death but reprieved & then sent on to the loathsome rat-infested hulks at Woolwich. This experience scarred him for life & he will never speak of it.

James encountered him as an 'educated convict' following his transportation to VDL at the age of twenty. His eye for a good man & the influence attendant on his position as magistrate in the colony permitted James to arrange his assignment as a tutor to our household shortly before we came to Norfolk Island. He has performed his offices admirably, playing the violin & harpsichord with remarkable intensity and to moving effect. Such a talented young man! He has also written a play & translated Racine's *'Phaedra'* from the French! There are many such stories of the wages of sin – sad defects of character manifesting in a genius, followed by the fatal commission of a crime & subsequent transportation to the colony.

The thought that Charlotte is of an impressionable age creeps in upon my mind but I banish it almost at once. We are entirely reliant on servants of this stamp & the female convicts are considered far worse than the men in vitiating their young charges. Such occurrances are frighteningly common, even among the most respectable families in the colony.

This afternoon my visitors – Miss Martineaux, Mr. and Mrs. Ommaney, Captn. Vale and Mr. Durlacher – repaired to the *conversazione room* to play the diverting game Counsel or Advice. I could hardly guess who advised me to *"give thought to a domestic establishment"* but found the amusement it aroused somewhat provoking. We then played the sensitive Chinese leaf which is put on the hand to try the character. I retired shortly after to work on the garland of wild-flowers & pearls I will wear in my hair at the ball to be given in the Officer's Mess tomorrow evening. My ornate gowns from Geneva are not to be shown off in this remote spot but I have more simple costumes from Lyon which will suffice & maintain my budding friendships without drawing unwelcome attentions.

Norfolk Island
November 26th. 1846

Great drama today! There was an earth tremor which shook the island for some seconds. Horses bolted & sheep ran in every direction, even I believe over the edge of the bluffs to their death. Tall pines toppled from the sheer cliffs. There was a tremendous commotion down at the Lumber Yard, but James walked in there alone without flinching & calmed the milling & cowering convicts. The buildings withstood the shaking except for minor cracks. Some said it was God's wrath on a sinful community *'steeped in crime to the very lips'*.

Norfolk Island
November 27th. 1846

The Ball was proposed by the 'Bachelors of Norfolk Island', better known as the Officers of the Detachment. The Ladies are to give one in return in the week before Christmas. But before I begin the account I must express I am in a great fidget with James as he has reacted most strongly to a slight degree of devotion shown me at the ball by the Polish Captn.

Zaleski of the 11th. Regiment who requested me for the *Waltz* & to march the *Polonaise*. Yet I cannot deny my heart is in a turmoil & fear the intimacies of this journal may fall under the eyes of those for whom it was not intended. But I must needs confide my inner thoughts to you, my dear friend & hope this close account does not fall into the wrong hands. Now to the ball & the cruel invasion of my sensibility it precipitated.

Fronds of the Norfolk Island Palm, Bats Wing Fern and branches of White Oak heavy with pink blossom created a veritable bower for our reception. Scores of small oil lamps were suspended twinkling like stars in the foliage & pine branches suspended over doorways and in window recesses. It reminded me forcibly of the little Indian Theatre which my dear father built for me in Bengal.

The room was exotic and enchanting with a light fragrance hovering over it like a sweet balm. The officers of the 11th & 58th in scarlet double-breasted coatees with bright green or black facings & white linen trousers together with the ladies of the Norfolk Island *haut ton* on their arms, descended the staircase lit by coloured lamps, the light playing on their simple ball dresses, *toilette* and *coiffure* (even here they manage it *à la Française*). Bullion tassels, belt plates, rows of gilt buttons & heavy epaulettes glittered opulently around the chamber. The refreshments consisted in tea & cakes, lemonade & orgeate, soup & punch. There was a stunning noise in the room and the music surprisingly attractive – supplied by two violins, a violincello, pianoforte and clarinet.

The order of dances was affixed in its own flowered frame to the wall. Captn. Zaleski approached & bowed to myself & James. I fear I suffered myself to shew my feelings when he requested the first *Montferine*. Of his costume I remember only the scarlet & green coatee with gold epaulettes & a fine gilt sword in a black leather scabbard. He is so gallantly pressing a personage that an *Anglaise* and an *Allemande* had passed before he handed me onto the bench, not freeing me until he had reserved the *Polonaise*. His carriage is noble & extraordinarily upright – he has a most aristocratic profile with waxed moustache & wears his fair hair rather long for a British regiment. His eyes are large & dark, seeming to conceal great depths & potential for melancholy. A most displaced personage to be sure! Spurs jingled & coat tails & crimson sashes whirled beneath the glittering lamps. My curls began to escape &

brushed his forehead and I became quite out of breath. I noticed a sabre scar on his left cheek as we circulated which much aroused my curiosity as to his background.

'You dance *avec grâce, Madame.*'

'Merci, Monsieur,' I managed to stumble out as he handed me back on to the bench.

C'est un jeune homme de beaucoup d'esprit.

Christina generously permitted me to lean on her and lay my elbow in her black velvet lap. She confided that James & myself were the object of much admiration among the officers & wives. I could only notice a degree of envy & some spite on the part of the other ladies despite my dressing down for the occasion. The evil behaviour of the murderous fiends not two hundred yards distant have come under strict control since James's appointment as the new Commandant. Everyone is vastly grateful for the increase in security but the domestic result has been a marked change in his mood & temper – he is becoming quite sensitive & critical.

During the ball animal spirits prevailed over the entire company. My emotions were forced & imprisoned beneath a feigned placid expression as I had been shot dead by a glance from Captn. Zaleski – I believe he is known with good reason as *'the Prince'* in the Officers' Mess. This is the first occasion in eight years of marriage I have permitted myself an access of feeling – it results from being too much in my own company. James was most assiduous & complimentary to me. He also dances in an accomplished style. In the complicated *Française* I found the figure terribly difficult and was *out* from beginning to end!

(Some lines heavily scored out.)

I felt bereft of life, moved by uncontained forces driving me relentlessly on, drawn like a moth to the flame. Christina only with difficulty brought me back to the Rational World & the information that supper had been given. Captn. Urquhart is a crusty old fellow & I heard him rail concerning the wild displays.

'These are the savage amusements of ungoverned life!' accompanied by a parsimonious grimace which distorted his features into an ugly mask.

The Master of Ceremonies had the delightful custom of giving out what was termed 'the flowers of distinction and *raillerie*' as the time for supper approached. One's name is called, the flower given (in my case the dark red-throated Philip Island Hibiscus) & you ascend to take your place at the table where others holding the same flower are seated. My heart throbbed with excitement when Mr. James Worth & Captn. Adam Zaleski were *both* called to receive Hibiscus. We would all be seated at the same table! What drama!

There are not words sufficient or proper to describe my state of mind during that memorable meal. Agonies of concealment, secret & ambiguous signs, fears & the dreaded monster jealousy worked me throughout. Was I conspicuous & too exacting in conversation?

James spoke to the assembled company at length about his father the 'Plutocrat' Sir Hawthorne Worth & their sugar plantation in Jamaica. On tour in Cornwall, George III once saw this flamboyant figure riding in a coach with three black postillions in tricorne hats & ostentatious livery. The King enquired how the gentleman aquired such vast wealth.

'Sugar, Sire,' was the reply.

'Sugar! Sugar!' cried the King in high indignation 'See to the tax on sugar!'

This anecdote gave rise to much amusement.

'Was your father an autocrat in domestic matters?' asked the prosaic Mrs. Webster.

'Everyone came under a firm hand in the household. Round about our estates at Crackington Haven he was loved on account of his being *outside* the law. Assisted the smugglers in their enterprises! Ha! Ha! Don't be shocked, ladies!'

James seemed to enjoy the discomforture this remark caused. He poured himself another bumper of claret.

'This is how I come to know the devils from the *inside* and get them to eat each other!' he gestured in the direction of the gaol in mock savagery.

'Have you had any *decent convicts,* James?'

'I've had some first-rate pugilists with me. I had Perkins, the 'Oxford Pet', with me. One of my lambs, 'Full-Breasted Mickey', had escaped from Eaglehawk Neck at VDL. He spurned the lines of fierce dogs, even those moored on platforms out to shore. Crossed the crushed shell and oil lamp barrier one night & swam through the blood dumped by us to attract sharks. Now there was a real pebble!'[69]

'You are a Balliol man, aren't you, James?' pressed Captn. Vane.

'Absolutely correct. Pulled stroke-oar. Sir Hawthorne was a tough perfectionist, taught me to read Latin & Greek in the original before I went up to Oxford. We had a fine library. Why, there is even a poet in the family! We are all great linguists. My brother translates from six languages.'

'Did you like Van Diemen's Land, Sir?' asked Mrs. Ommaney timidly.

'I am bitter about being *forced* to leave England – Wilberforce impoverished us. I miss hard riding to hounds early of an autumn morning when we clattered out of the yard through the sea-mist on a fine-scenting day. Hard riding it was in Cornwall – rugged fields, steep coombes, wind & sea, the cliffs. Built the character...'

His voice trailed off, his face clouded and the spirit ebbed away. He polished his monocle somewhat fiercely. Did I fancy tears appear in his eyes? This gentleman, so rough and ready with the men, has an almost feminine sensibility imprisoned within. His moods are mercurial & he instantly summoned up a hardness to tighten his eyes, quenching any flame in his heart, so that any warmth died before alighting on his lips.

'Come and hunt some wild cats and fowl with us, sir – we will take the dogs to Philip Island!' suggested Major Irwin, officer commanding the detachment.

'Capital! Choose some good men to get us across.'

Captn. Zaleski turned to me & smiled with his eyes.

'Mrs. Worth, I have a Mare in mind for you. A fine animal – part Arab & quite lively. I should like to bring her around to you tomorrow if you would graciously permit me.'

'Certainly that is most generous of you, Captain, but tomorrow is too soon. I require a side-saddle but shall attend to it presently.' I was instantly occupied with a keen anticipation of putting boredom to flight. Storm clouds seemed to gather over James's pale brow & he appeared most vexed, tossing his reddish hair ferociously. He indicated later that he was against me receiving presents especially from gentlemen, *particularly & especially foreign officers.*

But I cannot and will not be confined to Government House!

I should like to explore the island on horseback with this Polish Captain as my *cavaliere servante* – I certainly need protection from any convicts who may take the bush! James can proceed as much as he wishes with heroically flogging his desperadoes senseless on the triangles. The whole affair of punishment is too horrible & ridiculous for proper contemplation, even if the victims are incorrigibles. The Surgeon Dr. St. Aubyn told me James is obsessed with control & is concerned the convicts may make 'a rush', murder us all & abscond to Mt. Pitt! Hence the reports of excessive cruelty I have heard from the Officers who have some sympathy with the wretches. I shall accompany Archbishop Mollison to inspect the gaol when he visits us next year & discover at first hand the nature of their suffering – James will forbid me of course but I shall *demand* it.

It was past five when the party finally broke up. As we returned to Government House with lamps, some candles were to be seen flickering in the wards of the gaol.

'Some of the poor men are reading, James, look!'

'Well, I'll soon put a stop to that! Reading does not reform them. It's against the regulations!'

He left me to walk in alone with Major Irwin & went to raise the Chief Constable from a sound sleep in order to deal with the matter of *reading without permission*. He really is most vexing when the 'savage' mood is upon him & forcing 'concessions' from me.

CHAPTER XVI

'...as defined by the philosophers of the ancient world, Love is simply a certain longing to possess beauty;... and anyone who thinks to enjoy that beauty by possessing the body is deceiving himself and is moved not by true knowledge, arrived at by rational choice, but by a false opinion derived from the desire of the senses.'
Pietro Bembo in Book IV
'The Book of the Courtier'
by Baldesar Castiglione, 1528

As I read through this mutilated central journal I found myself less enamoured of the young Paulina, and more astounded at the curious double life being lived on Norfolk Island in the middle of the Nineteenth Century. Punishment, retribution and gratuitous delight in suffering was the prevailing philosophy within the prison walls. It would be interesting to read how she reacted to the visit by Archbishop Mollison, and whether her attitude to James, her love and respect for him, changed after seeing the existence of the prison inmates. During the balls, picnics and hunting expeditions, did the free citizens ever think about these wretched men, systematically tortured not five hundred yards from Government House? It appeared not... but then Kurt Franz, the last commandant of Treblinka camp, greatly enjoyed the 'first-rate vanilla ice-cream' that was available there. Convicts were not really members of the human race, just white slaves on assignment. These journals were becoming for me a chronicle of the mysterious co-existence of cruelty and romantic sentiment, allowing me a tantalising internal glimpse of the accepted fictions of history.

Nathan's illness had taken an alarming turn. He had left for Bali suddenly and clandestinely, without a forwarding address. Almira was desperate, and she was talking of travelling to Indonesia in the hope of finding him.

'God will help me,' she said, with heartbreaking faith. We thought this a misguided idea, but she was beyond persuasion.

My coffee bar was increasingly busy in the early hours of the morning, and it left me sleepless. It had become the only rendezvous for young islanders after the hotels closed and I was constantly being arraigned by the policeman for permitting public disturbances late at night. There were rumours of serving cognac to underage teenagers. I was losing money, because the temporary staff filched from the till and pilfered the food stocks. Ornamental candles were eaten by the intoxicated patrons, and teeth marks were often visible on those left behind. Whipped cream was squirted under the doors of my fellow shopkeepers.

One evening an islander was being chased by the constable. He drove up to the front door of the coffee shop, headlights blazing through the orange curtains, and he begged me to open the double doors and take the small Honda car inside the shop.

'C'mon, Haet! Do daa right thing, brud!'

We dragged the tables and chairs over the straw mats, and drove the car inside and shut the doors. I made a cappuccino on the famous *'La Dorio'*, the coffee machine shipped from the mainland, and I handed it through the driver's window. Candle flames wavered, and the light showed a poster of the young Terence Stamp costumed in a scarlet uniform. It was amusing to watch the police car cruising up and down outside, searching for the vanished mutinous crew.

'Wi gwen a' ghose party durn Channers' Corner – kam longfer us, Haet!'[70] Few customers were left so I left someone in charge and headed off to the party.

This was no way to run a business, and I began to get letters from the Commonwealth Bank demanding immediate repayment of my loans. The island life was eroding my character, and for the first time I began to question my presence there.

In the broadcasts I kept up a generally high standard, but I let commercial pop music programmes start to spoil the generally serious tone. Beer was spilt on the mixing console which justifiably upset the technician. The heavy breathing, drumming and explicit sexual congress of the song *Jungle Fever* made the Methodist Minister recommend my removal as Broadcasting Officer. Cows still invaded the aerial enclosure and forced the station off the air by locking horns with the transmission mast. Dogs continued to pee on the piles of records by the open door as I read the news, and birds flew through the studio and crashed against the glass window opposite the door. Our Italian guest chef regularly turned off the transmitter with her voluminous behind as she squeezed past the buttons on the control panel to deliver her cookery programme. The telephone continued to jangle on air.

My private life ceased to exist. The Hawthorn Green MG had been repainted Equipment Orange, after a small argument with a coral bank which damaged a wing. There would be no green paint on the island for some months, so for the repair I used some orange enamel left over from the construction of the airfield during the Second World War, a colour specially designed to be visible to aircraft at a range of twenty miles. I had to conceal myself more carefully when visiting Mareva at her shack on the windy hill above Kingston. She had also begun to visit me late at night at Blaydes, sometimes after basketball or netball at Rawson Hall, for a hurried and passionate hour.

My relationship with Mareva was turning into one of carnal pleasure, rather than one of commitment between the hearts of lovers. I visited her regularly, but it was clear we were slowly drifting apart. I became more intense in the expression of my affections, but this seemed to drive her further away. We were strapped on a pendulum of wild swings of passion.

CHAPTER XVII

Norfolk Nanwey
The Island of Feathers

*O*ne particular evening Mareva invited me to a dinner of Sweetlip and Nanwey, both favourite local fish. I tried to be unobtrusive when I drove down to Kingston from *Blaydes*. The shattered pediment of the Pentagonal Prison thrust grimly into the night sky as I doused the lights and coasted the last few yards through the gate, rustling through the rough grass to a position well concealed from the road. I sat for a moment listening apprehensively to the breakers on the reef. I clambered out of the MG and stumbled in the dark across dismembered passages of the gaol, shattered rocks and tussocks of grass, towards Quality Row. The colonial Georgian mansions nestled in their tropical gardens, slumbrous interiors glowing across the verandahs. Silhouettes crossed rooms, floated past the windows. I had to pass between two of these houses without detection.

It was a hard, dangerous climb up the hill that backed on to Kingston. Shapes I thought to be boulders turned into horses or cattle that suddenly reared up or shied away. I paused for breath on some damp grass, watching the phosphorescent line of the reef far below. Then I slid down the side of a culvert, tearing my clothes and bruising my hands, before I began the long push up the pitted track.

The sheer banks of the cutting suddenly echoed with the sound of a struggling car engine. Two beams of light wavered on the corners. Where could I hide? The walls were too high to scale. I threw myself into the rain channel beside the track, and I put my head between my knees. I was enveloped by coral dust glowing in the headlamps, and then the pinpoints of red light from the rear lamps disappeared around the corner. No-one had seen me, and I covered the last few hundred yards in a mood of elation. The window of the shack was lit by a single hurricane lamp, and it drew me like a moth to the flame.

Mareva did not turn in my direction. She was seated on a stool near the open window that overlooked a valley of pines to the lagoon and off-shore islands. She seemed lost in a reverie, but she had heard me on the road and my clumsy approach through the grass. I pressed open the door.

She was wearing only a dark-green shirt of military cut, loosely buttoned. One bare foot rested on the floor, the other on the rung of the stool. The short front fell slightly open to unveil her honey-coloured thighs and the source of my desire. Her profile showed an almost masculine strength of chin, but her brown eyes were large and warmly feminine, and the smile on her lips was enigmatic and unfathomable. She arched down from the stool, lustrous hair falling forward, the tail of the shirt catching up lightly to expose the curvature of her buttocks. She whispered over to me across the raffia mats like a lethargic cat, something of the panther in her movements.

'Wai yu bin take so long f' kam?'[71] she said.

'Well, I was reading Paulina's journals, and then I had to work at the coffee bar. They had a rush on.'

'Aa dinner es almost ready. Did you bring some wine?' A mischievous light came into her eyes.

'Yes, but I was lucky I didn't break it on the road. I had to leave the car down in the ruins and climb up here!'

'That's good. I don't want anyone to know about this night.'

'Why?'

'I've cooked wan little Sweetlip en wan big Nanwey. They have a great effect on your mind! Sex fantasies and dreams – we don't know what we might do!'

'Tell me what might happen, Mareva.'

'It is for you to time travel. I told you I dream of life on the island before the settlements.' she said. 'I know you think I'm changing, but not really. Just you wait!'

We sat at the table by the window, and she turned down the kerosene lamp. The room was bare, apart from the Polynesian woven mats and some watercolours of a princess descending the staircase of a castle. A few landscapes of the island also hung on the walls. Some of her painting things, brushes in bottles, squeezed tubes, were scattered about and unfinished paintings leant against a large glass float for fishing nets. The Norfolk Nanwey tasted strongly of seaweed ('Et contains aa love potion,' she informed me) and with wine it was delicious. The moon had risen over the valley and the blanched convict buildings seemed to float above the white water of the shoreline. It was difficult to concentrate on banalities, given the closeness of her almost naked body across the narrow table laden with rich food and wine. My hands drifted between her legs and our kisses became those of voluptuaries. We drank and ate slowly, discussing love affairs on the island. Mareva said 'Norfolk Love' was like the ball in a roulette wheel. Everyone would be involved with everyone else, if the cycle was given sufficient time and chance.

After the meal the wine glasses were knocked to one side, and she enfolded me in caresses of inspired passivity as we rocked gently and imprudently before the uncovered windows of the hut. Her skin was the colour of amber, preternaturally smooth and soft from countless hours lying naked in the sun, wind and sea. Her velvet tongue began its caress, soft and languid explorations of my body in slow motion. We glided towards the mattress covered with the dragon cloth, and I gently spread her dark scented hair over the white pillow. She stared at me through the eyes of the ancient past, a clear fertile power without sophistication, the enfolding eyes of a profound orgasm. The wind began to buffet the walls of the hut. As she reached across to turn the lamp down further, the scent of frangipani spread over me like a perfumed cloak.

Mareva seemed amused by my elaborations of lovemaking. To her it was a long, luxurious game, like swimming in a lagoon or bathing under a waterfall. A great deal of laughter and rippling pleasure was to be derived from it. Her notion of time was grandly extended in scale, moving at a different pace and rhythm to mine. I have never managed to recapture this slow, noble playing out of destinies. The Nanwey was drugging conscious thought, and I began to feel light and joyful, my mind flooding with colour, images and histories. Exhausted by the detonations of love, I beached myself finally between her thighs, my face pillowed in the scent of newly opened sea-shells, my tongue caressing their soft salty depths. Her body moved gently but inexorably against me, as powerful as the slow swells of the Southern Ocean approaching the shore. Moaning softly, she carried me unresisting on a voyage of innate natural rhythm, hours passing, before we gradually lapsed into sleep. My spirit seemed to flow from my body, above the depths of Oceania...

Dusk is settling over Matavai Bay and Point Venus, the moments before the sudden dark. The sea is as still as polished pewter. Palm leaves crown impossibly long and slender trunks that arch over the lagoon and islets. The high hills of shifting sands formed by the trade winds resemble the waves of the ocean. They are said to have been made by Hiro the Trickster, first builder of far-voyaging canoes. The tapa pennants and sails slung between the towering carved ornaments at the prow hang motionless. The war canoes drift in readiness for the coming conflict. As the swell gently respires, the twin hulls and decorated fighting platforms are savagely outlined against the mountains.

The tattooed body of the great Tahitian warrior and lover Puane gleams with coconut oil as he squats on the beach near the flickering flames of the candlenut torches. His skin is wrapped in these images to armour his body, protecting him from the gods of darkness and death. The lazily-moving arched patterns in dusky blue-black etched on his muscular thighs and buttocks, the representation of the emotions of his race, give deep sexual pleasure to the watchers. He is the teacher, the teller of original earthly knowledge. Young washed and oiled girls sit naked in a circle around him and display their more restrained decoration – delicate arabesques on their ankles, lips, patterns of lace on wrists and fingers, between their toes and other soft and secret places. He begins his recounting, accompanied by occasional music and poetry, of the enchanting tale of a voyage to gather scarlet feathers for the Royal girdle of investiture and war...

"The blind navigator Kaho Mo Vailahi sheltered from the squall in the hut thatched with fara leaves erected on the platform between the twin hulls, and lay down to analyse the Long Swells passing beneath the far-voyaging canoe. His own eyes had of necessity been replaced by those of his son Po'oi since they had been plucked out and placed into the open mouth of the new sovereign long years before. Po'oi stood on the bow platform behind the magical wave-splitter attached to the prow. He had lost sight of

his Key Star avei'a in the rigging during the night while the storm was gathering. He held an umbrella palm over his head as protection from the lashing rain and his tattooed skin glistened in the dim light. The moving patterns protected him from evil. Long feathered streamers lashed out from the polished mast.

Suddenly he called in the darkness that he had seen te lapa, underwater lightning. Streaks, flashes and momentarily shining plaques of light were flickering and darting beneath the surface of the sea. This phenomenon indicated that their destination, the Island of Feathers, was perhaps a hundred miles off, only one day of sailing in this large craft.

The mood of the crew changed from melancholy to joy. They had eaten well the previous evening, as some colourful flying fish had landed in the canoe during the day. The delicious flesh was cooked on a fire built on a bed of sand and stones on the deck. It was a welcome change from the exhausted stocks of fermented breadfruit, nyali nuts and pounded taro prepared before leaving Vaito'otia in Huahine. The fishbaskets attached to the sides of the canoe were empty, the bamboos and gourds filled with water were now almost dry. All the chickens, rats and pigs had been eaten long before. The High Navigator felt warmer after the feast of fish despite being in the cool southerly regions. It was almost a month since they had set out and now they were waiting for signs of their destination.

Rare parrots inhabit this distant island of pines, so remote as to be on the very edge of known far-voyaging. The plumage of these birds is treasured above all others, rich in colour beyond all comparison and their capture is dictated by the sacred requirements of our island chiefs and high priests. Their plumage is the shadow of Ta'aroa (The-unique-one) the ancestor of all the gods and he who made everything. From the infinity of time, he was trapped in an eggshell of darkness for millions of ages. He escaped through a fissure and shook off the red and yellow feathers that covered his body. They were transmuted into the trees and plants that grow upon the islands. A girdle of these feathers gives sacred fertility to the earth and is an image of the divine. In Oceania the making of it is an action of the greatest sanctity.

Thus the purpose of this rare voyage was to collect feathers for the maro ura – the scarlet girdle of the kings of Opoa and the maro tea – the white or yellow girdle of the kings of Porapora. Also for the feather house of the child god, used by the royal heir after his birth and dipping.

Now, the girdle is made in the following fashion. The feathers are closely sewn on to the banyan cloth with a long needle of polished human bone with tight lock-stitches, as to imitate the plumage of a bird. Patterns are formed to tell the name, character and acts of every monarch who has reigned in this land. The sacred needle is never removed. The dreadful to'ere drum is beaten with a stroke that indicates the beginning of human sacrifice. Men flee to the forests. The girdle will be worn to mark the coming human sacrifices before war. The promiscuous arioi throw themselves into wild, naked dancing on the raised platforms of their canoes to the thumping of shark-skin and blasts from the grandmaster's shell trumpet. Bunches of cocktail feathers flutter at the mast tips as the arioi urinate and defecate on the recently installed king to diffuse his heightened sanctity, this so that he may not contaminate and destroy those of us less sacred.

Fetch 'ura feathers in abundance
Let there be thousands resplendent
At the wall of jawbones
For the red girdle, O!

The blind Kaho Mo Vailahi, the greatest navigator of all, guided the momentous expedition to collect feathers for extensions to this garment of power. The High Priest of the Marae was also present in the canoe. He would select the birds. The rest of the voyage party, including the most seductive young girls, would trap the parrots, and carefully preserve the feathers according to ancient rite, and fish for food during the visit.

Koho Mo Vailahi grunted and moved to a squatting position on the lashed planks, so his most sensitive organ of balance, his testicles, might feel the correct interference of the complex swells. He had once previously found this island on the ominous edge of the known world with great accuracy. The task required all his sublime navigational skills. Hours later at dawn, he confirmed their course was correct.

They were caressed by the dry Uru or 'feathery' wind and they were sailing fast, the inverted triangles of the double sails filled with the energy of Raka blowing with his children through the holes at the edge of the horizon. Po'oi steered by sighting the sun, and his blind father by the heat of it on his cheeks. The astrologer chanted the influence of the stars.

Flocks of terns and noddies began to appear, busily fishing the ocean in company with a few red-tailed tropic birds and a solitary frigate bird. A shout went up from those aboard the canoe as the birds were seen – they are the shadows of the gods and are harbingers of land. Clouds hovered motionless on the horizon and Po'oi began to stare fixedly at them. He corrected the course of the canoe slightly towards a darker margin. Late in the afternoon the noddies headed for their roosts. They darted in and out of the wave crests while the terns flew above them and took a more direct course. The Island of Feathers soon appeared low and green on the horizon.

The land is densely covered in pine trees, creepers, palms and ferns and surrounded by precipitous cliffs. Two smaller islands are similarly covered in vegetation and difficult to land upon. The Island of Feathers cannot support visitors for long. The area is small and the plants are strange to our normal usages – a complete absence of taro, yams, coconuts and breadfruit make long settlement impossible. On a previous expedition banana plantains had been planted at the source of a stream. The fishing is unpredictable and dangerous and the shellfish are small and without true nourishment. The heavy forest which surrounds the island shore prevents deep journeys into the interior. Previous expeditions have told of the dangers of the reefs protecting the only lagoon and beach. One expedition never returned.

The Tokerau or 'spirit wind' drove them onwards. Ula the Master Wave-Reader now took his position on the prow platform. Paddles were handed to the strongest and they took their places along the hulls in rows. The magical wave-splitter would surely carry the sacred canoe safely across the reef.

Ula intensely watched the waves from the shelter of the thatched hut for a long while, sailing up and down before the surf. He suddenly signalled to the paddlers. The heavy pahi rose on the crest, and it was carried across the boiling coral into the lagoon that lay before the beach.

The golden tattooed girls leapt naked into the sea and swam laughing ashore in a cloud of perfume and spray. The darker men began to cut wood with their sacred adzes, to erect temporary shelters along the parts of the bay where the vegetation was less dense. Night was rapidly coming on. They would soon begin their search among the pines for the rare parrots. The tens of thousands of birds on this island have no fear and are easily taken. They remain almost still until they are lifted up and even then they scarcely make any effort to escape. This is the source of the enchanted reputation of the place and to those of us from Vaito'otia, a reason for amusement and fear. The High Priest made the birds defenceless with his spells and incantations.

Food was hard to find, and the courageous voyagers suffered cruelly from the lack of it. Sea and land birds were beaten and killed, and they helped supplement the inconstant source of fish. The plantain seedlings left by the stream years before had flourished, and they offered some variety, but the trappers of birds were often hungry.

The collectors of parrot feathers pursued their quarry deep into the interior of the island. It was tiring work, requiring great strength to clear a path into the mysteriously open groves of oak and pine. Parrots were also found in great numbers on the larger of the two near islands. Many adzes were broken and discarded during this exploration. The parrot they sought possessed feathers of most brilliant and variegated colour, red, yellow, blue, brown, green and orange. Such rare plumage is the veritable shadow of Ta'aroa. This bird flies through the treetops and it shines like a rainbow if seen in the sunlight. Sweet paste was applied to the trees, but many allowed themselves to be taken on the forest floor. Their hooked beaks collect a diet of flowers – the pink blossoms of the whitewood, the creamy petals of the magenta-throated hibiscus and the wild orchid.

The High Priest examined each trapped bird, and decided if its quality determined death or freedom. Birds with a rich yellow breast and orange cheeks are highly prized. Another is plumed in dark green with a red head, and blue edging to the wings. This royal shade of red is considered by the priests a perfect transmutation of the divine, appropriate for the girdle of highest rank. Each bird is possessed of only a small number of perfect feathers, so thousands must be trapped. But the birds of this island possess the most brilliant plumage of all the birds of Oceania.

Many months were spent collecting as well as laying down sufficient food for the return journey to Vaito'otia. The voyagers were sorely tried by the lack of familiar plants, but they baked fish, roasted doves and pigeons and made banana puddings. Storms and cold weather laid them low with melancholy yearning for their home. They captured flower lizards that lived on nectar and were the shadow of the fairies among the flowers

— gods to the royal Oropa'a family of Tahiti. No man has ever met with an accident or death while visiting the Island of Feathers.

Almost a year passed before the High Navigator Kaho Mo Vailahi tasted the sea and decided it was time to return to Vaito'otia in Huahine. The dried birds, parcels of feathers and lizards were carefully wrapped and stowed in the canoe. The food was also packed away from the ruinous water. The bamboo and gourds were filled to the brim. The High Priest uttered incantations over the remaining birds on the sacred island to preserve their beauty for the next generation of kings.

Ula read the waves for the difficult return to the open sea. The canoe was carefully lowered into the water from the edge of a low promontory on which stood a solitary pine. The collectors of feathers swam out through the surf to receive it safely on to the bosom of the ocean. The baskets were by now freshly stocked with struggling fish and lashed to the sides of the canoe. Captured parrots, doves and pigeons flapped in their cages. Po'oi set course by the sun and his wind compass which indicated the moist Marangai akavine or 'Marangai-gentle-as-a-woman' wind. The long voyage back to Huahine carrying the divine cargo was beginning."

The great warrior Puane falls silent as the great tale is told, and smooths more oil over his body. The firelight and candlenut torches are fading and he begins to sing a plaintive threnody. The moon has risen over Point Venus and the vahines slip away through the pandanus palms, their delicately tattooed bodies drifting like ornate moths into the niau-filtered light of their huts where the designs will be slowly traced by their lovers...

I woke from the paradise spun by the potent Nanwey, and I saw Mareva slipping naked outside the hut. She walked languidly across the grass to the tank stand and filled an enamel bowl with fresh water. Then she washed, in the open air, in the dim light cast by the setting moon and stars. Soon it would be daybreak and I would have to leave her before the island eyes began to ferret out secrets. I watched this primitive ritual of washing and oiling through the open door, still half asleep. The Polynesian nature was still strong within her, and yet the blood of Englishmen had set up swells of interference. She had already begun to drift away like a rudderless canoe, and I needed words from her to give direction to any future we might have together. She returned silently to the hut and she remained immobile, seeming not to wish to communicate. I felt she was urging me to go. I dressed swiftly, and I waited for some sign from her.

'See you at Music Valley this afternoon at two,' she breathed.

As I began the nightmare descent to Quality Row and the ruins of the prison, I glanced back at the illuminated window. I saw her standing there slowly buttoning her shirt over that unsurpassed beauty of skin. The scent of our lovemaking was still in my hair and on my fingers. By the time I reached Gallows Gate, dawn had broken over the island.

I sat listlessly in the car, sunk in that state of torpor that comes after a close brush with love or death. My nerves hummed and my body was numbed by the long voyage of the night. Through the shattered walls of the prison, I watched the first rays of the sun slant across the lagoon and pick out the solitary pine on the promontory. When I drove out of the stone entrance of the gaol, the sea was breaking in an ecstatic line of foam over the natural barrier to the lagoon. Suddenly I wanted a swim.

The early morning sand was cool under my feet as I ran to the shore, throwing off my clothes, the water sparkling at my toes. The seabed, stones, weed and tiny fish were visible with unnatural clarity as the water closed over my head. I dived and struck out vigorously for the pontoon anchored near the reef.

CHAPTER XVIII

Storms and Cyclones

'Laugh and lay down is the play
We'll fondle together,
To keep out the weather
And kiss the cold winter away.'
Scipio
The Castle of Andalusia
by John O'Keefe Esq., 1783

*C*hanges were taking place quickly now in my private life and on the island. The cyclone approaching the coast heralded drama in the weather to match the storms within the Administration.

Control over my personal life seemed to be slipping from my grasp. I had been violently evicted from Blaydes for rent arrears, and I was moving into an abandoned American satellite tracking station in a remote part of the island called Gannet Point. This building was curious for its almost complete lack of windows. The enormous front room had row upon row of shaded light bulbs under the ceiling, which used to illuminate the racks of equipment that tracked space vehicles. Even now, emerging from the enclosed room into the night under the myriad stars was rather like entering and leaving a space ship. One felt kindred spirits among the creation myths of Polynesia far out on these cliffs. I shared this idyllic spot with a diamond merchant from Burnt Pine, and later with a beautiful New Zealand philosophy student.

Electricity came from a petrol generator cranked by hand, and the water from an outside tank. The floor was covered with straw matting and a tiger-skin. By now I had come to want a piano badly, and I had recently shipped my fine Bechstein upright across from Sydney. Lashed to a lighter, it had bobbed heart-stoppingly in the surf, crossing the

Bar at Kingston. Then a fine layer of coral dust was wiped off the ebony case, and the passionate chords of the *Waldstein Sonata* were soon mingling with the birdsong among the pines. My relief at returning to the instrument was immense. A library, a gramophone and a large double bed completed the furnishing.

The house was near the cliff edge, close to an enormous pine, where I could sit and read Byron while gazing over the offshore islands and foaming rocks around Point Hunter. The nearest habitation was a small pottery, run by an English girl with a cultivated accent. Bach organ fugues or the B-minor Mass on my giant speakers placed in the open air bordered on the sublime. The white oaks that littered the cliff tops and valleys had a 'blasted heath' appearance suitable for musical drama.

This domain was the most peaceful and magical of my experience on the island. In the valley there were dense stands of pine, providing perches for the fairy terns that nested here in their thousands. They are confirmed risk-takers and lay a single egg in depressions or knots in the branch – they build no nests and the mortality of the chicks is high. Their white feathers were translucent in the sun, jet black eyes alert as they fluttered before alighting. Graceful on the wing in breeding pairs, these delicate porcelain birds communicate with a guttural '*yek yek*'. My desire for Mareva grew uncontrollably as I watched their courtship rituals.

The coffee shop business had been great fun, but difficult to control. Sometimes the patrons locked me out of the premises if I remonstrated about the noise, the impossible size of orders, the drink, the speeding, the munching of candles and the rest of it. The coffee studio had been hijacked by the mutineers.

'Twenty-five toasted ham en asparagus sandwich, Haet, en make et snappy, brud! En fifteen cups aa chino!'

'Ai es full es a goog en want ten cups o daa hot chocolate with plenty whipped cream on aa top! Get staaten! Yu es a bastard, Haet, with daa Mareva en yu es vairy lucky wi laik aa programme orn aa radio!'[72]

I was spending more and more time in the Reef Lounge at the Norfolk Hotel, worrying about money. I saw dark, ravening birds in my drunken dreams. The bank was pressing and I had not yet paid for half a ton of frozen macaroni cheese. I crawled under the floor of the coffee house one night to see if I could set the place alight to claim the insurance, but a kind thought for the adjacent premises restrained me from arson. I would need to sell it.

The purchasers were retired, elderly and diabetic, almost blind in fact. They must have been to feel encouraged by the set of figures my accountant showed them. I remember them stumbling around in whirling clouds of dust, when they raised the raffia matting to try to sweep away a year of concealed detritus. They toasted the pink dishcloth when I asked for a ham sandwich. She placed her distinguished grey head alarmingly between the huge metal plates of the industrial toaster as her fading sight necessitated closer inspection of the snacks. Boiling milk sprayed over the customers from the steam pipe of the 'La Dorio' coffee-machine in a vain attempt to make cappuccinos by touch.

'We want an interest in our old age,' they said benignly.

They would certainly have that. They named the place 'La Galette' and displayed landscapes by the island's amateur artists. Mareva sold at least two pictures through them. I fled before they could reconsider the purchase after the first challenge from the infamous *Bounty* crew, fresh from the Paradise Hotel at midnight.

Following the sale, I could give more time to my position as Broadcasting Officer. In the idyllic residence at Gannet Point, I wrote my long dissertation on the future of VL-2-NI. By now it was far more than an organ of shipping news and entertainment. It transmitted the proceedings of the Local Council, and it aired the political issues of the day. Transmission times had been extended to twelve hours, and the upgraded equipment extended the reception range to hundreds of miles. Extra announcing staff were needed and a technician was on permanent call.

We began to receive overseas fan mail.

'Late in the evening of 23rd. May, aboard my yacht anchored off New Caledonia, just before the transmission of the Radio Australia News, I heard what I believe to be the cacophony of a snoring descendant of the mutiny on the *Bounty*, followed by a toilet flushing. Do my ears deceive me? Was this an implied slur on the Commonwealth Government? Please expedite your reply.'

More seriously, a Royal Commission examining all aspects of Norfolk Island life had been set up under an Australian judge, and this involved the radio station. Hundreds of witnesses, exhibits and submissions were considered.

'This little island has more legal problems than continents. This is a real challenge. I'm fascinated by the situation here,' pondered the judge, and he rubbed his hands with professional glee.

The great issue was the constitutional status of Norfolk, the determination of which created sufficient mountains of paper and mystery, misinterpretation and lost Royal Documents to rival *Bleak House* by Charles Dickens. Questions of immigration status and company registration, tax avoidance and tax evasion, the provocative view of the island as merely a small Australian town run by the Department of Capital Territories, problems with tourism, the diffident airlines and the erosion of the very soil itself beset the Commission's investigators.

'I doubt if any Royal Commission in the history of Australia has sat in more delightful surroundings,' observed our judge afterwards.

This ephemera was my daily bread but the dense poetry of nature and the layers of history were my real existence. My love for Mareva gave me a deeper understanding of the island than would a thousand years of textual analysis.

Almira gave her views, which were full of affection for a doomed way of life and nostalgia for a more caring past. She began her address with examples. With an air of massive dignity she informed the commission that the old islanders would *never* borrow money, even to start a business.

'Money no use to me. You give me money, I throw it in the sea!' as was said on Pitcairn long ago.

She told them that *Almira's* was an old island home where there was no telephone and no licence. The paying visitors picked their own vegetables in the garden, assisted in making the jam and packed food for the dawn picnics. Her lilting voice with occasional words in Norfolk lay like a flower in the dark forest of political, commercial and bureaucratic self-interest. Her performance before the Commission made my heart sing for the Islanders of Pitcairn descent. Their frame of reference passionately excluded Australia, and they looked more towards independence and the maintenance of the deep historical links with Britain. I had been lucky enough to see this way of life before it disappeared forever.

The Polynesian character embraced humane values rather than material ones. These remained active on the island, although somewhat diluted by experience and indulgence. Throughout their history the Pitcairners had been accused of backwardness and laziness. This was used to justify gross abuses of property and failed to recognize their expanded sense of time; they felt there was nothing they *must* do, no temporal imperatives; intangibles were their main concern. There was always an ambivalent attitude to money on Norfolk Island. Vegetables, fruit and fish were often given as payment for services, or simply as a gesture of friendship. The social graces had achieved a high degree of refinement and subtlety among the older Pitcairn descendants. The bitter anguish concerning their rights lay like a glowing ember embedded deep in the heart, an ulcer that would not heal. These questions may never be resolved in the quagmire of vested mainland interests and divided loyalties.

The cyclone drifted closer.

I had recently taken up flying, and I went down to the airport to have my next lesson and check on the progress of the storm. The Meteorological Office predicted it would not pass over the island, but it would swing in close, say within fifty miles, accompanied by torrential rain and wind, some time tomorrow. The clear sky gave no sign of it, so I went ahead with my last lesson before my solo flight.

A Cessna light aircraft was available for pleasure or tuition. The almost complete absence of air traffic made my instruction pleasant. The runways were soft grass, and it was always a pleasure to bump into the air and then see the island shrinking beneath as I gained altitude. The witty instructor would gravely direct me to 'look out for other air traffic', and during emergency landings over water he would encourage me to 'look for a suitable field' to land.

The three islands that break the surface of the ocean here are the only visible peaks of the great mountain range that stretches from New Caledonia to New Zealand. Ultramarine craters of dark and mysterious water eat into the coast at Ball Bay. The beaches around the convict settlement appear almost tropical in their glittering whiteness. Coral roads wind through the island, passing by the half-hidden colonial homes lying among the stands of pine and oak. The dense jungle covering Mt. Pitt and Mt. Bates invites the explorer. The multitude of colours on Philip Island resembled an artist's oils. Flat Nepean Island, one of the outliers, had the finest beach. I practised my banking turns and stalls over this scene, and coming in to land I always feared the sudden drop in the turbulent air over the cliffs before the final run along the grass.

Mareva was waiting for me on her horse outside the fibro terminal huts when I climbed from the cockpit. The trees had begun to move slightly in the increasing breeze, and the birds were assuming strange patterns of flight. We needed each other more than we could admit.

Almira had been experiencing her own private storm. She had recently returned from Bali, where she had found Nathan in the grip of a serious illness. Now he was back in the island hospital. Her discovery of him was miraculous. She was relaxing in a restaurant at Kuta Beach after the long journey and was wondering in desperation how she could possibly locate him. She knew no-one and she had no address.

'I was at my wits end and then I looked up at the window and Nathan walked past it! I rushed out into the street but he had disappeared! I spent two days finding him in the town again. I managed to get him back on Norfolk, but it was no use.' She refused to weep in public, but the experience broke her spirit.

I visited him myself, and I found him pacing up and down like a caged lion. He reminded me of the descriptions of Fletcher Christian *in extremis*. 'He looked wild – his long hair was loose and his shirt collar open.'

'Hold your tongue, Sir, or you are dead this instant!' he said in an infantile voice. He laughed, and he saluted imaginary officers of the garrison who he assured me were passing just then. His beard was straggly and unkempt, his eyes were without focus. Harmless enough to approach, he was often to be seen wandering aimlessly. I liked him and thought his brilliance terribly misguided and finally wasted. We never spoke of Mareva again.

Almira was devastated by this tragic outcome of her dreams for her only son. She lost much of her joy in life from then on, and she began to withdraw from the active life of business. She submerged her grief within her faith in God, and she refused to speak of Nathan.

'He's gone,' she said flatly, her voice drained of the music of the language.

Cameron robustly approached her depression with his remedy of work. He began to build her a new house in a picturesque spot, and he distracted her with exciting plans. She edged ever closer towards him, and overcame her better nature even to praise him on occasion. I noticed they would walk together now among the lobster plants and palms in the old garden.

Suddenly the cyclone was upon us. The forecast was for winds of over one hundred knots. The clouds descended and the gale gained in strength. The pines up towards Mt. Pitt and Mt. Bates were swathed in mist, and dark clouds began racing across the island at low altitude. The landscape took on a curiously Scandinavian appearance, and the ominous harmonies of Sibelius suited this changed mood. Fairy terns and gannets were thrown into the air fluttering like autumn leaves, flying vainly against the punishing wind. Newly hatched chicks fell chirping from the branches. The palms lashed themselves and the rain filled the air with wild drumming on the glossy leaves.

After completing my session on the radio and drawing up a duty roster, I met Mareva. We watched the huge seas breaking over the long reef at Slaughter Bay and Point Hunter, driving gigantic arcs of spray and mist across the settlement and cemetery. The heavy tarpaulins protecting the roof of the Administration building under restoration billowed dangerously, ropes straining in the brass eyelets. The coast was inspiring in such wild weather and we drove round to Headstone Point. An enormous rainbow had appeared miraculously in the spray, and waves thundered into the caves and exploded fantastically with the build-up of pressure. She did some rapid sketches of these dramatic scenes in the car, completely taken over by this convulsion of nature. The earth beneath us trembled with the power of dynamited rock. The lugubrious name Headstone Point came after three privates from the 99th. Regiment were drowned while fishing off the rocks there, at the time of the Second Settlement. More prosaically, now, a huge rubbish chute hung above the sea and functioned as the waste disposal device for the island.

We drove up the muddy road to Mt. Pitt, laughing, the car sliding. The perfume of wet pines and ferns filled the air with a delicious freshness. I suppose it was dangerous but youth made us oblivious to fear as the mist rushed past and bruised leaves and flowers flattened themselves against the windscreen. At the summit, the view over the island was overwhelming and we could barely stand as the wind howled through the cables that braced the radio mast and the air navigation beacon. Noddies and shearwaters flew backwards out of control like discarded scraps of paper. The palms thrashed the air, fronds tearing away, spearing down into the drenched valleys of bottomless mist. The hairy boles of the tree ferns streamed. Heavy clouds engulfed us completely for periods, while the sea pounded the whole coastline extending the tempest far out from the shore.

It surprised me that the rain was so warm, and we kissed in a state of heightened passion, a sort of ecstatic dementia. I wrenched off Mareva's cotton top, and rivulets ran between her naked breasts and between her soft thighs as she lay in the grass. Her hair streamed over her face in long strands, and I drank the rain from her lips and licked it from her excited nipples and the tiny reservoir of her navel. I gently and then more violently entered her, and soon it was as if we were both voyaging across wide oceans, the wind singing in the rigging above. Such madness! Both of us naked on Mt. Pitt in the middle of a cyclone! But at least no-one was likely to come up there to find us.

All was forgiven. We would never separate. She would run away with me and leave her family. We would live together. We were crazy for each other and we drowned in the passionate naturalness of it.

'I dare you drive yus car naked through Burnt Pine with me!' she shouted.

'We'll be arrested!'

'So? Give them something to talk about!'

Although it was the middle of the afternoon, I decided to carry out this crazy idea. By sheer good fortune, I got the MG down the track running with rivers of mud. Torn branches flew low over our heads. Then on to the sealed road, and the naked drive through the main shopping centre. There was an insane exhilaration in the escapade and with the top down we were drenched, the interior of the car flooded. Perhaps we were not seen in the deserted streets, but the thrill of the possibility was satisfying.

We dried our clothes in Mareva's shack on the hill, and we watched the tremendous drama of the sea raging over Nepean Island. The hut trembled and shook, and I wondered if it would be flattened the next minute.

'We make love at any time, in any place!' she giggled happily.

We continued to laugh at our bravado and made a permanent friendship based on a sort of joint intoxication with the mad joy of simply being young, simply being alive. Truly we were deeply in love that day.

I had to report the progress of the storm at the radio station, so I tore myself away from Mareva and drove back to the studio. Ripped foliage was strewn across the roads, and madness was in the air. As I was driving along Stockyard Road, a figure rushed out and waved me down. I opened the passenger door, and he jumped into the car. He was carrying a small axe, and he seemed to have a bleeding wound in his forehead. It was the English artist Peter Green, who painted landscapes to sell to tourists. He was married to a slightly unhinged island woman named Mauatua. They had a famously volatile relationship and he was a slave to her wacky behaviour. John was a gentle person who escaped this dominatrix through alcohol and by retiring to a broom cupboard to paint secret erotic pictures of *vahines* frolicking naked in Tahitian sunsets.

'What the hell happened to you, Peter?' I shouted over the storm. I expected him to tell me a tree had fallen on his house.

'I was sleeping there peacefully, and all of a sudden, bang, she drove one of her stiletto heels into my forehead, right between my eyes! Bitch!'

'Good God! What did she do that for?'

'She said I didn't love her enough. God, how I *adore* these island women! Of course I was pissed out of my skull. But this time, I'm going to kill her. I've had enough. The worm has turned!'

He fingered the edge of the axe blade. 'Take it easy, man,' I said. 'You'll never find her in this murk.'

'Yes, I will. Just take me down to Middlegate.'

I let him out some way along Queen Elizabeth Drive. He rushed off through the howling gale down a lane near the Roman Catholic Church.

Transmission at the radio station had been interrupted by power failures, and the staff were sticking to their posts. We stayed on air day and night until the cyclone abated. It had curled menacingly around the island, and it had delivered a vengeful flick of its tail before slewing off across the Pacific. The tarpaulin protecting the roof of the Administration offices in the New Military Barracks was ripped wide open and the place was devastated by thousands of gallons of water pouring in. Rivers flowed down the stairs, ceilings collapsed, documents and records were lost in a lake in the basement. On my drive back to the tracking station, pines and oaks lay broken and scattered about the fields. One famous giant lay tragically on its side in a hotel garden.

It was only much later that I heard that Nathan had escaped from the hospital at the height of the storm. He was last seen loping up the road toward the summit of Mt. Pitt like a man possessed.

CHAPTER XIX

Government House, Norfolk Island

*T*he weekend following the cyclone, an invitation to dinner at Government House arrived. A mere cyclone would not deter this Administrator from social engagements. He was a Commodore in the Royal Australian Navy, affable, charming and intelligent. My broadcasting efforts during the cyclone had been noted, and the dinner was a reward. The Commodore had recently visited Almira in hospital, carrying two chilled bottles of champagne and three chilled glasses 'surreptitiously' wrapped in a tea-towel. This gesture appealed to her, and the champagne rapidly put her on the road to recovery. His wife was a vivacious woman with a keen interest in art, and in recording the histories of the older Pitcairn descendants. For an Administrator, he had a cultivated musical taste.

The lights on the verandah were blazing as I pushed open the picket gate. The house was built of coral limestone, surrounded by an extensive verandah in the Pitcairner Georgian style, with the roof supported by slim white pillars. The entrance was almost concealed by the spreading English oak on the lawn, but a housekeeper dressed in a black uniform with white apron was standing in a circle of light at the entrance. The Regency door-case and ornate fanlight looked elegant in the gathering dusk. Potted palms and ferns had been carefully placed on the maroon carpet, and a sentry box was set into the wall in the inner hall. The panorama from the windows over the Kingston ruins and the phosphorescent reef created a uniquely colonial backdrop to this social occasion.

The interior was warm and civilised. On the walls there were portraits of the Queen, a selection of naval crests, early maps, naive engravings of First Settlement scenes. The most spectacular pictures were watercolour illustrations of the regal *Nestor productus*, the extinct

Norfolk Island Kaka, or, more correctly, the Philip Island parrot. The Commodore in mess undress uniform was standing beside a perfect fire in the drawing room as his wife ushered me in. I was introduced to the other guests – the Assistant Medical Officer and his wife, a fellow naval officer who had served in the same ship as the Commodore, his wife, and a glamorous, tanned Australian legal secretary with long blonde hair, pearls and a little black dress.

We were taken on a tour of the house, shown the sentry balcony in the kitchen and the secret cellar tunnel that opened on to Emily Bay via a studded wooden door from the former Commandant's bedroom. We had drinks and we chatted about tourism and history. We looked at some artifacts of Maori life, and then we were summoned for dinner.

A huge cedar table of convict workmanship, set with fine crested silver and glass, adorned the dining room. Perhaps it was the same table mentioned by Paulina in her journal. Names, initials and messages carved into it were visible under the deep patina. They formed an excellent conversation piece and neatly filled the silence that descended at the commencement of dinner. Another perfect fire burned in the grate, and the candelabra flickered opulently. We were rather widely spaced along the twenty or so feet of cedar, but watercress soup and sherry soon assisted the beginnings of conversation.

'The Administrator's Office completely escaped cyclone damage,' beamed the Commodore. 'I arranged it all, naturally. The rest of the building was severly affected.'

'I believe it was the worst for ten years.'

'No-one was injured, but I suspect sensible people stayed indoors,' I commented.

'The knotty problem of excluding cows from the golf course is coming to a head,' said the Commodore's wife, who was a keen member of the Golf Club.

'I've heard it is the most inflammable topic on the island.'

'According to local rules, you *are* permitted to wipe manure off the ball before playing your next shot!' laughed the naval officer.

'It has become a question of class and democratic principle,' said the Commodore. 'Common grazing land for the Pitcairn decendants, or an exclusive golf course for the tourists and settlers, the eternal dualities of the island. I leave it with you.' He offered more Chardonnay.

'Yeah, I guess it's a bit smelly for the golfies,' put in the glamorous blonde. Her voice and appearance mismatched startlingly.

I was wondering who Paulina had entertained at Government House during the Second Settlement. Visiting Bishops, officers and gentlemen with their wives, I supposed. Would the conversation have centered around balls and calls? Probably nothing of the suffering in the cells would have disturbed their equanimity at dinner.

'I do love the painting *Blue Poles*,' commented the Commodore's wife. 'In fact I love Abstract Expressionism as a movement in itself.'

I felt this was my cue.

'Yes,' I said, 'although I rather like the Renaissance. The island is a bit like the Garden of Venus, don't you think?'

I had clearly gone too far and the table lapsed into deafening silence. Fortunately some Sauternes arrived with the fruit salad. The Commodore, ever the master of good form, suggested a return to the drawing room for coffee, cognac and music. He played a recording of Emil Gilels performing the rarely heard second of Tchaikovsky's piano concertos, and conversation resumed.

'The Kentia Palm industry is thriving, in fact, that chap Cameron has…'

'The new X-ray unit is *such* a welcome addition to our limited facilities at the hospital.'

'Did you know Liszt was piloted by Byron's gondolier in Venice?'

'They really must stop these "ladies of the night" visiting Norfolk. The latest one caused the longest queue for antibiotics I've ever had…'

'Bligh actually buried the drunken Surgeon of the *Bounty* at Point Venus in Tahiti. An alcoholic, apparently. Bligh simply had to carry on, poor fellow.'

'I've been getting a great tan here, have you? 'Biotherm' is by far the best oil to give you that amber glow…' She glanced down admiringly at her golden thigh, and she stretched her beautiful leg glistening with golden down.

The snippets of conversation flitted past. Now and then, the Commodore and his wife would call for silence during a musical passage and beat time with enthusiasm and approbation.

'Those grooves on the dining table were made by the high heels of a certain German Officer's mistress, trying to gain a purchase as she lay back and...' The Commodore was sailing in dangerous waters. His wife rescued him.

'Paul, do play us some Chopin,' she begged.

I could hardly refuse, so I never did discover the outcome of this anecdote. I gave a passable rendering of some waltzes and a ballade on the Broadwood upright. Later in the evening the Commodore took me aside.

'Paul, old chap, I don't really know how to put this, but it's about your radio programmes.'

'I hope you're enjoying them,' I said carefully, sensing something unpleasant was coming.

'Certainly on Sundays. It's just that sometimes your high spirits cross the invisible line. Take that reference to the Medical Officer's mistress and the piglets for example. You really can't speculate on such matters over the air. If they complain officially, I have to act.'

'Well, I've heard nothing untoward, but I'll keep it in mind. The Goons have a terrible effect on me.'

'Look, I've got some vintage cognac put aside for VIPs. Let's sneak a glass.'

The Commodore poured some fine *Château de Fontpinot* into brandy balloons. He crossed to a secretaire and returned with two *Montecristos*. The others were chatting on the verandah.

'Just take it easy,' he said kindly. We cut the cigars, lit up and sat silently puffing, listening to Gilels playing magnificently against the hush of the distant breakers. At about one o'clock the party began to break up.

As I came out on to the verandah, a fresh, salty breeze off the bay slapped my cheeks, and I breathed the pure air in deep gulps. We made our farewells. Flicking the MG through the curves on the ascent from Kingston to Blaydes, I felt this to have been a memorable evening. The amusing dualities of the golf course controversy came to mind again. At Gannet Point the terns were making their comforting night squawks. I reflected that Mareva had claimed a special part of me that would remain forever closed to the chattering middle-class culture however intelligent, sexy, charming or witty. She had placed me in contact with the silent divinities of the island.

My imagination was running at a high degree of historical excitement as I cranked the generator and turned in toward the tracking station. I was most anxious to take up the journals of Paulina Wellesley once more, and continue reading of her life in that same Government House I had just so recently left.

CHAPTER XX

'I slept till this morning like a diamond in cotton...'
Pedrillo
The Castle of Andalusia by John O'Keefe Esq., 1783

*'Pursue thy conquest, Love; her eyes
Confess the flame her tongue denies.'*
Belinda
Act I, *Dido & Aeneas,* Henry Purcell, 1690

*Norfolk Island
December 20th. 1846*

I was in a high state of nerves today – Captn. Zaleski finally brought the part Arab mare for me to ride & even to proffer as a gift! Nothing finer could have been given me for Christmas! I was in need of a side-saddle from VDL which took aeons to arrive on the *Lady Nelson* so my first canter was much delayed. I have called her *Tempter* as she seems continually desirous of being ridden & will *tempt me* out of the crippling apathy that descends on me in this dull island prison. She is a delicate pale grey animal spotted brown & possesses large beautiful eyes & an eager disposition. There is at last gaiety & love for a being in my heart!

James has been quite impossible in this matter showing an excess of gruff sensibility over intelligence but I have finally persuaded him to smile on such generosity – even if from a young *foreign* officer. After all he has many *foreign* convicts – Spanish legionnaires, Jews, Hindus, French, German, Poles, Swedish, Chinese & I even saw two Aboriginals from Australia yesterday. His father was a great breeder of thoroughbred horses in Cornwall so he cannot complain of me! *Actaeon* barked furiously around the mare which made her skittish – a degree of training needs to be attended to.

The children were happily at school under the care of their diverting schoolmaster & gentleman convict Hyacinth O'Rourke. He arrived here from Sydney on a private yacht called *Venus* and possesses a most distinguished aspect.

I was in high spirits today & suggested to the dashing Captn. Zaleski that we go on a *long morning ride* to a beautiful glen of palms in the direction of Mount Pitt; Mrs. Ommanney mentioned this *'Arcadia'* at tea on Tuesday. *Tempter* was frisking & anxious to be exercising – I would be be pleased to try her stamina in a climb. He advised caution as two convicts had taken the Bush the night before & he would not answer for my safety. I said that they were always absconding & if we were to dwell upon this matter we would *never* go riding. Captn. Whiteside will accompany us as he is familiar with the terrain & will carry a firearm. So as better to imagine riding through an English gentleman's park (the island is faintly reminiscent of a country estate) I chose to put off my normal cotton print dress & straw bonnet. I donned my bodice with the deep 'Polka' skirt, half-boots & tall beaver hat with long veil. My 'escort' was most complimentary towards my attire in that *suspect continental fashion* – dear me!

We passed the Agricultural Establishment at Longridge where perhaps 400 men were working peacefully in the open as well as 20 teams of bullocks and 3 teams of horses. The crops seem to be flourishing at this well-regulated farm. It is the most delightful spot on the island. There is little trouble here & I called on good Mrs. Treene, a plain, stout & short young woman – the wife of the Superintendant of Agriculture – to comfort her little daughter Priscy who has been seriously ill. James had made some broth for the sufferer. She is an eminently *pettable* child. Mrs. Treene was pleased of my cuttings of Bougainvillaea from the Government House garden but was embarrassed upon my arrival. I had caught her unawares & she fussed about & was effusive in her apologies at being not properly dressed before 9 o'clock!

Tempter is very sensitive & is not yet settled as to sheep but we walked on to Pettitt's Farm through Ledwich's Gulley & into the mountain forest on a narrow track. The palms grow thick together here & light is much reduced. The scrubs are all so heaped, jumbled & interwoven that progress was difficult. Suddenly we came to a clearing or glen. Ferns dissolve into the azure & feathery fronds filter the sunlight. Brilliant green parakeets screech & play their intelligent tricks in profusion! We were also accompanied by Hummingbirds, Wagtails & Scarlet Robins with emerald doves & pigeons soft-calling. Nature is at her most Elysian in such a remote spot.

'Let me take your hat, Madam, the branches will ruin it,' offered Captn. Zaleski, inclining toward me, *très gallant* in his scarlet shell jacket with bright green facings, rows of gilt buttons and smiling good looks of fathomless charm.

The rough Captn. Whiteside kept a weather eye open & patrolled for desperadoes. We dismounted in the glade, Captn. Zaleski handing me down.

'I would certainly like to sketch this beautiful glen,' I remarked & took out my books & pencils & set to work on the pines, ferns & parakeets. There were strange & sudden rustlings in the bush, but no wild men appeared. I engaged the young officer in conversation.

'May I compliment you on your dancing at our ball, Captain – quite the *virtuoso* – such grace was not learned in the Antipodes, I should say. Do tell me something of yourself.'

'Madam, you are too kind to a poor Slav. Yes, we Poles are passionate dancers! I was born in the Castle of Wiśnicz, in the South of Poland, to a family aristocratic but not too aristocratic.'

I smiled at his amusing turn of phrase.

'But why did you not continue to reside in your sad country – even fight for it?'

'As a young cavalryman, when Tsar Nicholas was removed as King of Poland in 1831 & the country was torn asunder, I was part of the Mission sent to London to offer the throne to a member of your Royal Family.'

'Why, this is a play, Captain – a piece of theatre – how impossibly Romantic!'

'Not ever, Madam. Only politics. Tsar Nicholas took a terrible revenge and confiscated our estates. Thousands of officers were sent by the Russians to the Caucasus. I chose to stay in England.'

'What could you do in England, pray, a tender foreign gentleman of your station?'

'I purchased a commission in a British Regiment – the 11th. Foot, known as the *Bloody Eleventh* after their distinctions in the Battle of Salamanca. My pronunciation is good?'

'Perfect, Captn., perfect. So when did you land on these distant shores?'

'I arrived at VDL in early November last year with my Regiment & Commanding Officer Lt. Col. Bloomfield, aboard the *Castle Eden*.' He spoke briefly to Captn. Whiteside, who seemed to be taking an excessive interest in our conversation rather than patrolling the bush.

'Did you not fight as a revolutionary, an *emigré* in Paris?' (I felt quite breathless in the company of this adventurous specimen & wondered at the *provenance* of the sabre scar on his cheek but would not quiz him on it for fear of appearing overly inquisitive.)

'Yes. I intend to return soon, but relief detachment is difficult. English officers avoid coming to VDL like the plague. Some even resign their commissions or go on half-pay to avoid it. Your drawing is very beautiful, Madam.'

'Thank you, Sir, and so is your wonderful mare *Tempter*. Look how content she is! Do you like my name for her?'

'I was in the National Cavalry in Poland, Madam. She is a fine animal from Bathurst in New South Wales.'

My beautiful mare tossed her head, neighed, and worried some flies that had settled.

'Christmas is almost upon us, Captn. Zaleski. We should get up an opera which would be *amusant, divertissant, non?*'

'*C'est une idée très intéressante, Madame.* But I do not know the English operas.'

The Castle of Andalusia is an excellent comic opera for such as young officers. I will look it out for your delectation & we will discuss it. The first theatre performances in Australia were here – we must keep up the tradition!'

My drawing was sadly deficient, but I had managed an agreeable likeness of the peculiar open spreading of the branches of this species of pine. The branches appear like ostrich feathers tipped with the brighter green of new growth. I sketched some passably interlaced fern fronds and walking tracks. My parakeets are flying with excessive *esprit* I fear.

'I think we should return to Government House quite soon, Captn. Zaleski. Charlotte will be fretting away from her Mama.'

We gathered up the stolid Captn. Whiteside, who was now fiercely patrolling the nearby scub, clearly betraying impatience at this civilised *tête-à-tête* between the Captn. & myself. Conversing & sketching midst the possible predations by barbarous murderers seemed insanity to him & we set off back to the Settlement. *Tempter* was intelligent & cautious on the steep descent, trembling in fear but carrying me safely with sure feet. How I love this animal!

How strange to speak of such matters as European history in a forest on this remote island in Oceania! Nostalgia and sense of distance are much in the ascendant of my thoughts. I was put in mind of my girlhood in Geneva, when the Poles were with Bonaparte. Through the good offices of my Uncle I aquired a splendid mount I called *Partner*, so named since he showed similar mischevious propensities to his infamous namesake.

I am so miserable sometimes! It is desperately lonely here & the almost complete absence of stimulation is wearing. But *at last* I have aquired a cultivated companion for my excursions & the protection of my person. Had I not come to VDL I would not now be in this *'exact replica of the infernal regions'* with vain-glorious *Mister Monocle* – married, children, duty & dreams. But hush, such violent thoughts – conflicting feelings are exerting an influence over me & I must desist. The island is beautiful of itself & yet this constant reminder of the Lower Nature of man is intolerable in the midst of such an Elysium. Concerning Captn. Z., I *must* cease to indulge my thoughts on matters that ought not to interest me as they once have done; to still the foolish licence of my pen; *'ce passé qui ne se répéte jamais...'*

Government House
Norfolk Island
Christmas Eve, 1846

Terrible events yesterday! Some Officers of the 11th. Regiment – Major Irwin, Captn. Dawson, Howey & Whiteside & James made up a party for fishing & visiting Philip Isle according to a long-standing arrangement. No fish were to be caught in the calm water & so they headed off to land on Philip. Here they shot a score of rabbits & scrambled about the dangerous cliffs tracking pigs & goats, ate an ample dinner & made to return to Norfolk Island. A sea had risen meanwhile & as they crossed the Bar they achieved a 'tremendous run' (as it is known) & the boat smashed to pieces on the rocks! Captn. Howey was lost & Dawson fearfully maimed – Charles St. Aubyn fears for his life. James was almost almost dashed to pieces but is a strong swimmer & made light of the drenching. The other officers clung to the remains of the boat & were fished out by soldiers of the Garrison.

On a walk late this afternoon with little Clara – the mite should take some air. Two Officers' carriages passed us at a terrific rate, returning from another pic-nic party at Orange Vale – young soldiers were hanging from them in all directions laughing & singing – I thought they were fit to capsize! Two officers were riding one horse! They shouted seasonal greetings & seem even to celebrate the death of their comrade lost on the rocks while fishing.

I have planned a Pic-Nic on top of Mount Pitt for Boxing Day. James has permitted the Settlement to finish work at 4 o'clock & he will join us (Charlotte, Adolphus & Clara) together with Charles St. Aubyn, the R.C. Rev. Valentine Onslow, Mr. & Mrs. Ommaney, Captn. Zaleski & Miss Martineaux & the schoolmaster Aeneas de Meuron. Mrs. Treene was to come but Priscy has taken a worse turn.

There was great excitement today with a shout of Brig O!! off the Beacon & the Garrison Colours were hoisted together with the secret signals that permit vessels to approach. I strongly anticipated some Christmas Mail & sent Septimus down to Cascades as the ship might stand off there. He returned empty handed as the vessel transpired to be a whaler. I am in the deepest dismals as it seems I am excessively abandoned by my correspondents in England and VDL. Preparations are going ahead with *The Castle of Andalusia* for performance on New Year's Day.

Norfolk Island
Christmas Eve 1846

James allowed the road & reef gangs to leave work at 4 o'clock. Many went to the Rev. Valentine Onslow or Rev. Charles Bedingfield for spiritual advice.

Much excitement within the family & preparation for Christmas. I was miserable much of the day on account of the separation from loved ones & cried much of the time.

Norfolk Island
Christmas Day, 1846

Much excitement with the children & attempts to forget my location in Oceania rather than Suffolk. The Ferrers managed to despatch some presents from Hobarton for them aboard the *Lady Franklin* on the vessel's recent visit. I sent them by return some perfect boxes made of the native woods of the island fashioned by that fearful amateur Hyacinth O'Rourke. Many 'Merry Christmases' were exchanged today with the simple and well-meaning folk who make up the settlement. Society is much restricted here. How I miss my dear relations & Lady Jane in particular! We invited some of the 'orphans' among the officers to share our Christmas dinner. However, looking around the festive table at so many unfamiliar faces created a mood of sadness difficult for me to dispel. I sat in the garden in a mood of great despondency watching the vanes of the windmill at Point Hunter slowly turning, my youth ebbing away.

Attended Divine service this morning. The Rev. Valentine Onslow gave an excellent sermon that I found most uplifting, although it was too long & tedious in places. He took as his meditation Philippians i. 23 verses 24-27. James had permitted convicts to attend & they formed the majority of the congregation. One demonaical specimen shewed his collarbones quite bare of flesh through numerous floggings – they were proudly polished to an amber sheen like two ivory horns. Some went to the cells beneath the curious sliding panels – the so-called *windows to heaven* – installed by Captn. Maconochie. They may listen to the service *if* they wish by pushing the panels back. James ordered that each man be served with one pound of fresh beef. I pray for all their souls & as a New Year Resolution I have asked Charles St. Aubyn to tell me something of their histories this season with a view to making a written record, a *Collection of Destinies*, rather as my aunt made collections of shells & animals in her menagerie in VDL. He warned me that it will be deeply discomforting if the truth be told, but I declared it would divert me from trivial concerns & fill the *deserts of time* at my disposal.

He reiterated as a meditation for Christmas some affecting stories told him by a Prison Matron at the Female Factory in VDL. One morning she was looking through the inspection window of a cell & perceived a female convict with her elbows on the table staring fixedly at an ordinary daisy. She had plucked the flower from the central patch of grass during her exercise period. The prisoner was a rude & repulsive specimen who would scarce be expected to harbour any feelings of the slightest sentimental value. She looked wistfully at her stolen prize. The wretched woman began to weep & her head fell to the table & in despair onto her hands. Bitter tears flowed noislessly, silently. Perhaps she remembered picnics with fond friends in the country. The creature then pressed the flower between the leaves of her Bible. The Matron saw the flower as a treasure she did not have the heart to confiscate, had there been any regulations concerning *'having daisies pressed between the pages of books'.* Another convict was inconsolable at the death of a mouse she had succeeded in taming. And yet another lured a sparrow to her cell & when the tiny creature came to an untimely end it broke her heart. Such stories bring tears of compassion to my eyes & are uplifting in hope over Christmas allowing us to dwell on the compassion of Christ.

Norfolk Island
December 26th. 1846

After church, set out in the 'convict carriage' for Mt. Pitt & the Pic-Nic. *Mister Monocle* strictly forbad me to ride *Tempter.* The path is narrow & we were forced to get out & walk the final distance. Glorious weather favoured us & we found most of the Party arrived well before our appearance. The Military Garrison were engaged in sports & lunatic games as we departed the Settlement. They had placed a silver watch on top of a greasy pole & were attempting to retrieve it as our carriage passed. The strains of their Regimental March *'We've Lived and Loved Together"* added to the general festive atmosphere in the barracks.

The first person to catch my eye on the mountain was Miss Martineaux who is excessively pretty, gay & ostentatious in her dress & has the tiniest waist I have ever seen – and the most absurdly large bustle! Tall & handsome Captn. Zaleski in scarlet shell jacket, blue forage cap & tasselled sabre galloped up on his chestnut in a cloud of dust. He cut a splendid booted figure with his fair hair, military moustache & spurs as he reigned in amongst us. He dismounted & led his horse towards our party.

'You are most kind to invite me,' he murmured & kissed my hand in *le style Polonais* whilst looking to me with those slightly wild blue eyes & radiant smile. I confess my heart leaped in my breast at this effrontery under the basilisk stare of James! A storm of vexation passed across his brow & he fiercely engaged Major Irwin in conversation, gouging his eye with his monocle. Charlotte pulled at the hem of my dress to gain attention. An island allows no privacy of relation!

We all rested in a small grassy clearing among the lemon trees, (golden fruit against dark green) & looked with the greatest pleasure upon the beautiful pine scenery, fern gullies & cerulean ocean containing the two outlying islands. Philip Isle is covered in thick wood with bare red peaks &

can be seen to great advantage from this elevated position. One feels entirely separated from civilization. Green parrots were eating violet berries & the Norfolk Island Pepper displayed its yellow cylindrical fruit & heart-shaped leaves among the star flowers. Pale green & tiny blue butterflies danced about in the sun. One could realize the vastness of our isolation in contemplating the wide sea to the horizon. Eliza & Louisa Lamb (our new domestic – she stole a quantity of lace in Bath but is not a plague or a danger) produced a fine *al fresco* luncheon; excellent wine was poured into the bumpers; James joined in with the children's diversions to the great amusement of all assembled.

Captn. Zaleski scarcely concealed his thrilling glances toward me on the mountain & I was put to a high colour despite my firmness of resolve. *Actaeon* played affectionately with tiny Clara & Adolphus produced his pet gecko from his pocket which escaped immediately into the Bush – tears followed & a stern rebuke from his father for weakening so under such a trivial loss. Some of the officers tried to slash a path down to Cascades but were prevented in their object by the dense jungle & darkness coming on. We were fortunate enough to reach the settlement without incident in the pitch blackness.

As we passed the entrance to the pentagonal gaol I noticed some flickering flambeaux illuminating a macabre scene. Shadows were cast on the archway decorated with horrid manacles & man traps. A poor wretch had been strapped to the triangles & was being *flogged by candlelight!* This was the first time I had seen such a gruesome thing by day or night & closed my eyes but not before I had seen that his back was a mass of bloody contusions. I could hear the deliberate count of the Constable – 'eighteen, nineteen...' & the hiss of the scourger as he laid it on in considered strokes. The poor beast shrieked towards the end of it. Superintendant Gaudin was handling the tails & I fancied I saw sparks of blood and flesh fly to his apron. This was not a sight for the children & I sternly rebuked them for staring upon it. I could hear the furious clank of irons from the dark cells as the imprisoned convicts protested at this outrage. Dogs barked mournfully, the ocean gave out low moans on the wind, the sentinel voiced his harsh cry & the gallows reflected the risen moon in a fiendish silhouette.

What a brutal end to a pefectly happy day! This pitiless scene has made me quite ill! I rounded on James & accused him of monstrous & blasphemous behaviour on the day after the Birth of Christ. He *laughed*, his face became confused & wrought & he said savagely whilst twisting his monocle:

'I'll flog the dogs when & how I like! Nothing is sacred to me. This foxy one's not half a pebble!' but he stopped the cart & I saw he interrupted Gaudin at the flogging. The Rev. Onslow was comforting the poor wretch.

'*Do* come and have a *petit souper* with us at Government House Valentine. Send this scum to the very devil!' James taunted the clergyman.

The Rev. Valentine commented as he stalked away in anger from our party towards his villa: 'One day these men will turn & kill their tormenter!'

'You have a deficiency of temper and discretion Mr. Onslow! I suggest you return among the crawlers!'[73] crowed James after him in a manner shockingly disrespectful to a clergyman.

It was a veritable scene from Dante that has been etched upon my optics *forever*. As we entered Government House past the cannons & pacing sentry he said in a gentle voice, suddenly full of sentiment & calm solicitude:

'My darling, they are the most fearful ruffians & desperate characters capable of concocting & carrying out any crime that might enter their heads. They have avowed to Murder everyone at the Settlement! I am creating a salutary dread in their hearts; it will protect us.'

'James, you are becoming a veritable *amateur of suffering!* Your behaviour here is a sanguinary farce!' I said vehemently & went to bed never to forget this terrible night. I fear he is two people at once & subject to mercurial changes of mood – such unpredictability is a plague to my heart & causes me the greatest distress.

What precisely is happening in this brutal island lair? Is James truly a good man? The questions haunted me through the small hours until the bell & bugle woke the wretched souls at dawn for yet another day of horrid torments.

Norfolk Island
December 30th.1846

Halcyon weather! We had a very pleasant visit from the two young boys and the daughter of the Surgeon Charles St. Aubyn and his wife Emilia. Charlotte & Adolphus were excessively pleased to have such a diverting interruption to their day. The children arrived in some style in a diminutive carriage drawn by four white goats. While they gambolled together on the grass near the pacing sentry I played a game of whist with Charles, Emilia & Mrs. Webster who had called on me earlier in the morning.

'Dr. St. Aubyn, how is Mr. Carpenter after that terrible incident? The island depresses him inordinately,' Mrs. Webster asked Charles.

'He tried to commit suicide while he was drunk – shot himself in the side when he dropped his gun. The wound is serious, but I have cleared it of debris, so he should recover within a few weeks. Drinking is the very plague in the Colony!'

'Whoever *once* gives way to it will never get the better of it,' commented Emilia.

'Yes, the most talented of young men – the *élite* of our society drown themselves in its horrors!' Mrs. Webster clearly saw catastrophe everywhere.

'Mr. Troublehouse the Magistrate was telling us some amusing convict stories over dinner the other evening,' I said, anxious to change from a painful subject.

'Do tell us, Paulina!' they said as one, pleased to be entertained and diverted.

'A man with a wooden leg named Clinch who was sent to Norfolk Island for throwing a stone at the King was sentenced to 25 lashes for *singing and smiling while on the chain.* He asked the Magistrate to direct that one half be administered to the wood! Such a clever riposte!

'Another *dog* was sentenced to 50 lashes for saying "Good morning" to a waterman & replied to the magistrate:

"Can't take off my jacket Sir to receive 'em."

"Well, take 100 lashes then!" directed our officer.'

'Oh! Most amusing!'

'They are quite incorrigible,' observed St. Aubyn. 'One I saw on the triangles had tattooed on his back the ghoulish message to the scourger: *"FLOG WELL AND DO YOUR DUTY".'*

'Some more tea, anyone?' Louisa effectively saw to the callers' needs.

'There have still been occasional robberies of houses & stabbings in recent weeks. Why, James's office was broken into in the middle of the day!' I added. 'I do anticipate beginning my *Collection of Destinies* soon with your help, Charles – it is sure to be vastly entertaining!'

'I hear you are putting on the comic opera *The Castle of Andalusia* tomorrow,' said Mrs. Webster.

'It will certainly take our minds off these rogues!' laughed St. Aubyn.

We made further ineffectual gossip & soon Emilia collected the children for their return to Cascade Station. James arrived at the house just as they were about to depart & suggested we accompany them on a *petite partie de plaisir* on account of the idyllic weather. The days have long hours of sunshine so we arranged the horses to be saddled & led out by our Chinese domestic Wu Li, his pig-tail bobbing about in a most diverting fashion. After dinner Septimus & Charlotte continued with music lessons in the parlour – some Sonatas by Joseph Haydn – Adolphus went shooting with his teacher Hyacinth O'Rourke, Eliza began putting little Clara to bed as we mounted up & headed off towards the Cascades.

The cart drawn by the white goats pattered along in front of us in perfect miniature style. *Actaeon* raced ahead like the wind. *Tempter* was frisking about alarmed as usual but I settled her quickly. We took the road that winds up through the hills above the Settlement to Pine Tree Flat and through the Sucker Ground Farm. A stream or rill bordered by copses & ferns descends from the pine-clad hills & winds among the grassy slopes which lead to an open valley. James (dressed in the *Stunner Tartan*) & Charles were conversing behind Emilia & me as we ambled along watching the children from horseback.

'Well, James, how are you?'

'I have dogs to keep the wolves off. The old trouble is returned – much preoccupied with the family in this Lazar House of crime.'

'My sentiments exactly. I hope my transfer to VDL is not further delayed. One breathes here the very air of convictism.'

'Charlotte & Adolphus need a proper education outside a penal settlement & company of their proper station. And this is no place for a Lady such as Paulina.' (I glanced back at him and smiled sweetly.)

'Have you been taking the medication I ordered?'

'Sleeping so much better after the drops, Charles.'

'The Settlement is now in excellent order after your strict coercions. The convicts are quick at *twigging a man*, James!'[74]

'That mass of corruption – Capital Respites – those we have here now must be kept down by a strong hand. The Rev. Valentine says I am pitiless. Well, fine feelings are lost on such wild beasts. His emotions are womanish! He resides near here at Cascades, but not for much longer, I'll warrant!'

I turned to Emilia as the talk of convicts distresses me.

'Did Miss Martineaux call on you last Sunday?' I remarked.

'Yes, she did call, with Captn. Zaleski as her dashing escort. They seem quite the pair! But we have *so* many callers on a Sunday after church that we cannot observe the Sabbath in any proper sense,' complained Emilia.

'I cannot say I like her *showy* appearance. She is what gentlemen call *very fascinating*,' I admit to a certain waspishness in this remark.

'I am no judge of fashion, my dear. Will you come & join us in a circle of cribbage on Wednesday?'

'I must take *Tempter* to the farrier and myself to the shoe-maker! I am riding all over the island at present!'

The loud voices of the gentlemen forced my attention back to what I have termed *The Black Books of the Settlement*. Charles worried the subject like a hound.

'Gaudin has a veritable passion for taking the tails. When I first saw a man flogged, every stroke made me flinch. Now one scarified back is like another – just press it down! Ha! Ha!'

'I have an utter aversion to the scourge, Charles, but I'm forced to it,' James complained. 'The *Lords Commissioners* spoil the sport by insisting that the island not only *pays its own way* but produces a *remunerative return*. They desire the introduction of coffee! As a gentleman & farmer I say it's impossible, arrant madness! The men will not do a bloody stroke without coercion by the musket and the lash – all that is left to me.' We were walking the horses past some fields that lay fallow.

'Look at those weeds! Who is going to grub them up so I can plant the maize? I haven't got enough willing labour.' James became emotional & his voice faltered.

'And that fool Denison has suggested introducing the white mulberry with the object of raising silkworms!'

'Take it easy, man.'

'James, do let the subject rest & delight in the beautiful vistas of the coral ocean. Look! We could be in Positano!' I expostulated with tetchy enthusiasm.

'My duty is my delight,' he stuffily replied.

We were passing a sheep station where some men were washing & shearing some of the thousands of island sheep in the goldening light. Some of the chimneys from a previous settlement still stand here & their old orchards have run wild with Vines, Guavas, Figs & Lemons in rampant confusion. Sugar canes grow beside the stream until it falls over rocks covered with delicate ferns. The brook, bordered by luxuriant plants, then runs through wooded hills until it flows over a flat promontory & falls tremendously some twenty feet to a beach covered in a profuse gallery of rounded boulders. This romantic cataract sounds effortlessly above the breaking waves.

'Scourging would *not* be necessary if I had more separate cells for solitary confinement.'

'Most men come and go from the island possessed of a cheerful demeanour, with no trouble at all.'

'Exactly! I have set up a hospital, postal service, regular school every night, soup for the sick. I even shewed them how to make tools & work at wood but you *cannot* reform a wild beast through principles & example.'

By this time James was pulling the mouth of his mount & acting most strangely. He was distracted, close to tears & my heart raced with a mixture of cold aversion for his person & true sympathy for his plight. Entwined around the trees nearby were the large purple flowers shot with red of the convulvulus plant & the copper-coloured Passion flower. A small & miserable group of wooden buildings abut the landing stage – only English prisoners are billetted here & those convalescing from winter ailments. We took tea in a curious & delightful folly. The centre of an enormous pine has been hollowed out and furnished with a large table and chairs.

'Do call on us at Government House, Emilia – Archbishop Mollison is visiting the island quite soon – do come to dinner.'

'Come to see us after the opera tomorrow!' James called as we turned our horses to make our way home. St. Aubyn was already unhitching the goats from the carriage in the yard of his farm, the children squealing & running in circles.

'Come, *Actaeon!*'

Tempter was quiet on the return to the Settlement, as if she sensed the atmosphere between James & myself.

'Do you remember *Risdon*, James?' I said quietly.

'Of course, my darling.'

'You pressed my hand as we fled the bushrangers.'

'I do remember.'

'You asked for a lock of my hair.'

'I have it still.'

'How our affections have been cruelly trammelled since then by this destiny.'

'Why, you are a constant companion of my thoughts. The haven of family life after a day in that Hell of duty & regulation is of greatest importance to me.'

'Cannot we soon leave this dreadful place, James? I fear for Charlotte, Adolphus & the little one in their constant concourse with convicts of whatever stamp, even Septimus.'

'Earl Grey has already requested Denison to break up the establishment. But it will take time, Paulina.'

'Cannot we return to England?'

'I have requested a place other than Australia, but my services are much valued *and* I have £800 a year which places me in most select company. Paulina, I have a reputation to preserve.'

We were approaching the settlement & James immediately stiffened & his demeanour changed dramatically. The monocle ploughed his eye & he searched the horizon intently. He had taken on his second personality. The Superintendant Gaudin rode up.

'Have those two devils been comfortably scrammed, Giles?'[75]

'Permanently muzzled, Sir!'[76] he said with a faint smile.

'Excellent work. Make sure of a good haul tomorrow & off you go.'

I know not what they were speaking of & James was furious when I requested enlightenment saying it was absolutely none of my concern.

Norfolk Island
January 1st.1847

Yet another year of my life has passed & the New Year is upon us. The Ferrers have written & will take up residence in July. I greatly anticipate this sojourn with my friends as the island life has insufferable *longeurs*. Major Ferrers serves with the 58th. Regiment, the *'Black Cuffs'*, and is to be assigned to temporarily augment the officers of the Military Garrison. This is somewhat unusual, but regiments are dreadfully divided up at present, I believe.

Intensive preparations were made for the comic opera *The Castle of Andalusia,* which was performed this evening. It went off excellently! The many airs, glees & choruses were much practiced by the officers, soldiers & their ladies who performed the work in the courtyard before the tremendous staircase of the Commissariat Stores. This severe building with minimal decoration & lit by flambeaux passed adequately enough as the *'Castle of Don Scipio'* on the coast of Spain. I gave them as much assistance as possible in the rehearsals of this witty farrago of mistaken identities. Our small orchestra performed wonders! Septimus was brilliant on the violin with true *Tzigane* melodrama & tone. Almost the entire free settlement crammed the space & I suspect even a few of our own convicts edged a view.

The First Act is set in a huge cave with the *Banditti* sitting at a table covered with a Tiger skin, singing & drinking. The first *Air* is quite singular to our situation:

Of severe and partial laws
Venal judges, Alguazils
Dreary dungeon's iron jaws,
Oar or gibbet, whips or wheels
How can we think
While we drink
Sweet Muscadine?
O, life divine!

Captn. Zaleski was playing the part of *Don Alphonso* & I imagined he gazed on me whenever he appeared. I have been *so* susceptible to the illusion of the playhouse since childhood but I cannot permit my heart this freedom & yet I seem inexorably drawn to him. I wished the earth to swallow me up. On this tiny island I cannot escape the prison of my distress. He inhabits the reflections of almost all my waking hours. In the second scene in the dark forest – all dark, hail & rain – the entire garrison sang Pedrillo's air & engaged in witty conversation with those on the stage.

A master I have, and I am his man
Galloping dreary dun,
And he'll get a wife as fast as he can
With a haily
Gaily

Gambo raily
Gigg'ling
Nigg'ling
Galloping galloway, draggle tail, dreary dun.

I was almost lost among the multitude of characters in the throes of mistaken loves, illusions piled apace upon each other. I would explain it but the farce appears too dull explicated on the page.

Captn. Zaleski was in fine voice for the *Air* sung by *Don Alphonso* & he seemed to fix his eye on me.

Love, sweet passion, torment pleasing
Pure delight in pain you give.
Thrilling anguish, flattering, teasing,
Ne'er from grief or rapture ceasing,
Yet I'll love, or cease to live.

Emotion crowded into my heart at this almost shameless expression of passion, but I forced my response below the surface & condemned it to languish there unbidden – the cost of giving freedom to this temptation is tantamount to entering the maw of damnation.

His friend Captn. Vane showed rare criminal spirit as *Spado*. Much shouting & cheering on the part of the garrison concluded the piece.

Ev'ry pure and chaste delight
Crowned with love this happy night.

Some of the officers & the St. Aubyns accompanied us back to the House for a *petit souper*. I trembled internally as the message from Captn. Zaleski was clear & he made to join our party after the performance. The snake-clasp on his black sword belt glittered in the light of the returning torches. I made desultory conversation with James as we sauntered through the balmy pine-scented night towards the lights of Government House, my luxurious cell. Charlotte & Adolphus grasped me tightly on either side.

'Mighty fine opera on a mighty fine night! We want for nothing on this island. What do you say, Hyacinth?' James observed suddenly.

'Certainly, Sir! Reminded me of my Oxford days as a dandy. Would wear my magnificent velvet-lined cloak to the opera on excursions down to London.'

'Then you would nail[77] a few waistcoats in Vauxhall I suspect! Ha! Ha! Ha!' James never failed to produce his sardonic humour. He treats Hyacinth O'Rourke with strange courtesy, considering his background as a *gentleman thief*. But then James used to delight in prowling the notorious *'Cat and Fiddle Alley'* in Hobarton before we were married & when he was learning the secrets of the criminal classes. I believe O'Rourke is possessed of a large property in Sydney & will soon move into his own *'Villa'* here on the island.

Actaeon scattered the ducks & geese & bounded across the garden to greet me. Eliza took the two children off to bed & the company repaired to the drawing room. Adam Zaleski stood with his back to the fire & adjusted his crimson sash & sword, his forage cap under his arm. He strikes a fine erect figure in his frock coat of undress military blue.

'Do play us something on the piano, Captn. Zaleski!' begged Miss Martineaux.

'Certainly, *Mademoiselle*. Allow me to play a piece expressive of the Polish soul, *"The Polonaise of Death"* by Michał Ogiński. The composer is believed to have committed suicide to this patriotic music when he discovered his unfaithful lover was dancing with another.' A tremor of expectation passed over the assembled company.

He performed this stirring piece with tremendous *élan* & romanticism, his square contour of face noble in the candlelight. My heart rose to it but I noticed James became terribly impatient & cast his eyes to heaven.

'I trust my voice has not given you a headache at the opera this evening,' Captn. Zaleski smiled with devastating charm.

'*Snook's Family Pills* will be sure to solve *all* my problems with *your* voice,' James remarked acidly, grinding his monocle. This caused great merriment among the officers but caused me to colour & Adam to pale & purse his lips, the sabre scar stretching taut over his jaw. He drew himself up erect.

'I beg to take my leave of you, Sir. Good night, Madame,' Captn. Zaleski bowed stiffly, bringing his heels together with a scarcely perceptible click & left the room abruptly. The gentleman & their ladies uttered controlled sniggers & clearly considered James had achieved a palpable hit.

'I have a heavy down on Zaleski, but do not ask me why,' James commented violently.

Are there no depths of wicked humour denied this husband of mine? Perhaps he thought that the Polish officer would not recognize that *Snook's Family Pills* are an *aperient*. I concealed my annoyance & left them all to smoke & play billiards, claiming weakness after the exertions of the opera. Louisa was quite capable of dealing with the ladies' needs in the drawing room until they broke up the party.

'Good night, my darling Paulina,' ingenuously remarked *Mister Monocle*.

As I made my way to my bedroom by candle I felt sure I saw the striped yellow & black convict costume of Septimus quit the door to Charlotte's chamber in some precipitation. Yet she was sleeping peacefully when I entered. What might this incident portend? Perhaps it was merely a trick of the light.

(The binding on this volume was broken and much of the journal had been mutilated.)

As the chill dawn light crept into the crevices of the tracking station I wrapped my silk Shinto smoking jacket closer about me and pulled on my pipe. I put down the battered volume beside the now empty bottle of Armagnac. Paulina's journals described a life on the island 'where Satan never sleeps', showing it from an unfamiliar perspective. Sensationalist history has painted an unbalanced picture of the penal settlement. Paulina provided a useful corrective in her depiction of joy, love, pleasure and despair among the officer class in the midst of convict suffering. But at the same time, she posed a moral dilemma for her phantom readers.

I remembered lines from *Doctor Faustus* by Christopher Marlowe, when Faust asks Mephastophilis:

F. '*How comes it then that thou art out of hell?*
M. '*Why, this is hell, nor am I out of it.*

Hell hath no limits, nor is circumscribed
In one self place. But where we are is hell,
And where hell is there must we ever be.'

Mephastophilis replies urbanely, and he indicates the seductive world all around them.

F. *'How, now in hell? Nay, and this be hell, I'll willingly be damned here! What, walking, disputing, etc.'*

The love gardens of our earth lie delicately suspended above the circles of Hell. A slight lack of vigilance of the heart, and we fall from the lawns of paradise like serpents through a crack in the rock, dropping through black space into the flaming bowels of it.

CHAPTER XXI

Best Three Potatoes
or
Things Seen from Right and Left (without Glasses)
for violin and piano by Erik Satie

A number of annual events of significance on the island demanded my presence. Now it was the Agricultural and Horticultural Show in and around the Rawson Hall. It attracted a cross-section of the community, and gave me the opportunity to speak to people I never normally met. Hundreds of prizes were awarded for detailed categories of endeavour – produce, cakes, preserves, tapestries, giant vegetables, riding, cattle breeding and others. The show had been established for more than a hundred years. It was part of my job to cover the event, and to announce the major winners. Mareva had been hunting around in her cupboards for some duck eggs that looked passable; a few wrinkled potatoes in the bottom of the bin were pressed into service. Taking part in the competition was what mattered.

'Can I come with you around the hall and see the prizes?' she asked me.

'You don't mind people seeing us together?'

She gave me an enigmatic look and a delicious kiss. 'I love you,' she whispered. Still, she insisted we drive separately to the hall. Her indecision about our relationship was driving me mad.

Hundreds of people were there, craning, inspecting and congratulating. The weather was glorious and a festive atmosphere filled the air. Hundreds read the small cards placed on each item, and a second prize had been awarded in many cases. I began to note down the categories and winners in all their absurd Rabelaisian prolixity:

'BEST 12 PODS OF PEANS, GREEN, DWARF, OR CLIMBING'
'BEST THREE CARROTS (LONG RED)'
'BEST THREE RADISHES (ROUND RED)'
'BEST LEMON PIE (WITHOUT MERINGUE – USING ISLAND RECIPE
WITH CONDENSED MILK)'
'BEST GENTLEMAN'S BUTTONHOLE'
'BEST PAIR OF KNITTED BED SOX'
'MOST ARTISTIC ARRANGEMENT – INSIDE A BOTTLE'
'BEST ARTICLE MADE FROM A SUGAR OR FLOUR BAG'
'PRETTIEST COVERED COATHANGER – ANY MATERIAL'
'NEATEST HAT, DRAIN FLAGS'
'BEST SAND POSY'
'BEST DUAL PURPOSE COW'
'LARGEST LANTANA STUMP – PULLED BY HAND'
'BEST STRING OR COTTON PICTURE'
'BEST BIG BOOB MADE OF WOOD'

Vertigo set in as I noted down the list.

I noticed Mareva had fallen into conversation with a tall man who looked like a business executive. Before I could see more, she was swallowed up by the heaving throng searching for the Best Head of Lettuce. She appeared again briefly with her companion, close to him, leaning on his arm, and then I did not see her again that day. The incident left me feeling uneasy. My imagination threw up indistinguishable threats, anxiety and suspicions moulded by childish fear and adult longing. In a word, I was jealous.

Almira wandered about with some of her mainland guests, introducing them to all her friends. People talked to me about my radio announcements, wondering when I would be dismissed by the Administration. I was scarcely listening to them.

I had all the results from the agricultural judges, and I headed up to the station to read the late afternoon news and notices. A Country and Western request programme was running as I took the microphone, and soon I was relaxing with a glass of wine.

'Here is a request from the Laundry Girls to the newly weds in the green Holden at the Southpac Hotel – *Great Balls of Fire* by Johnny Cash.'

The radio technician was becoming justifiably restive about my drinking on air during these sessions. An upset glass of claret some months before had already 'fertilised' within the mixing console, causing thousands of dollars' worth of damage. He had been reasonable at first, until I began to permit rock musicians and jazz fanatics their own alcoholic late-night programmes. The groups Slade and Led Zeppelin particularly upset him and the older listeners. Then he was diagnosed with cancer of the larynx.

'They took the lot,' he informed me laconically after the operation. I admired his courage. Now he communicated with an electronic vibrator held to his neck that buzzed in a strange disembodied tone, like a computer synthesising speech.

He flared up when he saw me drinking wine with the band leader in the studio, and he decided to switch off the transmitter. I received a phone call telling me we were off the air.

'Get out! Get out!' he shouted through the machine in synthetic, gothic sound. The situation was awful. I expected to be called in and sacked the next minute by the Official Secretary, and fled to *Almira's* in a mood of despair. She was asleep in the gloom of her little shack attached to the rear of the house, the bed covered in half-finished letters, suitcases disgorging clothing. Struggling up she smiled affectionately.

'Hello Almira! Watawaieh yu?' I asked in my best Norfolk.

'All the better f' sii yuu, darl! Kam in a' haus, you look like you need a drink! Have you seen a ghost?'

I had in fact seen a figure I thought to be Nathan pass through the garden. Probably my imagination. The whiskey was soon tumbling reassuringly into the glass, and the Tahitian fish was pushed out. I told her the whole story as the marinaded fish and alcohol soothed my emotions.

'You've got an evil streak, boy, but I love you furret. Storms pass. Not to worry.'

'Not this one, Almira. Anyway, thanks for the drink. Ai staartin home. Ai es pretty down,' I said. 'By the way, is Nathan back?'

Her face lost much of its joy. 'Yes, darl. He's working down at the crusher. Seems much better.'

'That's good,' I said.

At the tracking station I lay on my bed and stared at the rows of globes in the ceiling, the cobwebs, the slowly descending spiders, and reflected on the futility of explanations. I had never intended to upset this unfortunate man. Clearly my days as Broadcasting Officer were numbered if these reports became official complaints. And now Nathan was back.

I was due that evening at Drumminor for the final opera in the Fitzroy Douglas season – Verdi's *La Forza del Destino*. It seemed a great effort to 'dress warmly', drive across the island and light my mosquito coil among the elderly English. I took a seat on the verandah after a quick look at the cast list on the bistro blackboard. Clouds were scudding across the moon. Pleasantries passed by me unnoticed like night moths, but the music created an irresistible atmosphere under the shadowy bougainvillaea.

The three leaden hammer blows that began the haunting overture to the opera held a particular poignancy. I felt them as an obscure premonition, strokes across my heart. I tried not to dwell on this intuition, and I was soon distracted by a visitor to the island who was seated among the audience. Fitzroy Douglas seldom invited tourists to a performance, so I wondered who he and his pretty girlfriend were.

'Do approach the cold collation, old boy, guavas and ice-cream, tea and biscuits if you wish.' Fitzroy offered refreshments in his customary affable manner before calling me over to the brocade armchair. He introduced me then to David Rossiter, a young conductor on holiday, who was soon to begin a season at the Sydney Opera House with a performance of Wagner's *The Flying Dutchman*. Blonde-haired, Cambridge-educated, good looking and immensely talented, Rossiter was lamenting the small size of the orchestra pit in the Opera House and the difficulty of staging Wagnerian opera there.

'Oh, you're the chap who presented that erudite programme on Paganini the other evening,' he said.

'Well, I only played recordings of his violin music and read the account of his bizarre funeral,' I said. 'Thanks. It's good to know someone is listening.'

'Quite unexpected in this remote part of the globe. Perhaps I could visit you at the studio one evening?'

'Certainly. Come over on Sunday about eight. I'll be presenting some Erik Satie. Enjoying your stay?'

'A magnificent island...'

Alice, Fitzroy's charming and hospitable wife, was ringing the interval bell, which meant we were to return to the verandah for the final act. The green coils spread their killing perfume and the musical enchantment gathered again over the garden.

On the following Sunday evening I went to collect David from the *'Hibiscus'* holiday apartments. He appeared at the door bare to the waist in his shorts, with his girlfriend hovering in the lightest of dresses behind. One side of his face was covered in shaving foam, and he held a razor suspended in one hand. He looked young and full of energetic inspiration.

'I'm attempting to achieve that smoother cheek! Won't be a second!' he called jauntily and disappeared back inside.

We drove to the station, and as usual I had to shoo away the thin cows taking refuge under the awning at the entrance. I started up the transmitter, relayed the Radio Australia news and read the local notices before introducing the programme.

'Good evening, everyone, and welcome to another Sunday evening of classical music and drama on this beautiful South Pacific island. This evening we will address a few of the difficulties in approaching more modern classical music. Why do people resent it so, even denying it the appellation "music" at all?

'The origin of much alienating twentieth-century music remains a mystery to many. Consider that an important question had to be addressed as the century began. Where was music to proceed after the death of Richard Wagner? The music of Claude Debussy provided one avenue of development and that of Arnold Schoenberg another. Tonight we will examine the work of one of Debussy's friends, one who influenced him greatly, one of the most eccentric composers of *la belle époque* in France, the Montmartre piano player Erik Satie. Although not a "great" composer his attitude to art, life and his career provides us with an illuminating example of traits common to many misunderstood twentieth-century artists.

'He was born in Honfleur on the Normandy coast in May 1866 of mixed French and Scottish stock and died in Paris of cirrhosis of the liver in July 1925. Two hundred umbrellas and a hundred handkerchiefs were found in his sordid room after his death. Did they inspire him to embrace the absurd?

'The mosaic-like structure of his small scale piano pieces have an elegant simplicity. Many of his works present different places, times and states of consciousness simultaneously rather than the linear development of the more classical music we are familiar with. The furore he aroused among Paris audiences with his ballet score *Parade* and the dramatic symphony *Socrate* give us the first indications of a new musical aesthetic in the process of development that owes nothing to German Romanticism. Satie commented interestingly in one of his last notebooks:

'"Experience is one of the forms of paralysis." By this he meant that the accumulated lessons of experience tend to remove our spontaneity and ability to take creative risks. He was a humorous, passionate, most of all courageous advocate of freedom of form. In the *Guide du concert* for the first performance of the strangely static music of *Socrate* he wittily stated:

'"Those who do not understand are requested to assume an attitude of submissiveness and inferiority."

'His titles and instructions on interpretation were equally ironic – a piece instructed to be performed *"like a nightingale with a toothache"*.

'We shall begin with probably the most famous of his piano pieces, the *Gymnopédies* and the *Gnossiennes* written in 1888 when he was playing the piano at a cafe in Paris called the Chat Noir. They are curiously static, almost childishly simple and fresh – once heard they can never be forgotten – in a word an extraordinarily modern phenomenon in the contemporary world of Brahms and Verdi. They are played here by Aldo Ciccolini.'

As the first haunting bars floated through the ether over the island, David turned to me in surprise.

'Does the island audience appreciate all this?' he asked.

'Of course. There is an enormous love and understanding of music here. So few outside distractions means they can concentrate on the essentials of life.'

'Amazing. The operas at Drumminor are incredible. Alice and Fitzroy are wonderful people.'

'Well, Fitzroy has his moments. He's always writing to the paper about the cohorts of socialism taking over the island. Look, coffee and warm Apfelstrudel will be here presently from the Garrison Club. You are welcome to stay. In fact I'd love to have a long chat about music.'

'You must've studied music at some time,' he said. He naturally failed to realise he had touched a raw nerve.

'Gave it up,' I replied. 'No outstanding talent.' I smiled ingenuously, but I felt wretched with this casual admission of the failure of a cherished dream.

'Pity. Why don't we meet somewhere tomorrow?'

'Fine. I could take you out to the satellite tracking station where I live, and we could walk along the cliffs.'

'Excellent idea.'

'Perhaps we could voyage among the stars with Stockhausen and his mighty work *Hymnen* in the evening?' I suggested, very tentatively.

'Well… Messiaen and Boulez are about my limit! But of course conducting Verdi is my great passion.'

The encounter with David and my impulsive invitation made me realise that I was missing the possibility of intellectual companionship and conversation about music far more than I would care to admit.

CHAPTER XXII

*'What one dreads most in love inevitably
comes into being by an unknown law
that governs the consummation of fears.'*
Norfolk Island Journal 1972

Nathan never returned from his demoniacal ascent of Mt. Pitt
during the cyclone. The hospital sent out a search party, but
they were unable to track him down for some days. They combed the
dense rainforest on Mt. Bates near the magnificent Palm Glen and
King Fern Valley. He was finally found, very weak and ill, sheltering
in the famous hollow tree that had once concealed the legendary
convict Barney Duffy for seven years from the searches of the garrison.
Nathan was placed under strict control, although now this was hardly
necessary, as he had always appeared and acted like a gentle subversive.

It was necessary to fly him off the island for treatment and this
meant a special RAAF Hercules had to come from Australia. This
sort of mercy flight was not common, and the throbbing whine of the
huge aircraft alerted the whole population. His departure was public
and painful, and Almira was deeply upset. I spoke to Mareva about
it, and she was more worried that he had somehow been spying on us
up on the mountain during the cyclone. Perhaps that had driven him
to desperation.

'You don't know what he can do!' she said. 'Always silently
watching. He is a devil sometimes, intelligent and cunning. I'm not
sure he's even sick!' This surprised me, but I gave it no more thought
at the time. She seemed obsessed with hidden eyes, secret observers.
The island did erode your privacy.

'I had wan very strange feeling when we were up on the mountain.'
'When will he come back to the island, do you think?'

'No idea. When he wants I suppose. They can't detain him as he's not certified. He just wants wan trip a' Sydney,' she said. 'He just appears and disappears.'

A pause followed by a probe.

'Mareva, where have you been the last few days?'

'I had a lot on up at the hospital,' she said defensively. 'Those tourists are always falling off their motorcycles on to the coral road. Makes quite a mess of them sometimes.' She glanced away too quickly.

'Who were you with at the Show?'

'He works in ar Commonwealth Bank. Ai thort hi es riel gud an.'[78]

My stomach clenched instinctively. 'How can you *do* this?' I said. 'I thought we had a special understanding.'

'Well, one night I saw you talking so close with that girl painter from Australia who wears those red tights and micro skirt. The one who looks like a fish. And I saw you together laughing and talking with that blonde owner of the *Norfolk Hotel*, who is well past it.'

'That was nothing at all. We were discussing art.'

'Well, I was discussin what I was discussin with the tall man from the bank. I'm not a big intellectual like you.'

'Love has nothing to do with the intellect, Mareva. It's intuition, the coming together of two kindred spirits.'

'And I hate all this educated flowery talk! I just want to enjoy myself. You just go off to your 'Fish' en pat in.[79] Hope you enjoy the cold!'

There was hurt in her voice, and I did not quite follow the language as she lashed out in pain. I realised an additional rhythm had entered the pattern of our communication through lack of vigilance of the heart. If I removed my intense focus on her perhaps I could avoid the destructive erosion of jealousy. We agreed not to meet for a few days. The usual story, not at all exotic.

∞

There were many strange and eccentric characters on Norfolk Island to distract me from my heartache, but none more remarkable than William Forester. He had a Duty-free shop selling electronic equipment, not far from my coffee house, and he had a passionate love for the flora and fauna of the island. His shop assistant was an amateur historian of great wit. Missionary zeal shone from his bearded face. This and a slight stoop convinced me he was a naturalist truly inspired by faith. He vehemently opposed threats to the bird life posed by the rumoured arrival of jet services from the mainland, and he mounted a strongly reasoned defence concerning noise.

'Noise Exposure Forecast contours do not apply as ambient noise level is not really considered. People do not seem to fully appreciate this problem. Horses will bolt and carts overturn. Migratory birds will fail to nest,' he told the local newspaper, the *Norfolk Islander.*

William was a natural scientist in the eighteenth-century sense. He gave me the priceless gift of sight, the ability to recognize plants, birds and insects in the confused and overgrown jungle of the rain forest. I shared his passion, although he probably thought me a skater.

'If you look carefully, you will notice a curious symbiosis between the white oak, *Lagunaria patersonia* and the Norfolk pine, *Araucaria heterophylla.* They often grow together in a curious twinning pattern, see? Pines with their seedlings are like mother and child, aren't they?'

The afternoon that Nathan was flown out, William took me on a special tour of the reserves. We met at Cascade, near the Digestor of the old whaling station, and drove to the summit of Mt. Bates. The vista was more extensive than from the summit of Mt. Pitt, with panoramic views of Point Howe in the north-west of the island. A sense of the intense isolation of Norfolk, one of the most remote islands in Oceania, was quite pronounced from this elevated position. The tiny land mass contrasted strongly with the immense expanse of encircling sea stretching to the horizon. Paulina had described this vista in a similar way in her journal.

The air was soft, and metallic-blue butterflies danced in the sun above the flowering lantana lodged among ferns in an old American war excavation. We walked through a particularly dense stand of stately Norfolk palms, less disturbed by man and therefore more impressive than at Palm Glen. Immense King Ferns, Cabbage Trees and Tree Ferns almost blocked the light oases of dappled green. William referred to this area as Mt. Cross, the 'unknown' third mountain of the island. We passed gnarled bloodwood trees with nasty stains of blood-red sap dripping down the trunk, growing beside convict saw pits. Clouds of flying ants lodged in our hair, but William slashed on through the forest, oblivious to the bites, like a man possessed. Much of the reserve was choked by invasive species, wild olive, wild tobacco and red guava, introduced in convict times.

At last we approached the Captain Cook Memorial commemorating the discovery of the island, actually on my birthday, October 10th, 1774.

'As a child I would clap my hands and watch the sea-birds rise,' William said.

'It must have been wonderful to spend your childhood here. Tell me, William, why did Cook name it *Norfolk Isle?*'

'Before he left England, the Duchess of Norfolk made him promise to name one island after her that he discovered on the voyage.'

'Did he like the island?'

'He thought the pines could be useful for spars and masts. The Polish naturalists on board the *Resolution* thought the parrots were infinitely brighter coloured than anything they had previously seen in Oceania.'

We climbed down the gentle hills towards the Cascade Stream, which led past the site of another failed island industry, the Fish Factory. Avocado, certified bean seed, bananas, lemons, macadamia nuts, passionfruit, Tung Oil trees, poultry, fish, whale oil – all these potential industries had faded away, leaving tourism. The white oaks set against the slopes in an area nearby called the Cockpit looked like the vessels and capillaries of a giant human cell projected on the hillside.

The sun was setting as William introduced me to his mother, sitting peacefully on the immaculate brown-painted verandah of their Pitcairner home. Like many of the older people who had been born or lived on Norfolk for many years, Agnes looked radiant and beautiful. Her eyes gleamed blue and miraculously clear, her skin was pure and translucent. There was a fineness of vibration about her that defied analysis. The house had a strong atmosphere of goodness and devotion.

I had promised Almira that I would come to the airport to give her moral support when Nathan was leaving, and I slipped away briefly from the Forester home. Almira was sitting in her car, and she seemed low in energy, although she still looked elegant with that aristocratic poise she always possessed in a crisis. She pressed my hand to her breast where a hot water bottle nestled to combat the chilly evening coming on and tears flooded her eyes but did not flow. She was too proud for emotion to betray itself in public. Internally, I am sure, she was churning. Crowds gawked at the aircraft as a notable event in their otherwise unruffled day. The heavy rumble of the engines of the Hercules troubled the air after the loading was complete, and Almira left before take-off.

'Thanks for coming down darl,' she whispered.

I made my way back to the Foresters'. Agnes was making me some Valerian tea, and William was cleaning his shotguns. We were shortly to go hunting feral cats on the cliffs at Duncombe Bay in the north. We peeled some superb oranges, the finest I have ever eaten, from an old tree mulched religiously for years. The air over the entire island was pulsing now with the whine of the four great engines at full throttle. She was speaking to me in quiet tones about the Bible, and its message of the body being the Temple of God. Her voice was all but drowned out and the wooden house shook as the Hercules sped along the grass runway and climbed above the pines.

'We have a duty to care for the body… of the spirit,' she said then. 'We must love ourselves… this temple and tabernacle of Christ.' The rest of her sentence was lost in the clamour of trembling windows as the giant transport passed overhead, and the throbbing faded slowly over the ocean.

∞

William approached cat hunting not as a sport, but as a means to save the threatened species of island birds.

'We must conserve the brilliant Green Parrot,' he said. 'It is under terrible threat from the Red Parrot and these blessed cats. Just a few pairs remain. Philip Island could be used for an isolated breeding programme.'

'How many species of bird are extinct, William?'

'Probably six or seven. The Bird of Providence or Providence Petrel is returning. Almost two hundred thousand were eaten during the winter of 1790 by the starving penal settlement. The lighted torches were said to have attracted them down to their deaths like hail.'

'Good God!' I exclaimed. I was always amazed at the unconsidered massacres of fauna in those days. But if I had been starving, wouldn't I have done the same?

Early in my stay on the island I had noticed small depressions along the cliff edge where the feral cats had killed the seabirds – mounds of bloodstained feathers, munched wing roots or torn out burrows. The delicate fairy terns, robins and fantails were favourite prey. On the grassy slopes of Duncombe Bay they pounced on the little blackwinged petrel and fiendishly tore out only the breast of the bird to eat. Hunting through moonlit nights was popular, as the cats came out then in greater numbers. It was argued that their lives should be spared because they kept down the rat population, but William was having none of that. His policy was a torch shone from the path to trap a cat's glittering eyes its beam, followed by a shot through the head from the second hunter.

On this excursion we had with us an entomologist named Giles, dressed in a plastic anorak and bottle-end glasses. He was collecting and describing the island moths and insects, which had never been 'worked' by the national museums. He carried blue mercury-vapour lamps and large nets, which he set up then like isolated pools of waterlight among the trees and creepers of the rain forest. The swarms of flying insects and moths fluttered dementedly, trapped and imprisoned by their legs in the fine mesh suspended before the lamps. He carefully picked them off the gauze and placed them in the killing jars where they soon lay twitching, later to be classified. Some were given names associating them with island families – *christiani, buffetti...*

Early evening. We saw a few pairs of petrified eyes gleaming in the darkness, and I even got off a couple of shots at them. Then there were scampering sounds in the undergrowth, no bodies, perhaps just a drop of blood. The sighing of the surf below was accompanied by the shearwaters' mournful cries floating up from their burrows.

William's stooped form was silhouetted against the moon as he crept before me along the cliff, swinging his shotgun from right to left, following my torch beam like a military scout on alert. Sometimes we missed our footing on the crumbling edge above the raging sea, sometimes we broke through the roofs of burrows and wrenched our ankles. There were some close moments.

'There's one!' William hissed, as two points of reflected light were mesmerised in the torch beam. A shot echoed round the sheer slabs of basalt. With a piercing yowl the feral cat launched itself into the abyss, a dark form arching over the rocks in the moonlight to disappearing to a violent and unseen death far below. This ferocious hunt was all the while accompanied by the eerie moaning of the ghost birds and in the distance the spectral blue pools of Jeremy the *'mother'* floating within the gloomy forest. The sense of having entered an enchanted yet ominous world was inescapable. Beauty and cruelty hand in glove once again.

'Ah! Got him, the killer!' William would sigh each time, his duty towards the rare birds of Norfolk Island accomplished again.

CHAPTER XXIII

'Fish baiten guud!'[80]

*D*avid Rossiter had decided to come with me on a fishing trip, and we met one morning at the Kingston pier as dawn broke. Joe Christian was taking us out in his launch. The surf over the Bar was quiet, and the crossing uneventful. We headed towards the far side of Philip Island, across water marked on old charts as *'very foul ground'*, a distance of four miles. Philip Island was a man-made red desert, precipitous, waterless and the home of hundreds of rabbits. Some were carnivorous, and others had evolved long front paws to climb and feed on the few remaining trees. The pigs and goats introduced by the sporting garrison officers of the penal settlements had long since eaten the remaining vegetation and died out.

As the launch pitched in the strong swell, Joe pointed out the highest peak on this incredible moonscape. He told us about the mass escape of convicts to the island led by 'Black John' Goff in 1826.

'About fifty of dem stole aa boats from the settlement and rowed across. The exhausted and drunk convicts were all asleep when the military arrived on Philip early dar next day to catch dem. The convicts rushed up to the peak and hid in some caves up there. No food. No water. No boats.

'Black John' fought like a demon to the end, but he was finally brought back alive to Norfolk badly wounded, and sent to Sydney, and tried and hanged. Sharks got a lot of them who tried to swim across! One bored two holes in a door for his legs. His toes got bit off! Haw! Haw!'

The water around the edge of the sheer cliffs was stained rust-red by the eroding soil. It helped us imagine the feeding sharks.

'*Are* there many sharks in these waters?' asked David's girlfriend, Kirsty, in that particularly tremulous tone affected by the English when visiting the Antipodes.

'You bet! We'll probably catch one!'

Our hand lines had clusters of baited hooks, and we pulled in two and three sweetlip or trumpeter at a time. These would be delicious, cooked on the open fire of the barbecue I was planning for the evening. The baskets were soon full of struggling fish and their blood stained the water around the hull. The silver shadows of scavenging sharks began to rise from the depths. I was about to comment on this, when Joe's only fixed line snapped taut. He began to play the fish.

'Ai bin tal yu wi would catch us wan shark!' he shouted. 'Either that or it's a Japanese net.'

The shark was not huge, but when it finally reached the side of the boat it rammed its head at the planking.

'Hold the line and hand me the gaff!' Joe shouted.

He pulled the grey shark into the boat, and it began to thrash about. Its skin was scarred by battles, infested with parasites. He clubbed it across the head and it lay there twitching convulsively and emitting a stinking yellow fluid from its rear. The teeth were small, but they were evilly discoloured and razor sharp. He decided to fillet it immediately, and his knife quickly revealed the reeking entrails and shivering spine. He threw all that back into the sea, and other sharks rose to tear at the remains of their companion. My mind slipped back to Paulina's description of the mighty shark that was landed on the *Fairlie* when she sailed to Van Diemen's Land in 1836.

'How is the fishing in general, Joe?' David asked.

'The fish are getting less and less, poached by the Japs, mainly. We ask the tourists to give us the fish they catch but you're all right, 'Hat', keep dem – you're one of us bastards!'

The crossing of the Bar was more dramatic on the way home. Joe gunned the engines at the critical moment, and we surged across the reef slewing to one side. He would go out again later in the day, but we took a few fish each, left the rest and headed towards home for a late lunch.

'See you this evening for the barbecue, David,' I said. 'Pick you up around seven. I'll take you out to the tracking station from the *Hibiscus.*'

*'…each mistrustful scorpion generating the next,
more loathsome than before.'*
Norfolk Island Journal 1972

What was it made me take a turn along Emily Bay before heading off to Gannet Point? It turned out to be a fatal decision for my psychological equanimity. Perhaps I simply wished to swim and sunbathe, but as I got out of the MG I saw Mareva lying alone on the deserted beach. This was unusual, but I was excited to see her after our separation. I ambled past the ruins of the Salt House and along the edge of the bay.

Wavelets broke on the sand in quick succession. She was lying on her stomach, probably asleep, and so I admired her silently for a few minutes. She was wearing only a red crocheted bikini bottom, which revealed her superb tanned buttocks. Regular swimming had made them firm, and they were dusted lightly with sand and a few glinting crystals of salt. Her face was hidden in the crook of her forearm, with her thick hair fallen across it, cascading down her back like a *vahine*. Cicadas roughed their whirring scales in the coarse grass above the beach and a breeze blew wisps of hair in drifting filaments. I knelt before that golden body and brushed my lips lightly over her bottom, tasting her salty heat.

'Mareva, Mareva,' I murmured. She moaned slightly, and then she spun round as she woke.

'Oh, It's only you,' she said. She sounded disappointed.

'I missed you terribly,' I said.

'That's nice,' she said.

Grains of sand clung to her breasts, and the tiny lacework scarcely covered her impudent pubic hair. Her face was soft and warm from sleep. She flicked some curls from her eyes, and made a desultory attempt to put on her top, but it was so small that her nipples kept escaping, springing or pressing slowly through the open weave. It aroused me like fire. We both smiled uncomfortably but we did not kiss.

'I'm waiting for someone,' she said. 'But come now and swim with me.'

We dived into the bay and played like dolphins in the water, swimming between each others legs, nibbling and feather-touching the tender parts like fish. We swam to the tethered pontoon, and lay on the heated planks, breathing heavily. Her bikini clung tight and small, and the water cascaded off her powerful limbs and stained the bleached wood like spreading blood as she wrung her heavy hair. She lay down beside me then and pressed her cooled body against mine.

'Kiss me, Mareva. Kiss me. I'm desperate for you,' I whispered, and her lips and tongue sent me into a sort of waking oblivion.

'Can't we start again, from the beginning?' I looked into her closed eyes. Silence and the hush of the surf. She did not answer me. I lay on my back and stared into the sun, allowing it to blind my sight and scorch my body. The pontoon rocked gently as waves broke over the reef. We lay there slowly warming, listening to the hypnotic surf.

'How es daa "Fish"?' she suddenly said.

'All right I suppose. I have hardly seen her.'

'Dana lai! You spent the whole of the other night with that cold flesh. Yu two miek aut[81] all the time!'

'What?' I said. I pushed myself on to my elbows to look at her. Gulls wheeled overhead, cormorants dived for minnows.

'I know all about it. Everyone knows.'

'It means nothing. She's just someone to talk to. Why do you call her "Fish", anyway?'

'On Norfolk we have one nick-name for everyone. Shi es as cold as dead fish eyes. I can tell you everything about her! Yu gwen a' haew trabl lornga daa wan boy!'[82]

'You don't even know her.'

'She's one of those arty types,' she said almost with contempt. 'They're all the same, playing at nature, not part of it. Anyway, Shi daa morga.'[83]

'That's ridiculous, Mareva,' I said. 'Anyway, you're changing into a city girl yourself. The whole island is changing.'

'So? We're just as modern as you mainlanders!' she countered defensively.

'Well, you're losing that simplicity I love so much,' I said. 'You're becoming just a fashion plate, and all you talk about is money.' I knew this was unfair, but I kept on.

'Really? Hau peti!'[84] You said you loved me, but now I really don't believe it. You're lying again! You're so wrapped up in your own precious "artistic" feelings! Yu nor mien anaf f' mii.[85] Anyway, now that you've started to pat in with the "Fish" I've decided I'm free.'

'What do you mean, *free?*' I said. I was beginning to feel trapped like fishbait.

She laughed blithely, kissed me deeply again, and then dived into the bay and swam strongly to the shore. It seemed to take just seconds, her actions spinning out of my control. I saw her tiny figure walk up the beach and stop, and I saw it joined by a taller figure. I watched her, paralysed by indecision. Did they embrace, or was it just the effect of the shimmering heat rising off the sand? And then they were gone, and I lay back on the pontoon and tried to allow the tumult of emotions to subside. I hoped the sun would burn out the primitive jealousy that was growing in my heart. I lay there for some hours, following the clouds that had stalled over the island, generating unworthy scenarios.

CHAPTER XXIV

Chairman: *'There is another class of crimes too frightful even for the imagination of other lands… crimes which are notorious – crimes that, dare I describe them, would make your blood freeze, and your hair to arise erect in horror upon the pale flesh.'*
Molesworth Select Committee on Transportation
February, 1838

'Good God! If we miss the chance of punishing ten men, what will the Commandant say?'
Anonymous Constable
at Norfolk Island, 1846

*A*fter returning to the tracking station in this febrile condition, I was not anxious for a visit from David Rossiter or my friends. But the island had few telephones, so I could not contact them to suggest a change of plan. I put the enormous speakers out on the cliffs and set out some deck chairs – wine in the cooler and Tahitian fish on the table, coarse bread and freshly churned butter. Later in the evening we were expecting visitors for a barbecue. The steak was quietly marinading in a plastic bucket as I laid the fire.

I collected David from the Hibiscus Apartments, and we drove back to Gannet Point. Kirsty had a bad case of sunburn, and she was staying in bed until the evening. The road was bumpy and the holes in the passenger floor made the trip dusty and uncomfortable. The beautiful potter was standing by her studio window, and she gave me her usual wave. The late afternoon sun was setting as we drove up to the tracking station and large numbers of fairy terns were fluttering in pairs above the branches of the pines in the adjacent valleys, uttering their guttural 'yek, yek'. We sat in the deck chairs at the cliff edge facing out to sea. I poured some wine into large glasses and lit my meerschaum pipe.

'Listening to music on Norfolk Island is one of the finest experiences life can offer,' I said.

'It's a magnificent position to listen to Wagner. Such majestic cliffs.' He looked out over the vast expanse of gilded sea and sky to the horizon.

'Yes, particularly in moonlight at the dead of night. One can really ride the erotic oceans of his mind. Let me put on the overture to *Tannhäuser?*'

I could not reveal just how significant this opera was in my present dilemma, ensnared as I was within my own Venusberg. The powerful opening chords created an immediate enchantment. The narcotic effect of those melodies advanced inexorably over the spirit. The affirmation of the conclusion with its waterfalls of strings over rock delivered a monumental impact. We sat in silence at the close, darkness coming on, the sigh of the rollers on the reef, the terns like tiny angels in the pines above.

'Why did you come to this remote island?' he asked.

'To escape, I suppose. I rather lost my bearings.'

My voice failed me. How could I ever explain to this eminent musician my loss of confidence. Another drink, and we decided to stroll along the bluffs discussing pianists.

'Conducting at the Opera House in Sydney must be a wonderful experience.'

'Great opportunity for my career, and to see Australia. Although just between you and me, I'm more excited about the invitation to conduct Wagner at Bayreuth.'

'You lead a charmed life, David.'

But the conversation turned, as it invariably did, however eminent the visitor, to the convict past. We retraced our steps and the ruins came into distant view.

'This *is* an amazing place! Why did the British finally stop sending prisoners here?'

'Well, basically, it was too expensive to maintain the military garrison and the settlement was incapable of being self-sufficient. Then of course there was the prevalence of *the unmentionable.*'

'What was that?'

'Well, the place was known as *Sodom Isle* in the nineteenth century. The Victorians hardly dared mention the crime by name – *"inter Christianos non nominandum"*[86]. Many convicts were addicted to *"the unrestrained indulgence of unnatural lusts"*, to quote one colourful pastor.'

'The love that dare not speak its name and all that. Was homosexuality so rife then among the prisoners?'

'Absolutely! The men were herded together at night like cattle. Lights were forbidden in the barracks. There was an immediate scuffling from hammock to hammock as they sought a little human warmth and comfort. One fearfully crowded cell was known whimsically as *The Nunnery*.'

A trio of dapper Californian Quail suddenly ran fast into the undergrowth, top knots bobbing.

'Men addicted to it were known as *"fluters"*, *"madge culls"* or *"separate-treatment men"* in the prison.'

'I imagine the government of the day just wanted to shunt the criminal problem to the colonies.'

'Exactly right. Island possessions were immediately snapped up around the globe and investigated as convict settlements – Gibraltar, Bermuda, Mauritius. It was a mania, turning heavens into darkest hell.'

'The sexual horrors would have outraged the Victorians.'

'Of course, but reformers were sometimes unconsciously funny. One declared he felt that *"two is an objectionable number"*'

'Many convicts were young, weren't they?'

'That's right, in their twenties, scarcely criminals at all, petty thieves mostly. And in the final years of the settlement young offenders were sent direct from England to the island and mixed indiscriminately with the colonial Old Hands, those *"grown grey in crime"*. Young boys, known as *"colonial women"*, were simply raped and passed around like dolls. It was often a way of wielding power rather than sexual attraction. The old lags gave their vitiated young favourites the names of girls – Bet, Prudence, Kitty, Polly – announced their marriages and became passionately jealous if they as much as looked at someone else – that type of thing.'

'How appalling! What would the Victorians have made of modern life, I wonder?'

'Profoundly shocking, I suppose. Apparently the horror etched into the faces of the new men the morning after their first night in the barracks was gruesome. They believed it worse than Hell. Some attempted to blind themselves with cotton seeds, some ate sand. Many chopped off their own fingers and toes. Some contrived mutual suicide pacts. A convict in despair would arrange to kill his friend by cleaving his skull with his spade from behind and then the murderer would be subsequently hanged for the crime.'

A sudden gust of wind made the dark pines creak menacingly above us. Masked gannets were flying in from the sea to their night nests, passing close to where we were sitting.

'And the chaplains? Did they report these abominations?'

'The clergy believed that "the Almighty's scorching anger" would sooner or later descend on Britain for tolerating such demoniacal crimes against nature. The whole dreadful business was finally abandoned.' We stayed quiet for a time, mulling over such mysteries in our imagination as the ocean heaved inexorably below us.

'Were there any women convicts here?'

'Yes, but only during the First Settlement. They were normally imprisoned in the Female Factory in Hobart, which became a hotbed of lesbianism. Queen Victoria couldn't believe it. "No woman would do that," she was reported to have said.'

'How funny!'

'Yes, and how typically unrealistic. Moral life was utterly inverted here. A man was termed "Good" if he was an informer or depraved murderer and "Bad" if he preserved his moral conscience and attended church. It was a complete sabotage of the human heart.'

The last light of day dissolved as the blood-red sun dipped below the horizon. The sky had become a mass of crimson flecked with amber clouds.

'It was known as the *Ocean Hell*, wasn't it?'

'It certainly was. Convicts preferred death to banishment here. During one trial, a group of men who were reprieved from the scaffold but sentenced to Norfolk Island fell to their knees and wept, while those sentenced to be hung threw their caps in the air, kicked off their shoes and shouted "Hurrah!". They wanted to "die game" as it was said.'

We were looking down at the darkening sea breaking over a cluster of rock shards. Pines had collapsed at crazy angles, and other trees had been blown into extreme forms by the wind. The olive lichen hanging from the branches called *'Grandfather's Beard'* stirred in the breeze.

'I am continually amazed by individual cases. Some prisoners shammed madness to escape work, invented a preposterous "Welsh" language in which they failed to communicate with the constables. One convict they suspected of this "crime" was handcuffed to a bedstead; his head was shaved; there was a liquid, something similar to vitriol, that was put on it with a feather and then down the spine, over his two cheeks and the calves of his legs. His skin blistered instantly and the blisters ruptured. The man could not lie down and the wounds took a fortnight to heal. The process was then repeated. The prisoner suddenly became sane and ceased to speak in tongues. This was regarded as an especially clever ruse!'

The faint crackle of gnawing pine beetles in the stump we were sitting on disturbed the silence in a faintly ominous way.

'The convict returns indicate two and a half million lashes were administered in New South Wales from 1830 to 1837. After a flogging session, the sand around the triangle was soaked in gore. Their backs were lashed bare of flesh, sluiced down with a pail of water or their own urine, cooled by the application of banana leaves and then dried in the sun like crackling pork. Sometimes they became infected with sores and crawled with maggots. The stench of this putrefaction in the overcrowded cells at a hundred degrees, mixed with the stink of diarrhoea from overturned night-tubs, was stupefying.'

'Oh God!'

'And how the Victorian authorities abhorred homosexuals! The crime was considered as vicious as murder. One poor wretch had contracted *syphilis in ano* from his lover. The affected part was washed with a flannel and sand in a plunge bath. He said it was worse than death. They pushed a piece of flannel with caustic soda on it up his anus with a stick!'

'Paul, stop! Please! I don't want to hear any more!'

We turned and walked back along a path by the edge of the precipice.

'The atmosphere is spooky at night, though, isn't it?' David said.

'Yes, the air here is somehow infected with these memories. Sorry. I shouldn't have plagued you with all this.'

We wandered back to the tracking station. A fire was burning nearby, and I saw people clustered around it. I thought of showing Paulina's journals to David, because I felt that he would understand their significance. But something stopped me sharing the knowledge. I had actually become possessive of her, known only to me through her manuscript.

People began to arrive for the barbecue party, the pretty Australian painter minimally dressed, the diamond trader and his friend, a beautiful New Zealand philosophy student with Kirsty and two drama students from Whale Beach near Sydney who were smoking a joint. The music became funky. Mareva had said she might come later, but I doubted it. Certainly more people would arrive, many more, if it was a good night. Islanders did not mix readily with mainlanders in a social sense, not out of malice but as one told me, 'we just have a feeling of being of our own blood'.

'Isabelle, beautiful, did you get your temporary residence permit?'
'Sure!'
'And that waitress job at the Southpac?'
'Yeah, I was really pleased! *Wonderful* work setting tables and filling hundreds of bowls with fruit salad at breakfast, lunch and dinner. But the afternoon is free to go to the beach.'
'How long'll you stay?'
'Just for the uni holiday.'
'Still seeing Andrew?'
'Now that *would* be telling!'
There was a brief lull as some wine was passed around.
'Did you go to Millie's wedding at the Mission Chapel last Saturday?'
'Yeah. It was really nice. She wore this heavy white silk shantung gored skirt with daisy edging. She was carrying cream orchids. David looked so handsome.'
'They had the reception at that new restaurant called The Bounty Tavern. So many new places opening, aren't there?'
'Springing up everywhere. The food there was delicious.'

'Did you know they wrote their own vows?'

'Really! Can you remember any?'

'I think part of what they said was "I promise always to respect your needs and individuality" but I can't remember the rest.'

'How really romantic.'

Victor the diamond trader was putting steak, fish, prawns, sausages and potatoes on the grill above the glowing embers. The purple meat emerging from a plastic bucket dripping wine marinade appeared distinctly alarming. Mainlanders never managed to assemble the vast, stylish banquets the islanders miraculously produced. The music had fallen from Cream and The Electric Light Orchestra into the middle ground of Astrid Gilberto. I was surprised to see that Mareva had arrived and was talking to David and Kirsty. They seemed to be having a lively conversation, and I was quite pleased that David had met a real islander after all we had spoken about. I wandered over.

'So you came all the way from England to see us,' Mareva gushed. 'How exciting. I'd love to go to London sometime.'

'Well, not straight to Norfolk exactly. I came here for a holiday from Australia,' David said. 'I have a season conducting at the Sydney Opera House. The batteries are certainly being recharged in the Pacific sun.'

'He didn't want to bring me, but I forced him to,' Kirsty said, rather acidly, I thought.

'And now you've got sunburn,' David said unkindly.

'I pity Kirsty if you were alone on the island among the island girls.' Mareva was indulging her talent for flirting. 'You'd be gobbled up in a twinkling!' She gave him such a frank look, even I was surprised.

'What do you do here?' he asked Mareva.

'I work at the hospital and I paint quite a lot,' she said. 'I really want to go to art college. And I want excitement and travel.'

Victor joined us then from the barbecue. 'Of course I wasn't always a dealer in gemstones,' he was saying to Kirsty. 'I was in the New Zealand Secret Service for many years. Saved us from the machinations of the French in the Pacific.'

'Really! How dreadfully exciting. Do tell me more!'

'I can reveal nothing for twenty years, but I *can* say my phone was bugged and there were spy holes in the ceiling!'

'When David was conducting in Moscow his phone was bugged. Musicians are considered subversive there. Tell me, why do you live on Norfolk?'

Victor looked out over the dim form of Philip Island resting on the slate-coloured ocean. The pines soughed in a gust of wind.

'The friendly concern of people for each other. It's the peacefulness, the quietness. We're barely hanging on to what the rest of the world has lost, or is looking for. But this is beginning to disappear all too quickly now.'

'I think I'd be bored here,' Kirsty said.

'No! A vibrant social life awaits you. Last weekend four hundred people went to the Leagues Club Night Building Fund Raffle. They ate five hundred pounds of prawns and thirty chickens! Then there's the RSL Darts and the Calcutta sweep on the Melbourne Cup. The New Year Races at Kingston are fantastic fun.'

'It's all right, but not a *real* adventure,' Mareva said.

'How is Muriel?'

'She died recently.'

'I *am* sorry. How did it happen?'

'She got tired. She simply got tired of living with her husband and just died.'

Odile was half Spanish and half Corsican. She had studied stage design in Melbourne, and she was visiting Norfolk to help with the preparations for the Pageant. This spectacular show was to be a part of the Bi-Centenary celebrations of the discovery of the island by Captain Cook in 1774, with a visit by the Queen and the Princess Royal.

'Are the preparations going well?' I asked. 'I've heard that you begin rehearsals soon.'

'It's going brilliantly,' she said with bewitching effervescence.

She was quite alluring, in a blue coachman's jacket with boots over slinky burgundy Wolford tights. It was dark now and our faces were only lit by the fire and the house lights. We sat together on the grass, and her Venetian blonde hair glowed in the firelight. She did not strike me as being in the least like a fish.

'The red velvet curtain and pelmet is across the stage at Rawson Hall, waiting for the festoons of gold braid. But there are acres of sets still to be painted. In fact I shouldn't really be here!'

'Are you going back to the mainland after the celebrations?'

'No, I might work on the island for a while.'

'Why don't we have eat together one evening soon and discuss some possibilities. There's the *Commandant's Dinner* at the Garrison Club every Tuesday.'

'Great! What time will you collect me?'

Despite my own revenge flirting, I was painfully aware that Mareva seemed to have disappeared from the party, and I kept wondering where she was. More and more people were arriving, and we were likely to run out of food and drink. Nick turned up the music, and he wandered over to where I was sitting with Odile and a bottle of *Shiraz*. His smile looked dreadfully false.

'Hi, Paul. Listen, man, you have got to do something about the broadcasts of the Council Meetings.'

'Why, what's the problem?'

'All those papers moving about sounds like a washing machine, councillors talk across the table, bangs and wallops. The audience can't hear anything.'

'Could be an advantage, Nick.'

One of the managers of a Duty Free shop collared me, too.

'Hope you're advertising the Chicken and Champagne supper and the Fish Barbecue at the Golf Club next weekend over the air,' he said.

'Sure, sure. But I keep hitting my golf balls into cow pats or the drink! What can I do?'

'We're displaying the winning championship clubs at the shop just now. Why not buy a set and improve your game?' He looked genuinely expectant. His wife was intellectually frustrated with her life on the island, and she had started a regular discussion group with topics such as *'Roman Women – Their History and Habits'*.

David was talking with one of the drama students. They were sharing a bottle of wine on the grass by the fire.

'You must realise that women need to be able to freely exercise the option of independence in a relationship,' she said.

'Sleep around, do you mean?'

'They must feel free to act autonomously. This frees then from guilt.'

'Men are imprisoned in their roles, too. We are victims, too. Look at me, cooking on a barbecue fire!'

'You don't know the depth of your own hatred of women,' she said.

'What have you been reading recently, Paul?' asked David in an attempt to change the direction of the conversation.

'A love story by Benjamin Constant called *Adolphe*.'

'Love! Love!' cried the student. 'Romance is nothing other than the tool of male power that prevents women from understanding their oppression. Read *"The Redundant Male"* if you want truth.'

I tried to think why I had invited this frightful person to the party. It must have been because of her fine blonde hair. Fortunately the fish needed to be served and I rescued David from her arguments. I had come to the island to try to escape that sort of thing.

'Does the island have any political problems?' he asked me, as we moved the seared steak and fish around the grill.

'What a question! Norfolk inevitably becomes a *cause*. There are enormous differences of opinion between the various groups of people living here – the mainlanders, the islanders, the businessmen. Its like the stories of *Scheherazade*, an endless circle of tales postponing the final execution.'

'But the blood of mutineers runs in their veins!' David protested.

'Well a U.N. Delegation was asked recently by "persons anonymous" to investigate Australia's alleged "misrule" of the island. The "slave state" status is the perennial theme. Then there was the petition to the Queen. And now the islanders are selling their inheritance to outsiders and millionaires, and then complaining of the purchase. The island is changing irreversibly. Politics is pretty irrational here. I steer well clear of it.'

'Delicious fish, Nick.' I was tucking into some trumpeter.

'More wine, everyone, if you want it!'

'Isabelle! Did you catch that story of the man stealing ladies underwear from the line outside the Norfolk Hotel? He was fined and deemed *"knick-knack in the knickers"* by the Lions Club.'

'And did you read that dreadful letter in the *Norfolk Islander* where a lady complained that her children were continually called "Bounty scum" by a neighbour? She then questioned the legitimacy of the neighbour's children! Can you believe it?'

Many of Nick's guests crept up to the edge of the cliff in the gloom, glanced around quickly, and threw the disgusting purple steaks to the sharks.

I moved away from these small knots of conversation and wandered along the valley in the half-dark. The sea was still and the full moon reflected off it like a searchlight. Dark shapes moved around the fire, and the throbbing disco music encouraged a few to dance. The scene assumed the appearance of a primitive rite. Nick was rushing about in a frenzy arranging food and drink. David and Kirsty decided to leave early, and I saw them into their hire car.

'Sorry we have to go, Paul, but Kirsty feels a bit dizzy. Must be the strong sun,' David said. 'I'll take her home. I might come back in a while, we'll see.'

I had determined to visit Mareva in secret later. Curiosity gnawed away at me, and I had to find out what she was doing.

CHAPTER XXV

'Once Man was occupied in intellectual pleasures and Energies,
'But now my Soul is harrow'd with grief & fear & love & desire,
'And now I hate & now I love, & Intellect is no more.
'There is no time for any thing but the torments of love & desire.
Jerusalem, Chapter 3
Written and etched by William Blake, 1804-1820

*M*uch later that evening I made the decision to creep up to Mareva's shack on the hill and spy on her. Shame did not enter my mind, just the idea of finding the truth of my suspicions once and for all. I approached the hut from a new direction, and I parked in a small copse. It was not yet fully dark, so it was necessary to be vigilant. The same light stood in the window of the shack as in happier times, and I hid behind a dead tree so I could see into the room from a slight eminence. I put the lens to my eye.

At first I could only see shadows moving in the room. Then, as if a curtain had been suddenly raised, I made out the two bodies fiercely embracing. I was astounded to recognise David on the bed with her. He must have gone round there after leaving Kirsty at the apartments. How incredible! She's irresistible, a tropical *femme fatale*, I grudgingly thought.

Mareva was crouching over his mouth, her golden body, smooth and supple, moving rhythmically in the candlelight. She seemed to be throwing herself against him, her breasts touching his, striking his face, hungry for his body. He lay back entranced by her caresses. She was so wild with him, yet she had always been so romantically passive with me, this whole scene became an agonising revelation. I felt a fierce mixture of emotions – anger, betrayal, mainly desolation in the face of destabilised reality.

A car drove past, and I drew back instinctively. When I looked around the tree again, the harsh bark scratching my cheek, the sight of

Mareva's enjoyment, her fleeting expressions of sensuality glimpsed through her flying hair, struck my face like the lash of a jellyfish sting. Her movements became more and more violent and abandoned. I could no longer watch them approaching orgasm and crept away into the darkness. Had her need for new experiences, modern habits of freedom, seduced her into this? The wings of a dark, predatory bird hovered over me that night as I drove out to the cliffs. I sat staring for hours at a sea the colour of wine.

Now I avoided those parts of the island I knew she would visit. I shunned our customary places of assignation. I could no longer command her desire of me. She still maintained she loved me. Was this possible? Cryptic cards arrived in the post. We tortured each other with messages of promised meetings. I had never wished to stretch far beyond the body with Mareva, and it was her sheer *physical* presence that overwhelmed me when I was with her. The carnal was the source of my jealousy, and I knew the fault lay squarely within my own personality. I was being devoured by a sensual inferno.

The island began to lose the form of the ideal I had foolishly constructed, and the destruction of my illusions began apace. I began to drink more bourbon and smoke grass to blot out the pain, and I looked for other diversions. I was often too hungover to run the station. Broadcasts became unpredictable. Melancholy jazz took up an increasingly large part of my evening programming.

Jerry Jones, one of my colleagues looked up from the console, took the cans from his ears and buttoned up his floral shirt.

'This is Jerry Jones of the middle ground, handing you over to my so-phisticated friend Paul Seagrave, who'll keep you cool and amused into the small hours.'

'Thanks, J.J. Paul Seagrave now on VL-2-NI, bringing you mellow grooves till late and later. Close your eyes with someone you need to hold, settle back until the sun tracks over the beach. Lie by the tide, lovers, and float away high to Miles Davis, from his smooth as silk album, "A Kind of Blue".'

'You still bangin' that Mareva chick, man?' JJ said.
'I'm in love, man, in love.'

'Just you stay alive, man, keep cookin'.' He waved slightly as he left the studio.

The phone rang.

'Paul Seagrave, VL-2-NI. What are you in the mood for?' Soft and slowly spoken.

'Play me some Wes Montgomery, darling. Like "Windy".' Mareva's voice was caressingly gentle against the Miles, and I succumbed momentarily yet again.

Thefts of records from the library began to occur because I had forgotten to lock the studio. I announced this crime one morning, and I was suddenly surrounded by the Commonwealth Police, the Official Secretary, the Administrative Officer and finally the Administrator himself arrived in his Holden limousine. It was gratifying to find that the Establishment listened to my entertainments, but I remained wracked by guilt.

'Paul, you really must exercise some control over yourself,' the Official Secretary said. 'We can't have accusations flying around willy nilly.'

'I've warned you before, Paul. You're trying our friendship,' added the Commodore. 'We may have to let you go if things don't improve. I want a tight ship.'

'I can't help it if people are light-fingered.' I whined, terribly hungover and sick. 'I'll try to be more disciplined, I promise.'

But I hardly changed. I started revenge flirtations that I hoped would hurt Mareva. Even with Kirsty, until the unhappy couple left the island, Rossiter doubtless wielding his Wagnerian baton with abandon in Sydney. After broadcasting finished for the day, I haunted the piano bars at the hotels, playing blues till late, and picked up tanned tourist girls with bare midriffs in thin sarongs. Drunk, I drove them fast down to Emily Bay in the MG, only to vomit disgustingly on the sand, leaning against the chimney of the Salt House, robbing myself of certain pleasure. The girlfriend of a weightlifter was intensively quizzed on whether I compared favourably in the love department to her monstrous friend. Reckless drives alone along the coast at dawn. I was on a slide.

It was a philosophy student, though, who captivated me during this period of dissolution, and she set me on a straighter path. We could carry on abstract arguments at length while consuming dozens of oysters and drinking Mateus Rosé, naked and passionate in bed. The intellectual and sensual appetites were more in balance. Still, she was no substitute for Mareva. Cruelty and intoxication soon overwhelmed me yet again. I loved Mareva and I hated her simultaneously because of this terrible need, this almost physical dependency.

Weeks passed. Almira saw that I was despondent, and she jauntily suggested I get married to an island girl. She came to visit me at dawn one morning with a huge feast of fresh prawns for breakfast.

'You ought to get someone to look after you, boy! But taking you on would be no picnic. Ai es piiti her.'[87] And she expertly tore off the head of a prawn, cracked the shell and removed the tail in one piece.

I could hardly tell her about my problems with Mareva, and nor could I tell anybody else. My work on the station remained celebrated, and it became almost a sport to wager on when the notorious musician would be thrown off the airwaves. I played a lot of Schubert at Gannet Point in those intensely melancholic days and practised with a fervour previously unknown to me. Musical inspiration in compiling the Sunday evenings began to wane, and my life on the island began to lose its focus. Mareva had been an anchor, and now the chain was broken. She was drifting from my grasp, and she had begun to change, I feared permanently. Our love began to shrivel like a marooned starfish in the sun, I determined I had to leave soon, before the island also changed beyond recognition.

Late one moonlit evening Mareva appeared at the door of the tracking station, drunk and tearful, begging a reconciliation. She was wearing black lace-top stockings, sneaking out from beneath the hem of a tiny black lycra skirt, the briefest peach knickers, red cotton top clinging like skin. She seemed an absolute parody of the unaffected natural spirit I had encountered upon my arrival. We kissed lightly.

'Why are you dressed like this?' I said irritably.

'To draw you to me,' she said, draping herself over my shoulder.

'Don't you realise the exact opposite is happening?' I said desperately. 'We've drifted apart. I don't want you all painted and sophisticated.' The moonlit sea was dimly visible through the pines.

'Play the piano for me, Paul. I love your music.'

'And David Rossiter's for sure.'

My remark hurt her. 'I was curious,' she said. 'He was English, and I just wanted to see what it was like. Will you take me to London? Play something, please.' And she ran on and on.

'I will, I will, but we must talk.'

'All this talk! You just think I'm not intelligent enough for you. The "Fish" is a great talker, isn't she? Does she talk when you pat in?'

'Please stop this, Mareva, please. I want you as you were!'

'How was that?' She pressed her face close to mine.

'Natural, unaffected, timeless…'

She put a finger across my mouth, and her lips devoured me. We fell to the tiger-skin rug on the floor, and once again took our rapacious pleasure of each other under the battery of lights. But we could feel by then something common in our sex, the illusions had departed. In some unavoidable way we had corrupted each other. The residual tremors of emotion would be required to run their course before we could release each other completely.

One of my consolations at this time was to read from the final volume of Paulina's journal. She would never permit me to be dismal. The final slip-case had given up its treasure, but the green morocco binding would require repair if it was to be preserved. At night, as I threw myself on the bed under the lights of the tracking station, in despair of ever retrieving Mareva, I could always reach out to Paulina and follow her destiny.

CHAPTER XXVI

'The maize hitherto used for the pigs would thus become available for the
subsistence of the prisoners, which would be highly desirable...
and turned to profitable account...'
George Maclean
Commissariat, Van Diemen's Land, 1848
concerning the piggery on Norfolk Island

'...You will call this cruelty, I call it curiosity, that curiosity that brings thousands to
witness a tragedy, and makes the most delicate female feast on groans and agonies.'
Melmoth the Wanderer by Charles Maturin, 1820

*L*istening to Mozart's *Don Giovanni* and reading Paulina's journal
in the sun had became one of my favourite occupations. My hours of
broadcasting had been cut by the administration. Now I was restricted
to the classical programmes, so I had plenty of time to read and dream,
if not to make love. One glorious morning I was repairing the binding
of the penultimate volume and rearranging the torn pages, when I
noticed a slightly raised thickening of the leather. Something had been
hidden between the board and its calf covering. The ornate seals had
been carefully preserved. Some dessicated petals of an unknown flower
fluttered over the cliff in a freak gust of wind.

Officer's Quarters
Norfolk Island
November 30th. 1846

My dear Paulina

At the ball you asked me to write to you concerning my moods and my
service on Norfolk Island as we are so rarely alone to speak freely. I offer a
brief sketch of my preoccupations.

I remain an outsider and an exile in the Antipodes, yet I am not entirely abandoned to my fate as a former cavalry officer much drawn down by destiny. The *tremendous swell* Captain Vane is my solitary friend among the general boorishness of the officers and soldiers. Their mess is amusingly known as *'The Never'* on account of it never having been cleaned! Thirteen dozen of wine can go in there in the early evening and in the morning a scene of prostrate intoxication, wrecked furniture and broken bottles fascinates the eye. Many hunt wild cats on Philip Island and the heads, paws and tails decorate their rooms as trophies! Plovers, curlews and Lowries are all hunted with passion. But we must nevertheless excuse their low morale. Our regiments are in effect *banished* from Great Britain. A soldier may expect to spend three and a half years in his native land out of twenty-eight years service! Their families are cruelly chosen by ballot *'to go'* or *'not to go'* to the colonies. Only twelve wives are permitted to each one hundred soldiers embarking and there is never sufficient room on the ship. If left unattended in England the family may likely starve. These men are *wrecks* after thirty years service! Their sympathy with the convicts is more surprising then than the more anticipated hatred one would expect.

But Captn. Vane and I often ease our military buttons after parade, smoke our Giant Hungarian pipes together and take more than a glass of Tokay on the cool verandah of the Officer's Quarters overlooking the ocean. In a mood of elegant boredom we hunt, ride, play cricket and cards, read Lord Byron or Bingley's Animal Biography, study languages, drink and yawn together – how we do drink the old Military Port in what one of our officers has named *'The Pongo Mess'* – until the chairs begin to fly like flies around the room! Then there are the balls or *'hops'* and the pic-nics and dinners when we are at it till six o'clock! The other day we fished for Turtles in Cresswell Bay and watched some thrashing killer whales near the coast. In fact we are inseparable companions and have solved all the problems of philosophy, love and horsemanship!

I look out over the Settlement and see fallen men going to their forced labour holding up crossed chains with thongs of leather. They carry lime, boil salt and mine coral. They tear the food with their fingers and drink from the water buckets like beasts. The Military are morally polluted by these degrading spectacles. Why, one young subaltern struck his Commanding officer in the face with his cap hoping to be jailed alongside his convict mistress! The plan failed and he was shot for the offence! The heroic wives of soldiers share the *urine tubs* for natural functions which are then rinsed out and double for washing! The most ribald language falls upon their ears. Corrupt constables and overseers who were once convicts ride the island with portable triangles to flog the victim bloody for each passing misdemeanour. I must desist, for one as you should remain ignorant of such disagreeable facts.

Guarding convicts in such conditions is not my idea of Soldierly Duty, Paulina & I am desperately unhappy.

Yet the background to this hell is the paradise of nature, one of the most beautiful on earth, the setting in which our mutual affection can grow. The sea breaks over the reef in wonderful cleansing whiteness as I write.

Paulina, I have *my duty* to consider above all else. As an Officer in my Regiment I am shamefully neglecting it. The military garrison have great sympathy for these injustices against the convicts. We are ordered to take harsh measures which we avoid and are constantly on the *qui vive* with loaded muskets. And yet if the prisoners escape, God help us!

(This first letter from Captain Zaleski to Paulina, informative rather than romantic, appeared to have some leaves missing so I returned to the journal. Perhaps she kept it just out of sentiment.)

Government House
Norfolk Island
August 30th. 1847

The Ferrers are at last arrived on the island from VDL! After many delays they finally sailed from Hobarton aboard the *Tory*, a barque that formerly carried convicts. We went to Cascades to assist in their landing & they required planks to cross the chasm of rocks boiling with surf! All were fearfully drenched! Major Ferrers made his usual humorous quips in fractured French concerning the vessel & the voyage as he stepped ashore.

'L'odeur "bétail" s'y trahissait de la manière la plus pronocée.'[88] Fanny is heavily with child but will prove a confidante for me in this time of stress & disillusionment. James & Claude were excellent companions in Hobarton so I trust this old friendship will improve James's mood which has become

increasingly distracted of late. We are to take them on their first island picnic to Orange Vale when they are settled in.

The Rev. Valentine has been dismissed from his post! He wrote letters critical of James's methods which reached the ears of La Trobe. The Administration deemed him unqualified for the particular difficulties encountered here. I too found his holier than thou attitudes & specious soft address insufferable. Archbishop Mollison makes another visit to us quite soon & so we must rely on the Anglican chaplain Rev. Bedingfield for the present.

To be in the direct society of Captn. Z. now causes my heart the greatest turbulence. I wake in the middle of the night thinking of him & feel the pressure of this enforced separation from my love. His evident agitation when in my presence & his heightened emotion would betray us in an instant, so I attempt indifference which deceives the spectator, but is often felt by him as cool detachment. *One* of us must contrive to control emotions & I am more naturally equipped by upbringing. His handsome smile no less than his soulful & artistic qualities have thrown me into this love, a disturbance of the spirit that I felt had died long ago. We must maintain a *Platonic* love, the most difficult kind, despite his pressing moods. I continually imagine his lips on mine... and am so desperately ashamed! I cannot escape the island & am perforce thrown into his company almost daily & *must* see him, converse with him & cannot fly my conflict of spirit & temptations. His youthful society captivates me but plunges me into a desperation of vanity at my superior years – I am almost thirty-five! I dare not write my true feelings – I hardly know them – on the chance my journal is discovered. Our convict bookbinder has prepared some fresh journals for me covered in green Morocco – how I yearn to fill them! I have been reading with intense interest that master-piece by Benjamin Constant – the brief French novel called 'Adolphe'. It is an inspired, melancholic & tragic story concerned with the dangers of *borrowing the language of love*. Does Adam truly love me, or is he simply casting around for an occupation of idle hours, playing with my heart as the young Adolphe toys with the sentiments of the older unhappy Ellenore?

(I recently misplaced the key to the lock on my journal, hence the gap of some weeks in the entries.)

Norfolk Island
September 23rd. 1847

Alarums all over the island today! The French are coming! Flags &
coded messages were run up at the Signal Station at Point Ross. Canons
were fired. A number of ships – Nine Sail – appeared on the horizon &
were thought to be the French enemy. They have colonial ambitions in
New Zealand & Tahiti & our security is greatly threatened. One frigate
could devastate us! We are completely defenceless. There was a deal of
activity down at the Settlement where I believe the Irish prisoners – all
considered traitors – were locked into the gaol for fear they would turn
treacherously on the Constables if the enemy attacked. The ships stood off
for five hours when it was finally recognised they were American whaling
vessels in fleet formation searching for one of their number which had been
blown off course.

Norfolk Island
September 30th. 1847

James is become intractable, monstrous & increasingly cruel. He is
desperate to fulfil his duty on the island against the impossible odds of
the system. I understand *why* this is happening but it cannot excuse his
peremptory manner to me. His attitude to the dismissed Mr. Treene, the
Agricultural Superintendant, is shocking to relate.
As previously mentioned, Priscy, the daughter of Mrs. Treene, had been
poorly for some time. I rode out to Longridge Farm to visit her & take
some broth to the little one. Upon arrival, the house was in an uproar with
Constables brutally searching the property. The notorious bushranger
Martin Cash had paid a short visit & was quickly deprived of some eggs
which he had come to collect. Mrs. Treene was beside herself with alarm at
the attitude of the Constables. This was the *second* search by the Police – the
first was at ten o'clock last night. The frightening nature of this ransacking &
subsequent tumult of barking dogs & chaos *without warning* has considerably worsened Priscy's condition.
James is believed to have given his authority for these outrages, citing
that the Regulations must be observed to the letter. The Shepherds &
Stockmen must destroy their gardens in which they take such pride & from

which their health clearly benefits. Mr. Treene feels James wishes to persecute him into resignation & feels much maligned. After quitting the Farm I promised them I would take it up with him at least on the sick child's behalf. James is under a malignant illness of the mind at present & seems ready to knock down everyone! I taxed him with this case this evening & his reply was caustic & irritable.

'Paulina, you are too soft with these people. You must understand that discipline was out of hand on the Island & privileges have proliferated. Treene must be set up as an example to the others. *Fear* is the only force that makes them hop!'

'And their sick child?'

'I told the Constables expressly not to wake her! Paulina, my work is not your concern. *Just do your duty as my wife!* You are taking after Lady Franklin & look what that achieved for Sir John – shameful dismissal. I do not wish the same. I have a proud name in the colony!'

With this fusillade he quitted the room for his study & I was left with a violated heart & a strong sense of injustice. Captn. Z. is the only consolation & refuge for my sentiments now. James is become hard & unapproachable. I must speak to Charles St. Aubyn about his state of mind.

Norfolk Island
November 6th. 1847

There is at last some joyful news! Fanny was delivered of a healthy baby daughter last week & today the infant was Christened by the Anglican chaplain Rev. Bedingfield. We had a small reception here at Government House & were all pleased to observe that God gives life even in the midst of the fallen from grace. Mrs. Webster, Charles St. Aubyn & Emilia & Mr. Ommaney took tea with us as well as some military officers who were friends of Major Ferrers. Mercifully Captn. Z… was absent as my heart could scarce have taken further wrenching.

Charles looked exhausted & has lost much of his former vigour. He says he has enormous quantities of work to perform as the number of punishments is increasing, particularly flogging. Also the prisoners require more nourishing food & are constantly ill with dysentery through lack of a proper diet. One overturned his full night tub & stood on it in the fetid darkness of the cell to read a smuggled book at a chink of light through the door hinge!

Charles tells me the horrors he deals with daily cannot be conceived & are inspired by the devil. Anything & everything can be made a flogging charge. Tobacco has caused an almost insane degree of lashing. The Penal Settlement begins to *utterly dominate our waking hours & our entire thoughts*. He told me a terrible story as we sat on the verandah in the sun.

'A convict attempted to hang himself in his cell, having been accused of indecency in the Lumber Yard. He was discovered just before expiring & James ordered fifty lashes for the offence. I explained the man was near to death & that I would not answer for his life. James then ordered him *strapped down* for six weeks! I remonstrated with him but to no avail. 'One scabby sheep spoils the whole flock, Charles!' he shouted.

I visited the convict some weeks into the punishment & he could scarcely speak but moved his lips like a gasping fish. I placed my ear closer to his mouth in order to hear. After some concentration I could apprehend the words 'Loose me – oh, loose me.' I answered that I dare not against the Commandant's order. He gave a deep sigh from the profound crypt of his soul & tears trickled down his sunken cheeks onto the steel frame to which he was bound. Paulina, it was ghastly. I cannot go on...' I thought Charles would break into tears.

James's work impinges now on my life to an excessive degree because of the concentration of island society. I must escape & help these poor wretches in some way, but I am trapped, imprisoned myself! It is weeks since I have strayed even one mile from Government House. One can so easily forget the therapeutic virtue of Nature's gifts in the shadow of the gibbet.

Norfolk Island
May 3rd. 1848

Halcyon weather today! Last night I read over my Italian journal of eighteen years past when I was at Florence in May 1830. What days of sacred innocence were those! To recapture some of the *brio* of that time I decided to don my Raymond-blue riding habit & take my first truly long ride on *Tempter* for many months. Adolphus was left in the capable hands of our dear friend Hyacinth O'Rourke & I determined before departing that his school work had been well planned. Charlotte & Septimus were deeply engaged at the instrument on some Nocturnes by John Field. I invited Mr. & Mrs. Ommaney from *Victoria Farm*, Mrs. Webster & the Rev. Bedingfield to a pic-nic at Orange Vale. We were accompanied by Captn. Zaleski & his fellow officer Captn. Vane.

The cool air reminded me of the Malvern Hills in spring & with the officers I was soon far ahead of the carriage carrying the rest of the party. Captn. Zaleski & I flew like the wind along an endless romantic avenue of pines – some four hundred trees I believe – towards *Longridge Farm*. *Tempter* trembled with the thrill of galloping at long last. We were quite breathless with excitement at the end of it! I reflected sadly on my last visit to the farm to comfort Mrs. Treene. Priscy passed away shortly before Christmas & was buried in the cemetery at Kingston. I promised to care for the child's grave & keep the flowers always fresh. Mr. Treene & his wife are now returned to VDL. There is a dearth of produce in the yards since they departed, just a few miserable stacks of straw.

I willfully banished all melancholy thoughts, swept up my veil and with *Tempter* tossing her mane in pleasure cantered the short distance down to the stream that runs through the Commandant's garden. The officers could scarce keep pace with me & I laughed at their tardiness.

'Gentlemen, I should join your regiment in the guise of Durova the Cavalry Maiden! Would you have me as an officer?'

'As long as your gender could remain our particular secret Ma'am!' Zaleski was in excellent spirits & a glance from his eyes shot me dead once more.

We set our feast under the cinnamon tree as a change from the oak. Winter is coming on, although the weather hardly deserves such an appellation in this Eden. The presence of banana plantains, lemons, loquats, the dense foliage of the India rubber plant together with the remarkable beauty of the coral trees render it a fairy realm.

Norfolk Island
May 4th. 1848

I was forced to break off the narrative of yesterday as the excessive fatigue of my exertions overtook body, mind and pen.

After our luncheon in this enchanting gully I suggested we ride further along tracks and parts of the coast I had not yet explored. The remainder of the party preferred to tarry & loll in their sunlit bower so I set off with Captn. Zaleski whilst Captn. Vane, giving us a cavalier expression of *killing* complicity, volunteered to stay with them *en garde*.

'A couple of desperadoes have absconded to the glens & have not yet been turned in. One of us should remain on duty here. I'll indulge my rest in the orange grove! *Allez Zaleski!*'

This appeared so natural & charming an offer that the least suspicion could not have arisen so Captn. Zaleski & his sweet devotee cantered along the track towards some tracts of cultivated land called '*One Hundred Acre Farm*'. Much of the soil in this region is a rich rust colour. The area is considered the *bijou* of the cultivated sections of the island & has been cleverly managed in the way of clearance & provision of wind-breaks. Wonderful vistas were provided us in this portion exceeding all imagining. The cultivation of grain resembles lofty lawns suspended above the ocean.

'Paulina, this is the first occasion we have managed to be alone together & in the company of Nature,' remarked Zaleski as we trotted towards the track leading to Anson's Bay. He cuts such a fine figure on his horse dressed in a dramatically short scarlet shell jacket with green pointed cuffs & the blue forage cap of his regiment. His tight breeches caused my heart to race and his boots gleamed in the stirrups.

'Let us take the the full advantage of it!' I cried & urged *Tempter* into a canter as we recrossed the stream flowing from Orange Vale & rode back onto the track down Barney Duffy's Gulley & past the Marjoram Farm. Occasionally we glimpsed the Delft-blue ocean through the pines until we gained the open space above Anson's Bay. It was a magnificent ride through undulating forest with many unexpected panoramas.

Panting for breath I dismounted & contemplated the running swell breaking in massive billows on the crags that stretched along the coast. *Tempter* was slightly lathered & her flanks trembled with the exertion. Captn. Zaleski trotted up & let himself down beside me on the grass. We sat in silence for a time, leaning against the trunk of a vast pine & listening to the crashing of the surf on the boulders far below.

'The sea rages over the rocks like the passion in my heart,' he whispered ardently with disconcerting intensity.

'Adam, you must not speak of these feelings – already I can neither eat nor sleep. At any event some desperate assassin may be watching us!' I countered in a not altogther convincing manner.

'When you received my second letter, how did your heart respond?'

'It contained all I had forever hoped.'

He reached into the pocket of his scarlet jacket.

'I have here a small gift for you,' he told me & pressed into my hand an antique silver pill-box of the finest workmanship with a rampant horse engraved on the lid & the date *1686*.

'It has been in my family for generations but I give it to you as a sign of the depth my true affection,' he murmured & gently kissed me on the forehead. I shamefully confess to collapsing in his arms. He removed my riding hat, his fingers toyed with my curls & his lips lightly brushed my cheek. I loosened the piece of cherry ribbon I had tied about my neck & pressed it into his palm.

'Keep this to remember our love, dearest Adam.'

We lay watching the infinite waves breaking over the jagged basalt shards far below. I traced the scar on his cheek gently with my finger.

'How did you come by this, Adam?'

'A matter of honour in the Caucasus,' he murmured & did not venture more intelligence. I shivered despite the warmth of the sun.

The mystery of this *'assignation'* – if it be so termed by the envious – is that I gave myself so unreservedly to such pleasures without a single thought for James. There is something in the air of this island that affects the sensibility in unaccountable ways.

'Your habit fits you like a glove, *mon amour*, but I must confess to being privy to other secrets.'

I instantly flashed around.

'What exactly do you mean, Adam?'

'Well, it was in this manner. One sultry evening after mess, I was strolling along Military Road for some air, in the direction of the Burial Ground, when I noticed in the twilight that you were grooming *Tempter* in the garden. I made my way towards the stables intending to draw you into some little conversation. Suddenly, I was challenged by a sentry.

'Who goes there?'

'Your Captain you d..n fool! Are you blind?'

'I must challenge everyone Sir, even Mrs. Worth,' he dutifully replied.

By the time I passed the gate you had already placed the mare in her loose box & disappeared inside. I was about to return to the Officer's Quarters when I noticed a light burning to one side of the house. I moved around to obtain a clearer view & found myself looking into your bedroom. You had not yet drawn the curtains & I could see your activities quite clearly.'

'Adam, there are so many sentries about the house, you must be mad!'

'Yes, but so desperately in love as to risk all! I persevered with my quest & noticed that you had taken out the sketches that you executed on our first ride to Mount Pitt. You had included a horseman in one of the views & stared at it for a long time before kissing it tenderly.'

'Yes, I remember this occasion now. How shameful of you to spy upon me, Adam!'

'But most promising to my cause, Paulina, you began to weep – for what reason I know not.'

'Because I felt my heart & soul imprisoned by my fate.'

'Your maid hurried in & began to undress you. Your shoulders were draped in a loose camisole while she brushed your hair in the light of the oil lamps. Directing her to leave, you then removed the rest of your costume except for the most transparent chemise. Naked you stood before your mirror & embraced your body as if by a lover. Turning, you looked at me directly with your face to the darkness of the glass, blind to the exterior world. Only then did you realise the dangers of exposure & quickly draw the curtains.'

I stood up briskly. 'How dare you, Adam! You are not a man of honour, sir! We must return immediately!' He smiled & gently pulled me back down to the grass.

'I have never & will never forget this vision of beauty. It haunts me, Paulina. I am & will ever be your slave.' He kissed me passionately until my heart was pounding & I was fit to expire. The dizzy height above the cliffs added to my discomforture & I believe I almost fainted away. When I regained this world he was cradling me in his arms. The terrible dangers of this situation suddenly dawned forcibly upon me & I struggled to my feet, my hair tangling in the snake clasp on his belt.

'This is madness! You revel in such risks, but James has spies everywhere! We really must return to Orange Vale at once!'

He assisted me to mount up & we headed back along our previous route. On this occasion I was utterly insensible to Nature's gifts & could scarce keep my composure. Captn. Vane rose to meet us. They were ready to depart.

'We had given you up for lost or imagined you taken by some blood-thirsty characters! Time to return to the settlement before dark, I think.' The carriage loaded up with the festive party & set off with the escort. I am quite unable to give an account of myself or even remember any detail of that return journey.

I will retain the above history, the most detailed I have written in this journal, to peruse in my age & reflect that once at least in my life I was rapturously loved by a young man of passion, nobility & grace. And that this great love was ardently returned.

Government House
Norfolk Island
May 30th. 1848

Archbishop Mollison finally arrived on the island today after many delays. There was a parade of the Military Garrison to receive this distin-guished personage. He is staying with the Rev. Bedingfield on Quality Row. An inspection party will be formed to visit the gaol tomorrow & I have insisted that I am included in it. James opposed this most strongly, insisting that such sights of male convicts were not for women & he would not answer for my health & nervous disposition. I answered that if Lady Franklin could deal with such sights in VDL there was no reason why I might not attempt something of the same on Norfolk Island. He stormed off in one of his 'savage' moods.

Norfolk Island
June 1st. 1848

The Archbishop insisted on visiting the Gaol early this morning. Our party set off soon after breakfast. The group consisted of James, Charles St. Aubyn, Major Ferrers, the Rev. Bedingfield, Giles Gaudin the Superintendent, the Chief Constable Mr. Baldwin & myself. James has begun to sport a Malacca cane with a silver knob carrying the Royal Coat of Arms. How he gets himself 'up' to worry the poor devils!

We began with a visit to some of the cells. I trembled at the thought of seeing at first hand the victims I had wondered on for years. An overseer opened the door to the first dungeon of horror & a sulphrous-yellow gas streamed out like the exhalation from an animal's den. As it drifted off I could ascertain it was produced from the bodies of some men chained to the wall by three ring bolts, hanging with arms outstretched.

'This is the *spreadeagle* position, Sir. Takes the flash out of 'em!' Giles Gaudin was a repository of information. The men immured there without proper ventilation presented a most haggard & desolate appearance. I was close to fainting, but the Archbishop went inside to comfort them with the word of God. James threw back his coat revealing his pistols stuck in his belt, & commented, 'You don't know what desperate men these are, Sir.'

We walked over to where a man was strapped down on a stone, the grim traces of crime etched deeply into his countenance.

'How would you like a hot mess of steak and onions, Jack?' James asked menacingly. The man replied with terrible imprecations & strained and shook his manacles like one insane.

'You see, Sir, just how unreasonable they can be!' quipped James & I noticed the rest of our party smiled unpleasantly.

'Give him the gag!' he ordered one of the constables. A wooden cone with leather straps was produced, which had a hole drilled down the centre for air. Mercifully we turned away before it was applied. Choked shrieks followed us.

Archbishop Mollison also wanted to visit the Lumber Yard. Before James became Commandant it was a fearfully dangerous place ruled over by *The Ring* – an abhorrent group of demon-like old lags or *'flash-men'* who concocted the most infernal crimes & protected the guilty with knives. James had broken this hotbed of pollution & would face down the desperadoes alone. *The Ring* now broken, the convicts clustered around the Archbishop like children, tugging at the cloth of his cassock. They pressed him concerning when the religious services might be held & pleaded that he might hear their confessions. To contemplate Hell heavy with guilt must have sorely tried their sanity. Some held back, clearly embarrassed to appear *soft* before their peers. Others wept that the Archbishop was taking a sincere interest in their immortal souls. To see their blanched, pleading faces upturned to the man of God, their attenuated bodily appearance shuffling along in heavy irons, was desperately affecting.

They cowered before James & he showed a curious propensity for an exact knowledge of each, commenting on this or that punishment or offence in his curious language. The party made towards the hospital ('a whited sepulchre') & the exempt wards under the guidance of Charles St. Aubyn in order to inspect the excoriated backs of flogged men. We at first examined the heavier *double* cat-o'-nine-tails or *thief's cat* used on Norfolk Island, which has a double twist of whipcord, with each tail possessing nine knots. I ran my fingers over these hideous strands with their regular tumours thinking of the whipped men strapped to the triangles & bleeding into their shoes, before turning away in horror from the formidable device. After being flogged into a bedridden condition with this instrument, only bread & tea are provided to sustain the sufferers.

'The blood sloughs off and the backs heal up soon enough!' claimed a jovial constable seeing my discomforture.

'I told you this was no place for you, Paulina,' James whispered in my ear.

'No, James, it isn't. I really must return to Clara.'

I could not face the offensive experience of scourged skeletons in the heat of the day, despite Lady Franklin's superior charity in this regard. Major Ferrers escorted me back to Government House.

'James is a man of commanding presence & completely without fear, Paulina. He has the strength of one of these great pines around us & is an English gentleman to the core,' he remarked as we walked along Military Road.

'I'm sure the island is excellent for James & his reputation, but this is a terrible place for monotony & horror, Claude. I am desperate for some *gentle amusement!*'

'Quite. But you know it is a type of earthly paradise, my dear. We are such a happy family together, almost one might say, a *"social common-wealth"*. Everything edible is in abundance here, & free, moreover – poultry, vegetables, fruit! I shall be sad indeed to leave so soon. My Regiment is to try a little fighting with the maneaters of New Zealand & requires my services. Our regiments are so dreadfully cut up & disorganised in the colonies!'

'Claude, you are a dear man, but will never understand what a woman of my stamp requires.'

The afternoon stretched out before me like a desert. I decided to begin work on my study of the irreclaimable demons. I take as my motto an extraordinary remark reported to me:

'I love my fellow prisoners as I love my life.'
Uttered by a Convict aboard the 'Rodney'

A Collection of Convict Destinies
begun by Paulina Wellesley
Norfolk Island – Oceania – 1848

No. 1 – Charles Anderson

Destiny the first is that of the celebrated convict Charles Anderson born at Newcastle-on-Tyne. Orphaned early in life he was sent to the workhouse and at the tender age of nine went to sea on a collier. He then joined a man-of-war and was severly wounded at the Battle of Navarino. This brought on fits of violent criminal excitement and the reward for his courage and sacrifice resulted in transportation to Goat Island in Sydney harbour.

After much indiscipline from an ungovernable temper this modern Prometheus was chained by his waist to a rock for two years with trumpet irons on his legs. A hollow was carved in the rock for a bed which was covered each night by a board with holes, locked down with wing bolts and then removed in the morning. Covered only in rags, he would scramble for food pushed towards him at the end of a pole from a boat. Curious visitors from passing ships would throw him pieces of bread or biscuits for amusement. His back was covered in sores from innumerable floggings, maggots feeding on his flesh. Rain caused him to roll about the rock in terrible agony. He was forced to carry baskets of lime at Port Macquarie, absconded and lived with the aboriginals before he was finally sent to Norfolk Island for life, having committed murder.

Our friend Captain Maconochie was the enlightened Commandant at this time when Anderson had already been convicted of numerous violent assaults. He was only twenty-four but appeared to be fifty. This rare Christian Commandant set him to work with a bullock team. The good Captain then partially cleared the summit of Mount Pitt – the area of our pic-nic – and erected a hut and signal station for him to operate. His pride burgeoned with the trust and responsibility and he dressed himself in a dapper sailor suit, telescope under his arm and imagined himself returned to active service on the man-of-war. He tended his own garden and proudly brought basketfuls of magnificent flowers to dress the captain's dinner table.

The highest in the land were amazed at his transformation. Anderson regained his self-respect under Captain Maconochie but after this good gentleman was withdrawn from the island for being too lenient and recalled to England, Anderson's excitability rapidly became insanity. His final rest was a lunatic asylum where he spoke incessantly of Captain Maconochie and his family.

The good Captain & his curious ideas & behaviour are a source of derision for James & the colony. But the attitude to convict matters held by *this* naive English girl, who left England in 1836 at the age of twenty-four, has now turned away from a slavish acceptance of the bleak views of her husband. Reformation cannot come through the use of the scourge; everyone is debased by it. I would prefer not to dwell on pestilence & moral plague, but the limited society on the island forces me to turn terribly in upon myself. I will add to my 'Collection' as I learn more of these tragic histories.

No.2 – Extract from an unknown prisoner's letter
An ill-fated Husband
Dated 'Norfolk Island, 11th April, 1835'

'My dear Wife and beloved Children,
Through all the chances, changes, and vicissitudes of my chequered life, I never had a task so painful to my mangled feelings, as this present one, of addressing you from this doleful spot, – my sea-girt prison, on the beach of which I stand, a monument of destruction; driven by adverse winds of fate, to the confines of black despair, and into the vortex of galling misery. I am just like a gigantic tree of the forest, which has stood many a wintry blast and stormy tempest; but now, alas! I am become a withered trunk, with all my tenderest and greenest branches lop'd off...'

(I unfolded a letter from the collection secreted in the morocco binding, carefully preserving the rose petals. I opened it carefully, and the unrestrained emotion of the contents in regular minute handwriting leapt out at me from the page.)

Officer's Quarters
Norfolk Island
Lundi Janvier 11, 1848
L'heure du diner

Mon ange aimi

How can I not love you after your rapturous letter after the opera! You revealed all the beauty of your lonely and noble soul. I am seated on the *balcon* of my quarters reading some poems of Lord Byron having just arrived in from a ride after dinner. I look towards Government House hoping malevolent fate will grant the slightest glimpse of you. Your golden-haired son is playing on the lawn with *Actaeon*. You knew I was singing *Don Alphonso* only to you – singing of the sweet torments of my heart. How I long to run my fingers once again through your beautiful curls and trace your lips with my fingers. *Mon bel oiseau*. I see in you all the natural beauty that surrounds me. How I loved you in your light-blue riding habit when last you rode *Tempter* spiritedly up the steep track to Pine Tree Flat above Kingston!

Forgive the presumption of the ardent lover. I write because we cannot speak so readily alone. My Polish *esprit* runs away with me. Only Englishmen possess that '*ironie aride qui souffle comme un vent de mort sur les jouissances du coeur*' [89] in the fine words of Mme. de Staël. Such uncivilised and bearish officers surround me. One even arranged the transportation of a man so he could have his way with his wife! My thoughts fly constantly to you. The isolation of the island makes me feel *we are alone together in the world* and thus is my love more real, more deep.

But what can you and I contrive in this cruel separation? We have met at a time when neither is free to pursue the affections of the heart – I bound to my nation and my regiment, you to your husband. We can always ride the magnificent tracks to the mountain or along the crags at Duncombe's Bay under pretext of visits, pic-nics or exercising the horses. But we are so often in the company of others!

We belong together. We must grasp what pleasure and love we may – an hour here or an afternoon there in this paradise within hell. After our last ride to Point Ross I returned to the carriage at the barracks and in the dust on the seat slowly traced your name...

Ours is such a small *knowing community* Paulina, guarded by sentries night and day! We must take care, my love. Your husband has his spies everywhere and harbours most unnatural suspicions of everyone. But Hyacinth O'Rourke is a fine Irish gentleman and can be trusted to the death with our missives.

Your letter was strained and full of tears – some had even fallen and run the ink – and yet you remain so outwardly calm in company, in fact bear such *noblesse de naissance* that I cannot but sacrifice all for you. You write of the shame of your *perverted* feelings for me and of the dangers to your soul. Your voice is crushed in the throat. It makes me sad to see you suffer so.

In this Garden of Eden, how can we *not* love each other? I remember when first I saw you in the sunlit doorway of Government House, radiant in a straw bonnet and carrying a basket of flowers you had recently gathered. Your face lay in part shade beneath a cream parasol and your long satin dress presented so elegant a figure. The sunlight caught your auburn curls while the exertions of your outing had flushed your cheeks. Your hazel eyes danced with light and your lips slightly parted in a smile revealing pearls. Do you remember letting fall some flowers in surprise? The affinity of our hearts was clear from those first precious moments. The terrible sights and sounds of Norfolk Island are not for one as you, *mon amour*, who I would wing back like an eagle to my castle in the frozen North, to the Great Hall before the roaring fire, to ride with me in golden October through the vast forests of birch and aspen. I hold you close *kochanie*.[90]

Je suis seulement dans un rêve.[91]
Je t'aime.

Adam

Detruis cette lettre![92]

(I was not exactly surprised by this letter from the *beau sabreur*, as her journal had already mentioned it. Still, for a married woman to have crossed a certain threshold was remarkable at that time. The dangers of an affair for the wife of the Commandant scarcely bear imagining. The geographical isolation and the air of the island have a curious influence on behaviour, all inhibitions fall away.)

CHAPTER XXVII

'...How were they to free themselves from their intolerable chains?
"How? How?" he asked himself, clutching his head. "How?"
And it seemed as though in a little while the solution would be found,
and then a new and glorious life would begin; and it was clear
to both of them that the end was still far off, and that what was to be
most complicated and difficult for them was only just beginning.'
(Fade up *Soirée de Vienne* No. 6 – Schubert-Liszt)

'*Y*ou have been listening to *"The Lady with the Little Dog"* written in 1899 by Anton Chekhov, in the translation by Vladimir Nabokov.

That brings to an end this Sunday evening's programme of music and drama from VL-2-NI Norfolk Island. Next week we will continue our exploration of the *Great Piano Virtuosos of our Time* with the remarkable career of the Russian pianist Vladimir Horowitz. The programme will include the astonishing recording he made of the Liszt B-minor Sonata in 1932. Before we close here are the Local Notices:

Arrangements to obtain a Coat of Arms for Norfolk Island have now reached the design stage. Suggestions in writing with a sketch are sought by the Administration for submission by the Council to the College of Arms in London. They should be received before 5pm on Thursday, 31st. October.

Tickets are available for the Debutante's Ball in period costumes of 1770 from the *Playboy Pharmacy* in Burnt Pine.

A consignment of the special bottling of wine – Claret and Moselle – to commemorate the Bi-Centenary of the discovery of Norfolk Island will be available next month. Orders should be placed at the Administration Offices, Kingston. Drink up, gentlemen, and do your duty!

Thank you so much for listening. I wish you an *exotic and erotic evening* – I will certainly have one. *Gud nait* from VL-2-NI, broadcasting on a frequency of 1570 kHz from Norfolk Island, the nipple on the soft bosom of Oceania. Until close down a number for a special lady – Tammy Wynette with her melancholic song *"Pregnant Again"*.'

The telephone on the mixing console rang almost immediately. It was an official voice.

'That's it! I've had enough of these sexual innuendos – *and* on a Sunday! Come and see me tomorrow down at the Administration Offices.'

The next day I was permanently relieved of my duties as Broadcasting Officer.

So it had finally come to this. Without employment, I would not be able to stay indefinitely on my residence permit. As I drove up to the tracking station from Kingston I realised my days were numbered. I consoled myself with the treasure of Paulina's journals, which would be a fine permanent reminder.

Later that afternoon I decided to visit Almira. She could always lift me out of my despondency with a wry observation, a whiskey and some Tahitian fish.

'Es ai hau glehd f' si yuu,' she said as I came into the kitchen. 'Wataim yu gu orn a' bied laas nait boy?[93] You look terrible!'

'Ai es need wan drink, Almira. I've lost my job on the radio station.'

'Tal es jok!'[94]

I explained as best I could and with a degree of embarrassment.

'Yu kaa duu.[95] What are you going to do?'

'I've been here almost three years. It might be time to move on.'

'Yu es right orn daa point, darl. You can still make a career in music at your age, but not f' much longer. Unless yu gwen maeri wan Norfolk girl and live happily ever after!'

'That's not very likely, Almira. I just wish it was. I have to pack up so much stuff, ship the piano, pack my books, sell the MG. It'll be impossible for me to leave quickly. I just so love Norfolk. They will have to tear me away.' I stared down gloomily at the raffia mats.

'Darl, go up Mount Pitt and get me a couple of lemons, will you, and then come back and have dinner. I've got some beautiful trevally to cook tonight. Stay with me for a little.'

I drove up into the reserve and picked some lemons and yellow guavas. It was always peaceful wandering through the rain forest, but my connections with nature were now tinged with the melancholy of imminent departure. As I returned down Mission Road, a motorcycle passed me at tremendous speed, cutting me up violently. It was Nathan, and to my surprise he waved cheerily and laughed. I waved back, but I felt something ominous in his random appearances, like warning signs along a treacherous mountain path.

Almira's was a haven of peace for me. The joy that embraced one there sealed time in a tight knot. Laughter and humour still bubbled around the kitchen table but it was not as I remembered it from earlier days. Almira had appointed a manager for the guest house and there was a new stove in the modernised kitchen. She could deal with more guests now, but the price for efficiency was a decrease in human contact and in that particular feeling of simple improvisation that had welcomed me when I first walked up onto the verandah, bruised by the city and looking for escape. The sense of family had disappeared, perhaps forever. Almira now often had violent spasms of coughing. Cocks crowed in the dead of night.

After a marvellous dinner, she impulsively suggested we go for a late evening drive. The guests had drifted off to bed, after offering doubtful advice on future island policies and the conduct of the residents. She was babysitting a young island boy and took him with us. She wanted to see the moon rise.

The first stopping place was Bucks Point, the site of many a festive dawn breakfast, where at night the enigmatic and mysterious white oaks and whitewoods stood like ghostly sentinels under the stars. Down then to the Lone Pine at Point Hunter, where the moon rose over the coral banks and swell of Sydney Bay, yellow at first, then silvering as it climbed higher into the night. This solitary pine was present in every old photograph I had ever seen of Sydney Bay. Then to view the moon suspended over Government House and the pale settlement from the landing place at Kingston, the area teeming with shades, and lastly to Longridge, to see it poised above the convict stone arches.

'Ean't that beautiful Ali, e'n dem cows es lookin' orn,' came the small voice of the boy.

I remember the morning I finally decided to leave. I was dozing against the wire wheels of the MG in the warm sun at Rocky Point. Red-tailed tropic birds, black noddies and grey ternlets, were wheeling and diving, skimming the surface for fish. The pines were soughing in the gentle breeze, and the clouds were suspended motionless above Mount Bates. Bees were humming after pollen among the wild flowers, competing with the tiny white butterflies for nectar. Thin cattle with twisted horns and withered teats were meandering perilously close to the cliff edge, as usual. The sea was a glittering ultramarine, the surface a mirror of abstract swathes of light and shade stretching as far as the horizon.

I had come to the conclusion I was wasting my life in this voluntary isolation. Could I justify dropping out completely from a promising career? I had to study *something* in the present competitive job climate. All these questions tumbled through my brain. The feeling of claustrophobia had been growing for some time and my privacy had now almost vanished. The island had gradually become a psychological prison for me, just as the mainland had.

While I slowly packed my books, recordings, rugs and velvets out at the tracking station, I began to see more of Mareva again. We had both changed during the time we had spent together. However we still compulsively sought each other, unable to resist the attraction of opposites. She had become more sophisticated, more concerned with clothes, cosmetics and potential husbands, all the delights that the new money flooding the island could buy. The hospital had rewarded her excellent work with promotion and a promise of managerial training. Television broadcasts had become more frequent, opening the window to the outside world, dragging the island into the communal hell of mass communication and information overload. Mareva was spending less time engaged in the simple island pursuits I remembered from our early days.

On the other hand, my involvement with her had made me incapable of taking a conventional mainland life seriously. Now I knew an alternative philosophy of the senses and an expansion of time beyond the accepted controls. This sort of consciousness, though, was passing away with the older islanders. Mareva and I had made each other unable to accept the lives to which we had been born.

We now hardly ever searched for shellfish or made love as a natural expression of affection. We wandered the rock pools and the reefs in the transparent light, and sometimes we saw the reef fall in shade, Philip and Nepean Islands dramatically spotlit by shafts of sunlight. A white-faced heron landed near me on its long legs, and gazed elegantly in my direction. We had our last picnic beside the Watermill Creek in the former Arthur's Vale, where reeds grew in water as blue as the sky, and purple and red Tarler birds and strutting cocks displayed their plumage among the lilac water hyacinth. A rare green parrot speared towards an ancient plantation of bananas at the head of the valley. On wet, grey afternoons we strolled along a tiny beach known as Beefsteak and collected wave-polished pebbles, which Mareva took home for keepsakes. We went fishing at the Cord and off the rocks near Monty, from the plateau and pool at Black Bank. Now Mareva was wearing fashionably sexy clothes, and I remembered with nostalgia the fragments of simple cloth slipping down over her unsurpassed beauty of skin.

Our last barbecue together was to have been out at 'aa Stieshan' near Point Howe in the north of the island. Because of strong winds, it was relocated inside the grey walls of the old Prisoner's Barracks. Only islanders had been invited, and there was some tension when I appeared.

'Ai es herd yu s' gat yusaelf wan nyuu toela, Haet![96] Why are you with Mareva?'

'Ai es leavin' Norfuk soon, Hoof. Es wan sad dieh.'

'Ai gwen a' glehd yu s' gorn, brud.'[97] Everyone laughed in a good-natured way.

There were so many friends to take leave of. My farewell call to Government House was on a magnificently sunny day. The Administrator's wife welcomed me at the rear entrance and offered me coffee on the verandah. The view was glorious over the creaming rollers and glistering blue ocean, pines acutely etched against the honey-coloured stone.

'The stories of the older Pitcairn descendants are so humorous and beautiful,' I said, 'they should be preserved and written down. A whole generation is passing with no-one to preserve this nobility of soul.'

'Yes, Paul, you're right. I know it is tragic, but who will do it?' she said. 'The tradition is an oral one. It is probably already too late.'

We both fell silent and listened to the breakers on the reef. 'So many of the younger ones consider themselves *Australians*. They are losing that gentle charm of the older Pitcairn descendants,' I said.

The Commodore returned from guiding some eminent Cocos Islanders around Norfolk. He immediately invited me to lunch with his customary naval hospitality. He uncorked a bottle of chilled White Burgundy.

'I overheard you as I came in,' he said. 'Yes, the Pitcairn personality is slowly being diluted. Commercial interests are bound to destroy the character of the island in the end. I've just had a meeting with the Council concerning tourism. They are all terribly divided.'

'People are just too greedy. Not like the original Pitcairners who declared, if I remember, "Money no use to me. You give me money, I throw it in the sea!"'

'Yes, I remember that quote. Did you know that they are threatening to allow jet aircraft to service the island? Perhaps once a day?'

'Well, that certainly *will* be the end of the idyll.' We all became thoughtful.

'I'm sorry about the recent events, Paul, but I did warn you.' The Commodore was friendly and sympathetic.

'I know. I've always broken the rules,' I said.

'It's out of my hands, unfortunately. Bureaucracy will have its way, now that a complaint has been officially lodged,' he said. 'I can't really intervene. We'll miss your music, the educational side. Sorry.'

'That's really kind of you to say that.'

'Shall we have some food and music?' his charming wife suggested. At that moment, a small table appeared, set with shining silver, glasses and a dazzling cloth. A superb fish pie of scallops, trumpeter, prawns and oysters materialised as if by magic, with a delicious green salad. What a perfect setting for lunch! Through the slender white pillars of the verandah, I could watch the red parrots bullet through the pines towards the entrance to the New Military Barracks. Vast acres of white water were laid out over the torquoise beyond the reef. The green-gold wine glowed in the crystal glass, beams of trapped sunlight springing to the eye. A Mozart Piano Concerto floated out from the Georgian interior to complete this Elysian scene.

The South Pacific is such a warm, enfolding and essentially feminine ocean, quite unlike the Atlantic, which is masculine, aggressive, wild, uncompromising, brutal and green. The Pacific foam which bathes the warm and voluptuous people of the islands of Oceania is of a different texture and character to that of the north, nurturing a different temperament. It was at that moment I realised that although my body may have been leaving Norfolk Island, my spirit would be forever present there.

'Play us something on the organ, Paul! We'll go out to St. Barnabas Chapel.'

On the way we collected Almira and Aunt Connie as they both loved music, particularly the organ. The Mission Chapel at dusk was an oasis of spiritual calm. The tarler birds were *'kreking'* from the nearby swamp and the fairy terns fluttered like tiny angels between the dark oaks surrounding the chapel. Incense, walnut, cowrie shell and marble trembled in the filtered interior light. A stupendous sunset shone through the stained glass, creating a numinous atmosphere.

I switched on the bellows, and the sonorous tone filled the perfumed interior, the mechanical tracker giving a remarkable timbre to the simple range of stops. The passionate voices of a three-part fugue by Nicolas de Grigny answered each other in perfect counterpoint – the wrought pattern of the island forged in sound. François Couperin and Sebastian Bach so perfectly articulate that fine line that separates the physical from the metaphysical, a line I had constantly traversed like a spiritual acrobat during my residence in this enchanted place. At length we emerged into the deep night of birds and insects in an uplifted mood, and bid a final farewell on the chapel steps.

I had my last dawn breakfast at Simon's Water with some islander friends. The waterfall was like a Japanese formal garden, with reeds, rushes, rivulets trickling over brown rocks, forming a stream cascading into the sea far below. Even the youngest played with the barbecue fire and long knives, while the parents remained indifferent to the dangers. Liver, sausages, tomatoes, eggs, bacon and bananas were all cooked on the hotplate. The children rode the wild horses that roamed near there, and I saw amazing scenes with hooves flying and bodies tumbling. The sacred kingfishers gave their staccato call. Translucent terns flew against the light as the rising sun exploded over the Pacific.

CHAPTER XXVIII

'I must marry another – and yet I must love this; and if it lead me into some little inconveniences, as jealousies, and duels, and death, and so forth – yet, while sweet love is in the case, Fortune, do thy worst, and avaunt mortality!
John Dryden
Marriage-a-la-Mode, 1673, Scene 1.

*J*chose a day of perfect weather to conclude my reading of Paulina'a diaries on the cliff-top at Steels Point, not far from Simon's Water, known in convict times as The Big Flat.

Government House
Norfolk Island
June 12th. 1848

My hand shakes in writing this entry & my heart races with the fear of recent events. Dark foreboding washes over me as the future is not yet clear. The delicate web of my love is cruelly shredded & torn – it blows in the wind like violated lace. My dearest friend may soon lie dead or mortally wounded & I feel compelled to chronicle the events that have led to this most bloody of sunsets.

The Archbishop was soon to be leaving the island, so a visitation dinner was arranged at Government House in his honour last evening. James sent out cards to most of the illustrious residents (if they can be deemed such in this remote spot) ranging from the Civil Officers to the Military Garrison. Covers were laid for twenty.

It was a clear evening & by seven our guests began to arrive on horseback & by carriage from the more outlying stations at Longridge & Cascades. Our young negro Rose, colourfully dressed in the old postilion livery from *'Trevalor'*, occupied himself lighting the flambeaux along the verandah while Eliza & Louisa welcomed the guests into the hall. The sentries & cannon made a singular contribution to this glittering scene. Some members of the regimental band in scarlet jackets formed a quartet at one end of the verandah & played some charming airs & dances. For the first time since arriving I decided to wear one of my low pink gowns from Geneva.

Charles St. Aubyn & Fanny arrived early & were soon followed by Mr. & Mrs. Ommaney, the Rev. Bedingfield accompanying Archbishop Mollison, Mr. & Mrs. Austen from *Antonio's Farm* & the crusty bachelor Mr. Greenside with his collapsible top hat accompanying Mrs. Webster. Captain Vane of the 11th. Regiment accompanied the governess Miss Martineaux, dressed in a ravishing gown of blue & white striped *gaze de Chambéry*, her waist shrinking by the minute! The military officers arrived *tout le monde ensemble* & made a spectacular dress entrance in their scarlet coatees with bright green facings & tails with white turnbacks, gilt buttons & white buffalo sword belts – Major Irwin commanding the detachment, Major Ferrers of the 'Black Cuffs' & Fanny. Finally my *énergique* Captain Zaleski made his entrance wearing his Karabela sabre, carrying his shako with the white over red pom-pom upright under his arm, on it the brass sunburst *'XI'* winking in the firelight. The drawing room only just managed to contain the dazzling throng. Few presentations required to be made except to the Archbishop, as our island community is of the *'so intimate'* variety. It was generally hoped that he would deliver us of an uplifting sermon on Sunday. The want of French I thought to be a great limitation. The domestics, assisted by our little negro & the pig-tailed Chinese Wu Li, served the champagne that James had so painstakingly collected over recent months. A fine fire burned in the grate.

I spoke to Fanny about her infant & gave her advice from my recent experiences with Clara & her illness. Adolphus ran about saluting the officers madly, darting between their legs & generally making a nuisance of himself. The gong sounded. I must admit to being foolishly miffed when Captn. Zaleski stepped up to offer his hand to Miss Martineaux. Major Ferrers escorted me into the Dining Room & the company took those places I had carefully contrived for them at the enormous cedar table.

The Archbishop, who was seated in the middle of one of the long sides, bowed his head & said Grace. A pair of candelabra had been lit & the crystal glasses, decanters & silver glinted in the flames. The burgundy Minton service, which had miraculously survived the voyage from Devonshire Street to Oceania intact, was displayed to great advantage. Another excellent fire burned in the fireplace below the portrait of the Queen & Prince Albert. Our convict domestics were severely limited in number & ability so dinner was served *à la Russe* with the main meat & bird course being set before James to carve. The tiny orchestra had moved into the Drawing Room to entertain us during the meal. The fine company thus assembled made one almost forget the dutiful reason for their presence on the island, the grim outlines of which could be glimpsed through the bars on the windows as the moon rose behind the pines.

'This island must be one of the most beautiful places on earth!' observed the Archbishop finishing his soup.

'A veritable cornucopia of Nature's gifts,' added Major Ferrers.

'Certainly we are vastly more fortunate than the poor wretches in Ireland living through the famine in the bogs,' thundered James. 'I try to dun this into the prisoners skulls, indicate the advantages of our salubrious climate & conditions, but they'll have none of it.' He massaged his monocle and set to on carving the duck.

'My Uncle writes from Exeter that Clarendon apparently referred to one Irish M.P. as *"a very ridiculous but not ill-disposed savage",*' laughed Major Irwin along with the rest. The bumpers of claret were refilled. Charles St. Aubyn smoothed his moustache before observing, 'Revolution is brewing at our door. The Orléanists have been routed in France and a Republic declared. Louis-Philippe and his Queen shelter in England in disguise under the titles *Comte and Comtesse de Neuilly.* Awful events, my friends!'

'Your Foreign Secretary. Lord Palmerston or Pumicestone, I'm not sure of the pronunciation, has always been sympathetic to the Polish cause,' the dashing Zaleski smiled.

James replied in rather a surly manner, 'We British aren't revolutionaries and don't hold with throwing up the barricades.' Many at the table evidenced agreement & nodded energetically.

'We Poles will joyfully fight Austrians, Russians & Prussians to liberate our country wherever they are!' Captain Zaleski seemed possessed of an excess of patriotism & adopted a suitably erect military posture.

'My dear Zaleski, Poland is just an *idea*, not a *nation!* Well, not any more – Haw! Haw! – You should be off fighting for it now!'

James arrogantly fired off this broadside & Adam visibly stiffened & paled. The corners of his moustache quivered. His eyes sought mine in fury but I glanced down at my plate in full betrayal. He massively controlled himself against this grievous insult.

'If the Continent is aflame, will the conflagration spread to England?' ventured the tremulous voice of Mrs. Webster.

Mr. Austen owned *Antonio's Farm* near Rocky Point – one of the most productive on the island. He glanced thoughtfully at his broken fingernails before observing:

'Agricultural distress and starvation are the matters that cause revolutions. Blight on crops lays us waste even here.'

'I warn you that supporters of Feargus O'Connor have been given new blood at Kennington Common. Anything may…' Captain Vane was cut off in mid-flow.

'We can be sure such politics will have scant effect on *our* distant Paradise,' Fanny cut in gaily.

Major Irwin gave her a severe riposte as the lively *Radetzky March* floated through from the Drawing Room.

'Quite the contrary, my dear. Lord Grey requires the military to be on service at home in England and will shut up this tin pot shop soon enough – there are four hundred thousand Frenchmen under arms – colonial defence is too dashed expensive. Too many departments!'

'Exactly so! The colonists should pay to defend themselves,' added Major Ferrers.

Captain Vane attempted another flight.

'I beg to differ, Sir! That runt Russell has left us defenceless in the colonies with his parsimony towards the military. We have been issued pop guns for salutes from yachts!'

'Calm yourself, Sir! Remember there are ladies at dinner,' inveighed Major Irwin.

The Rev. Bedingfield spoke in quavering tones.

'There could be an outbreak here that would astonish the civilised world.'

A silence descended over the party as we reflected on our plight among the reckless & depraved convicts, immensely distant loved ones in danger, the perils of a misguided colonial policy & Europe aflame in revolution.

'Peel should never have halved the duty on sugar!' James suddenly shot out. A subject of historic family significance continued to eat away at him like a cancer.

'Please, James, you can be so dull! During all your catalogue of horrors, Johann Strauss has been touring England playing his spirited waltzes and causing a sensation among the ladies according to my correspondents.'

I was unable to restrain myself from this return to lightness. The dinner conversation was in danger of a descent into *grave seriousness*.

'I once danced a waltz & polka in Vienna at a Court ball with the Prince Schwartzenberg! I became quite giddy with the delight & the champagne,' gushed Miss Martineaux, much to the approbation of all the officers present who found her even furtherly *very fascinating*. We had reached the array of tropical fruits which were brought forward with the abundance of a Polynesian market. Rich cream from the dairy compelled us to luxurious indulgence.

'Your Grace, you have not given us the benefit of your wisdom at table. How runs the devil's ministry?' remarked James, rather disingenuously to my mind.

The Archbishop smiled & nodded slowly, preparing his 'peroration'.

'An active clergy is the most efficient of police. Religion has more profound effects than politics or war. Here on this island amidst the suffering of the pestilential mass, we Christians must recognize His image, mutilated though it be, He who will come to judge us all on the last day, both prisoner and gaoler. Every hand is raised against the prisoner – we must provide the balm of compassion.'

A reverent silence descended upon us all at this moment.

'I shall never forget the inhuman expression of those thousands of faces turned up at me.'

The delightful strains of a Strauss polka filtered through from the Regimental musicians.

'We are grappling with the devil at the very gates of Hell! Close combat face to face, foot to foot,' the archbishop concluded heroically.

'Some of the *crawlers* – excuse me, your Grace – the *prisoners* are subject to religious visions. Bernard Duffy – convicted for assaulting a constable – told me he had received an order from *'On High'* to refuse food. I prepared a juicy steak smothered with onions and took it down to his cell. As I entered the den I communicated the following to him:

'I have a message for you. The ban is off – you have permission to eat. And look, here is a little something sent down to you from *"On High"* to begin with.' My cheery voice caused the fellow to fall to & quickly resume eating. This anecdote caused much amusement around the table.

'I truly believe, Your Grace, that some of these men should be treated as lunatics rather than criminals. Heredity plays a fundamental part in the determination of their character.' James trailed off, seemingly distracted in his own mind.

'Fear of punishment is no way to prevent crime. They commit further horrors out of sheer wretchedness,' observed Charles.

A natural pause in proceedings allowed me to suggest that the ladies, the Archbishop & the Rev. Bedingfield repair to the drawing room for some uplifting conversation & leave the gentlemen to smoke and finish their port. Mrs. Webster smiled benignly towards Mrs. Austen & Mrs. Ommaney while Miss Martineaux flashed a lightning glance over her pretty shoulder into the eyes of Captain Vane. Zaleski sat like a stone. As I passed through the arch & smelt the first cigars I heard: 'Buzz the decanter, James! Now, when are we to hunt some cats & parakeets on Philip Island?' energetically fired off by Major Ferrers.

The band had now fallen silent & moved into the Dining Room with the gentlemen. The Archbishop engaged us in conversation. 'Tell me, ladies, do you observe your religious duties without difficulties in this flawed paradise?'

Mrs. Ommaney spoke up readily on this topic.

'After church on Sunday, there are vexatious numbers of visitors which makes it difficult to observe the Sabbath in the proper manner of contemplation.'

'I will mention this abuse – without names naturally – in my sermon and suggest that communion with one's own soul is the way to reform & the path to immortality,' unctuously replied the Archbishop.

'The island is often in a state of alarm with absconding convicts. It is enormously difficult to raise children under the influence of convict tutors in these conditions.'

The assembled company gave each other knowing *cast down* looks, which clearly related to Charlotte and the *common suspicions* concerning the congress with Septimus during music lessons.

'How is dear Charlotte, Paulina?' asked Fanny quite innocently.

'She is making remarkable progress at the instrument. She will doubtless take her place in the very best society when we return to England.' I attempted to appear unconcerned but was weeping inside.

'Speaking of music, do sing for us, Miss Martineaux,' urged Mrs. Austen, who spoke little but listened a good deal.

Miss Martineaux coloured up but required no further persuasion, and sat down at the small *Stodart* instrument in the Sheraton case I have so painstakingly transported about the world. Her voice had been trained in Italy as mine was in Florence many long years ago. She began with some Mozart sacred songs, I believe for the benefit of the clergymen present. The voice was pure & light & her auburn ringlets tumbled onto her shoulders. The *voix de sirène* charmed the officers from the Dining Room in a trice.

'A man without hope is a desperate man... death is the only change he can expect... that or escape... eventually the convicts become useless machines.' Major Irwin broke off as he entered the room.

They sat respectfully for a time listening to the ethereal harmonies but then requested some airs from Bellini. I rummaged in my music cabinet and produced Norma's invocation to the moon – *'Casta diva' ('Chaste Goddess')* – from Act I. That the silver orb itself was visible through the barred windows, suspended over the settlement above the lofty pines, seething ocean & languishing souls made this music deeply affecting. The applause was deafening despite her clear difficulties with the technical demands.

They pressed us to perform the duet of Norma & Adalgisa from Act II. *Prince Zaleski* stood stiffly erect at the back of the party near the bronze bust of the Duke of Wellington against the Solomon's Seal curtains. He looked at both of us with a penetrating glance as we took our places under the portrait of Queen Victoria. I played the piano on this occasion as Miss Martineaux owned to being a poor sight-reader. As the music progressed, the passionate avowal of unity between the two women in the opera had a profound effect on the performers. Much between us had remained unspoken concerning our mutual affection for our Polish hero over many months. We had of necessity been forced to inhabit each other's company by virtue of the restricted compass of the island. Tears welled up unseen as we concluded the piece & gazed with forgiveness into each other's eyes. More tremendous applause & then sudden raucous calls, affected by the port, champagne & the charms of Bacchus.

'Don Alphonzo! Don Alphonzo! A song from *The Castle of Andalusia!*' they chimed & the officers sang in occasional unison their favourite chorus:

'Oar or gibbet, whips or wheels
How can we think
While we drink
Sweet Muscadine?
O, life divine!'

'Zaleski! Zaleski! Sing for us! Sing!'

Even the ladies & the Archbishop were amused by this sudden outpouring of infectious animal spirits. Captain Zaleski smiled, smoothed his blonde moustache & walked through the throng towards the piano.

'No! No! We have a surprise ladies! *"The Battle of Prague"* by Kotzwara. I shall be the narrator & now so to action! Is our military quintet ready?'

A stirring *Prelude* begins the piece. I clapped my hands at this rousing climax to the concert. The description of the battle is presented with musical illustrations accompanying the narration of warrior scenes.

'*The word of command!*' Serious chords on the pianoforte.

'*First signal cannon. The bugle-horn call for the cavalry!*'

'*The attack!*' Agitated violin, trumpet, flute & pianoforte.

'*Prussians! Imperialists! Heavy Cannonade!*' Captain Zaleski played & narrated like a man possessed. The ladies breasts heaved & hearts pattered including my own.

'*Fire bullets!*' They flew about the room in sprays of sound! Scales rippled from the pianoforte in imitation of *Running Fire.*

'*The generals hatch a cunning plan.*' Insinuating & dark insidious chords throughout.

'*Attacking swords! Light Dragoons advancing! Horses galloping!*' A farrago of tempestuous music.

PAUSE

'*The cries of the wounded.*' A melancholy dirge on the bass viol with souls ascending depicted high on the pianoforte. Zaleski appears troubled in spirit, moustache drooping.

'*The Trumpets of Victory!*' Powerful martial music with intimations of the Wedding March. Posture erect!

'*God Save the King!*' The assembled company stood perfectly to attention.

'*Turkish music!*' A sudden revival! Our military quintet did their best at cacophany borrowing the cutlery and punch-bowl & imitating Janissaries! *Actaeon* madly chased his tail.

'*Go to bed. Home.*' Calm harmonies & a fitting *finale* to the battle & the evening. The audience clapped & cheered rapturously as *Prince Zaleski* stood beside the instrument & acknowledged the applause. Miss Martineaux & myself were panting with excitement. But as '*Our Hero*' was about to take his seat again for an *encore* a monstrous occurrence took place. James suddenly said loudly for all to hear.

'Charles, did you bring the *Snook's Aperient Pills*? We're bound to require 'em shortly!' adjusting his monocle & quizzing the victimized Captain Zaleski insolently.

The significance of this remark was lost on most of the company except a few of the officers who had been present on the previous occasion of insult & now looked dark & their festive spirits rapidly drained away. Captain Zaleski was as stiff as a ramrod & pale as a ghost. The scar on his cheek turned an angry purple. His eyes glittered ferociously as he approached James with determined strides & bowed.

'You are a Turk, Sir! You have insulted the honour of my country, my regiment & myself. This cannot be tolerated!'

The room fell as silent as the tomb & only the turmoil of the reef was to be heard. My heart had stopped beating & I was near to fainting. The entire company was staring at the noble figure of Adam, proud in his scarlet & gold. James seemed to expand with confidence & quietly replied in that menacing voice I had so often heard with dread, that curious feature of his relations with the sensual & malicious demons of the prison.

'Well Sir, you are *quite* the foxy General! We'll see if you can meet it my joker.' He adjusted his black coat, slowly removing the monocle from his eye & polishing it on his swansdown waistcoat with massive effrontery.

Major Irwin grabbed Captain Zaleski by the arm & whispered savagely, 'Guard your tongue, Sir! You can be cashiered for such threats as these. Captain Vane, get him to bed. He's a disgrace to the Regiment!'

The members of the 11th left soon afterward, Adam trembling with fury. Their boots echoed horribly distant & hollow along the wooden verandah & the bullion-fringed epaulettes with the Queen's Cypher glinted evilly in the flambeaux. The Archbishop & Rev. Bedingfield shook their heads sagely & the ladies whispered deep asides. James turned to Major Ferrers.

'Damme, these excitable foreign officers shouldn't be allowed to clutter our Regiments – revolutionary talk, luring our wives with their horses, pretty poetics & simpering manners – he needs a good thrashing!'

Miss Martineaux had burst into tears & I wished the earth to gape & swallow me up. The after dinner conversation continued only as long as decent courtesies would permit. The company rapidly dispersed, with no sympathy in evidence for Captain Zaleski & much for the discourtesy experienced by James & myself. I must needs conceal the tumult that drove my heart like a pounding engine towards an internal explosion. Destiny had hurled me violently into the buffers at the termination of the line.

Government House
Norfolk Island
June 15th.1848

Again I sit trembling at my mahogany desk looking out through the barred window to the wide Southern Ocean & stands of pines fringing the beach. It is a beautiful late afternoon on the island but suffocating simooms & tornadoes reign in my heart. Words are barely adequate to depict the events of today, the most anguished of my life.

Following the terrible altercation with James, Captain Zaleski was nowhere to be found. I sought out Captain Vane but he was not forthcoming with any intelligence concerning his friend & fellow-officer. I did not wish to appear unnaturally inquisitive & fortunately, with what I regard as extraordinary sympathy, Charles St. Aubyn sought me out. As we walked in the gardens of Government House he gave me to suspect that Adam had delivered some type of challenge. I could hardly breathe, dreading the outcome.

'Captn. Zaleski has elected fight on horseback, he being the injured party & once a Polish cavalry officer.'

'On horseback! Oh my dear Charles, give me your arm.' I do believe I was near to fainting.

'Fear not, Paulina. Captain Vane & Hyacinth O'Rourke are likely to achieve a *réparation d'honneur*. We are not at "The Dove" tavern in Hammersmith where the sign over the door reads "Pistols for two, champagne for one".' He smiled reassuringly.

'Hyacinth O'Rourke?' I was most surprised to hear the name of our emissary, *confidante* & family tutor named as a second.

'James is as close to him as anyone on this island. Both are gentlemen, you see.'

'But he's a convict! He's what you might call a "half-mounted gentleman".'

'An amusing phrase, Paulina, but a forged cheque on Robarts Bank doesn't make him any less of a gentleman in James's eyes. He's an Oxford man, Paulina; they attended the same college. O'Rourke is a thief of circumstance.'

'If a reconciliation is effected, how will I know of it?' I asked nervously.

'I promise to tell you anything I can glean in the interim. I know how worried you must be about James in this gruesome matter. Take heart. He's one of the strongest men in the country!'

'*Worried about James*', I thought to myself – more that my heart was throbbing with a frightful mixture of love for Adam & guilt concerning my husband, the father of my children. The island had become a simmering cauldron of passions. The rest of the day I spent in a distracted state in my bedroom. Little Clara was brought in to me on a number of occasions by Eliza, which gave at least some semblance of normality to the day.

Why did Adam feel compelled so to defend his honour? I realised in a painful access of dismay that jealousy in the hearts of both antagonists – more horribly, jealousy of *me* – had probably brought about this confrontation. But Captain Zaleski was a fierce patriot & James's ill-considered remarks at the dinner table had pushed him over the edge. I feared he would not withdraw the challenge. James, with his marked peculiarity of temperament & humour, would positively revel in this situation.

I scarcely touched my dinner, although James ate with gusto and quizzed me on my downcast mood. I remarked that I would be taking to my bed as I had felt unwell for much of the day. I lay in the semi-dark & sleep was denied me as I tossed & turned over the melancholy events of recent months. *Actaeon* lay on the floor beside the bed and would occasionally rise & place his muzzle on the edge of the counterpane, whimper & look up into my eyes with what I fancied was deep understanding of my pain before flopping down again with a slight scratching of claws on the *parquet*.

I must have finally fallen asleep, because I woke suddenly to hear James's footfalls moving about the house. The bracket clock read 4.30 am in the faint light of dawn. With a thumping heart I rose & crept about the house to ascertain his activities. It appeared he was going riding! The impossibility of this as a pleasure excursion struck me like a thunderclap – a far more sinister event was about to transpire. He had buckled on a sabre, the very sight of which was like a shaft of ice plunged into my deepest organs. Hyacinth O'Rourke was also up & saddling a horse. They remained silent & merely nodded a greeting to each other. Impulsively, I decided to follow

& slipped quickly into my riding habit. *Tempter* whinnied as I approached her loose-box, but I quietened her & took only a few minutes to put on her saddle. *Actaeon* obediently stayed in his kennel.

James & Hyacinth walked their horses along the track that leads to the right of the house, past the soldiers' gardens to the lugubrious thickets & weeping machineels of the *Burial Ground* & then up the steep path to *Piper's Farm*. The Government House sentry appeared to have slumped asleep in his box & as this path did not pass through the Settlement or any inhabited area the strange departure was probably not spied upon. I held *Tempter* well back & checked her pace despite her friskiness in the cool air of early morning. Light was just beginning to break over the vine-covered hills & mist clung to the ground in filmy sheets. The sea had been stained a deep indigo by the night. On the high ground to the eastern side of the island the gentlemen rode on through dense stands of soaring pines towards *Steele's Point*. I realised they were heading towards an area bounded on one side by sheer cliffs of black lava & the other by open grass, known in the Settlement as *The Big Flat*. A few sheep were quietly nibbling the grass near a deserted shepherd's hut & charcoal burner's camp. I halted *Tempter* near the bole of an enormous White Oak. The air rang with the birdsong of the morning chorus & green parrots flashed noisily through the trees that were growing at broadly spaced intervals over the parkland.

Two military figures dressed in scarlet shell jackets with bright green Prussian collars & blue cloth forage caps had dismounted & appeared to be deep in conversation. I distinguished the identity of these gentlemen without difficulty as Captain Zaleski & Captain Vane of the 11th. Foot. Following this leap of recognition, I could scarce avoid that sudden stricture in the throat as I became sensible of this grave unfolding of destiny & the vagaries of chance. I tied *Tempter* to a huge creeper that snaked down from an oak not far from a small stream. A chill breeze rustled the leaves above me as I stood concealed by the low branches among the tangled roots that spread over the ground like the ribs of a fan. Cobwebs glistening with water crystals stirred icily near my cheek.

Captain Vane & Hyacinth O'Rourke as seconds were engaged in close conversation & I thought an *amende honorable* may have been achieved, that the duel may have been in some way averted. However, with the heavy gait of formal deliberation, each second took one pistol over to James &

then Captain Zaleski. I wondered if these were the same pair of Balkan pistols with the inlaid grotesque motifs that Adam had shown me one happy afternoon on the verandah of the Officer's Quarters. As the light increased & the first fitful rays of the sun transformed the drops of dew into jewels, I was discomforted to see the surgeon Charles St. Aubyn standing somewhat apart with his back to the duellists, looking out over the ocean swell, apparently oblivious to the events taking place nearby. The mist slowly dispersed from the grass. James & Adam had both lit cigars & stood talking to their seconds, blowing clouds of smoke into the chill morning air with a demeanour of the greatest composure. Finally, they walked over to their horses & mounted. Dappled sunlight fell on the mottled bark of the tree upon which I was leaning.

For one wonderful moment I thought they had decided not to proceed & to sensibly withdraw, their honour satisfied by an appearance. In trepidation I watched them walk to opposite ends of a long avenue between the White Oaks that led to the cliff edge. They turned their mounts to face each other. I looked in the direction of Hyacinth O'Rourke who was standing at the halfway point, holding a white handkerchief aloft. Vapour issued in jets from the nostrils of the excited horses as they pulled against the reins & restlessly pawed the ground. Captain Zaleski sat nobly in the erect posture of the cavalry officer, while James was rather heavy for his mount & took more of a hunter's seat. The handkerchief fell & both steeds leapt forward directly into the canter. As they galloped towards each other the riders raised their arms, pointed their outstretched pistols & at the point of closest distance, fired. Parrots screeched wildly at the sudden report & rose fluttering into the air before darting away into the pine forest. The horses pranced & twisted as they halted, throwing up small clods of earth. The smoke cleared & I was desperately relieved to see that both contenders were unhurt. Pairs of white butterflies danced above the daisies.

Captain Vane & Hyacinth O'Rourke crossed over to their respective principals. Surely they would terminate the duel now, honour having been satisfied? I could scarce restrain myself from running forward in an access of joy. But it was with horror that I apprehended another *tilt* was planned – the pistols were being reloaded. This dramatic method of duelling as if in the ancient lists must be in the Polish or German chivalric tradition of the 'reiter' – to my mind it was quite unknown in England. I was fascinated & terrified at once at the ghastly novelty of it.

The ground vibrated with the pounding of hooves as the handkerchief again fluttered to the grass followed by the raised arm, loud report & puff of smoke as the pistols were discharged & the combatants passed one another. On this occasion Adam put his hand to his temple & slumped over the withers of his stallion. Blood ran in a scarlet rivulet down the grey neck of the animal & it tossed its head wildly. The acrid odour of gunpowder drifted in my direction. I thought he had been mortally wounded & it chilled my soul.

Rising upright once more after what seemed an endless moment, he looked at his bloody palm & was as if galvanised by an electric charge. He threw the pistol to the ground, drew his sabre & trotted back to the end of the avenue, turned & waited. A dark meander coloured his cheek & lay matted in his fair hair. James & Hyacinth O'Rourke were now deep in conversation. My mouth was dry & my own blood was coursing through my veins like a throbbing tempest. Captain Vane beckoned O'Rourke to join him & they held serious discourse. Vane returned briefly to communicate with Captain Zaleski. James drew his sabre, walked his horse with some deliberation to his own end & turned to face his adversary. Hyacinth O'Rourke took up his allotted halfway position once more. I wanted to scream out for them to desist from this barbarism yet I stood transfixed by the strange nobility of it. Wisps of cloud appeared in the heavens, blown like diaphanous rays in a mighty headress.

Both horsemen set off at a precipitous canter as soon as the hand-kerchief floated down. The flashing blades of the upraised sabres caught the rays of the rising sun & I shut my eyes in terror. The harsh clang of steel stung my ears. When I opened my eyes both were still mounted but James was holding his left shoulder & *smiling*. Charles St. Aubyn rushed across to the central glade with his medical bag, both combatants dismounted & engaged their seconds in animated conversation. To my absolute surprise they all seemed in good spirits & even loud laughter rang around the natural arena. *Tempter* was more than restless & I feared we would soon be discovered so led her off to a more remote spot beyond the stream. I was shivering as if struck down by the ague. Within minutes the gentlemen had mounted up & disappeared from *The Big Flat*, trotting along the track down to Kingston.

My consummate abilities as an actress carried me through the remainder of today but I trembled from head to foot continually & was subject to fainting fits. James told me that he had been stabbed in the Lumber Yard by a convict who had concealed a knife & made a rush. Charles called on him to bind his shoulder & confirmed this incident. My evident distress – though from an entirely different cause – disconcerted them both I think. What will become of us when this crime is discovered? We will be forced to return to England in shame or worse! James will face a trial! And what will happen to Captain Zaleski? Will he be cashiered? If I am separated from him I cannot answer for my state of health. My pulse races in panic. I write late at night unable to sleep, my loyal *Actaeon* lying beside me. None of these questions has been affirmatively answered.

(The absence of entries for the subsequent period of four years greatly fed my curiosity and I decided to research the destiny of this spirited woman when I returned to Australia. The realisation that Paulina had been resident on the 'Island of the Damned' for perhaps seven years made me wonder at the mental stamina she so clearly possessed to continue writing the chronicle at all.)

Norfolk Island
October 11th. 1852

James remains insistent that the accusation by Lieutenant-Governor Denison of his excessive use of the lash on the desperate wretches is grossly unfair. The most incorrigible convicts culled from Gibraltar & Bermuda, from Millbank, the Hulks, Pentonville, Portland & Parkhurst, even dangerous convicts from India are now resident here & will respond to corporal punishment alone. All compute their chances or *price* of detection in lashes before committing the crime or breach of regulations – especially pertaining to misuse of tobacco. He requires more isolation cells – the finance & the will to build them is notoriously absent in London. James is exhausted & overworked – his health is collapsing & the island has a mysteriously debilitating effect on his mental faculties overall. I really must do my duty as a wife & support him throughout these reversals.

The gold rush in New South Wales & Victoria has caused many of his junior officers to resign. Increased remuneration will not be forthcoming from the Government to keep them at the penal stations & convict overseers would be impossible to contemplate. The former island Commandant, Captain Foster Fyans, has told La Trobe: *'You are aware of all the gold fields – the ruin of the colony.'* It is of deep irony to my person to realise that the *Polish* Count de Strzelecki was the first person to demonstrate the existence of gold in Australia ten years ago. The ideal charms of the infant colony, that pastoral *Arcadia*, must now give way to the march of civilisation – the metamorphosis of the *'bon vieux temps'*...

(Words had been scored out and the glue on the binding had given way as if a clutch of pages had been forcibly removed.)

Charlotte ran to me in the drawing room weeping.

'But I love him Mama, I love him!'

My worst fears were confirmed about the congress of Septimus & Charlotte through the inflamed emotions created by music. I sent for Septimus instantly & he came in with his head bent low. He looked beaten down in his drab convict garb. A tremor of sympathy passed through my heart as I was put in mind of my own shameful situation.

'What has happened here?' I tried to be resolute yet kind.

'Ma'am, I have *again* succumbed to the temptation of a lady above my station. I love your daughter!' He looked across at her sobbing on the chaise-longue & sighed deeply.

'Please, Septimus! Never utter such a thing within my hearing again. You will bring down the wrath of Jupiter when James hears of this.'

'Must you tell him? I am so ashamed to appear thus before you in magpie clothing & not as the gentleman I am. I have committed the crime of forbidden love. I'm *profoundly* sorry for this sin against her youth & beg forgiveness. I cannot answer for myself when such passions are upon me!'

'Mama, leave him alone! Must Papa hear of it if we stop the lessons?' Charlotte was weeping uncontrollably. It was at this terrible moment James entered the drawing room.

'One of the traps told me something has been crabbed.[98] What is it?' He stared penetratingly at all of us through his monocle, his massive frame filling the doorway.

'Septimus – has – fallen – in – love...' my voice failed me.

'Well, we'll soon have those delicate feelings out of him! Who is this *bleached mott*, this *flash piece of mutton*?'[99]

'Charlotte... in love with... Charlotte...' Silence grew heavy like a great stone in the air. My pounding heart prevented speech. The stone fell like thunder.

'What! My own daughter! I knew we had to get out of this d....d Hell but... *you,* Septimus after my saving your hide in VDL. You... you... you are a disgrace to human nature!'

'I want to marry your daughter, Sir – after I get my ticket of leave & set up on my own account.'

'Set up! Set up on your own account! I'll muzzle you, my joker, & thrash the flashness out of you! Why, I should hammer you down like a bullock! Constable! Constable!'

'Yes Sir!'

'Give this scowbanker[100] a feeler[101] – he's only half a pebble and most likely won't meet it[102] – then take him out to that hell within a hell, Philip Island! Leave him to rot. Then you can listen to the wild dog's music as long as you wish, you *dog!* Dear God – my own daughter!' I tried to reason with James but he was beside himself with fury. Charlotte was inconsolable.

'Mama! He'll go mad out there! He's too sensitive a soul for that! Please don't flog him Papa, please!' She broke down completely.

'You, young lady, are going back to England to your cousin in Suffolk. To your room! This Lazar House of crime infects all of us! The sooner we depart this Hell the better!' James pounded outside, mounted up & rode furiously towards the Settlement in a cloud of dust.

Such a day of terrible suffering and dismay! Charlotte is desolate about returning to England & broken-hearted over Septimus & the ghastly pain he will now suffer on her behalf. She looks out to Philip Island & despairs! I am sick with grief & have refused all callers pleading illness. The greatest horror is that she may be developing *gonorrhea.* Charles has promised secrecy after examining her but James would hang Septimus for it!

If this business of mine with *Captain Zaleski* is discovered... James will kill us all! He has been much upset & preoccupied – as have we all – by recent *événements.* I think it preys disconcertingly upon his mind. Fanny has been most accommodating in *all matters* concerning the imminent scandals. Whenever I look out at that perfect view across Sydney Bay I dwell on thoughts of Septimus abandoned to his terrible fate on Philip Island. It has quite ruined the once beautiful vista.

Norfolk Island
December 5th. 1852

Charlotte departed today aboard the *Martin Luther* & I have been weeping almost constantly.

The ship arrived here from Sydney & will sail directly to England. It will be an almost empty convict ship on the voyage home & I have persuaded one of the Ferrers' governesses to accompany her. The surf was running high & we only just managed a crossing of the Bar. The ship was riding such a swell, we had to hand the luggage on board overhead & I was prevented from assisting her to stow it & arrange her cabin. I cannot write – I am in despair of the fate that has brought me to the reaches of this dark cave. *If we had followed a normal life farming in VDL none of these tragedies would have come to pass.* As a mother I feel I have lost a child – there is no greater agony than this. It could take a year to receive a letter from England!

She wept hysterically & her pale pinched face barely cleared the rail of the vessel, as we pulled away in the skiff. The governess smoothed her hair out of her tearful eyes. From the landing place, I watched for long hours with little Clara & Adolphus, as the ship tacked & slipped beyond the horizon. To watch your daughter drifting across the ocean... away... away... from your reach... is a painful laceration to the heart. Her lover now suffers atrocious horrors in isolation. How she must have gazed yearningly upon Philip Island as she sailed past & how it would have torn her heart.

I learned before her departure that the mysterious infection has been cured. Thank God! Poor dear Charlotte!

What could possess James to be so cruel! Throughout this strife he remained the adamant tyrant – Charlotte *must* leave for England despite her heart-rending pleas to return to Hobarton with us quite soon. I had to prevent him from *flogging her!* The demons of punishment have turned his brain into a pitiful cauldron that feeds upon horror. His physical presence is odious to me & *still* I must needs perform those duties of a wife & *more vile practices* words cannot begin to depict.

I have retired to my bedroom with *palpitations of the heart* & am *determined* to continue to suffer them to avoid his loathsome touch...

Norfolk Island
Christmas Day 1852

Norfolk Island is soon to be completely *abandoned* as a penal settlement! I could not have received a better Christmas gift than this piece of glorious intelligence! James is completing a study of the suitability for yet another type of experiment, the resettlement of the Pitcairn Islanders, those pious descendants of the mutiny on the ship *Bounty*. The Queen is to give the island to them as a gift in order to preserve their unique identity without external influence.

We are decided firmly upon return to VDL & my heart leaps at the realisation of it. We may even return home to England & my beloved Suffolk! How wonderful it would be to embrace my dearest daughter once more! Social diversions are become invisible here – the officers of the 99th. Regiment are considerably dull compared to the dramas & antics I remember of the *Bloody Eleventh*. I missed my dearest Adam unconscionably for many long months after he departed Norfolk Island – my heart cruelly torn, unable to write my journal & to fit to die. Cold waves of loss still pass over me when confronted with a mounted officer in a short scarlet jacket. But I am recently become more reasonable & forcibly ceased this flow of unproductive romance.

The impossibility of properly educating Adolphus, Clara's tender years & my present pregnancy all militate against a further term. I feel more contained now that I am reconciled with James as his wife. I fondly hope we can return to the farm in the Huon River District. *Actaeon* will accompany us & I would never be inveigled to part with *Tempter* however hard the passage to VDL. I have written to the Ferrers in Hobarton in the greatest excitement! We will be aboard the *Lady Franklin* within a few days, crossing the Bar for the final time! To have survived these many years in paradise among the greatest offenders in Great Britain – *the true aristocrats of crime* – is an experience that has forged my soul.

Government House
Norfolk Island
Morning of the Last Day in Paradise
January 18th. 1853

(Here to my disappointment the bound journal ended. I looked up from this engrossing final volume to find evening rapidly coming on. There were no more pages to read, and I felt as though I was dangling over a precipice. The dreadful courtesy of the duel and the banishment of the young lovers dominated my imagination as I gazed into space. Nature was laid out in a panorama before me, the sea as indifferent to human destiny now as when this adventure had befallen Paulina a hundred and thirty years before. Terns sought their night nests as they had done for thousands of years. Dido was singing in inconsolable despair as Aeneas sailed away. Carthage burned in the sinking sun.

'Remember me, but ah! forget my fate.'

Purcell's noble opera finished and I began to wonder. There *must* be some clue to what had become of Captain Adam Zaleski. And what of the intervening four years, and the eventual fate of James and Paulina Worth after departing Norfolk Island? There were two more letters to read and I approached them with the voraciousness of a lover. The first turned out to be little more than a note written in Zaleski's fine hand.)

Officer's Quarters
Norfolk Island
July 12th. 1848

Paulina *mon amour*

I am drinking a glass of vodka on the verandah and thinking of our love as I look towards Government House. I miss your laughter and joy most painfully. My heart is wounded in its deepest chamber. Linked as it is to yours it can only be violently ripped away. We have been torn apart by my excesses of impulsive passion. I have been denied a court-martial and will be *transferred* quite soon to Port Phillip with the present detachment of the 11th Foot who are to be replaced by the 99th. I will sell out my commission. At last I will be free and am yet still young enough to fight and die for my country. Such are the cards dealt to me.

Paulina my perfect darling, you will forever occupy a special place in my affections. I am cruelly divided between my duty and my love of you – it fills me with despair. Despite the insurmountable obstacles to this love we *will* somehow continue it. I wear the cherry ribbon you gave me at Anson's Bay pinned inside my jacket next to my heart.

I kiss you *kochanie*

Adam

(The second was a bizarre piece of large dried leaf covered in crabbed handwriting in strange brownish ink.)

Whomsoever finds this letter give it to Mrs. Paulina Worth
Philip Island
Christmas 1852

Charlotte my love!

Abandoned in pine branches I make some ink of banana leaves & juice to write to you my love. A wild dog that worries me with mad & evil eyes in the night – my lips search for you in darkness. I am torn from your heart by cruellest fate – your ship I saw pass like a slow knife moving along my soul. Hot rivets struck in my irons fiercely burnt. "That's nothing to the burning you will get in Hell!" cried the Constable. In the dumb cell the weavils fell through the ceiling crawling over my hands, face & neck & into my mouth making sleep impossible. The flogger took it slow to put me to the triangle. Yes. He slaked his thirst for the hot work from the black bottle of porter – yes – slowly he wiped his dripping mouth with the back of his brown, heavy hand & bent to the brine tub for the cat – yes – & slow & deliberate laid it on for two dozen, calling each stroke. Thrown to Philip Isle in rags – violent rain, salted pork & a putrid cask I crawl about an animal but I still translate Racine at leisure. I will love you till I die – the millstone crushes the rose within my breast – your lips – we will embrace & play music again my love

Septimus

(This tortured letter made me think sadly of the blighted love of Septimus & Charlotte. The language showed a distracted mind. Did they meet again in England? Was he taken off that second circle of Dante's Hell or did he die insane? There were no further clues to any of their ultimate destinies.)

CHAPTER XXIX

'But this man's heart was full of anger against his own people,
full of anger existing there by the side of his desire of her.'
An Outcast of the Islands
Joseph Conrad, 1896

'My purpose is to tell of bodies which have been
transformed into shapes of a different kind.'
Metamorphoses, Book I i
Ovid, 43 B.C. – A.D. 17
(tr. Mary M. Innes)

'Mareva, yu gwen sor ef yu sti aut iin aa san noe klorth.'[103]
We had gone to Second Sands to swim and sunbathe. The settlement
at Kingston was laid out in a breathtaking panorama, looking almost
as it would have been in an engraving of the period of Paulina's
residence. Mareva lay naked in the sun like a fallen idol.

I had spent the weeks since my dismissal in sunbathing, drinking
and gazing at the horizon over the reef, trying to tear myself away
from her and the island. I was as brown as a Polynesian. An endless
round of farewell parties and requests on VL-2-NI had sapped my
energy. A 'philosophy of inaction' began to control my mind. My
ambitions for a concert career dissolved again in the spume blowing
across the shore. Nearly all my possessions had now been disposed of or
shipped back to the mainland, yet I was still living at the empty
tracking station, unable to depart. My final opera on these cliffs was
'The Flying Dutchman', and the history of the *Bounty* came to mind as
the passionate harmonies flooded the moonlit ocean below the pines.

The perfume of Mareva's body drifted over to me on a gust of
wind. I stroked her skin and we made love on a shimmering patch of
sand between two boulders. The harsh shapes of the rocks sunk in the
sand reared against the sun.

'I love you, Mareva,' I said, 'but I must do something with my life. Twenty-three is too young to retire to a paradise. Can you understand that?' I looked again into the eyes of the ancient past.

'No, I don't understand! You are only interested in the "Fish" and all that intellectual rubbish! Yu es nehsi![104] Yu es huihui![105] You know where you really belong, *forever* with me on the island, my lover in chains!'

Her hair lay about her face in wet gleaming strands like the snakes of a Medusa, the Gorgon taken in sex by Poseidon, lord of the sea; the sight of her horrid yet mysteriously graceful features had turned men to stone. Silver trunks of dead pines lay about on the sand, the ends of the broken branches like laughing devils, horns emerging where the wood had split apart. Turnstones tripping on brilliant orange legs busily flipped shells and seaweed with their beaks, in a compulsive search for food. The island was becoming an unreal construction in my mind, now that I was set on departure. I baked in the heat, fascinated by Mareva's sensuality like lured prey and yet longing for escape.

The following morning I arranged my passage out on the flying-boat. That was also the day I gave Almira a hand-coloured engraving of Thursday October Christian, the handsome son of Fletcher Christian and his Tahitian wife Mauatua, wearing a straw hat ornamented with black cock's feathers. She was touched by this small gesture.

'Won't be long before you come home, darl,' she said.

It was also the day that a horse leapt from a bank at Mission Road on to the MG and wrecked it. The new owner had taken delivery only two days before and I took the incident as a clear omen of approaching punishment.

Mareva had insisted we spend my last night on the island in each other's arms. On our last walk through the rainforest she took me to a section I had never before explored, at the top of Grassy Road. As we climbed over the fence we entered a magical and curiously evil place, unlike any other I had visited.

The entrance was through an archway of wild lemon, the yellow fruit in brilliant contrast with the dark green of the tree. Massive cables of creepers were hanging from the topmost branches of giant whitewoods, singly and in heavy braids, like plaited snakes or the collapsed power cables of a city after a cyclone. These Samson's Sinews trailed along the ground in massive loops, forming abstract festoons. We came to a sunlit glade fringed by Norfolk palms, ancient tree-ferns and hanging purple *ipomoea*, the air perfumed by jasmine. Fantails accompanied us spinning like tops, close to our faces and feet, while the occasional vivid red flash of a scarlet robin illuminated our walk. The sun was setting through this perpendicular maze, reflecting old gold from the chaos of buttressed roots and magnificent specimens of ironwood, sharkwood and bastard oak that would have surprised even the curator of Kew Gardens. I kissed Mareva and told her she was not of this world. We clung to each other in sterile yet passionate desperation, the form of her naked body exposed through the thin cotton of her long dress, her supple curves under my palm, the creeper known as Devil's Guts catching up in her perfumed hair. We fought the unrelenting passage of time to my departure.

Tremendous lichen-covered boulders littered the valley floor in this unearthly garden. We wandered further into the paradise, losing ourselves finally among the Big Creepers, an atmosphere like a primaeval forest. It was warm, moist and airless, the scent of heated foliage unsettlingly erotic. Frozen in time, motionless, we held each other under the ferns, before turning back and struggling through the heavy undergrowth out into the open air of Mission Road.

'See yu laita orn,' she whispered, and her tongue caressed my ear.

We had arranged to stay the night at a hotel on the bluffs above Anson Bay. I said my farewells to the diamond dealer at the tracking station, packed my last suitcase and drove up to the hotel in a hired jeep, similar to my first transport on the island. Paulina's journals were wrapped in waxed cotton, safe among my soft clothes. Mareva was to meet me there secretly after dark, with three sharp raps on my door. I awaited her in a mood of bittersweet trepidation.

The night sky was calm and moonless, with innumerable stars pricked into the vault. My room overlooked the ocean and during the late afternoon I turned over Paulina's journals again. The antique feel of the morocco bindings made them like a treasure.

'...great excitement today with a shout of "Brig O!!" off the Beacon and the garrison Colours were hoisted together with the secret signals that permit vessels to approach. I strongly anticipated...'

Three sharp knocks interrupted me, and I put the journals aside. I pulled open the door and I was confronted with a woman who had undergone a complete metamorphosis since the afternoon in the rainforest. Now she was wearing make-up for the first time, coral gloss lipstick and slate eyeshadow, a faint trace of glitter on her cheeks. Her dark mane of hair cascaded wildly about her shoulders. She had on a short stretch-denim dress with a full-length zip down the centre, open to partly reveal her breasts, and on her feet a pair of delicate high-heeled gold-rope sandals. She clutched a cold bottle of Laurent Perrier champagne and two glasses. I could hardly believe this was the same girl who had bent over the mineral-blue pools collecting shellfish years before. She now looked so attractive in a sophisticated and polished city sense, that I was thrown into a conflict of horror and desire.

'You look wonderful, Mareva,' I said. 'Come in, darling.' I opened the champagne, and I poured two glasses.

'It's a pity this is our last night,' she said. 'And it's all your fault for leaving.' She was genuinely upset yet petulant. 'Do you really have to go?'

'Let's not talk too much,' I replied. 'To us,' she said, and we clinked glasses. The lively mousse instantly lifted my spirits.

'Do you think you might go to Sydney and study art?' I said. 'We could meet there sometime.'

'You still want to see me again? Do you? Do you?' She leant against me, whispering.

'You might become a great artist, you never know.'

In the silence tears welled in our eyes as we gazed into the chasm dividing us. 'You are such a crocodile,' she said. 'Anyway, I don't love you any more, do I?'

We were soon embracing on the divan. The zip sang down to its base. This time she was wearing seductive underwear. A satin strapless bra shaped her breasts to delectable fullness and softly contoured her nipples. A silk thong edged in cream lace was ironed to her golden skin, darker shadows nestling tantalisingly behind the scalloped flowers. I traced with my finger the flow of the filigree over the skin, the sleek cheeks of her bottom, the tiny triangle of French gauze snuggling into the tanned cleavage. I noticed a small

Indian tiger tattooed inside her thigh as *Tabu* perfume drifted over me.

The feline grace of her former lovemaking, the langorous elaborations of beauty were abandoned on this night in a more frenzied search for immediate pleasures. She was more experienced now, and she rushed me breathlessly along the slopes of passion. I remembered the time I had watched secretly through the windows of her hut, and it set me aflame. Her powerful body arched above me, hungry for satisfaction, shuddering with rapidly achieved pleasure. Her hair fell like a warm scented tent enclosing our faces, and her breasts caressed my cheeks. Her lips crushed mine, and I tasted the blood from her bite, her tongue exploring me carefully like a bruised fruit. We drifted to sleep fitfully in a haze of orgasms and champagne.

I awoke suddenly in the dark, and I was choking on smoke. Hardly able to breathe, my lungs searing, my eyes streaming, I struggled to get up from the bed.

'Mareva! Mareva!'

I could not find her in the room. Stumbling over furniture, I careered into the wall and felt my way along the smooth boards, finding the door with a surge of relief. I wrenched it open, and I was almost knocked flat by a blast of superheated air and a scorching flare that roared down the corridor. I called her again until my throat closed up and I choked. Lurching along the blazing corridor, bumping into things, I reached a fire door and slammed down the bar. I burst out into the open air near the swimming pool.

Through my streaming eyes, I could just make out the low buildings engulfed in fire, flame darting out from the windows, sparks spiralling high into the night sky. The pines around the hotel were cast in flickering silhouettes, and some flared up suddenly like pagan torches. Only a few people were about, and I frantically searched among them for Mareva. The one fire engine on the island was garaged at the airport, and it would take at least fifteen minutes to arrive. It was impossible now to enter the collapsing building; flames licked through the asphalt roofing and glowed off the surface of the swimming pool; people stood in dark groups, fascinated and paralysed. I was despairing of seeing Mareva alive again when I heard a voice call me haltingly from the dark.

'Paul! Paul! Ai es hier!'[106]

Mareva was lying naked on the grass in the malignant light. I kissed her lips, but they tasted now of ash and charcoal. She was coughing and tufts of her hair had been singed away. Her beautiful skin looked blackened and burnt on the arms and legs. I suddenly realised I was naked too, and I managed to find a couple of sheets in a laundry outhouse. We hobbled towards the jeep and I set her precariously on the rear bench.

'Where *were* you?' I said. 'I couldn't find you!'

She only moaned in reply. Then I remembered Paulina's journals, still in the burning room. My world seemed to collapse. I started up the jeep and bumped along the track towards the road.

We passed Nathan, bare-chested on his motorcycle, wheeling in demented circles around the lawns and paths in front of the blazing hotel, punching the air with his fist as if he was urging the fire on. I saw him speed off in the flickering dark towards Point Vincent. Mareva was moaning on the open rear seat, so I drove at speed to the hospital. I sat in the casualty room in despair, while the doctor dealt with her.

'Looks far worse than it is,' he said. 'Mainly superficial burns and smoke inhalation. Don't worry, she'll live.'

Everybody on Norfolk soon knew I had been alone with Mareva at the hotel. Now she was hurt, all her friends and acquaintances visited the hospital. The islanders always reclaimed their own in a crisis.

Rumours abounded as to the fire's cause. People had seen Nathan lurking around the public rooms of the hotel late that night, asking if Mareva was staying there. Some had seen him riding his motorcycle. Other people suggested the fire had been set deliberately, out of commercial desperation. The hotel was in difficulties and a successful insurance claim would have solved many problems at a stroke. The destructive passion of jealousy or commercial exploitation were equally reprehensible. For me, the worst part was that Mareva had been severly injured, perhaps permanently disfigured. I felt an unfocused sense of guilt and I thought of the purgatorial fire that had destroyed the *Bounty*. As for Paulina, her relics lay lost in the ashes, the wind already blowing away the last traces of her soul.

At first light, after borrowing some clothes, I headed back to Anson Bay to search through the smouldering ruins. Smoke was still rising above the pines, dispersing out to sea. Incinerated wooden frames reared up from the scorched earth, and the pines in the garden had shrivelled into agonised shapes. I found the burnt shell of our room, and I began to sift through the warm ashes. I thought everything was gone, but then I came upon the long zip from the front of Mareva's denim dress and the charred remains of Paulina's locked journals. The morocco bindings had protected the interiors to some extent, but the edges of the paper were burnt, some pages entirely scorched. The beloved handwriting sprang at me from the page, the blackened edges like mourning stationery.

'I willfully banished all melancholy thoughts, swept up my veil and with Tempter tossing her mane in pleasure, cantered the short distance down to the stream that runs through the Commandant's garden. The officers could scarce keep pace with me & I laughed at their tardiness.'
'Gentlemen, I should join your regiment...'

I picked a hibiscus from a crevice, and went down the zig-zag path to the beach. I sat for hours in the arms of a rock sea-monster known as the Pulpit, looking out along the majestic coast. Fortunately I had salvaged the charred zip and the scorched diaries. Paulina could be resurrected from the ashes, and Mareva at least was still alive. The long rollers broke over the jagged rocks in clusters, falling into patterns of three followed by brief passages of calm water. I counted these patterns absent-mindedly for hours. In my reverie, I imagined Mareva as a new-born Venus riding to the foaming shore on her shell.

During my period of residence on Norfolk Island, a curious operation of tripartite time had emerged, a system of three realities contained within one island, contained within one heart. It had been like the phenomenon in physics called *interference*, where waves of light or energy reinforce or neutralise one another when their paths meet or cross. Wave followed wave of time, the dreams of prehistory, Paulina's journals and Mareva's links with the *Bounty* – like the rollers pounding this coast. Each wave had its own separate identity, but interacted with the others. The unity of place combined with disunity of time produced unexpected insights and historical harmonies, resonances, and unsolicited patterns of irresistible beauty, like a fugue in music. Why, Paulina with pounding heart, had embraced her Polish officer on the cliffs just above me!

I stayed on the island until Mareva was discharged. The doctor had been correct and her burns healed without any scars. She retained the beauty I remembered from the beginning in *Almira's* garden. However, we never recovered the fire of our original passion. The transformation was complete. Mareva had become a civilised and sophisticated lady at last, taking her proper place in the modern world.

CHAPTER XXX

'Ideo amor ab Orpheo sine oculis dicitur, quia est supra intellectum.'
(Love is said by Orpheus to be without eyes because he is above the intellect)
Conclusiones in doctrinum Platonis (No.6)
Pico della Mirandola

'I cannot agree, Phaedrus, with the condition laid down for our speeches,
that they should be a simple and unqualified panegyric of Love.
If Love had a single nature, it would all be very well,
but not as it is, since love is not single;...'
Pausanias in *The Symposium* (180c)
Plato, 385 B.C. (tr. Walter Hamilton)

*D*usk. The *Pacific Trader* rode at anchor outside the reef. The sun had laid out the cloth of her setting over the slow-breathing ocean. Mareva and Almira had both come to say goodbye, and the three of us stood on the jetty at Kingston, unable to speak, watching the sea breaking over the long coral shelves at the margin of Slaughter Bay.

'Don't you leave it too long to come back home,' said Almira, and she gave me a squeeze. 'Thank yuu for all the beautiful music on a' radio – and out a' Mishen Chaepl.'

The majesty of her carriage and her noble profile always left me searching for words. Her lustrous eyes looked at me sadly from uncharted depths.

'Yu es got yus Tahitian fish, Guava jelly en that Norfolk stamp collection?'

I assured her they were safely packed in what was left of my luggage. In so many ways she represented all the islanders for me, everything that was best in the older Pitcairn descendants, simplicity, generosity, respect, trust, wry humour, intense love of children and tolerance of the foibles of men, all accompanied by the redeeming vice of devilment. Now, the island and its people were changing forever. I could feel the irresistible commercial forces bulging beneath the surface. I wondered if I would ever see Almira again. But in the words of the Pitcairn hymn:

In the Sweet by-and-by,
We shall meet on that beautiful shore.

'Ai gwen back a' car,' she said. 'It's cold here. Kiss your old Valentine, darl.'

I held her close, this lady of the noble spirit. Tears welled in her eyes and I fought to control my emotions.

Mareva stood alone with me then on the pier. The unnaturally calm sea lapped gently against the breakwater.

'Paul, yu always did make me laugh! Ai will remember everything, will you?'

'Mareva, you will always have a special place in my heart – no one else could ever enter there.'

'Yu always were romantic.' There was that ironic smile again, those soft, far-seeing eyes framed by the wonderful mane of hair. As we kissed I was enfolded for the last time in the sweet scents of Oceania.

'Daas et!'[107] I sighed, and I climbed down into the launch, clutching Paulina's scorched journals. Mareva quickly brushed her eyes with the rapidity of pride and my throat tightened with the pain of imminent separation.

The flying-boat rocked gently on a sea of gold as I was taken over the Bar for the last time. Mareva dwindled in size, and behind her the buildings of the Penal Settlement on the 'Isle of Death' glowed distant and honey-coloured. For me, now, they were peopled with ghosts from the time of the beautiful Paulina Wellesley, the third lady of my heart. Dashing Captain Zaleski still rode wildly through the pines to meet his forbidden love. Commandant James Worth, laden with impossible duties by the British Government, possessing the qualities of a Victorian general but doomed to a perverted destiny of cruel convict supervision, witheringly adjusted his monocle as he ordered the lash. I looked out to blood-red Philip Island, that hell within a hell, and I saw Septimus Thorn, the gentleman convict and translator of Racine, driven mad by blighted love and music among the wild dogs. Beauty and cruelty possess a curious symbiosis.

Every actor on the stage of Transportation had a personal tragedy. Convict and gaoler alike were faced every day by their own limitations and perversities. All were victims of a cruel and misguided System. The tragic history of convict times has remained a partial account for too long. Refined manners, joy and the trails of love also endured among the demonised British custodians and settlers; the contribution of their colourful destinies should be recalled to balance the account.

I felt I had gained in wisdom from this interaction of nature and human history. Besides, I had been given the strength to face life. I now had the self-confidence to resume my studies. The secret was all in this learning to give, to the composer, to the listener, finally to myself. That you remain imprisoned within the confined shell of your own personality and the limits of its development no matter where you live, was a simple but fundamental lesson. In the words of Benjamin Constant in the Red Note-Book, 'Circumstances are of little importance, character is everything; you cannot break with yourself.' Now the islanders were grappling with new demons, the devils of commerce, 'face to face, foot to foot'.

The island was greater than all the human players in this tale, a timeless domain of purest air where the human felt at one with nature, free at last. For years I had lain in the sun on the glittering sand before the reef, gazing at the horizon over a peacock sea, playing and listening to music at night on the ocean cliffs. We should remember we are but tenants in this ageless landscape. The enchanted isle had ultimately become a living being for me, layers of history and love in constant metamorphosis within the Garden of Venus, a swirling dance of the Graces – sensuality, beauty and virtue.

Clouds of spray fogged the windows as the outer engines opened to full power. The regiments of pines on the sheer cliffs skimmed past in a haze of sea spume and tears. The flying-boat pulled off the surface of the gilded lagoon and climbed laboriously into the dwindling light. We circled briefly over Norfolk Island, so curiously shaped like the human heart, and then set course for the mainland, the cycle complete.

NOTES

1 'Well, am I glad to see you! Come inside, darling!'
2 'I'm Almira.'
3 'You'd like a whiskey, wouldn't you? Join the family!'
4 'Try a piece of this fish, darling.'
5 'Tahitian Fish darling. Go on, have some more! It's good, isn't it?'
6 'How are you darling?'
7 'Help youself to a whiskey, go on.'
8 'Are you going to dawn breakfast at Buck's Point tomorrow?'
9 'We are going out on the cliffs, watch the sunrise over the ocean and have breakfast around the fire, aren't we, Teio?'
10 'You should start learning to speak Norfolk as soon as you unpack your bag!'
11 'Peli has got a sheep (slavish admirer) that he doesn't want.'
12 'Who is it?'
13 'She'd follow him to the ends of the earth and further.'
14 'This is mada darling. Green banana dumplings cooked in milk. Help yourself to some.'
15 Tahitian for 'Silence!'
16 'Would you like some sweet potatoes?'
17 'That may be true darling but there are plenty of devils on Norfolk!'
18 'It's delicious!'
19 'You must've had plenty of time on your hands and not much coffee!'
20 There is conflicting evidence on how the ship was burnt.
21 'Are you going up in the sticks today?' (the area around J.E. Road, Red Road and Selwyn Pine Road in the north).
22 'Mind you take that stuff to Sarnum's on J.E. Road.'
23 'That's my boy Nathan.'
24 'Come inside and light up the fire darling.'

25 'Darling, take a pineapple and some carrots down to Government House – go on.'
26 A visitor to Norfolk – a person can be a resident for thirty years and still be considered a 'blow-in'.
27 'How are you? I'm Paul.'
28 'You can speak Norfolk well, can't you?'
29 'I'm going.'
30 'I'm going swimming.'
31 'What have you been doing?'
32 'Is there anything in it?'
33 'Open up the thing! There may be treasure inside!'
34 'He worked for the Administration at Government House, in the gardens mostly. He was an expert at pretending to work. He was usually flat out on the bed – tired or faking sickness.
35 'Oh no! It's just some stupid old books.'
36 'See you tomorrow.'
37 'Too much reading brings on an early death!'
38 Convict officialese for 'homosexual'.
39 Convicts backs were often infested with maggots after a flogging or from carrying lime.
40 'Hat'.
41 'How are you all?'
42 'You're speaking poor English!' On Norfolk great pride is taken in speaking excellent English.
43 'You're drinking too slowly!'
44 'He was sometimes mad with jealousy and imagined things.'
45 '…he was incredibly angry!'
46 Kissing.
47 'I'm going. I'll catch it if I'm late.'
48 'I'm not going to the cemetery! I'm afraid of the ghosts in Kingston.'
49 There are many ghosts to be seen on Norfolk Island – Billy Tin is one such that appears near the Royal Engineer's Office at Kingston.

50 'Are you going for a swim?'
51 'Don't be mad!'
52 'Something ran over my foot! It's a sea eel!'
53 Convict argot for smart or knowledgeable felons.
54 'Are you drinking up or slowing down?' (always meant as a criticism)
55 'Would you like a beer?'
56 'See you later, brother.'
57 'Nathan, you must be mad!'
58 'Now it's dead we can't ask it to testify!'
59 'She's had it some time!'
60 'All the tourists just love Norfolk!'
61 'What have you been doing?'
62 'Have you ever made love on a gravestone?'
63 'Are you going to the Bounty Ball tonight?' This ball is one of the social highlights of the year.
64 'Background' in the family, cultural and educational sense.
65 Brother, I'm going to flog the ears off your face if you don't stand aside!
66 Convicts often bit off each other's noses in fights.
67 Convict argot for 200 lashes.
68 'The stone' was a form of torture where the convict may be spread-eagled over it for some days in all weathers.
69 Convict argot for a tough man who could take a lashing without flinching.
70 'We're having a ghost party down at Channers' Corner. Come along with us, Hat!'
71 'Why did you take so long to come?'
72 'I'm completely drunk and want ten cups of hot chocolate... Get going! You're a bastard with Mareva, Hat, and you're very lucky we like your radio programme!'
73 Convict argot for felons who complained or moaned to the authorities.
74 Convict argot for discovering someone's motivations.
75 Convict argot for executed.
76 Convict argot for executed.
77 Convict argot for 'steal'.
78 'I think he's really nice.'
79 'Pat in' is a phrasal verb in Norfolk meaning 'make love'.
80 'Caught you out!' (when someone reacts to a taunt)
81 'Make love'.
82 'You'll have trouble with that one before long, boy!'
83 'She's so bony.'
84 'What a pity!'
85 'You're not man enough for me.'
86 (A crime) 'impossible between Christians'.
87 'I pity her.'
88 'The cattle odour reveals itself in a most pronounced manner.'
89 'That arid irony that blows like the wind of death upon the joys of the heart.'
90 Polish for 'darling'.
91 'I am only in a dream.'
92 'Destroy this letter.'
93 'What time did you go to bed last night boy?'
94 'You're joking!'
95 'That's no good.'
96 'I heard you got yourself a new girlfriend, Hat!'
97 'I'll be glad when you've gone, brother.'
98 'One of the constables told me something has been discovered.'
99 Georgian English for female convicts – 'blonde & beautiful'.
100 Convict argot for 'blackguard'.
101 Convict argot for 200 lashes. 'Black Box' was 500 lashes and usually resulted in death.
102 Convict argot. 'To meet it' meant to survive the lashing with some equanimity.
103 'Mareva, you are going to burn if you lie naked in the sun.'
104 'You are nasty!'
105 'You're grubby!'
106 'I'm here!'
107 'That's it.'